KAPU ʻĀINA

FORBIDDEN LAND

A BIO-TERROR THRILLER

BOOK THREE

BY

TERRY FRITTS

Kapu 'āina is the third installment in the bio-terror series featuring the Hawaiian Islands. *Kapu 'āina* continues the saga of the Red Summit terrorist organization and the agents who joined together to end its reign of terror. *Taka,* book one in the series, was released in November of 2006. *Kona Snow,* book two, was released in June of 2007.

For those readers familiar with Michener's *Hawaii*, you will no doubt see the homage I pay in Chapter one to this incredible author for the inspiration he has given me to write about the islands

This book is a work of fiction. Any similarity between characters in the book and real people are coincidental. The events and disasters in *Kapu 'āina* are from the author's imagination, but are all within the realm of possibility.

Terry Fritts is an author, musician, and teacher who resides with his wife Pauline in Riverview, Florida.

Terry can be reached at tfritts01@aol.com or visit his website: terrywfritts.com

KAPU ʻĀINA

FORBIDDEN LAND

BOOK THREE

KAPU 'ĀINA
FORBIDDEN LAND

CHAPTER ONE

Present time

"Gigolo is such a crass word. I prefer to think of myself as a beach boy," Marlin whispered to the stunning brunette dripping with diamonds. Marlin was one of those fortunate males with the God given charm, physique, looks, and, of course, equipment to satisfy the most demanding socialite. He smiled that enchanting smile that had taken him from the beaches of Waikiki to the main ballroom of the *Grand Maui*, Hawaiian Cruise Line's spectacular flagship. Of course, it took more than his smile for him to reach the pinnacle of his chosen career. "We should talk later," Marlin said, not wanting to keep his present lady waiting.

Marlin would brighten any room that he entered. Men and women both could not help but stare when they saw his dazzling smile. Women desired him and men envied him. At least the men who didn't also desire him. And, for a price, a very steep price, Marlin was happy to oblige their most amorous desires.

Among the elite clique of beach boys that still populated the luxurious haunts of the finest resorts and beaches of Waikiki, Marlin was one of the best. Then again, it had always been his destiny. His father, Max, was legendary in his abilities to woo the rich and famous. His grandfather, Kelly, had been one of the original surfing beach boys that made Waikiki famous in the late 1940's and 1950's. This new breed of post-war Hawaiian men was known as the Golden Men. Kelly was one of the finest. He had been in the service of some of the richest women from the mainland during his prime. Divorcees and widows seemed to be drawn to him. Before long he had established quite a reputation, built on glowing and enthusiastic referrals. He almost lost his life when a tsunami hit the North Shore in 1948. He and his lady friend had spent the afternoon sharing each other's pleasures. He had just dozed off when she awakened him to look at the ocean which had receded several dozen feet off shore. In an instant, he grabbed her arm and began running frantically towards the car. She pulled her arm away, not used to being so forcefully treated. It was that split second that cost her her life as the tsunami thundered ashore. It was Kelly's prowess as a surfer that saved his own life as he was hurtled inland by the surging waves.

Max was Kelly's only child and resulted from one of his socialite flings. A young heiress to a well-known hotel chain mogul became infatuated with Kelly during a visit to Oahu in the late fifties. Max was the consequence of this well-kept secret affair. Kelly was paid an annual stipend to raise his son as well as guarantee his continued discretion and silence.

Marlin, on the other hand, was not the result of one of his father's affairs with the rich mainland socialites. It was a one-night stand Max had had with a gorgeous hula dancer from the luau show at the Royal Hawaiian. The dancer realized even before Marlin was born that Max was not husband or even father material. She moved to Pearl City soon after Marlin was born. Max made no effort to find her. Marlin was almost seven years old when he found out who his father was. His mother decided to marry a sailor who was moving back to Iowa and who wanted no excess baggage. Marlin was excess baggage. His mother packed a small suitcase and, without a word being said, dropped Marlin and the suitcase on Waikiki Beach at the foot of Kelly's beach towel. Thus, began Marlin's education. Marlin would spend his summers and weekends watching his father ply his trade on the beaches of Waikiki, life lessons he would never forget. That is, until Max's premature death at the hands of a drunken tourist. It seems the man grew jealous of the attention his wife was paying Marlin's father. A fight erupted that ended in Max's heart being pierced by a buffet serving fork. He died before he reached the hospital.

Marlin was only sixteen years old. He moved into a small trailer with his grandfather on the North Shore until Kelly also died of tuberculosis later that winter. Though young, Marlin had acquired the skills necessary to continue Kelly and Max's legacy.

Marlin had matured into one of the finest escorts money could buy. He viewed it as his duty to take these wanton socialites for every cent he could. He had grown to hate them along with the rest of the tourists who were destroying his island and whom he blamed for his father's death. Though he certainly didn't act like it.

"I'm clear!" Toyoyuki yelled to the three men loitering near the baggage cart. His supervisor waved his acknowledgement and went back to his conversation. It was the supervisor's job to check the seal of the gas intake, but as usual he was too busy. Toyo got out of his truck and went back to double-check the fueling cover. Everything seemed to be in place. The 747 was fueled and ready for its return flight to Korea. This was the second 747 Toyoyuki had fueled that afternoon. He still had one more to go. All were preparing to return hundreds of tourists back to their homes. That was how it always was on Sundays. Thousands of passengers hurrying home at the last minute. Most headed back to work on Monday so they could brag about their incredible vacation in Paradise. "Paradise lost is more like it," Toyo said quietly to himself.

"Yoyo! Bring me some coffee after you park the truck. There should be some left in the lounge. If not, fix a new pot. Mahalo!" Again, the supervisor turned away before Toyoyuki could respond.

Toyoyuki hated the name Yoyo. Why his boss insisted on calling him that he couldn't understand. He had told the boss to call him Toyo but his boss just laughed. Now everyone called him Yoyo. Toyo kept his mouth shut and seethed inside. He had grown to hate his job along with this haole who ordered him around.

"You are by far the most ravishing beauty aboard this ship," Marlin said, smiling as he rejoined Barbra Chenoweth, his lady friend and the heiress to a vast insurance conglomerate. Her concern about his absence seemed to melt away when she saw his hypnotic smile. "I come with gifts," Marlin continued, as he handed his lady a perfect 'Rosa Cyclop'.

"It's absolutely gorgeous! Where on earth did you find such a rare specimen?"

"I ordered it special for you from the Geschwind Estate. I know how you love roses. It arrived a few hours ago by boat," Marlin said, exuding charm. He did know how to romance his lady friends.

"It must have cost you a fortune having it sent here from Romania."

"Nothing is too good for you, my love." Marlin gently lifted her hand to his lips and kissed it without breaking eye contact. Her knees felt weak as she swooned in anticipation.

Of course, Marlin had charged the entire expense to their suite. He would spend nothing for his act of loving generosity. Barbra knew it as well, but it made no difference. It was the thought that won her over.

The wine steward brought them a bottle of Dom Perignon Rose 1996.

"I ordered the Rose to match the color of your rose," Marlin explained. The steward poured a small amount into one of the glasses for Marlin's approval. "Fabulous! Only the finest for your lips, my love."

"But of course, Marlin. That's why I chose you," Barbra Chenoweth smiled wickedly.

They sat close to each other sipping their champagne, watching the beautiful people show off their bodies at poolside.

"Why do you keep looking at your watch? Do you have to be somewhere?"

"I need only to be with you, my love. Nowhere else," he replied. "Why don't we retire to the cabin for a bit of afternoon fun?" Marlin suggested.

"Momentarily. I rather enjoy the view. Look, you can see whales off to the side. Isn't that wonderful?"

"It truly is wonderful. But not nearly as wonderful as you. I cannot wait another minute to be with you. I insist we go to our cabin at once."

This was not how a beach boy should act and Marlin knew it. He hoped Barbra did not notice. It was his job to cater to her wishes, not the other way around. Marlin again looked at his watch. He was growing edgy.

"You are in a frisky mood today," she replied. "I guess we do need to get properly dressed for this afternoon."

"Right after I get you properly undressed," Marlin replied.

"I certainly hope so," she replied, laughing. She didn't notice as he once again checked his watch.

"Sorry to bother you, Ms. Chenoweth," said one of the *Grand Maui* officers who was standing at the table with an envelope in his hand.

"Yes, what is it?"

"I was asked to deliver this invitation to you. The Captain also instructed me to wait for your reply."

"He did, did he?" She took the envelope, removed the invitation and began to read.

A burst of laughter exploded from Barbra. "Tell the Captain of course we would love to go and he is assuredly more than welcome to join us. That is, if the ship can do without him for the evening."

"The Captain will be delighted to hear your reply. And rest assured, the ship will be fine until you return." The officer hurried away to relay the message to the Captain.

"What was that about, my love? Are we going somewhere?" Marlin asked.

"We have been invited to a most fabulous party. A helicopter will be here in an hour to take us to Bill Casey's estate-warming party on the Big Island. The Captain will be joining us since Bill is a major shareholder in the company that runs this ship. Isn't it fabulous?" Barbra could not hide her excitement.

"Do you mean William H. Casey, the computer and investment tycoon? Didn't he buy half of the coastline between Kona and Waikoloa last year?"

"That would be Bill, but I doubt if he settled for only half. We must hurry if you still plan to get me properly undressed like you promised."

"But of course. A gentleman never breaks a promise to a lady." Marlin kissed her hand as they headed towards their suite.

"I forgot your rose," Marlin suddenly said as they reached the suite. "You go in and I will run back and get it. It will only take a moment."

"Of course, my love."

Marlin whispered into his cell phone as he hurried back to the lounge. "A fortunate turn of events, my friend. There is no need to risk sending the helicopter for me tonight. The lovely Ms. Chenoweth and I will be leaving the ship along with the Captain early this evening. More than an hour before activation. It couldn't have worked out better. I will contact you when this is over."

"Excellent!" was the only reply Marlin heard before the phone went dead.

Toyo's shift ended at five in the afternoon. He had pumped the fuel to several inter-island flights and four international flights, including the last three 747's. He had also made a pot of coffee and delivered it to his boss, just as he had been told to do. He had also performed three other tasks just as he was told to do. The difference was that it was Satochi who had instructed him to do these tasks.

Satochi was an assassin. A very effective assassin, but not infallible. Satochi had been in hiding for months. Time needed to recover from the plastic surgery on his face and the reconstructive surgery and therapy on the tendons of his right leg. He almost lost his leg when Eddie Popp, a CIA agent, used Satochi's own weapon to almost sever the leg just below the knee. Had his boss, Aioka Matsuura, head of one of the world's most violent active terrorist organizations, not pre-arranged for a boat to be at the ready in the Avalon Harbor in Catalina, Satochi surely would have lost his leg. Even after the extensive surgeries, he still had a pronounced limp and needed a cane to walk. A very limiting handicap for an assassin. But not for Satochi. It did require him to give up the weapon he had used to kill so many men in the past. His 'Lei O Mano', or tiger shark tooth koa club, was no longer practical. It required close combat and a firm footing to properly kill your opponent. Satochi now used a more logical weapon befitting his injury. He now carried a cane that sheathed a samurai-type sword. The hand grip converted to a barbed claw opposed by a razor-sharp giant Tiger shark's tooth, both for ripping or slashing open the throats of his victims. The sword was capable of severing limb or even the head with one mighty blow. A very bloody and messy means of killing, but it was the way of the Polynesian warriors. Blood only made the warrior stronger and Satochi was a warrior.

Satochi was Aioka's most trusted assassin. At least he was until the fiasco in Avalon that almost cost him his life and ruined Aioka's planned anthrax attack on Los Angeles. Of course, it wasn't entirely Satochi's fault, but Aioka had lost much faith in the man he now secretly called bikko. Satochi had heard rumors of this and, even though he was a cripple, it was the tone which Aioka used when saying the word that troubled Satochi. What he hated more was hearing that Aioka sometimes referred to him as "rokudenashi", meaning one that is not worthy or no good. One day he would confront

Aioka about dishonoring him, but not until he got what he wanted and needed from Aioka.

Toyo placed three precisely formed devices that fit perfectly to the inside of the gas intake tank of a Boeing 747. At least they were supposed to fit perfectly. He had difficulty screwing the aluminum outer cap on the Korean jumbo-jet. The outer cap wasn't necessary to keep fuel from leaking out because the inner cap would not allow that to happen, but it was noticeable if it wasn't replaced. He was able to turn it just enough for the cap to catch in the receiver. Toyo knew it would vibrate out as the jet accelerated down the runway. He only hoped it wouldn't fall out before the ramp controller cleared it to push back. It would probably go unnoticed if it fell out while taxiing and, if not, it wasn't serious enough to order the plane back to the terminal. At least Toyo hoped it wasn't. Each device contained a timer and enough C-4 explosive to blow the wing apart. But that was not its purpose. Its purpose was to explode the hundreds of gallons of jet fuel in the newly filled primary tanks, turning the entire plane into a giant fireball. All three planes.

Toyo hurried to leave. He knew all three bombs were wired to explode at any moment. Exactly when that moment was, he had no idea. He did know two of the jets had already pushed back several minutes before and the third was due to leave immediately. Toyo intended to be as far away from Honolulu International as possible when that moment arrived.

Aioka Matsuura, like Satochi, had returned to the Hawaiian Islands and, like Satochi, he also had extensive plastic surgery in an attempt to hide his previous identity. There were several counter-terror organizations with agents assigned to finding Aioka and Satochi and putting an end to their Red Summit terrorist organization. They were both very cautious and rarely ventured out in public. Aioka had moved into a house near Hilo on the east or wet side of the Big Island. It is spread across the slopes and canyons of a Mauna Loa lava flow from the 1800's. Hundreds of small enclaves and individual homes are hidden in the dense rainforest that covers the area. A very private and remote environment ideal for people seeking to stay private and anonymous. The only real excursions away from the house were either for business or for his semi-weekly visits to the *Back to the 50's* diner located up the highway in Laupahoehoe, about 20 kilometers north. The 50's diner reminded Aioka of a Hurley's, the name of the chain of burger stands he had owned back in Japan or, more precisely, that his dead brother had owned and founded. It had the same fifties theme as did Hurley's and the chef, Chris, would even occasionally venture out tell a few jokes and maybe even sing a song for you. Besides, Aioka thought they had the best Mahi sandwich found on the island.

Aioka's new house was not like the extravagant mansions he was used to staying in. It was a remote semi-secluded house on the Honoli'i Stream. The house was almost directly below the tall bridge overpass of Highway 19, the Mamalahoa Highway connecting the Hilo and Kona sides of the Big Island. The house was an ideal hideout for Aioka. Honoli'i Cove was one of the most popular surfing beaches on the east side of the island. That meant there were always people around. Lots of people. Enough people that visitors to Aioka's house usually went unnoticed. The house was on the bank of the river and had direct access to the ocean by both wave runner and small speedboat, each of which Aioka maintained at the ready. The highway bridge above his house offered the perfect landing spot for a helicopter if that should be needed in an emergency. Aioka kept a small jet at a hangar at the Hilo airport along with his helicopter. He was used to, and preferred, the luxury a private jet provided. Lately he used commercial air transportation to keep a low profile. Too many private jets were coming in and out of the Big Island airports, especially the Kona airport. The airport authority realized what a huge money maker taxing these planes could be and were monitoring them much more closely than before. Aioka would only use his jet if it were absolutely necessary.

No one would have expected him to move back to the Big Island after all that had occurred over the past two years. His ranch near Hawi, of course, was confiscated after the mad cow-tainted cosmetic plot was disrupted by the FBI. He was left blameless of any involvement with the Red Summit terrorist organization that was responsible for the attack. That was when he still was known as Taka, the name he stole from his brother when he murdered him and had the real Taka's body thrown into the molten lava of Kilauea. Then, only six months ago, his safe house was discovered along with the lava tube tunnel leading from the hidden anthrax lab below the Paleaka Ranch down to the ocean. Almost all of his weaponized anthrax was lost as was over a million dollars in cash. The cash was of little consequence, but the loss of so much anthrax was devastating. He and Satochi did manage to remove several canisters, but three were wasted in the failed attempt to rain death down upon Los Angeles and one was destroyed when his yacht *Kona Snow* was blown out of the water by the Navy Seals team in Catalina. He still had four canisters remaining, more than enough to wreak havoc and kill tens of thousands of Americans. And it would start today.

One lesson Aioka had learned from his bio-terror attacks of America over the past years was that Americans didn't consider slow death by disease real terrorism. Thousands were affected by the Bovine spongiform encephalopathy or BSE-tainted lipstick terror plot and were doomed to die an agonizing death, their brains rotting away, turning into sponges with no hope of recovery. A horrible death, but not horrible enough to induce terror. Nor did he expect the male gendercide, that the abducted Russian scientist created with his GMO coffee beans, would prove terrifying to America. Still, it had been a brilliant plan that would significantly alter the population of the United States for generations. A brilliant plan that had not yet run its course. And wasn't that always his ultimate goal, to stop America from growing, exploiting, and stealing the resources of the rest of the world? To put an end to American Imperialism and the American culturalization of his Japanese heritage as well as other unique cultures now at risk? None more so than the Polynesian culture almost extinct on the Hawaiian Islands. He had sworn to put a stop to it. That was why he had found so many willing to join his terrorist cause here in Hawaii. The native Hawaiians were losing their land and their way of life. They were on the brink of not being able to afford to live on the islands. Their islands! The islands of their ancestors, the islands of great kings, now the islands of the four million-dollar condos and the thirty million-dollar houses, the islands of the wealthiest men in the world.

Aioka swore that would change. He felt a kinship to these Hawaiians.

Terror, real terror, was body parts lying in the streets and blood running down the gutters. That was what the media called terror and that is what Americans came to believe. Aioka would give them such terror, terror like they had never before witnessed on American soil, terror that would blind them to the real attack he had always planned. More blood than they could ever imagine.

"Who's minding the ship?" Marlin asked the Captain as they prepared to enter the waiting helicopter.

"My First Officer is more than qualified to step into my place. Besides, who am I to turn down such an invitation? Especially since it is from the majority stock owner of the cruise line. I will have the helicopter return us to the ship before it is halfway to Fanning Island."

"Bill has offered us one of the beach bungalows at the Four Seasons, so we won't be returning with you," Barbra told the Captain.

"I am sorry to see you leave the *Grand Maui*, but we are almost at the end of the cruise and I think the Four Seasons, though not as nice as your suite aboard ship, is an excellent choice. I will have one of the valets pack your belongings and forward them immediately."

"Thank you so much, Captain. I cannot tell you how much I have enjoyed your ship." Barbra was looking at Marlin when she made her last statement. The Captain knew her comment wasn't necessarily said for his benefit.

It was a short flight from the helipad on the *Grand Maui* to the Kohala Coast and the estate of William H. Casey. Casey had amassed a fortune through shrewd business deals and was now one of the ten richest men in the world. One of his most recent investments had been the purchase of several miles of coastline on the Big Island. Only the State of Hawaii and Parker Ranch owned more of Hawaii than Bill Casey and not everybody was happy about it. Bill had built two new golf courses on his land. One course was for the guests of the several resorts he now owned or was building, along with the owners of the extremely high-end condos and homes that were now covering much of the black lava. The other course was for him and his closest friends, insuring he would never have to wait for a tee time.

With the onslaught of houses and condos came the onslaught of traffic. It now could take up to two hours to travel from the Kailua-Kona airport in Keahole to Captain Cook, a distance of barely 20 miles. Locals called it the Kainaliu Crawl, more aptly called the Kailua Stall. Taxes had skyrocketed along with housing costs. Most Big Island residents couldn't afford to live in the Kona area and had to commute as much as two hours to get to their jobs meeting the needs of the flood of mainlanders and foreigners. Discontent was growing at a pace greater than the building boom on the Big Island.

At exactly four-thirty in the afternoon, not more than ten minutes after the helicopter departed the *Grand Maui*, a timer in a small package placed inside the air conditioning vent in the main dining hall activated an aerosol spray. Every fifteen minutes a burst of the deadly contents would be sprayed into the air drifting almost weightlessly throughout the massive hall. Eventually these micro molecules would float gently lower attaching themselves to any available surface. If that surface happened to be a proper host for this deadly and fast-acting strain of anthrax, it would be only a matter of hours before preserving the host's life would be impossible. Survival depended upon a quick regiment of massive doses of Cipro. Even then, survival was not guaranteed.

"Honolulu ground, Korea Air 16 spot six taxi with alpha."

"Korea Air 16, follow American 137 to runway 26L hold short spot nine."

The Korea Air 747 moved slowly into the taxi line behind the American 767. The captain continued to respond to the first officer's scripted challenges.

Aboard the ITOP 747, the CSR confirmed the passenger count while the two pilots continued checking the maintenance logs and fuel sheets.

Do you have all the paperwork?" the CSR asked.

"I think we're set," the copilot responded.

"Cabin ready, people seated," the flight attendant informed the captain.

"Thank you, Susan," the captain replied as the attendant closed the cockpit door.

The CSR closed the cabin door while two other flight attendants armed the door escape slides. The pilots continued their checklist confirming all doors and windows were closed and locked slides armed and cabin ready.

"Ramp tower, ITOP 370 ready to push from gate 26."

"ITOP 370, cleared to push and stop at the top of the alley." It was now the tug driver who would communicate with the captain and get the massive jet safely away from the gate.

"AMG 204, winds 260 at 15 Fly runway heading, runway 26L cleared for takeoff."

"AMG 204 cleared for takeoff, runway 26L."

The pilot moved the thrust levers to takeoff position and steered the airplane to the centerline with the rudder pedals. The 747 lurched forward.

"80 knots, thrust set," the copilot called out.

Without warning, the plane exploded in a massive fireball incinerating the 387 passengers and crew aboard the plane. The airwaves erupted as the tower controller, ground controller, and several pilots taxiing their planes for take off, all began to speak at once. Suddenly, Korean Air 16 holding at spot nine in the taxi line exploded into flames. Parts of this plane ripped huge holes in several other planes waiting to take-off. It became chaos as all of the pilots turned their planes in any direction reasonably free of debris in an attempt to get away from the burning airplanes and other planes near them. Several of the taxiing planes started emergency evacuations and passengers began running helter-skelter across the runways and tarmac for safety. Inside the terminal everyone ran to the giant windows to witness the hell transpiring before their eyes. The ITOP 747 was being pushed back from the gate by the tug when the first plane exploded.

Toyo was just leaving the tarmac when he heard the thundering clap. From where he stood, he couldn't see the plane. His boss and several other workers ran out to see what had happened. There was no way for him to leave without arousing suspicion.

"Yoyo, what's going on?"

"Sounded like some kind of explosion to me," he responded.

"No shit dumb ass," his boss replied. Before Toyo could respond the second plane exploded. This time the men could see the fireball as it rose into the sky.

"Get us back to the gate, now!" the ITOP pilot radioed the tug driver. The driver knew not to question the pilot and started to pull the large jet back towards the terminal gate.

"Everyone to a truck," the boss yelled. "People are going to need help. Watch out for the ITOP, it looks like it is pulling back...." Toyo, his boss, and the other workers were all blown apart before the boss finished his warning as the ITOP burst into a blinding fireball. Large sections of the plane

16

ripped through the glass walls of the terminal killing dozens of people who had rushed to the windows to view the tragedy unfolding. Burning jet fuel covered both the inside and outside of the terminal. Honolulu Airport had turned into a war zone. Body parts covered the runway and the tarmac. Burning airplane parts, luggage, and bodies were everywhere. Inside the terminal, parents were screaming for children who were no longer there. The injured were being trampled as they slowed the progress of the screaming mobs fleeing for their lives. No one knew where the next bomb would explode. They only knew they needed to get far away from the airport as fast as possible.

"Hi, I'm Eddie, Eddie Popp, you know, like in soda pop."

"A pleasure to meet you, Eddie." Barbra responded, putting out her hand. Eddie gently took her hand in his, bringing it to his lips and softly kissing it. "Oh my, such a gentleman," Barbra replied, eyeing Eddie. Had Marlin not been her chosen friend this trip, she surely would have made Eddie Popp her escort these past weeks in Hawaii. He was as charming as Marlin, but had somewhat of a bad boy aura.

"Barbra, my dear, I see you have met my special friend, Eddie Popp."

"Seneca, I didn't know you were here on the islands. You should have let me know. I would have loved for the two of you to have joined Marlin and me on the *Grand Maui*."

"Oh, I did that cruise last year, but thank you anyway. Eddie and I have had a wonderful time here at the Four Seasons this past week. Eddie has taught me to surf and I have taught him the finer points of cheating at golf." Barbra and Seneca both laughed.

Marlin and Eddie excused themselves and went to the bar while their two lady friends bragged and reminisced.

"Nice to meet you, Eddie. Been doing the circuit long? I don't think I've seen you around before," Marlin inquired.

"If you mean rubbing elbows with the rich and famous, no, I haven't been. I've been on the Big Island taking care of a friend's house and dog while he's been away for the past few months. I just kind of fell into this good fortune while hitting the island night spots."

"Well, you must be pretty good at it if Seneca Willows has kept you around for a week. That's typically not her style."

"You sound like an old pro at this," Eddie replied.

"I am, third generation beach boy in fact. I cannot think of anything I would rather do."

"You won't get an argument from me. A guy could grow to like this kind of life," Eddie said.

"You have no idea," Marlin replied. The two men continued in their conversation throughout the evening. Of course, neither neglected their lady friends that had brought them to the party. They were both the perfect escorts.

The party was in full swing at one of Bill's resorts just north of the Four Seasons, the Kona Village Resort. It, more than any resort on all the Big Island, gave you the real feeling of old Hawaii. All guests stayed in authentic thatched huts scattered along the beach and around the lagoon in a tropical paradise setting. Visitors were not allowed to even drive close to the resort. A guard house a mile inland kept curious tourists away. The resort boasted having no televisions so as to shield you from the reality of the world while you escaped. Cell phones were strictly forbidden, though enforcing the rule was difficult with the famous and high-end clientele that frequented the resort. It was this lack of connection with the outside world that delayed notification of the guests as to the terrorist bombings at the Honolulu airport.

"Damn, I hope that is you vibrating with anticipation and not that damn phone of yours," Seneca said, only half-joking.

"Sorry sweetheart. You know I have to keep this with me."

"Yes, yes, I know. My secret agent lover."

Eddie looked at the caller ID. He knew that it had to be important if the FBI watch officer in Honolulu was calling on a Sunday evening. Eddie walked away from the crowd of people dancing by the pool before he answered the call.

"I guess you found me," Eddie answered.

"Jesus Christ, Eddie, haven't you been watching the news? It seems like all of Hawaii is under attack," the watch officer said frantically.

"Whoa, slow down a bit. Just what are you talking about?"

"Turn on a freak'n television, Eddie. Three planes fully loaded with passengers were blown up at Honolulu International just a couple of hours ago. All air traffic has been grounded in the United States until further notice. And now that goddamned anthrax virus you guys worked on is back and worse than ever. The cruise ship, the *Grand Maui*, has sent out a mayday requesting immediate medical assistance for the whole damn crew and all the passengers."

"What are you talking about? I just talked to the Captain of the *Grand Maui* twenty minutes ago. He didn't say anything about it."

"That's because they haven't been able to reach him. You better let him know what the hell is going on."

"Are you sure it's anthrax?"

19

"Positive. The same ship's doctor who discovered the anthrax-infected bodies on that dive boat last year identified the symptoms as being exactly the same. The Navy is rushing a medical team there as we speak. I just hope they make it in time. The doc says some people are already covered with lesions and many others are sick. Jotty Joplin called from Washington and wants you on that ship ASAP! I thought you guys destroyed all the weaponized anthrax when you discovered that lava tube and laboratory in Hawi?"

"I did too, but apparently we were wrong."

"I've got a pilot and a copter ready to go. Just tell me where the hell to send it."

"Have it meet me at the 18th green of the Four Seasons golf course. Right next to the club house. I will head there now and light a flare so the pilot knows where to land."

"You better bring the ship's captain with you. The doctor told me he had the series of anthrax shots after that last run in. His pilot is too sick to fly. And you might want to take a look at the shit happening at the airport. It is still complete chaos there."

Eddie immediately went to the ship's captain to inform him of the situation. The captain was stunned by the news. Eddie then explained the situation to Seneca. At least part of it.

"Oh my God, Eddie! Barbra and Marlin came from the ship. Do you think they are infected?"

Without answering, Eddie hurried over to the bar where Barbra and Eddie were chatting with another couple.

"Excuse me, but could I speak to the two of you privately for a moment."

Barbra was a bit perturbed until she saw the serious expression on Eddie's face. Marlin sensed trouble and tried not to look nervous.

"Are you both feeling alright?"

"We've never felt better," Barbra replied for the both of them. "Why do you ask?"

"An outbreak of anthrax was just reported on the *Grand Maui*. The captain and I are headed back there now."

Marlin caught Barbra as she swooned. "Do you think we have it? Marlin asked, concerned.

"No, I think if you did, we would know it. Just in case, keep an eye on each other to see if you notice any strange sores or if you begin to feel ill. I will be in touch with both of you when I find out what's going on." Eddie didn't want to ruin their night any further by telling them what happened in Honolulu. He wasn't even sure himself what was happening there, but he damn sure planned to find out.

CHAPTER TWO

One year earlier

Mahmoud lay on a blood and vomit-soaked blackened mat inside the makeshift tent. If it wasn't for an occasional moan, you would think he was already dead. His eyes were open, but clouded in a frightening vague stare. His skin had lost all elasticity and hung on his fragile skeletal frame. Droplets of blood had formed on his nipples. Fresh blood stains covered the white shorts matted to his legs. His hands, cut by years of working the gold mine, bled continuously, his blood unable to clot. Blood trickled from his nose and ears. The virus would soon end his life, just like it had the ninety miners before him who had also lay in this tent. Mahmoud prayed it would be sooner than later. In a separate tent, five other miners lay in various states of the disease, none as ravaged as Mahmoud. Six miners had somehow survived the initial symptoms, though their recovery would be difficult and not guaranteed. One survivor was blinded and another had his testes explode. The others would not fair much better, yet they would live. Mahmoud would not be so fortunate. Only his wife was by his side. Occasionally, the nurse would look in to see if Mahmoud was dead yet. The mat was needed for others who were too far along to remain in the communal tent. Randall was the young physician assigned by the CDC to treat these most recent victims of the filovirus, but he refused to see Mahmoud. He was too frightened. He never expected to be placed in such peril when he signed up with the Doctors without Borders. The one local doctor who had worked at the small government health center in Durba had himself died of the virus. Randall had already radioed the center to let them know he would be leaving when the next landrover arrived with medicine and supplies from Kinshasa. There was no telling when that might be. Travel was severely limited and dangerous because of the several armed factions fighting for control of this region of the Congo. It could not be too soon as far as Randall was concerned.

Randall was smoking his fourth cigarette of the morning when he heard a vehicle approaching. Usually this meant trouble. The armed guerrillas and the aide organizations were the only ones with vehicles capable of reaching this CDC outpost and Randall had received no message about supplies being delivered. Still, his hopes were high that this could be his ticket out of this death trap.

"Anybody alive here?" a voice called out from the landrover as it stopped in a cloud of dirt.

"English! Somebody is speaking English," Randall said, as he rushed out from behind a stand of trees where he had been hiding. Suddenly, he stopped when he saw several armed men taking a defensive position by the vehicle. "What do you want?" Randall called out timidly.

"I'm looking for Dr. Randall Carson. Are you the good doctor?" a man replied with a German accent.

"I am Dr. Carson from Doctors without Borders. I'm here helping with the Ebola outbreak. How can I help you?" They were trained to tell strangers who they worked for in hopes of keeping from being killed by the guerrillas.

"I am Günter Marx from the University in Marsburg, Dr. Günter Marx," a rather large man replied as he climbed out of the front seat. "I was sent here to collect blood samples of the victims to compare this outbreak to other strains we have collected."

Randall didn't immediately reply. "You need to contact the CDC if you need samples." He had been warned about terror organizations trying to acquire samples of the virus. The Aum Sharikyo cult had sent forty members to Zaire in 1992 offering medical assistance in an attempt to get the virus. Ebola was a Category A biological terrorism agent and capable of posing a severe threat to the health of a country.

"That's preposterous," Günter replied. "We have been obtaining our own samples from these outbreaks since our initial filovirus scare in Marburg in 1964. We have a more complete sampling of strains than the CDC could ever hope to collect. They come to us when they have questions."

"I have heard of your facility and its reputation," Randall replied.

"Of course you have," Günter replied emphatically. "Please, just give me several samples so I can be on my way. The air here is thick with death and I do not wish to stay here any longer than necessary."

"My sentiments exactly," Randall replied. "I had no idea it would be this bad when I volunteered to spend my vacation time working with Doctors without Borders. I cannot wait to leave. In fact, I plan on going with the next supply truck due to arrive next week. My life is just too valuable to waste here."

"A real humanitarian," Günter thought to himself. It was obvious Randall belonged in some HMO clinic treating headaches, not here in the Congo treating real diseases.

"I still will have to contact my headquarters before I can issue you those samples and that may take a while. Those are the rules," Randall said.

"To hell with the rules," Günter replied. "Armed guerillas were seen headed this way early this morning. Why do you think I brought all this firepower? I will not wait and you would be a fool to stay here. You should come with us. My guards will keep us safe."

"I cannot just leave. I have patients who are dying."

"And what are you doing for them that these local nurses cannot do. You know there is little chance of recovery. It is dangerous in this area, especially for an American. You could stay in Watsa a few days until the fighting stops and it is safe to return. I'm sure they could use a good doctor at one of the hospitals there."

It didn't take long for Randall to realize Günter was correct. What good was he doing here? He was already planning to leave. Why even bother to stay in Watsa? "When do you plan to leave Watsa and return to Germany?" Randall asked.

Günter knew he had him now. "I have a twin-engine Cessna waiting for me at the airstrip just south of the village. I plan to fly to Tanzania as soon as possible. I have a Marburg University jet waiting for me at the Kilimanjaro Airport in Arusha."

"You wouldn't by chance have room for an extra passenger?" Randall asked. "I really don't think I can take this place for another day."

"If you help me, of course I will help you. You will find Germany to be a much friendlier place than Durba. Not so many people with machine guns running around killing people." Günter laughed loudly at his own joke.

"How many blood samples do you need?" Randall asked.

"As many as will fit in this container," Günter replied, pointing to a large special ice chest one of the guards was taking out of the back of the landrover.

"Just give me a few minutes to gather my things. We already have several samples in our cold chest from the victims who died. We were preparing to ship them to the Special Pathogens Program at the National Microbiology Laboratory in Canada for diagnostic testing. I'm sure nobody will miss them. I will have the nurses start drawing blood from the patients in isolation." Randall knew that leaving Doctors Without Borders in the middle of an assignment would not look good on his resume, but at least he would still be alive. Africa was not what he had expected.

Two hours later Randall sat next to Günter in the rear seat of an old, but reliable, Cessna 310. The filovirus samples were secured in the luggage compartment along with the few personal belongings Randall refused to leave behind. The armed guards stayed behind in Watsa. The pilot sat alone in the front.

"I am so damn glad to be out of that place," Randall said.

"So much for your Hippocrates Oath," Günter snidely replied.

"I beg your pardon! Who are you to judge me? I always considered the good of my patients and treated them according to my ability and my judgment. I never did harm to anyone. There is nothing further I could do for those sick miners but keep them comfortable. It doesn't take a doctor to do that."

"That's not the part of the Oath I am talking about," Günter replied. "I'm talking about the part that says you will give no deadly medicine to anyone who asks."

"What are you talking about? I have never done such a thing," Randall replied.

Günter didn't reply.

"We have just entered Tanzanian air space," the pilot reported to Günter.

"Look down there Randall. We are halfway across Lake Victoria. It almost looks like an ocean from up here."

Randall was still too angry to respond to Günter, although he did look out at the vastness of the lake. When he looked up, Günter held a 9mm semi-automatic Glock pointed at his head.

"I'm afraid it is time for you to leave us, Dr. Carson," Günter said.

"What are you talking about?"

"You broke your Hippocrates Oath and now you must pay the consequences." Günter replied. "You gave away the Ebola virus to someone who plans to use it in a very deadly way, me!"

The color drained from Randall's face. "You can't be serious."

"Oh, but I am serious," Günter replied.

"The nurses back in Durba know I left with you. They will contact the authorities when I cannot be found," Randall said.

"Who will even bother to look for a doctor who ran out on his commitment to help the sick? Besides, the nurses at the CDC outpost are already dead. I had those guerrillas who escorted us to Watsa return and kill everyone. Actually, I did you a favor. You will be considered a martyr rather than a coward."

"I can pay you." Randall was now desperate.

"I've had enough of your pathetic behavior," Günter replied. "Get out!"

"If you think I'll jump from this plane, you're crazy," Randall replied.

"If you don't jump, I will shoot you, and then throw you from the plane. I am giving you a chance."

"Some chance," Randall replied.

27

"Men have survived such falls in the past, especially into water," Günter said.

Randall lunged at Günter, but was stopped short when the bullet exploded into his chest.

"Dammit, Günter, you'll get blood all over everything," the pilot complained.

Günter quickly pushed forward the empty copilot's seat and opened the door. Fighting the onrushing air, he shoved Randall's body through the narrow opening. "I believe I got him out before any of his blood soiled the seat," Günter said to the pilot. "It looks to be another beautiful day on the Serengeti. I'm going to miss Africa."

The Cessna landed at Kilimanjaro International Airport and taxied to spot five on the far eastern side of the outer boarding tarmac where a small Lear jet was waiting. Kilimanjaro Airport has five boarding areas. Four are on the inner tarmac near the terminal and available only to the few commercial flights that arrive and depart daily. The fifth, or spot five, is where private jets and larger private aviation propeller planes load and unload their passengers. Swiss port had fueled the small jet and a custom's official was waiting by the door of the jet as the Cessna taxied to a stop. No commercial flights were due for another two hours, so the agent was passing time talking with the jet's pilot until the mad rush of an arriving flight started again.

"Dr. Marx, your pilot informed me about your research into tribal genetics. It sounds truly interesting. I understand you were in Tabora collecting blood samples of the local tribesman. I hope you were successful," the agent said.

"Remarkably so," Günter replied. "My pilot is bringing the samples now if you would care to inspect them."

"That won't be necessary. Enjoy your flight back to Germany." The custom's agent didn't even bother to look at Günter's passport.

As soon as Günter was aboard, the jet requested clearance for take-off and received it.

"If you look off to the left you can see Zanzibar," the pilot announced over the intercom. Günter didn't hear the pilot's message; he was already fast asleep.

Günter awoke when the tires of the Leer jet screeched as they hit runway 18 of the Helsinki-Malmi Airport. It was the primary general aviation airport that served the Helsinki vicinity. All commercial flights flew into the newer Helsinki-Vantaa Airport located about 5 km further north from the city centre. The Malmi airport is much more convenient for business travelers and lacked the congestion and delays often found at Vantaa. A corporate limo was waiting for Günter as he exited the jet. The limo and the jet both belonged to Zetanutra, one of the largest nutraceutical manufacturers in all of Finland. Customs agents rarely bothered to inspect or question corporate jets landing at the Malmi Airport. Today was no exception.

The limo drove the short distance down the E75 to Somainen where Zetanutra had their warehouses and manufacturing plant. The Zetanutra executive offices were located in the city centre. A ten-foot chain link fence with razor-wire on top surrounded the perimeter of the Zetanutra warehouse and manufacturing facility. Such a fence was typical of all the businesses in the Somainen area. Zetanutra had an unusually large number of security cameras monitoring the area. There were three warehouses on the property and a complex of several manufacturing buildings, all designed for the production of specific types of Zetanutra products. The warehouses appeared identical and there were no windows in any of the three. The middle warehouse, however, had a much more sophisticated security entrance system than the other two. Both vehicles and pedestrians entering the building had to go into an inner holding area and wait until the outer door sealed before being allowed access to the warehouse. Very few workers were even allowed access to warehouse two. Zetanutra told its employees that the security and secrecy were due to the extremely competitive nutriceutical industry and the constant attempts at stealing company research secrets. A highly plausible and believable scenario.

"Aioka, my friend, it is so good to see you are safe and well," Günter said as he climbed from the car.

"I was very surprised to receive your call so soon. When you said you would have the virus within the week my scientists had to scramble to acquire the Biosafety equipment to deal with a Level 3 agent. They are still finishing the installation," Aioka replied.

"I told you we would be doing business again very soon," Günter replied.

"You do realize I will not be able to fulfill my side of the bargain for several more months," Aioka replied. "It is all arranged and it would be impossible to speed up the process."

"Of course, our agreement was that the exchange would occur in a year. I was just fortunate that an outbreak occurred in the Congo. I was afraid I was going to have to break into the facility in Canada to get you the samples. Here, they are yours," Günter said, as he passed the chest to Aioka.

Aioka refused to take that chest and signaled for one of his scientists to take it. He quickly placed it in a biohazard bag and took it directly into a Biosafe laboratory built in the middle of the warehouse. This inner building had no outer windows, although there were windows between the several lab and work rooms inside the free-standing structure. It also contained a complete Biosafety Level 3 laboratory with the so-called space-suits for the scientists to wear while performing their tasks and proper decontamination chambers outside the entrance.

"Did you have any trouble acquiring the samples?" Aioka asked.

"If you mean, did I leave any loose ends or witnesses, the answer is no. I still have several loyal mercenaries in the region that made sure there was no one left alive at the CDC outpost in Durba. I personally took care of Dr. Carson, who so graciously supplied me with the samples. There is no way anyone will even know filovirus samples existed, let alone were taken, from the outpost. It will appear that everyone at the outpost was killed by guerrilla factions warring in the region."

"That is excellent," Aioka replied. "Have you considered my offer to watch over my interests here in Helsinki while you wait for the completion of our bargain?"

"I have and I will," Günter replied. "I also met with those four jailed men in Texas you told me about. They would make excellent foot soldiers for our attack on America. That is, if you can get them out like you say you can."

"I wouldn't have offered if I couldn't," Aioka replied. "Now let me explain what I need you to do for me here."

CHAPTER THREE

One week earlier

"I love you so very much," Haruko said to Jotty as he held her in bed.

"And I love you more than you can ever imagine."

"I don't know, I have a pretty big imagination," Haruko replied as she pulled Jotty on top of her.

"Thank God for herbal supplements," Jotty thought.

Only five months ago Jotty could not have imagined Haruko lying next to him, let alone beneath him, in bed. He had dreamed about it since he first saw her, but never thought it would actually happen until Aioka was brought to justice. At least that is what Haruko had said those many years Jotty had professed his love to her. Jotty Joplin was head of the Far East division for the National Counter-Terrorism Center in McClean, Virginia. He actually was drafted into the position from the FBI. Almost everyone in his office had been drafted from various agencies. Haruko was an expert on Aioka Matsuura and the Red Summit. She had come to the NCTC from the Japanese National Police Agency where she had been their head of counter-terrorism, a position that lacked any real authority and the respect she deserved for her abilities and accomplishments. She had previously worked with Jotty when he put together an international team to breakup the Red Summit. Jotty had been in love with Haruko since then. When both their governments declared the Red Summit officially non-existent, Haruko spurned Jotty's professed love and returned to Tokyo knowing they had not seen the last of the Red Summit and determined to show Taka was not who he seemed to be. She was proved correct last year when the Red Summit resurfaced and Aioka revealed it was he who assumed Taka's identity and led the Red Summit. Jotty's NCTC was able to stop the terror attacks, but Aioka got away, as did his chief assassin Satochi. Haruko knew Aioka could never return to Japan, so she agreed to join the NCTC and move to America to once and for all end the Red Summit's reign of terror.

"Can I get you some tea?" Jotty asked as he climbed out of bed.

"That would be lovely," Haruko replied, "and don't forget to take your supplements."

Jotty rolled his eyes as he walked into the kitchen. He was several years older than Haruko and not in nearly as good of shape as she was. That was something she was working on. She had tried to make him a vegetarian, but failed. She had managed to get him to stop eating red meat, or at least she was partially responsible for that. Jotty lost his taste for beef after the mad cow-tainted meat surfaced in several American cities as part of the Red Summit's first attack on America. Haruko had started Jotty on a strict regimen of vitamins and herbal supplements to go along with his daily jogs and his twice-weekly martial arts training.

"Green or black?" he yelled to Haruko.

"Green, of course," she replied from bed. It was Saturday and Jotty always treated her to breakfast in bed on Saturdays.

Jotty started the water and began to lay out the dozen or so vitamins and capsules Haruko had insisted he take. Not all of them were taken everyday and Haruko had taped a chart on the back of the cabinet door for him to follow. He wasn't sure what half of them were for, but he had his suspicions about a couple of them. Since he started taking these supplements, he was more virile and had more stamina than he could remember having in years. He wanted to mention it to Haruko, but was too embarrassed. "What if it wasn't the supplements?" Jotty thought to himself. "How would I explain that?" When he had the time, he would do a web search to see what these various capsules were designed to do.

"Have you talked to Jim lately?" Haruko asked as he brought her breakfast.

"I was going to call him today," Jotty lied.

"I think you're too concerned about what Jim is going to say about us living together."

"I feel guilty! You know he loved you too," Jotty said.

"He only loved the idea of loving me. He never really loved me the way you do and he knows that. Call him, see how he is doing."

"I know I should. I did read the reports by the company psychologist about his recovery. He seems to be doing much better, but even the psychologist isn't sure how he would react under fire."

"Maybe it's time to bring him back to work and find out. I bet Eddie is getting pretty tired of taking care of Jim's garden back in Hawaii."

"I'd be willing to bet everything that that garden died three months ago. From what I hear, Eddie has found the nightlife on the Big Island to his liking. It's about time to put him back in the field. Brazil, possibly! Isn't that where you think Aioka may be hiding out?"

"That is what I used to think. I have the feeling he has moved somewhere else, but Brazil would still be a good place for Eddie to start looking."

"I'll give him a call first thing Monday morning," Jotty replied.

"You mean Monday afternoon? Remember there is a six-hour time difference now that daylight savings time is here."

"You're right! I should probably wait till Monday evening to give him a chance to wake up from his partying. Boy, is Eddie in for a shock!"

"You had better hurry if you are going to make it to your martial arts class," Haruko reminded Jotty. "By the way, I gave Ellen some of your supplements for her husband to try last week."

"Ellen, who's Ellen? You don't mean that overbearing obnoxious lady in the South American research section, do you?"

"That would be the one, and she is not obnoxious. Overbearing, yes, but not obnoxious. She is married to Wallace in threat analysis. You know, the one in your martial arts class."

"Oh yes, the hen-pecked one," Jotty retorted. Haruko threw a pillow at Jotty.

"I'll see you for lunch. I love you," Jotty said, as he hurried out the door to avoid the pillow. Jotty didn't like the idea of everybody knowing about his supplements, but he wasn't going to question Haruko about it. He just hoped it wasn't what he thought it was, or he was going to be mighty embarrassed.

Director Cheney was not the least bit happy with the way the INS agents were handling their prisoner population. There had been several accusations about sexual misconduct by some of the INS guards and now the media was starting to take notice. Cheney ran the 551-bed Rolling Plains Regional Jail and Detention Center in Haskell, Texas. It was a privately-owned for-profit facility that housed both men and women for the Immigration and Naturalization Service, the State of Wyoming, and Haskell County.

"That damn woman," Cheney said to his secretary. "She goes off spouting all that bullshit and now the Feds are sending in a special assessment team. They can assess this as far as I'm concerned," Cheney said grabbing his crotch.

"If they don't, I will," his secretary laughed, giving her boss a kiss and a squeeze.

"You feel hot," his secretary said, "are you feeling alright?"

"Never felt better," Cheney lied. Three days ago, he woke up with a severe headache, fever, and muscle pain. He thought he was coming down with the flu, but didn't want to tell his secretary. He enjoyed his special evenings with her too much to have a little flu get in the way.

Ver Dell Cheney was a happily married forty-five-year-old man with two children and a mistress. He also was a big fan of "tongkat ali," a stamina producing herb from Malaysia. It had done wonders for his golf game and for his sex life, a sex life that he preferred to keep secret from his wife. He ordered a free sample after a friend told him how it had completely restored the romance in his life. It proved to be everything his friend had said it was, and more. He became a regular customer reordering a supply every other month. He had the supplement delivered to his office at the detention facility just to make sure his wife had no reason to become suspicious. Ver Dell and his wife were getting along better than ever, and he was keeping his mistress very busy, two things he didn't want to screw up.

"Are you sure you are okay? You look really flush," his secretary said.

"I am feeling a little peculiar. I think I had better..."

Ver Dell dropped to his hands and knees and began to vomit blood.

"Oh my god, Dell," the secretary was frantic, "I'll call the facility doctor." Ver Dell could only raise one hand to signal he understood before more bloody vomit spewed from his mouth.

When the doctor arrived, Ver Dell lay shivering on the floor of his office.

"Take him to the infirmary, immediately," the doctor said to two of the guards who came to assist. "And try not to get any of that blood on you." Both men looked at the puddle of bloody vomit and the vomit-soaked clothes Ver Dell was wearing, and then looked back up at the doctor. "Well, at least make sure you change your clothes and wash your hands after you get him into a bed." There was no way they would be able to not come in contact with the blood.

Ver Dell was actually feeling a little better by the time the guards got him to a bed in the infirmary.

"Doc, I think I just need to go home and rest. I got some kind of damn flu bug," Cheney explained.

"Let me have a look at you first, your eyes look a little red."

"It's just this fever I've had the past few days. I'll get over it."

"Uh-huh!" the doctor said, as he continued his examination. "Bill, I'm sending you to the hospital."

"No way, Doc, that won't be necessary," Cheney replied. "I got that team coming from Washington today to check us out. I need to be here."

"You need to be in a hospital. That was blood you were vomiting. That's not a good sign. You also seem to have some kind of a maculopapular rash."

"What the hell does that mean?" Cheney said.

"It means you have little red spots with pimples in the middle covering your body. It looks like it might be measles."

"Measles? You got to be kidding. Only little kids get the measles. I had them when I was little," Cheney replied.

"That's why we need to get you to the hospital to see what it is then. No more arguments," the doctor insisted.

Ver Dell was not going to argue because he again doubled over in pain and threw up a vile bloody mixture all over the bed.

"Where's Wallace?" Jotty asked his instructor hoping to head off any embarrassing comments in front of the class.

"He's pretty sick from what I hear," one of the other students said. I think he took a pretty hard hit at practice the other night. I heard he was peeing and throwing up blood."

"I didn't hear about that. I better give him a call. All of you start stretching, I'll be right back," the instructor said as he headed to his office.

"Wallace was telling me about some supplement your wife gave his wife for him to try," one of the other men in the class said. "He said something about it giving him the stamina of an 18-year-old boy. Of course, he phrased it a little differently, more like..."

"I really don't think the ladies present want to hear that kind of talk," Jotty said interrupting.

"No, as a matter-of-fact, we would love to hear about your magic aphrodisiac Jotty," one of the ladies giggled.

"Me too," another piped in, "my husband's energy could stand to rise a little if you know what I mean." Her comment got most of the people in the class laughing.

It was turning out worse than Jotty imagined. He was never more relieved to see the instructor rush back into the room. "How's Wallace?" Jotty asked hoping to change the subject.

"If erections last more than four hours, see a doctor immediately," someone in back called out, making everyone laugh. Everyone but the instructor.

"I'm afraid I have some bad news," the instructor announced. "Wallace is not expected to live. He has been diagnosed with some form of a hemorrhagic fever."

"What is that?" one of the women asked.

"It's a very serious disease." The instructor responded.

"Just how serious?" Jotty asked.

"Serious enough that anybody who was with Wallace in the past week is required to report to building D at the Virginia Hospital Center in Arlington, and I believe that includes everyone in this room," the instructor said. "As a matter of fact, they are sending a bus over to pick us all up."

"This does sound serious," one of the students said.

"Isn't Ebola another name for hemorrhagic fever?" someone asked.

"Whoa, let's not get carried away and panic everyone," one of the students said. "Just because it is a hemorrhagic fever doesn't mean it's Ebola. Let's not start that kind of rumor. Let the doctors tell us what it is."

"The bus will be here shortly so everybody change back into your street clothes. Call whomever you need to call to let them know what's going on, but the bosses said we want to keep this out of the media for the time being. We need to know exactly what it is we're dealing with before we say anything," the instructor explained.

No one gave a second thought to Jotty's herbal supplement. The word Ebola was now screaming in everyone's head.

It took three days for the doctors at Haskell Memorial Hospital to diagnose Ver Dell with hemorrhagic fever. Everyone on the staff was at a loss as to what was causing his condition. Results of his blood analysis from Dallas confirmed the diagnosis the same day Ver Dell died. It also confirmed that it was a filovirus that caused the condition. There were only five known filoviruses, the four Ebola viruses and the Marburg virus. All extremely deadly. The entire Haskell Memorial Hospital was quarantined, as was the Rolling Plains Regional Jail and Detention Center, until doctors from the CDC in Atlanta arrived. No one went in and no one came out. People in Haskell County were afraid to leave their homes. Haskell, Stamford, Rule, Weinert, and Throckmorton became bigger ghost towns than they already were. Business came to a complete halt as the word Ebola was bantered about.

The first CDC team arrived by van at the Haskell hospital. They brought equipment capable of dealing with a Biosafety Level 4 agent. The spacesuits that the CDC physicians wore did little to aid the anxiety felt by the entire county. A second team of doctors arrived by helicopter at the detention center. They did not wear the same biosafety suits with breathing apparatus like the other medical team, but did wear a similar suit without the head helmet. They did have on face masks similar to those available at any home supply store. They ordered the facility into a lockdown and instructed the guards that were still under quarantine at the facility to take them to the section of the center that housed the county inmates. As they walked past the individual cells, one of the doctors held a device that looked similar to the medical instrument Leonard 'Bones' McCoy carried on the original Star Trek television series. It had some flashing lights and would emit an occasional beep. In a matter of minutes, these CDC doctors had identified four prisoners infected by the Ebola virus and ordered them to be placed in the helicopter before they infected the rest of the prisoner population. They would be rushed to the hospital in Abilene which the CDC had set up as their headquarters. No one questioned the doctor's orders and the guards were more than happy to see the infected prisoners taken away.

"How bad is the outbreak?" Jotty asked the head of the domestic counter-terrorism division at the NCTC.

"It seems limited to the six locations we originally identified. Fortunately, in only one case did we have a secondary infection. All but one of the original infected subjects died. Looks like the wife who got it from her schoolteacher husband in Cudahy, California, will pull through, as will the insurance salesman in Detroit. Wallace of course died, as did the schoolteacher in California, the vet down in Florida, and the chef in New York."

"What about those four prisoners missing in Texas, any word on them?"

"We do know it was no CDC medical team that took them away. It looks like a well-orchestrated prison break. It only makes sense that whoever caused the infection of the original six victims did so to break these guys out. What do you know about these four guys? I was told you're the one who originally busted them on a terrorism charge."

"I can't believe it's those same yahoos Jim and I arrested several years ago for trying to steal the bomb ingredients. You know we were able to pin several of those southern church bombings on those guys," Jotty replied. "What were they doing in a county facility and not a state or federal prison?"

"Way too much overcrowding in the state facilities is why. This was a privately-operated prison holding several types of inmates. These guys were angels compared to a lot of prisoners."

"Somebody went to a lot of trouble to break them out," Jotty said. "You got any ideas or leads as to who did this?"

"I was kind of hoping you might have a few," Jotty's counterpart replied.

"I can tell you that from what I hear those four guys who broke out are pretty bad news. Some kind of an offshoot of the Aryan Brotherhood I believe. They possibly have some ties to international terrorists. It seems they each had a visitor several weeks ago. He said he was their new attorney, but the guards report he spoke with some kind of an accent. There may still be a video of him, but no one at the detention center was sure. I'll get some of my people working on it. Any word how the virus was administered?"

"None as yet, but we'll find out. I've got to brief the boss in ten minutes. Anything else you want to add?"

"Nothing for now," Jotty replied, "I'll let you know if I hear anything."

A thorough search was conducted by federal CSI teams of all the victims' homes and offices, but no source or even a trace of the Ebola virus was found. All the reports were sent to the FBI for analysts to look over to see if they could come up with some kind of connection. Jotty had hoped to get a chance to see the files, especially since Wallace was one of the victims, but that was not to be.

Almost a week had gone by since Wallace was first diagnosed. There had been a funeral and a lot of concern at NCTC headquarters. Ebola was a word that seemed to strike fear in everyone. Whether it was the gruesome visuals of the bodies hemorrhaging and blood flowing from every orifice, or the fact that there was no cure, didn't really matter. What mattered was that Ebola was a Category A bioterrorism agent and someone now had access to it. Who that someone was had become the NCTC's priority investigation.

"Günter what the hell happened? Why did the disease not spread?" Günter could tell Aioka was not prepared for the results of the initial test.

"It went exactly as planned, well, almost. That NCTC agent, what was his name? Oh yes, Jotty Joplin, he was supposed to have been infected. Apparently, this Wallace somehow got hold of the capsule containing the freeze-dried Ebola. However, we were successful with all the other targeted individuals."

"He was the one I wanted the most! He is the one who has interrupted several of my previous plans. I wanted him to die a horrible death in front of his friend, Haruko, then I wanted her to suffer as well," Aioka responded.

"According to his ordering data, he will submit another order in two months. When he does, we will place another tainted capsule in his bottle of supplements."

"How can you be sure we will be successful then?" Aioka bellowed. "You can't."

"Then I'll have the new cell members we just freed handle it themselves. I'm sure they'd enjoy killing the man who put them in prison," Günter replied.

"Have them kill that other agent as well, the one who is on leave in Canada, Jim Rikey, but not the girl. I want Haruko to live to see the two men who loved her die. I want her to suffer and I want to see it for myself. I will deal with her in due time."

Günter grunted his acknowledgement.

"Now what can we do about the Ebola? Why did others not die and why didn't everyone infected die?" Aioka asked.

"The media has distorted the reality about Ebola. It is true that it usually has an 80% fatality rate, but it requires direct contact with infected body fluids for transmission. It also kills so quickly that the host is dead before much transfer can occur."

"So, it will only be effective if the person actually swallows the supplement capsule?" Aioka asked.

"As a stand-alone agent, yes. However, if we turn it into a chimera virus by breeding it with another virus, like small-pox or even the common cold virus, then millions would die," Günter explained. "It's technically called virus duplexing."

"What would it take to do that?" Aioka asked.

"Acquiring the small-pox can be accomplished with a little bribe to the right Russian scientists. We have the connections to accomplish that. Our lab in the warehouse is capable of creating the chimera, but not safely. Ebola is overrated as a Biosafety Level 4 agent. Our Level 3 safety equipment is capable of dealing with it. However, adding the small-pox virus will require us to upgrade to Level 4 suits. Not doing so is too great of a risk. The lab itself is not really as airtight as necessary either, but I'm willing to take a chance with it," Günter explained.

"How long will it take to make sufficient amounts of the freeze-dried chimera virus?" Aioka asked.

"That can be done in less than a month. However, it will take at least two months to get the lab safely equipped to handle the job."

"I need it sooner than that. They'll eventually figure out how the initial outbreaks occurred. I need you to have it

ready and packaged in two months. Do whatever it takes,"
Aioka instructed. "By the time the chimera is shipped, you
will have the weapon I promised you.

45

CHAPTER FOUR

One day earlier

Romeo could feel the beads of sweat running down the nape of his neck causing it to itch as if fire ants had left their burning white pustules slowly trailing down his back. Moisture began to gather along his waistband. Yet he didn't dare scratch or wipe the sweat away. That would be tantamount to blinking and Romeo never blinked in the face of danger. He stared it square in the face. Unflinching, stoic, and unafraid. He could still hear the crackling static coming from his earpiece. He had to remove it when they began jamming all the electronics and radio frequencies on the airplane. The white noise was just too distracting and Romeo could not afford to be distracted. He stood at the ready, poised at the foot of the portable boarding stairs blocking access to any unwelcome visitors trying to attempt to board the plane. The door to the plane was shut and the last transmission from his counterpart on the other side of that door before the radio was jammed ordered Romeo to allow no one, absolutely no one, to board the airplane without approval of the senator. That was all well and good when Romeo could converse with the men on board the plane, but that wasn't possible now. Romeo was on his own. The safety of the crew, politicians, and their aides was dependent upon Romeo's judgment and ability to stay focused and reserved. A difficult task with over twenty Kalashnikov automatic rifles aimed at your head.

Jesse Romeo Gonzalez was a marine. More than that, he was a lifer in the marines. He had served two deployments

to Afghanistan and was part of the initial attack on Iraq. He
lived to be a marine and almost died in the process. Romeo
was one of the first to learn the power of an IED. It was one
of these improvised explosive devices that killed two of
Romeo's comrades and nearly blew his head apart. He was
riding in one of the early Humvees just outside of Sadr City. It
was a Humvee supplied to the occupying forces without the
needed armored protection. Part of the front wheel exploded
into pieces from the blast and a large section of the wheel
shattered Romeo's skull. Smaller pieces of plastic, rubber,
and metal tore through his uniform and into his skin. Actually,
Romeo died, but medics happened to be riding in the trailing
vehicle and were able to revive him. He needed several
operations to repair the damage to his head and his brain.
The doctors had difficulty controlling the bleeding in his brain
and had to reenter the skull several times. These operations
left a three-quarter inch scar from ear to ear across the top of
his head. Even if they could have, Romeo insisted they do no
plastic surgery to try to hide the scar bisecting his skull. It was
his badge of courage. His medal to prove to the world that he
indeed was a battle-tested Marine. Ooh-rah! Surprisingly,
Romeo recovered quickly from his head trauma and was
anxious to get back into action. His commander didn't see it
that way and recommended an honorable discharge, a
discharge Romeo fought untiringly. It took the intervention of
his congressional representative to insure Romeo would
remain in the military, although his combat days were over.
Romeo was assigned duty as a military escort for senators
and representatives on foreign junkets and fact-finding
missions. Romeo could live with that. He would have
preferred uniformed duty, but that would not be the case in
his new assignment. A low profile was preferred by the State
Department. A marine in full uniform didn't always convey a

popular message these days around the world. Despite several requests, Romeo refused to grow his hair long enough to cover his glaring scar, nor would he shave his head to help hide his war wound. He wore it proudly for the world to see.

Viktor Cheznov was not a happy man. Viktor was a colonel in the Federal Security Service, the FSB, formerly known as the KGB. He was in charge of overseeing the security of Russia's secretive research facilities in and around the Perm region. It had been a very trying year for Viktor. One of Russia's top scientists from the genetic research lab in Perm was kidnapped last year by a Japanese terrorist group. Several people had to die in order to retrieve the scientist and protect the secrets of his research. The scientist was recaptured, but much of his research fell into American hands. Unfortunately, several American and Canadian missionaries had to die in the process. The Kremlin was not happy with the results, nor were the American and Canadian governments happy about having their citizens massacred. The killings were blamed on Chechnyan rebels, but the intelligence agencies for both countries knew better. Now another potential crisis threatened Russia's security and Viktor's honor. Four suitcase nuclear weapons were missing from the facility southeast of the city in a remote part of the Ural Mountains, the same facility that the delegation from the United States visited two days ago, the delegation that now sat in a plane on the tarmac before him. Two United States senators and four Congressional representatives along with their support contingent were now being held captive by Viktor as he awaited word on how to proceed. Two armored personnel carriers blocked the American Boeing 747 from taxing to the runway. As if that really mattered. The Perm public airport also served as a military airport, as did most

Russian airports. Lining the runway were over forty bunkers, each with a Russian MIG fighter ready for immediate takeoff. The only way the 747 would be leaving Perm would be with the government's permission. Viktor did not see that happening any time soon.

He had ordered a sophisticated radiation detector be brought from the storage facility, but it would still be five or six hours until it would arrive, and there was still no guarantee it would be effective. The suitcase nukes were housed in cases designed to keep radiation hidden. The only way it could be detected was if someone were to open one of the suitcases. He had ordered that all electronic and communications be jammed aboard the airplane. He wanted to use the electronic pulse-weapon that had been so effective in Hawaii in destroying all non-shielded electronic equipment. Doing that would be like declaring war on the United States, for there were several very influential American politicians on the plane. Still, if the stolen nuclear weapons were on board, it could prove to be catastrophic for the present American government. These were decisions that needed to be made by someone above the rank of colonel. For now, as much as he despised doing so, Viktor would just have to wait.

It was by chance that the world found out about the U.S. Congressional plane being held by the Russians in Perm. A group of British students had been in the Ural Mountains visiting several of the summer camps spreading their Christian message. As they were boarding a plane to Moscow, they saw the drama unfold. As soon as they landed in Moscow, one of them reported what they witnessed to BBC News. Within an hour the standoff had reached a world stage. Aioka was not pleased at what he heard about the situation. He had a lot riding on the success of this mission.

Nor was the Kremlin pleased when their President received an urgent call from the U.S. Ambassador concerning the plane's detention. Aioka, too, had made an urgent call to an acquaintance in the Russian FSB who had been on Aioka's payroll for some time.

Viktor's cell phone began to ring. "Yes, what is it," Viktor replied to the caller.

"Colonel Cheznov, it is Boris Ivanoz from headquarters. We have just been ordered to allow the American plane to leave. Do you understand? They are to be allowed to leave immediately."

"Under whose authority was this command made?"

"President Putin personally called with the command. It has become a serious international incident. He ordered them released at once."

"That is ridiculous," Viktor responded. "Does he understand what they may have taken on the plane?"

"He understands fully what you believe they have, but has ordered that you follow his decision. If you fail to do so, you are to be arrested."

"What is the President thinking," Viktor mumbled. "Tell him I will do as instructed, but I want you to repeat the order to my assistant so there can be no misunderstanding. I will have him record the order."

"Do whatever you wish, just as long as the plane is allowed to leave," Boris replied.

Viktor tossed his phone to his assistant. "Record the order from headquarters, I cannot believe what they are telling me, but I shall comply."

Viktor ordered the two armored vehicles to move and the men to return to their trucks. He walked up to Romeo standing erect with his hand still on the handle of his gun.

"Halt, sir" Romeo ordered. "Come no closer!"

Viktor did as Romeo asked. "I have been told to allow you to leave. I disagree with the order, but I intend to follow it. I hope you know what has been stolen from us. I know it is on your airplane. I don't believe your Congressmen on board are even aware of what has taken place. Are you part of this plot?" Viktor said as he stepped towards Romeo.

Romeo tensed, "I'm ordering you to step back, Colonel." His hand touched the butt of his pistol.

Viktor wanted to slap Romeo for his ignorance, but had to respect him for doing his duty as ordered. "I don't believe you were part of the plot. I believe you are being used as much as the politicians you are protecting are being used. Someone has committed a grievous crime and you, either wittingly or unwittingly, have helped them succeed. May God have mercy on your soul if you are part of this. I would be careful who I told this to on the plane if I were you. No telling who your real enemies are." Viktor turned and walked back to his waiting car.

Romeo's expression did not change. He continued to guard the steps of the boarding ramp. Suddenly, the earpiece Romeo had removed from his ear stopped buzzing and he could hear the Marine stationed inside the jet calling his name.

"Romeo, Romeo, get your ass in here, Romeo. We've been cleared for take-off. Let's get the hell out of here." The hatch at the top of the ramp opened. Romeo quickly glanced over his shoulder and saw his partner waving for him to come inside. Slowly he backed up the steps keeping his hand on his pistol. By the time he reached the top step the plane's engines were both on and the Russian ground crew was preparing to attach the tug to maneuver the plane to the taxi way. It would be a joyous flight home for the politicians on board. Of course, they would still have to make their scheduled stop in Bangkok to refuel but, according to the pilot, they would make it in plenty of time to attend William H. Casey's resort-warming extravaganza in Kona. The mood was jovial as the jet raced towards Thailand, jovial for everyone but Romeo. Viktor's words cut deep in his thoughts. "Just who were the real enemies Viktor had referred to? And exactly what was it that was stolen and brought aboard the plane? Or was it all just a ploy and political posturing in order to scare the Americans?" But the words that cut deepest and scared Romeo the most played over and over in his head, "may God have mercy on your soul if you are part of this." What would cause a man to make such a warning?

CHAPTER FIVE

Ten hours ago

Jim Rikey had spent the last five months on a leave of absence from the NCTC. He was staying at his uncle's house outside of Edmonton, Canada. This was the first time Jim had visited the house, although he had often been invited. He just never seemed to have the time. Now that he was there, it was to dispose of a lifetime of memories his aunt and uncle had collected, for they both had been assassinated by rebels in Perm, Russia. Jim had not expected it to take so long to sort through all their possessions and find an appropriate way to dispose of them. With every drawer opened and every box packed, came memories of Jim's own childhood in Texas. Both wonderful and painful reminders of the happiness he and his brother shared, and the sadness of his brother's death. Jim wasn't in the healthiest frame of mind when he decided to come deal with his uncle's estate. He had prided himself on his excellent shooting ability. An ability that had got him out of several jams, won him plenty of money, put lots of bad guys in jail or their grave, but most recently caused the death of an innocent man in front of his wife and children. Jim had not worn or fired his six-shooters since that tragic accident six months before. He had been attending weekly counseling provided by the NCTC and was in fact much happier than he had been since the tragic accident in Princeville. The affairs of the estate were coming to a conclusion and Jim knew that he would soon have to return to work. However, he had decided he would not be returning to the NCTC or to the Hawaiian Islands. He wanted to return to Haskell, Texas, and the comfortable slow life he enjoyed as the Farm Service Agent for Haskell County. He was through fighting terrorists. The only things he wanted to fight were boll weevils. Jotty, Haruko, and Eddie could hunt down Aioka and the rest of those Red Summit terrorists without his help.

Jim was still a little gun shy, but was looking forward to the opening of mule-deer season in Alberta, him and about ten thousand other hunters. He had recently received an upgraded bullet-proof vest that NCTC field agents were now being issued. It was a rather unusual design in that it was made of a series of overlapping scale-like ceramic plates that contoured to the body. It was called Dragon Skin and was touted to be the best body armor on the market. "Just as long as it protects me from any crazed hunters," Jim said to himself as he dressed for his hunting trip. As he headed out to his car with his rifle and supplies, he failed to notice the truck parked down the road with two men inside.

"Looks like he's a goin' huntin'," the man with the binoculars said to his partner.

"That's good," his buddy replied, "it'll look like an accident. People will think he was shot by some over-anxious hunter. This will be a piece of cake."

"That sum' bitch deserves to die for what he did to us," the first man said.

"Well let's make sure he does," his buddy replied. He started the truck and followed Jim as he headed towards the foothills. "Looks like we be a goin' huntin' too."

"No way! Absolutely not! There is no way I'm going to stay here and take care of that dog and this house for another day."

"Little bro', it's just one more day. I promise I'll be back tomorrow. I'll even go with you to the North Shore for some surfing. I'll even pay for the flight and the room for one night."

"One whole night? What a philanthropist you are!" Michael replied snidely.

"Okay, two nights, but you've got to pay for dinner," Eddie replied.

"It's a deal," Michael said, "but if you don't show up by late afternoon, I'm out of here and I mean it." Michael Popp was Eddie Popp's younger brother and looked and acted just like Eddie. In other words, he was a blond-headed surfer and womanizer who loved to party. Michael had graduated from the University of California at Santa Cruz where he had studied marine biology and surfing, not necessarily in that order. He was visiting his brother in Hawaii as part of his year of play before he faced the reality of the working world. Michael was not happy that his brother had put him in charge of Jim's house while Eddie frolicked with that lady at the Four Seasons Resort. Michael had been staying with Eddie for three weeks and the Big Island was starting to feel small. He had surfed several of the hidden spots Eddie had told him about and even the popular Honoli'i Park near Hilo. It was there that he had a bit of a run in with some of the locals who didn't care for vacationing haoles dropping in on their waves. Surfers are very territorial about outsiders coming in and 'stealing their waves'. This often times led to some ugly confrontations usually ending in a fat lip, or worse, from a fist or a surf board turned into a lethal weapon. Michael was savvy enough to walk away when he had his confrontation in Honoli'i, but not before exchanging some expletive-laden conversation with the locals.

"I just have to grab a few more things," Eddie explained taking a dinner jacket out of the closet.

"Must be a formal affair," Michael said. "Shouldn't you take along some socks? It is formal, right?"

"Not that formal," Eddie replied, and they both laughed.

"You sure this rich hot one doesn't have a friend?" Michael asked.

"I'm very sure! You're not quite ready for the big leagues yet, bro'. Keep practicing with those mainland school teachers and secretaries down at the Malolo Lounge at the Hilton or those beach bunnies that hang out at Huggo's or Lulu's down in Kona. You'll have no problem finding comfort there," Eddie said.

"I haven't yet at least, but the same faces keep showing up and I don't want any of them to grow too attached," Michael explained.

'See bro', that is exactly what I'm talking about. You have to use that attachment to your favor. When you can do that, you'll be ready for the 'bigs'. I'll see you tomorrow and stay away from those punks down at Honoli'i."

"Later!" Michael responded. "And don't leave me hangin', cause I will bail."

"Adios," Eddie said, as he jumped into the rented convertible.

"I know it's been a very trying week, but you promised last weekend that you would call Jim. You really need to do that today," Haruko insisted.

"I will, I promise. You know this Ebola thing and the prison break have stirred things up at the office," Jotty replied.

"Even more reason to call Jim," Haruko argued. "He needs to know those white-supremacists escaped from prison. And we could sure use his help with all the extra activity that seems to be brewing. There has been a ten-fold increase in suspected terrorist chatter intercepted these past two weeks. I know it has to do with those Ebola breakouts. We could use his help and besides it's time you tell him about us."

That was the part Jotty was dreading the most. He didn't want to tell Jim that he and Haruko were living together and planning on getting engaged. He didn't think Jim was emotionally strong enough yet to deal with that kind of news, although the company counselors who had been working with Jim said he was pretty much fully recovered from his trauma. "Okay, I'll give him a call as soon as we get home."

"Why not now on the cell phone?" Haruko asked. "I would like to hear what you say to him."

"That is exactly why I will make the call from my office at home. With the door shut. I feel pressured enough just having to make the call, let alone trying to double-think everything I say so I don't say the wrong thing to either of you."

"I can understand that," Haruko replied, "just as long as you promise to make the call."

"I promise," Jotty answered, as Haruko leaned across the seat and kissed him sweetly on the cheek.

"You know I do love you," Haruko said.

"I know you do," Jotty replied, "and I love to hear you say it."

"You're supposed to say 'I love you' back to me," Haruko said hitting him on the arm.

"I know that," Jotty replied, "but I like it when you get fired up."

They both laughed as their car neared their house.

Jim headed west on the 16 out of Edmonton in his uncle's older jeep Cherokee. Not far behind were the two men following in their newer Toyota Tundra pickup. There were several such vehicles on the road, this being the first day of mule-deer hunting season. Jim was headed for McCay. Actually, he was headed for a remote spot just east of McCay near Chip Lake. Right before Jim reached the 751 turnoff, he turned right on an old logging road that was nearly impassable. Jim had chosen this area because he had read about the record setting mule-deer that was shot in this area by Ed Broder back in 1926. It was scored 355 2/8 points by the Boone and Crockett Club, a record that still stands today. Jim was just hoping to get a decent shot at a big buck in this rugged terrain. He didn't notice the Tundra make the turn behind him onto the logging road.

"Stay back," the passenger said to the driver, "we don't want that sum' bitch to see us."

"He ain't gonna see us, and if he does so what, he'll just think we are a couple of other hunters out looking for a kill," the driver laughed at his own lame joke.

Jim turned into a turnout and stopped the Cherokee. He would walk towards the river from here. He watched as the Tundra drove past.

"Don't look at him, the driver said, "he might recognize us."

"He ain't gonna rec'nize us," his partner replied, "besides, if I don't wave, he might get suspicious." The man smiled and waved as the Tundra rushed by the turnout.

Jim paid the two men in the truck little heed, though he didn't care much for the idea that there would be other hunters nearby. "I hope those two are smart enough to drive on a couple of miles," Jim thought. "I don't want anybody getting shot by accident, especially me." Jim pulled on his backpack with two day's worth of supplies, grabbed his uncle's older Remington Model 700 30-06, and headed down a trail towards the river that runs into Chip Lake. The trail was difficult to traverse as it followed a stream that formed a series of magnificent waterfalls as it rushed towards the lake. Jim walked along the edge of a ridge about sixty feet directly above the rushing stream.

"Stop right there and drop your rifle," a voice called out from behind a clump of trees to his right.

Jim turned slowly towards the voice.

Bark from the pine tree next to Jim's head exploded before he heard the report of a high velocity shell fired from a rifle directly behind him. "My friend said drop the rifle, so drop the damn rifle," another voice called out.

Jim had no choice but to do as he was told.

"Remember me?" the man said as he came out from behind the trees holding an M-16 that had been modified to be a sniper's weapon.

"I'm afraid I don't," Jim said.

"Maybe this will remind you," the man said as he rolled up his sleeve to give Jim a clear view of his mangled hand that was missing two fingers. "You did this to me."

"I'm afraid I have done that to several people. You are one of the lucky ones that didn't get it through the heart," Jim replied.

"Asshole," the other man said as he walked up behind Jim and kicked him hard behind the knee.

"A couple of brave boys you are," Jim said, trying to anger them. "Now I remember. You two were part of that group that tried to steal the bomb-making ingredients from that farm in Texas. Is that what this is about?"

"You know I was going to use this sniper rifle to shoot you from far away, but then I started think'n, I wanted to see your face as I killed you," both men raised their rifles. Jim was about to leap off the ridge and into the stream below when both men fired not ten feet in front of him. The two shots hit Jim almost simultaneously, striking so hard that his body flew backwards off the trail and down the sharp incline into the stream below. Before the men could reload, Jim's body was caught in the swift current and hurtled over the falls and was lost in the rapids.

"You think we should look for the body?" one man asked the other.

"Hell no, didn't you see that sum' bitch fly when those bullets hit him? He's deader than shit! Let's go get a beer 'for sum'body comes lookin'."

"First, I gotta make a call," the other man dialed the phone as instructed to do.

"Yes?"

"We killed him. We killed him good," the white supremacist replied.

"Are you sure?" the voice asked.

"Sure as shit," the man replied, "twice in the chest at close range."

"Did you put a bullet in the head as instructed?"

Both men looked at each other.

"Just like you said to do," the man replied.

"Good, you know what to do next."

Satochi had been to the house before. He had come here in search of the genetically modified potato that was not there. What he did find was a Russian FSB agent searching for the same thing. Satochi quickly dispensed with the agent in his preferred bloody manner, using his Lei O Mano. The agents head was nearly ripped from the torso and blood covered the floor and desk where the agent had been sitting.

It was a grisly sight for Jim to discover when he arrived home. This time Satochi had come to finish a job he had failed to do at both the Princeville Hotel in Kauai and the Busy Bee Restaurant in Avalon on Santa Catalina Island off the California Coast, and that was to kill Eddie Popp. It was Eddie who had crippled Satochi with his own Lei O Mano in Avalon. Satochi did want vengeance on the man who had done this to him, but he would not have considered it without Aioka's approval, which he did not seek. It was Aioka who wanted Eddie dead, for Aioka wanted the world to see that no one was beyond his reach. Besides, Eddie lived on the Big Island as did Aioka and Satochi, and neither could afford a chance meeting with Eddie Popp.

Michael heard the car pulling into the gravel driveway. He, like Eddie, had never bothered to close the gate when they were home or going out for the evening. In fact, Michael wasn't even aware that there was a security system on the gate and the house. He walked out to greet the visitor.

"Aloha, how can I help you," Michael asked.

Satochi quickly got out of the car and approached Michael. He was ready to pull the pistol from the holster hidden beneath his sports coat if Eddie recognized him and tried to run. Satochi stared at Michael somewhat confused. "Why don't you run?" Satochi asked.

"What are you talking about? How can I help you?" Michael asked again.

"You are more stupid than I imagined," Satochi replied. "Or perhaps my plastic surgeon was more talented than I thought."

"Look buddy, I don't need any grief. I'm here on vacation. If this is about that punk 'braddah' that I punched who tried to throw me off Honoli'i beach, I'm sorry, but he deserved it."

The mention of Honoli'i beach startled Satochi. That was where Aioka's new hideout was. What all did this Eddie Popp already know?" Satochi wanted to torture Eddie to find out what he knew, but Aioka had given him strict orders to kill Eddie and quickly return to the house.

The driver stepped out of the car and Michael turned to look at him. As he turned Satochi pulled out his pistol.

"Whoa there bud." Michael said as he saw the gun. He turned to run just as Satochi shot him in the side of the head. Michael dropped straight to the ground, dead.

"Turn him over and rip off that shirt," Satochi ordered his driver. Satochi put the gun away then turned his cane upside down so the giant Tiger shark-tooth was resting on the dead man's chest. The tooth dug deeply into the skin of Michael's chest, but no blood flowed. His heart had long stopped pumping blood and gravity had begun to pull the blood downward. Carefully Satochi carved an ancient Hawaiian symbol on Michael's chest. "Carry him back inside and place him precisely where I told you. I want them to know who is responsible for this."

Satochi wiped the torn skin and muscle tissue from his cane. He watched as his driver placed the body in the chair by the desk in the same position as the Russian FSB agent that Satochi had also killed months before. "You lived longer than you should have, Eddie Popp. Now Satochi ma-ke die dead." Even the driver laughed at Satochi's pidgin comment.

Satochi pulled out his phone and pushed one button. Almost immediately Aioka answered.

"Is it done?"

"Eddie Popp is dead," Satochi replied.

"Good! I will send out the announcement to the media that the Red Summit is back and has started to purge those who tried before to stop us. The world must know that no one is safe from our vengeance. After today, all of America will know the meaning of terror!"

"You go on in, I'll bring in the groceries," Jotty said as he and Haruko arrived back at their condominium just outside of Falls Church, Virginia.

Haruko carried in a bag of the frozen items from their shopping and began putting them away. Jotty had not yet come in. She was about to go out and check on him when the phone began to ring.

"Hello," Haruko answered.

"Hey bitch," a voice said over the phone, "how could a white man ever love a slant eyed pan-face bitch like you?"

"Who is this?" Haruko demanded, "how did you get this number?"

"Look outside if you want to see your lover before we kill him," the caller said.

Haruko pulled back the curtain and looked down to where she had left Jotty unloading the groceries. Looking up from the parking lot three stories below were two men with guns. Jotty stood wobbly and dazed next to the men. One was supporting Jotty's arm to keep him from collapsing. As Haruko looked on, one of the men put his gun to Jotty's temple and pulled the trigger. The right side of Jotty's head blew away in a spray of blood, brains, bones, and tissue. Haruko screamed as Jotty's body collapsed to the ground in slow motion. Her phone began to ring again.

"You are dead-men walking," Haruko shrieked into the phone.

"You're next bitch, be seeing you soon," the man threw the phone at Jotty's limp body lying next to the car and ran with his partner down the street. Already sirens could be heard in the distance.

Haruko grabbed the gun from her purse and ran down the steps to where Jotty's shattered body lay. She was blinded by fury, prepared to kill the two assassins, but they had already disappeared. She sat down next to Jotty's body, took his hand and began to cry.

The assassin dialed a preprogrammed number on the cell phone.

"Is he dead?" a voice asked.

"Absolutely!" the man responded. "Jotty Joplin is dead!

CHAPTER SIX

Present time

"Where is that helicopter?" Eddie said impatiently as he scanned the night sky.

"There," the Captain pointed, "coming from the South."

"Light those flares so we can get that bird down safely," Eddie shouted to several of the hotel workers told to assist in any way possible.

One of the security men hired for the party ran out from the bar at the Hualalai Grille. "Eddie, Eddie," he called as Eddie was preparing to board the copter. "News reports are saying over fourteen hundred killed at the Honolulu Airport today and I just heard the first report about something happening on the *Grand Maui.* The FAA has grounded all non-emergency aircraft, so the news stations won't be able to send a copter to check out the ship. Good luck."

"Thanks for the info," Eddie replied.

When the helicopter finally reached the *Grand Maui,* things were worse than Eddie expected. Over one-third of the passengers had already died and the Coast Guard response team had run out of Cipro. Before the night ended another one hundred passengers would die.

"How did this happen?" the Captain asked. "Where did the anthrax originate?"

"This appears to be the same strain that the Red Summit used in their terror attack on Los Angeles last year and the same one found by your doctor on that dive boat," Eddie responded. "This weaponized version is a fine mist that will float in the air, then slowly settle on its intended victims. Were there any fireworks shot off tonight?" Eddie asked the ship's doctor.

"We have never shot off fireworks from the ship," the Captain replied, "although, we do occasionally watch the displays from some of the larger resorts like the Hilton Hawaiian Village, but we haven't even done that recently."

"Then it probably came from the ship's air circulation system. We need to check that right away," Eddie advised.

"We have no crew members available to do it, they are all dead or dying," the Captain replied.

"Find me the chief medical officer with the Coast Guard team," Eddie told the doctor.

"That would be me, I'm Doctor Lambetti."

"I'm Eddie Popp with the NCTC, on loan from the CIA. I need you to call the Coast Guard Air Station at Barbers Point and tell them we need more medical personnel and security personnel. We will have them look for the source of the outbreak," Eddie ordered. "As of now, this is an NCTC investigation and I will be in charge until you are told differently."

It was a bold move by Eddie taking command of the situation, but a decision he knew he had better clear with Jotty pretty damn quick. He walked out of the grand dining hall which was being used as a triage area so he could make the call in private. It was four in the morning back in the Washington D.C. area. Eddie knew better than call Jotty directly at home, so he called the operations desk at NCTC. He would let the night officer take the heat for waking Jotty.

"This is the NCTC," a serious voice responded.

"Hi, this is Eddie Popp in Hawaii, I need to get a message to Jotty Joplin head of the..." Eddie was abruptly interrupted.

"Who is this and how did you get this number?" a stern voice demanded.

"What are you talking about? This is Eddie Popp. I'm on loan to Jotty Joplin from the CIA to work the Red Summit case." There was silence on the other end of the phone.

"Is anybody there?" Eddie asked.

"Could you please give me your social security number, Mr. Popp," the officer in-charge asked.

"What the hell is this? Nobody has ever asked for my social security number before. Did I get the wrong number or something? Did I accidentally call my credit card company?"

"Please, Mr. Popp, just give us your social security number."

"Hell no, I won't. That's all I need is for someone to steal my identity and put me in debt forever," Eddie hung up the phone. Before he could decide whether to call back, his phone began to ring.

"What is it?" Eddie responded harshly.

"Hello Eddie, it's Mike Olitz."

Mike was Eddie's old boss at the CIA. "Mike, It is you, I recognize the voice. What the hell is going on? Has everybody in Washington gone crazy?"

"Maybe not in Washington, but definitely at the NCTC everyone seems a little whacky. I was just awoken by a call from the head of the NCTC security team. It seems you refused to properly identify yourself and they needed someone to confirm your identification. So, just to be sure, tell me the name of the boat you used in Thailand."

"Amnesia, she was called the Amnesia," Eddie replied.

"Good, now call the NCTC back and straighten this mess up," Mike said.

"What mess?" Eddie asked, but Mike had already hung up the phone.

"This is really weird," Eddie said out loud as he again dialed the NCTC number.

"Please hold while we transfer your call, Mr. Popp," the desk officer replied.

"Eddie, thank God you're alive." It was Haruko's voice.

"Haruko? What the hell is going on?" Eddie asked.

"Where are you Eddie?" Haruko asked.

"I'm on the *Grand Maui*. I believe the Red Summit attacked it with anthrax. I'm afraid most of the passengers will die before sufficient help arrives. That is why I called. Is the Red Summit behind the bombings in Honolulu as well?"

"As of yet, no group has claimed responsibility, but we are sure it is Aioka and the Red Summit. Eddie, we were told you were dead." Haruko explained.

"Dead? Who said I was dead? I need to speak with Jotty. I bluffed my way in charge of the investigation here and need Jotty to back me up and get some more agents here ASAP. Maybe we can get Jim here, he's the expert on anthrax." The phone was silent. "Haruko, did you hear me."

"Yes, I heard you. Jotty is dead. We were told you were dead as well, and Jim is missing."

"Oh God, I'm so sorry, Haruko," Eddie said, "but why did you think I was dead?"

Haruko paused before she answered, "Because we sent a police officer to Jim's house when we couldn't reach you and he reported finding your body inside."

Eddie almost collapsed. "Oh my God, my younger brother was staying there watching the house. He looks just like me." Memories flooded Eddie's mind as his entire body went numb.

"Eddie, I'm so sorry," Haruko replied. "Several of our people should be arriving in Hawaii within the hour. I will send one to replace you immediately. You need to go be with your brother."

Eddie screamed so loud it scared several of the medical personnel tending the victims inside the grand dining hall. "I am going to kill that son-of-bitch Aioka." Then Eddie remembered Jotty was also dead and how devastated Haruko must be about that. He quickly composed himself.

"Are you now in charge, Haruko?" Eddie asked.

"Only temporarily. I'm so grateful you are still alive, though I am truly sorry about your brother."

"What about Jim? You said he is missing."

"We had someone check his house when we realized Aioka was seeking revenge. Jim's car was gone, but we heard from neighbors he was planning on going deer hunting on opening day, which was yesterday. The Canadian mounted police are searching for his car in the area where we believe he planned to hunt. So far we have heard nothing."

The Dragon Skin proved stronger than Jim ever could have imagined or hoped for. The bullets from the two rifles were designed to pierce standard Kevlar body armor, but not the new ceramic Dragon Skin style armor which was now available. Two of the ceramic pieces did break, but the integrity of the vest held. The force of impact did break two of Jim's ribs and knocked him unconscious and backwards off the cliff. He would have some severe deep bruising to his chest. Had the bullets been shot directly towards the heart, the blow could have quite possibly stopped his heart. His body was like a rag doll as he tumbled down the steep cliff cushioned by the backpack he still wore. Hitting the icy water quickly brought him back to his senses, but he was in too much pain and too confused to stop himself from going over the falls towards the rushing rapids below. Fortunately, the pool was deep at the bottom of the falls and Jim was able to avoid being sucked down the raging torrent of rapids. He lay quietly under some shrubs near the stream for almost an hour, occasionally blacking out from the immense pain in his chest. Jim eventually managed to remove his backpack to find some food. He tried a granola bar, but the pain from chewing and swallowing was not worth the effort required to eat it. After another hour, he was able to sit up despite the intense pain. He knew that the two men who shot him would have made their way to his position by now if they were still looking for him. He wanted to remove the vest, but trying to do so was impossible with his injuries. In another twenty minutes, he had regained enough strength to begin his slow trek out of the forest and back to where he left his Cherokee. He only hoped the two gunmen weren't waiting there for him to return. It was a chance Jim was willing to take.

The assumption at NCTC headquarters was that the Red Summit was responsible for Jotty's murder and the killing of Eddie's brother.

"Why do you think they allowed you to live?" One of the department supervisors asked of Haruko.

"I have no idea. They did say that I would be next."

"That's what you told the police who first responded as well, I see," the man said, pretending to read the report.

"That's because it is true!"

"Of course," he replied insincerely.

Haruko was getting angry with what the supervisor seemed to be implying. "Just what is it you are trying to say? Do you think I was somehow involved in Jotty's murder?"

"No, not at all," he replied, backing off his accusatory tone. "It's just curious that they allowed you to live."

"It's not curious at all if you knew how Aioka thinks. He wanted me to suffer. He wanted to take the most important person in my life and make me watch as he murdered him right before my eyes. Now that he succeeded at killing my soul, he will try to kill my body."

"I think we need to remove you from this investigation. It has become too personal."

"It has always been too personal. It would be absurd to remove me from the investigation. I know more about Aioka Matsuura and the Red Summit than anybody. This is just the beginning. This has been a warning as to what is about to come. No, you need me more than ever on this investigation."

"That decision is not for me to make. I can only make my recommendation, and my recommendation is to reassign you until you have a proper perspective of the situation. Until then, you are to remain temporarily in charge of the Red Summit investigation, but if it were my decision, I would have you reassigned."

"Well, thank God it's not up to you," Haruko said as she left the office slamming the door behind her.

"Idiots, they're all idiots," Haruko was heard saying as she stormed back to her office.

CHAPTER SEVEN
Seven hours ago

"Are we there yet?" Henry asked for the third time.

"Jesus Christ, Henry, how many times are you gonna' ask? Does it look like we're there yet?"

"If I knew what 'there' looked like, I could better answer that question. But since I don't, I have to ask."

"You read the article just like I did, and you saw the pictures just like I did, so you should damn well know, just like I do, that we aren't there yet!" Donald replied.

"Are you sure we parked in the right place? It didn't look like the picture to me." Henry continued.

"I'm positive. We parked on the right-hand side of the road between mile markers 46 and 47, in an area on the mauka side of the road that fits four or five cars, and there is a dirt road directly across the street just like the article said," Donald explained.

"Yeah, but how do you know that the guy who posted the article is telling the truth? What if it's a trap or something to get tourists down to some 'braddah's" pot farm and then shot?" Henry said.

"Look around you, Henry, what do you see?"

"Black lava," Henry replied.

"Exactly, miles and miles of black lava. We stopped seeing any plant life when we left the road back at those stacked rock cairn trail markers. Do you really think this lava would support a pot farm?" Donald explained.

Henry didn't answer. "What's with the air? It's like we were back in L.A. smog."

"Close, it's called vog. It forms when the volcanic gases from Kilauea mix with oxygen forming this haze. It won't kill you any more than the air back home will."

"Well that's reassuring," Henry replied facetiously.

The two men hiked on in silence for another ten minutes until they saw the fence.

"There's the fence," Henry said.

"And there's the Great Crack," Donald replied.

"Holy shit, that thing is huge. It looks like it goes for miles."

"It does, over eight miles, and be careful where you step, there are a lot of loose rocks near the edge and I keep hearing hollow echoes from my foot steps in several places around here. We are probably walking on the roof of some pretty big lava tubes," Donald said.

"That could be ugly if the ground gave way," Henry replied.

"Stay alert and watch your steps," Donald lectured.

Donald and Henry walked along the edge of the crack for almost a mile. There were several areas where they could go down into the crack and explore. There were also several lava tubes that opened up at the bottom of the crack.

"Man, we should have brought flashlights. I would love to walk into one of those tubes," Donald said. Henry didn't respond for they had reached an area where lava obviously recently flowed out of the crack. It was a smooth black surface which meant the lava flowed very quickly out towards the ocean.

"Your wish is my command," Henry said, smiling and holding up a flashlight.

"Where did you find that?" Donald asked.

"Right here with all this other stuff, look at it all."

Henry had found a huge stash of equipment and food hidden in a lava tube opening. There were ropes, several flashlights and lanterns, a lot of canned food, some clothing and, most disturbing, a case of dynamite and several boxes of ammunition.

"I don't think we better mess with that," Donald said. "I think it best if we head back towards the car and away from this area."

"Eh bra, found da kine stash," the man looking through the binoculars said to his partner.

"Satochi say we gotta go kill em fine um," his partner replied.

"Den we gotta kill em and lose da bodies."

"Watchu like do wid the caa dey go come in?" the second man said.

"Call Satochi, he gotta know what do."

"You know, I saw this special about tsunamis that talked about the Great Crack," Donald explained to Henry as they started walking back. "They say that if the island split apart at the crack from a big earthquake or something and fell into the ocean, it would cause a tsunami up to a mile high. They called it a flank collapse. Can you imagine all the damage that would cause? Millions could die from something like that. Hell, that tsunami in Indonesia was only 20 feet high and it killed over two hundred thousand people."

"That's bullshit," Henry replied, "it would have already happened. They had that big earthquake just last year and nothing happened.

"But you never know," Donald replied. "How do you think all of these great cliffs around the islands were formed? Hell, even over by the condo, Kealakekua Bay was formed by a big flank collapse. They say it caused a tsunami over 250 feet high that wiped out Molokai. They even have evidence of a tsunami over 1100 feet that hit Lanai around a hundred thousand years ago."

"Ain't gonna happen in our life time!" Henry replied.

"Yeah, but if it did you could kiss California goodbye," Donald replied.

"That's the same thing they've been saying about the San Andreas Fault for years, and it still hasn't happened."

"You never know, bro'," Donald replied.

"Well, I guess that would be one way to solve the immigration problem," Henry laughed.

"You racist asshole," Donald replied and joined in the laughter.

"Check that out," Henry said pointing towards a helicopter in the distance. "It looks like it's headed our way."

The helicopter continued straight towards the two hikers until in was circling overhead.

"Man, I hope we aren't in too much trouble. Do you think we were trespassing?" Henry asked.

"I'm not sure, but I believe we're about to find out," Henry replied, as they watched the helicopter slowly settle on the smooth lava.

As the blades of the copter began to slow, one well-dressed Asian man and a second smaller man using a cane exited the passenger side of the helicopter and slowly approached the two hikers.

"Nice day for a hike," Aioka said, "were you guys checking out the Great Crack?"

"We were," Donald responded cautiously.

"Yeah," Henry added, "we were following a map from an article we read about hiking to the Great Crack on instanthawaii.com. It tells about all sorts of hikes."

"It's just so unfortunate that you didn't choose one of those other hikes," Satochi said. "If you had, you wouldn't be in the trouble you're in."

"What trouble?" Henry said. "There were no signs saying we were trespassing. Even the article said it was okay to take this trail. If we were trespassing, then I'm very sorry we came on your land. We won't do it again."

"I am sure you won't," Satochi replied. "And according to my two men standing behind you, your curiosity got the best of you and now you'll have to pay."

Donald and Henry both turned around to see two Hawaiian men walking up the trail behind them.

"I'm not paying you any money for hiking to the Great Crack," Henry said defiantly.

Donald sensed they were in trouble. "We're sorry for any inconvenience we may have caused you, and I promise neither of us will say anything about what we found in the lava tube."

"Oh, I'm sure you won't say anything," Aioka replied in a sinister voice nodding towards Satochi.

In a quick and fluid motion, Satochi unsheathed the sword hidden in his cane and slashed the throat of the stunned Henry. Henry's eyes got very wide and he tried to speak, but only gurgled. Donald who was standing slightly behind Henry bolted as fast as he could run down the old road towards the ocean. He knew he could not outrun the helicopter, but knew he could outrun the two men in 'slippahs' and the small man with the decided limp. His hope was to find help before the helicopter could give chase. Satochi handed his sword to one of the men now standing next to him and pulled his Glock 19 from its holster. He handed the gun to Aioka. Aioka lifted the Glock, aimed, and slowly squeezed the trigger. Donald was not able to outrun the single bullet that buried itself in his brain. His forward motion caused his dead body to tumble ahead for several more feet.

"Bring me his body," Aioka demanded. The man holding the sword handed it back to Satochi who used it to cut the t-shirt off the dead hiker. He used the shirt to carefully clean his sword before sheathing it.

"Remove his shirt," Satochi ordered as his men brought Donald's body and laid it next to Henry. Satochi turned his cane over and rested the large tiger shark tooth on Henry's chest. Very methodically he carved a design in both Henry's and Donald's chests.

"There is one car at the turnout. It is a rental and must belong to these two. Place the bodies inside, then drive the car to Punalu'u and hide the car in the weeds just past the beach, but not too well. I want the bodies found and the message sent to all these mainland tourists that they are not welcome on this part of the island," Satochi instructed.

"Make sure you place the bodies in the front seat," Aioka added.

"Yea boss."

The two Hawaiians carried the bodies to a stand of bushes near the turnout. They found the car keys in Donald's waist pack and used them to unlock the trunk. Neither man spoke as they threw the bodies in the trunk, then started the car and drove the twenty miles till they reached the Sea Mountain/Punalu'u turnoff. Sea Mountain had been a grand plan that never came to fruition. The golf course was still in operation, although the temporary club house and snack bar were in such poor repair it was finally abandoned. Several of the condos had been abandoned, as had several houses in the area. The jungle was slowly taking back many of the lesser used roads. In spite of all of this, tourists still poured into the area during the day. Punalu'u Beach was a major stop for all the tour buses that circled the island. The draw was the black sand beach and the giant turtles that spent the day sunning themselves on the black sand. It was a beautiful spot, but one that was not a safe place to be after dark. Even many locals from Hilo, Kailua-Kona, and Waimea dared not visit the area after dark. This was the part of the island where tourists and tourist dollars were not welcome. This was the area ruled by the native Hawaiians, the Hawaiians who were tired of their lands being sold off to the super-wealthy who were anxious to buy their own little part of paradise, the Hawaiians who believed their land was stolen from their Queen, the Hawaiians who swore to some day receive the recognition they deserved and demanded, the Hawaiians sworn to taking back their lands by any means. Along with those Hawaiians who grew some of the best marijuana in Hawaii and want no one treading on their 'Hawaii nei.'

It was easy to find an overgrown area next to the road to semi-hide the car. As one of the men moved the bodies to the front seat, the other straightened the weeds bent by the car driving through them. The men had no sooner finished their job and started walking up the road when a van stopped to pick them up.

"Eh brah, I get pakalolo, you like smoke?"

"Shoots, we go!" the men replied as they climbed in the van and headed down to the beach to watch the sunset and scare the few remaining tourists away.

CHAPTER EIGHT

Six hours ago

It was early afternoon and the jet roared as the pilot reversed the thrust on the engines slowing the large plane as it neared the end of the Kailua-Kona runway. The pilot continued to roll the jet down the long runway till he reached the jet port at the South end of the airport grounds. There were more than two dozen private jets already parked in the area. A parking place near the exit and hidden behind several large fuel storage tanks had been saved for the Congressional jet. It provided some protection from the curiosity seekers along 'U'U Road hoping to catch a glimpse of the rich and famous as they arrived for the party. Barricades were also in place barring traffic from driving further past the jet port down 'U'U Road. There was no need for customs to board the plane or question the passengers since they were some of the most prominent Congressmen in the country returning from a trying fact-finding mission to Russia. Romeo was first off the plane as he always was. The necessity to secure the area for the dignitaries on board was not so pressing now that they had returned to American soil. Still, he stood at attention at the bottom of the boarding stairs as the Congressmen slowly exited the plane and made their way to several waiting limousines provided by William Casey. They were all to be his guests for the next two days at one of his new resorts along the Kohala Coast. Each of the Congressmen had at least two assistants and several of them had even more than that. They of course would be provided places to stay at one of the other resorts in the area; however, most of them would not be attending the gala party William Casey had planned. They would be shuttled from their hotel to where the Congressmen were staying to attend to business in the morning except, of course, for those few special assistants who would be discretely shuttled to Casey's resort to meet with their Congressmen that night to attend to other business.

As each official walked down the boarding steps, Romeo gave a crisp salute welcoming the Congressmen back to U.S. soil.

"Romeo, you are a true soldier, America is proud of you my boy," the senator from Mississippi said.

"Yes sir, thank you, sir," was Romeo's reply.

"Now that we're back in the United States, it won't be necessary for you two marines to guard the plane. Mr. Casey arranged for rooms for the both of you at the Hilton Waikoloa Village, all expenses paid," the senator explained. "Airport security will take over the responsibility for our plane for the next two days. You boys enjoy yourself, you hear?"

"Alright, good buddy," Romeo's partner Jeff said after the last Congressman had entered one of the waiting limousines, "we get to live like the rich people for a couple of days."

Romeo was not so enthused. Viktor's final words were still echoing in his brain. He wanted the opportunity to search the plane to see just what it was Viktor was so concerned about.

"Jeff, I am kind of worried about something," Romeo said, deciding to share his concern with someone. "Back in Russia, that Colonel who stopped us from leaving said something about a grievous crime being committed as if someone on the plane stole something really important or did something really bad."

"If that was the case, they never would have let us leave. We would still be sitting in Perm freezing our asses off while our governments negotiated. He was just playing mind games with you. Nobody stole shit from the Russians. Hell, you saw the state of their country, what do they have that anybody would even want?" Jeff replied.

"Maybe you're right," Romeo replied.

"Of course I'm right. That's why I outrank you my friend. Now I'm ordering you to grab your suitcase and get your ass into that limousine so we can have two days of fun in paradise."

"Shouldn't we wait for the rest of the assistants to load the Congressmen's luggage before we go?" Romeo asked.

"Hell no, we have only two days and I damn well plan to squeeze every possible second out of those two days, so let's go," Jeff ordered.

It just didn't feel right to Romeo. Maybe Viktor was right when he told him to be careful whom you talk to, for you never know who your enemies might be.

"So, somebody better give me a straight answer and give it quick or there'll be hell to pay," Viktor shouted at the room of mid-level FSB staffers and technicians on the fourth floor of the infamous 'Tower of Terror' that once served as KBG headquarters in Perm. During the Cold War, thousands of Russians who entered the famed Tower were never seen again. It still struck fear in the hearts of most Perm residents. Now it was the fear of Viktor's wrath that had the room of staffers silent with fear.

"We have already told you, Boris disappeared shortly after the standoff with the plane of American Congressmen." Several of the staff members knew the trouble Viktor was in.

Four suitcase nukes, originally designed and made for the KGB, were missing from the storage facility outside of Perm in the Ural Mountains. Each of these bombs contained from ten to twelve kilos of fissile material, capable of producing an explosive charge of .75-1 kiloton nuclear blast. That is the equivalent to one thousand tons of TNT. It could destroy everything within a half-mile radius if denoted at ground level. It would not produce a large volume of radioactive fallout, limiting danger levels to within three kilometers of the blast. Prevailing winds could greatly alter that contamination area.

"Wasn't Boris at the storage facility the day the American dignitaries toured the facility?" Viktor asked one of Boris' co-workers.

"Yes, he always accompanies visitors to the storage facilities."

"When was the last time any of you saw Boris or his family?" I saw his wife Polya at the train station last night around 11:00. I thought it peculiar she was out so late. When I asked, she said she was going to visit her sister in Yekaterinburg."

"Pull up the train schedules," Viktor said to one of the workers seated at a computer. Within seconds, Viktor held a list of all trains arriving and leaving Perm.

"There is no train leaving for Yekaterinburg last night, only one arriving from there. Let's see a list of all passengers boarding trains leaving Perm last night."

The worker had predicted the request and immediately handed Viktor the information. "There is no Polya Ivanov on this list."

"But there is a Polya Blokhin, and as you know Blokhin means full of ticks..." the worker began to explain.

"What what are you trying to say?" Viktor said impatiently.

"Boris' wife, Polya, was a veterinarian. She would of course always be dealing with animals full of ticks."

Viktor thought about the technician's interpretation. "What is the destination of the train Polya Blokhin boarded?"

"St. Petersburg, with at least six stops in-between. She bought a ticket for one of the sleeping cars," the technician replied.

"I want an FSB agent at every stop that train makes. Make sure they have a recent picture of Boris and his wife. Do we have an agent on board that train?"

Again, the technician typed rapidly on the computer keyboard. "Valyntina Sergeev. She is one of the provodnitsa that oversee the private sleeping cars. Valya, I believe, is the name she goes by."

"Contact her immediately. Find out if our friend Polya is still on board. I want to know everything she does and everyone she talks to. With luck, Polya will lead us to Boris." Now a more daunting task lay ahead for Viktor. He needed to call the Kremlin and give them some very bad news.

Romeo was quiet on the ride from the airport to the Hilton Waikoloa Village. Viktor's words gave him no peace.

"Why did the Russian colonel keep them from taking off? What could be so valuable that he would risk an international incident over it?" Then it came to Romeo.

"Could someone actually have smuggled a nuclear bomb on the Congressmen's plane?" he said softly to himself.

"What did you say?" Jeff asked.

"Nothing, I was just thinking out loud."

"Well, I order you to stop thinking and start drinking," Jeff said as he poured Romeo a large bourbon on the rocks. Romeo smiled and grabbed the drink from Jeff's hand.

"Here's to America," Romeo said raising his glass.

"Home of the free," Jeff replied, as they clinked their glasses together.

"We heard from Valya," Viktor's assistant said. "She reports that a woman, who seems to match the photograph one of our agents gave to her at the last stop, is in the berth and cabin assigned to Polya Blokhin."

"Looks like her or is her?" Viktor thundered, "which is it?"

"The provodnitsa isn't specific, the woman was asleep," the assistant replied.

"Dammit, we need to know if that is or isn't her for sure. We cannot afford to lose our only lead to Boris," the Colonel explained. Before anyone could answer, another of the FSB agents assisting in the search for Boris quickly entered the room.

"We have found Boris Ivanov," the agent began to explain, "his body was pulled from the Kama River less than an hour ago. He had been shot once in the back of the head."

Viktor rubbed his face to relieve the stress that felt like a vice squeezing his head. He remained silent for a moment, as did the others in the room waiting to know how Viktor would react to this very bad news.

"Arrest his wife at the next stop and have her flown here," Viktor calmly requested. "And be careful, she may be armed. I want the entire train searched for the bombs. Let's hope we get lucky." Viktor knew the bombs would not be there. He was sure they were already out of the country and in the United States by now.

"Could it be an attempt by the Americans to show how better safeguards are needed for our nuclear weapons?" The assistant regretted it the moment he said it.

Viktor glared. He would be the first to admit that tighter security was needed and he informed the Kremlin of that very fact on a regular basis. Their reply always referred to the political cat-and-mouse game constantly being played between the two countries. The United States had invested billions of dollars in upgrading the facilities and security for nuclear weapon and waste storage throughout Russia. The Kremlin insisted more money was needed to complete the upgrade and the Americans continued to insist that Congress had cut off the funds to do so. That was why so many American Congressmen came to visit the facilities and why Russia continued to encourage the practice. It was now up to Viktor to discover how this occurred and who was involved

"Hilton Concierge, how may I help you, Mr. Gonzalez?"

The concierge calling him by name surprised Romeo until he realized that the phone no doubt showed who and what room was calling. "Yes, I would like you to arrange for a rental car as soon as possible."

"Of course, Mr. Gonzalez, may I recommend a convertible since it promises to be a spectacular sunset."

"Whatever is cheapest," Romeo replied.

"But sir, we were given explicit instructions by Mr. William Casey's secretary to make sure you only get the best while staying with us."

"Whoa, are you sure about that?" Romeo replied.

"Absolutely, Mr. Gonzalez, how soon will you be picking up your convertible?" the concierge asked.

"Immediately, if possible."

"It's possible. I think you'll find that it'll take you at least fifteen minutes to reach the lobby from your room in the Ocean Tower. I'll have the car ready. All that will be required of you is your signature and a driver's license."

"Yes, of course, thank you," Romeo replied.

"No, thank you sir, it is our pleasure."

Just as promised when Romeo reached the lobby, thirteen minutes later, the car was waiting.

"Ready to go for you, Mr. Gonzalez, just sign here," the concierge said, "and enjoy your drive this evening."

It took Romeo almost thirty minutes to get back to the Kailua-Kona Airport. He parked as near the Congressional jet as possible, but it was still a bit of a walk to the security clearance office near the private aviation area.

"May I help you?" the security guard at the gate asked.

Romeo pulled out his identification and clearance papers. "I left a suitcase I need on the plane."

"No problem, Mr. Gonzalez, they are still unloading some of the Congressmen's luggage. I believe the compartment is still open and accessible."

"Thank you, I'll only be a few minutes," Romeo replied.

"Take your time, you're in Hawaii now. Things move a bit slower on the islands," the guard said smiling.

As Romeo approached the jet, he saw an assistant to one of the Congressmen loading a large suitcase into the back of a van.

"A little late for unloading luggage, don't you think?" Romeo said as he cautiously approached.

"Oh, hello Romeo," the assistant said, obviously startled, "I was aaa..., I was a, I was just taking the Senator's luggage to him. He needed his formal wear and it's packed in a different suitcase."

Romeo could tell the man was lying. He moved his hand nearer to his sidearm. "Why don't you step away from the van while I have a look inside? Keep your hands where I can see them."

"What...what are you talking about? I'm...I'm just getting the senator's luggage," the assistant stammered.

"Please step back, I won't ask again," Romeo repeated pulling his pistol from its holster, but not yet pointing it at the assistant. The assistant quickly moved backwards. "That's far enough. Keep your hands where I can see them," Romeo said, moving towards the rear of the van. He glanced quickly in, trying to also keep an eye on the assistant. "What is all this?"

The assistant didn't reply, but started slowly moving to the right.

"I asked you a question. This is not the senator's luggage. What is in these suitcases? And stop moving," Romeo demanded aiming his sidearm at the assistant.

"Suitcase nukes," the assistant replied. "I was paid a lot of money to get these on the Congressmen's jet."

"So that's why the Russian colonel wouldn't allow us to take off. He knew. He knew someone had stolen nukes, but couldn't risk an international incident if he boarded the plane and was wrong," Romeo surmised.

"I was sure we were done for when those trucks blocked us in," the assistant said.

"Who's we?" Romeo asked, but the assistant didn't answer, but again started slowly moving to the right.

"Stop moving," Romeo demanded.

"You won't shoot me. I'm a covert C.I.A. agent. Stealing the nukes was my assignment. The President wants to show how easy it is to get a hold of tactical nuclear weapons. He wants to force the Congress to allocate more funds for Homeland Security and for better securing the Russian nuclear storage facilities."

"I don't believe you," Romeo replied.

"Putin is even in on it. Why else do you think that colonel would suddenly allow us to take off if he knew we had nukes on board? It was all prearranged by both presidents. Somehow that FSB colonel found out about it and almost ruined everything."

Romeo was confused. Could this man be telling the truth? Was this whole junket just a ruse from the very beginning? Romeo reached in the van and unlatched one of the suitcases to open it.

"You've got to believe me," the assistant pleaded, "you are about to make a career ending mistake."

The assistant's last statement got Romeo thinking. The last thing he wanted was a discharge back to East L.A. and to the gang life that sucked the soul out of most of the boys growing up there, at best leaving little more than a drug addled brain housed in a tattooed and scarred body. Romeo had no desire to be an emaciated shell of a human being wandering the streets or wasting away in a prison cell like the majority of his childhood friends. No, that was not the life he wanted. But he did want to see if these suitcases really contained nukes and not drugs or artifacts. He slowly lifted the lid of the suitcase. Romeo was not an expert, but it did look to be some kind of a bomb.

"How can I believe you? How can I be sure you work for the CIA?" Romeo said stepping from behind the van's back door.

"He can't," a voice said. Romeo quickly turned his gun in the direction of the voice, but the gun was gone. Romeo barely caught the glint of the blade that sliced cleanly through his wrist removing his hand along with the gun it was holding. Before he could scream, a second swing of the blade slit his throat to the spine. Romeo crumpled to the ground.

The assistant turned and vomited. "Quickly," the voice commanded, "pick up his body and place it in the truck." Another man came out of the shadows and with the help of the assistant they put the body next to the suitcase nukes.

"Don't forget the hand."

The assistant picked up Romeo's hand which still gripped the pistol and tossed it into the van. "Wipe up some of that blood before the security guards come back around," the voice ordered. The man next spoke to the driver, "take one of the suitcases to the plane in Hilo, you know where to take the rest."

"Yea boss," the driver replied.

"He opened one of the suitcases," the assistant said, but the voice didn't seem to understand. "When do I get the rest of my money?" the assistant asked. "They'll know it was me who helped steal the nukes. I need the rest of my money so I can disappear."

"I guess you should have thought of that before you sold out your country," the voice said. "But I can help you disappear."

"What are …," but the words turned to a gurgle as the assistant's throat was ripped away.

"After you drop off the bombs, take both the bodies to the worksite, and throw them in one of the lava tubes."

"Yea boss," the driver replied.

"Give me his jacket," the voice said. The driver handed him the assistant's suit coat and he wiped the blood from his sword then sheathed it back into the cane. He would clean the spattered blood from his body later.

"It's not her," the FSB agent said to the colonel, "it's not Polya Ivanov who was on the train."

"Why am I not surprised by this news," the colonel interrupted, "who is the woman?"

"We don't know, the woman is dead. When one of our agents boarded the train, they found her still lying in the berth where the provodnitsa had earlier seen her. She appeared to have been dead for quite some time," Viktor's assistant reported.

"Have her body flown back here immediately. I want to know how this woman died," Viktor said.

"I'm afraid I have more bad news," the assistant continued, "Polya Ivanov took a late-night flight to St. Petersburg. A check with Tamojhnya shows that she caught a hydra-foil to Helsinki. She should be arriving there shortly."

"Have some of our agents in Helsinki wait for her to arrive and detain her in a safe house until I arrive." Viktor instructed.

"And if that's not possible?" his assistant asked.

"Then he is to watch and follow her until I arrive," Viktor responded. "We cannot afford to let her get away. Make that very clear."

Viktor knew that Polya did not have the bombs. He did not need to go to Helsinki, but to the United States. The sooner the Kremlin realized that fact, the better chance Viktor had of retrieving his four nukes and the safer the world would be.

The two Navy hydrogen planes that had been high above the Pacific monitoring the waters around the Hawaiian Islands had been redirected to do 1500-foot fly-overs of all the major airports on the islands. They were sniffing the air for possible explosive chemicals that would reveal the presence of other bombs that may be hidden or set to explode. Since all air traffic had been stopped, it was safe for the plane to make low and silent passes above the airports.

"Sir, we have an anomaly," the technician said to the naval duty officer.

"What kind of anomaly?"

"One of our hydrogen surveillance planes just picked up a radiation signature on the Big Island," the technician replied.

"Is it still there?"

"No, it just flashed for a few seconds, but there is no denying it was a positive identification."

"Are you sure it just isn't some poor soul who just had a radiation treatment?"

"If that was the case the signal would still register. This one disappeared! That means it's shielded in some way."

"Can you pinpoint it for me?" the officer asked.

"19.65 North latitude, 156 West longitude. That's the Kailua-Kona International Airport," the technician replied.

"Shit," the officer replied. "It's not as if we have enough already going on today. Call the airport security and have them take a look around. I need to call Washington."

CHAPTER NINE

One hour ago

It was three in the morning when Jim finally made his way back to his parked Cherokee. Instead of walking directly to the car, he carefully circled the parking area staying hidden in the trees. He wanted to make sure his two wannabe assassins were not waiting to complete their failed task. After a half-an-hour of lurking in the trees, Jim could no longer wait. He needed to get to a hospital for some x-rays. He wanted to make sure it was only a couple of broken ribs and two very bad bruises causing him all the pain. Once in the car, Jim felt a sense of relief. He quickly turned around and headed down the rugged logging road grimacing in pain at each bump. When he reached the main highway, he turned towards the east and floored it, trying to put as much room between him and anyone who may be waiting or trying to follow. The roads became windy so he had to slow to a more reasonable speed. It didn't take long for the headlights to appear in Jim's rearview mirror.

"Damn," Jim said as he pushed the pedal to the floor. "Where are my damn six-shooters when I need them?"

The lights behind continued to grow nearer. Jim's older Jeep was no match for whatever was closing in behind him. Even though there were occasional houses and stores along the road, no stores were open in the middle of the night and Jim knew better than to stop at one of the cabins or houses. Chances were nobody would be home or answer the door before the car chasing him closed in. Even then, he didn't want to chance getting someone else killed by the two crazy men who had tried to kill him. Jim's only hope was to keep going and hope he reached a more populated area before he was run off the road.

The road straightened as he crested a small hill. It was a straight gradual descent for at least a mile. About half way down the hill were two police cars blocking the road with their lights flashing.

"Yippee," Jim shouted wincing as the pain of his yelling burned his ribs. "Thank God for the Mounties." Jim continued speeding till the last minute then slammed on his brakes skidding to a stop just a few feet from the two Canadian mounted police cars.

"Out of the car, with your hands in the air," one of the Mounties shouted.

"With pleasure," Jim replied. He awkwardly climbed out of his car keeping an eye on the approaching car. "Shit," Jim said as the car that had been following him came to a stop. It was a Canadian Forest Service truck.

"Are you Jim Rikey?" the man said as he climbed out of the truck.

"I am," Jim turned to face the ranger but the exhaustion and injuries from the past sixteen hours finally took their toll as he stumbled and fell unconscious into the arms of one of the Mounties.

"I guess we got our man."

Portable flood lights lit up the Honolulu International Airport like it was the Super Bowl. Hundreds of emergency vehicles and personnel moved like ants around the runway, tarmac, and terminal, very orchestrated and deliberate ants. Massive grids had been set across the entire area, and a matching set of grids had been placed in several of the larger hangars to carefully place and plot every minute piece of airplane, baggage, and body part. Of course, the actual body parts were not placed in the hangar, only a written description and identification number that correlated to a specific plastic bag holding the actual tissue, limb, head, or whatever other part was found.

Hundreds of flights into Honolulu were being canceled around the globe. Those planes that were already too far into their flight to return were directed to land at the airport in Lihue on Kauai or Kahului on Maui. The several thousand tourists already on Oahu would be spending a few more days while arrangements were made for their flights to depart from Dillingham Field or John Rogers Field in Kalaeloa. Neither of these airports could handle the larger commercial aircraft, but were able to shuttle passengers to airports on the other islands capable of handling the big jets.

The military supplied the personnel for the clean-up and cataloguing of the debris at Honolulu. The FBI was in charge of the investigation for the moment until it was determined which division of the NCTC would be in charge. It would have fallen under Jotty Joplin's purview had it not been for his assassination earlier that same day. The director of the NCTC did not feel Haruko nor Eddie had the experience and qualifications to step in as head of Jotty's department. Haruko was adamant in her disagreement with that interpretation, but her arguments fell on deaf ears. Had she been a citizen of the United States, and a man, the circumstances would have been much different. As it was, her argumentative attitude had forced her supervisors to exclude her from the search for Jotty's killers as well as what was no doubt a terrorist attack most likely perpetrated by Aioka and the Red Summit. She had been assigned to work on the six Ebola outbreaks and to determine if they were a coordinated terror attempt. It was also obvious to all that it was Eddie Popp the murderer was looking for when his brother Michael was killed at Jim's house in Hawi. With Jotty having been killed, it was not a stretch to think an attempt would be, or already had been, made to kill Jim Rikey. So far, none of the authorities had been able to locate Jim or his Jeep, though they had narrowed the search area based on interviews with neighbors in Edmonton. The NCTC director, former Senator Conyers, hoped Jim would be found safe and was ready to return to lead the NCTC team that Jotty had put together. The director already met with the psychologist who had been treating Jim's post-traumatic stress syndrome and knew Jim was mentally fit to assume the post if he was willing to do so.

There was much debate as to the intended target of the bombings at Honolulu International Airport. Several agents in the NCTC thought it was aimed to disrupt military operations at Hickam and was part of a bigger plot. Others thought it might be al-Qaeda following through on their threat to bomb several planes, a threat that was discovered and disrupted by a joint Filipino US Intelligence in 1995. Several agents linked it to the Pan Am flight 830 out of Tokyo, that was bombed on final approach to Honolulu by what is now believed to be an early faction of the Red Summit. Consensus was that the Red Summit was responsible for the bombings, especially since several of the NCTC task force assigned to investigate the Red Summit had come under attack. Now with the anthrax attack on the *Grand Maui*, there was little doubt it was them. Aioka put an end to any doubt when he released his claim of responsibility and his warning that the worst was yet to come.

Eddie had left the *Grand Maui* and returned to Jim's house in Hawi as soon as an FBI supervisor was flown to the ship. Several more medical teams had arrived, but they were too late to save the majority of the passengers. The ship would remain quarantined and at sea for several more days while the bodies were removed to a secure location at the Coast Guard facilities on Oahu and the ship thoroughly sanitized to remove all potential deadly anthrax spores. Giant refrigeration units were being set up in a hangar at the Coast Guard base to preserve the bodies until cargo space became available to return the bodies to their mainland homes, which could be quite some time due to the airport bombings. All morgue facilities in Honolulu were at capacity dealing with the thousands of body parts from the airport bombings. When Eddie arrived, his brother's body had already been removed to the North Hawaii Community Hospital morgue in Waimea and a forensics team was meticulously scouring the house in search of clues. After hearing about what had happened to Jotty and being told about the petroglyph carved into his brother's chest, Eddie had no doubt who was behind the murder and needed no forensics team to tell him. He knew it was Satochi. Eddie swore to finish the job he started in Catalina when he almost ripped off Satochi's leg with his own weapon. Now it had become very personal, but he couldn't show his feelings. He did not want to be removed from the case like he knew Haruko would be. She was too much of a firebrand and everyone, including her bosses, knew it. Eddie's main concern was who would be put in charge of the Red Summit investigation and how big of a part would he get to play? All of this would no doubt be resolved after the funerals for Jotty and Michael.

"Jim, thank God you are alright," Haruko was crying as she spoke to Jim over the phone. "We were so worried. We thought you might be dead."

"How in the world did you find out that somebody tried to kill me and why was everybody trying to find me?" Jim asked puzzled. "Did the Mounties tell you about my injuries?"

"The doctor did tell me about your broken ribs and the severe bruising on your chest. They also said you had quite a few cuts and abrasions."

"Yes, that usually happens to me when I'm shot, then fall off a cliff into a stream and get swept over a waterfall and down several rapids," Jim said, trying to be funny.

Haruko was in no mood for Jim's humor. She remained silent.

"What's wrong, Haruko?" He could tell something was not right by her silence.

"Jotty is dead. We believe he was murdered by two of the white supremacists the two of you arrested in Texas."

"I'm so sorry, Haruko," Jim said. He didn't know that Haruko and Jotty had become lovers and were living together, but he had his suspicions when they both stopped calling to check on him a couple of months back.

"Someone also tried to kill Eddie at your house in Hawaii," Haruko started to explain.

"Is he alright?" Jim asked interrupting.

"Eddie wasn't there at the time, but his brother was."

"Oh my God, they killed Eddie's brother?" Jim asked.

"They did. Eddie thinks it was Satochi who did it," Haruko said.

"Aioka's assassin?"

"Yes, that's what he believes. There have also been two major terrorist attacks that Aioka has now claimed responsibility for. Over half of the passengers and crew of the *Grand Maui* were killed by the same strain of weaponized anthrax that Aioka used for his attack on California."

97

"That's awful news," Jim replied.

"It gets worse. Three jumbo jets were blown up within seconds of each other at Honolulu International Airport late Sunday afternoon in Hawaii. Almost 1700 people were killed with three hundred more injured in the terminal."

"And Aioka did this?" Jim asked.

"He released a statement claiming responsibility for the terror attacks," Haruko replied.

"How do the white supremacists tie in with Aioka? It was two of them that tried to kill me as well."

"The four of them all escaped last week from the correctional facility in Haskell. It happened during what I think may have been a trial run for the Red Summit's next big attack."

"What kind of attack?" Jim asked.

"Six cases of Ebola hemorrhagic fever were reported within a week at six different locations around the country. One of the victims was the warden at the Haskell facility. During the panic, a medical team claiming to be from the CDC arrived by helicopter and claimed four of the inmates had been exposed and needed to be removed immediately from the facility. After what happened to the warden, nobody was about to argue with them."

"Are the six cases related?" Jim asked.

"They all are the exact strain that originated a few months back at a goldmine in Durba in the Republic of Congo."

"How in tarnation did it get from the Congo to the United States?"

"Well, it wasn't by accident," Haruko replied. "One of the victims was an agent here at the NCTC."

"Sounds like that wasn't by accident," Jim replied.

"I don't think so either," replied Haruko, "but I intend to find out for sure. I know Aioka is behind this as well, but I haven't shared that with the bosses. They're not very happy with me right now."

Knowing Haruko, Jim could understand why. "When is the funeral?"

"Tomorrow, here in Virginia." Haruko replied. "Will you be well enough to make it?"

"Sure I will," Jim replied. "I will catch the next available flight out of Edmonton."

"That won't be necessary," Haruko replied. "Director Conyers has authorized one of the company jets to pick you up. I think they want you to head up the team."

Jim wasn't sure how to reply. He assumed it would be Haruko who would take over for Jotty. She knew the most about Aioka and the Red Summit.

"What about Eddie? Will he be able to come to the funeral?" Jim asked, trying to avoid the subject of who would lead the team.

"Eddie will be attending his brother's funeral back at Santa Cruz in California. Because of the tragedy in Honolulu, air traffic to and from Hawaii is a nightmare right now. The NCTC arranged for Eddie to bring his brother's casket home on a military flight returning to California after dropping off a team of doctors and medical technicians to deal with the anthrax outbreak. The director told him to take some time off, but he refused. He plans on meeting you here the day after tomorrow, right after his brother's funeral."

Jim noticed that she said meet him, not us, when she was talking about Eddie. "It sounds like you don't plan on sticking around for the meeting."

"I don't. I've been asked, or should I say told, that I need to step away from this investigation. They're sending me out to track down that Ebola virus."

"I thought you said we already know where it came from."

"We do, we just don't know how it got to the six victims, or where the doctor is that was working with the original victims in the Congo. No one was found alive at the CDC outpost where he was working."

"They all died from the virus?" Jim asked.

"Not all of them. According to the report we have, most of the bodies found there had been shot several times. The doctor was nowhere to be found. Some local villagers reported seeing several armed rebels leaving the area in two trucks. One of them with two white men inside went to the local airport where they boarded a plane of some bush pilot. We have people working on that information. Doctors without Borders, the organization he was working for, told us he had requested to leave several times. The reality of the situation was a little too overwhelming for the doctor to handle."

"The doc here says if I'm flying back there tonight, I need to get some rest, so I'll talk to you when I arrive," Jim said.

"I'll pick you up," Haruko said, her voice beginning to crack.

"Haruko, I'm really sorry about Jotty, I know you both loved each other very much. We'll all miss him. Remember, I love you too."

"I have never forgotten. Goodbye," Haruko replied softly.

For a moment Jim had forgotten about the physical pain he was in, at least until they began to wrap his ribs.

"Quit crying, it can't hurt that bad," the nurse said.
"If you only knew," Jim replied.

CHAPTER TEN

A pall came over the well-heeled party-goers as news of the airport bombings and anthrax attack on the *Grand Maui* began to spread at William Casey's party.

"Friends," Bill said addressing the crowd from the bandstand, "by now I'm sure you've heard about the tragic attack on three passenger jets at Honolulu International Airport earlier this evening. I have also been informed that passengers on the *Grand Maui* were purposely infected with a form of anthrax. Needless to say, hundreds were killed in the attacks. I know many of you would like to contact your love ones back home and let them know you're alright. Many of you may have lost friends in one of these attacks, but I'm infinitely thankful that my good friend Barbra Chenoweth decided to attend my party and was not on board the *Grand Maui* when the attack occurred there. You all are welcome to stay here at one of my resorts until the situation calms down later this week. Those of you, who came to the Big Island on one of my private jets, or one of your own, will have no delays when you decide to leave the islands. As for those of you who flew here on a commercial flight, I would like to offer the services of my pilots and jets to return you home, but not until you are completely comfortable with the situation. For those of you staying at the Kona Village Resort, I have arranged to have televisions brought in for those of you who desire them. I know many of you will want to follow this horrible tragedy as it unfolds. However, the band will play on and you all are welcome to stay as long as you like and enjoy the party."

"My God Marlin, we would be dead if Bill hadn't invited us here tonight," Barbra said, swooning.

"Let's hope it's not as bad as Bill described it, my love. Perhaps we should take a walk on the beach to calm our nerves," Marlin suggested, as he poured Barbra another glass of champagne.

"No, I think I just want to sit and listen to the band and sip champagne," Barbra replied, "don't you just love slack-key guitar music, Marlin?"

"Indeed, I do," Marlin replied, wondering how Barbra could so quickly put the terrorist attacks and her near-death by anthrax so quickly from her mind. It was as if such tragedies were meant for, and only affected, the common folk.

"Now don't you drink too much, darling, I expect great things from you tonight," Barbra said winking.

Marlin smiled his most charming smile as an answer. It was automatic, for the only thing on Marlin's mind was the thought that he was responsible for the deaths of all those people on the *Grand Maul*, and somebody was bound to figure it out.

Günter recognized the two FSB agents the moment he walked into the Helsinki terminal. He knew they had come to stop Polya and he was not about to let that happen. Polya had been busy the final two hours before the hydrofoil reached the terminal. Her long and stringy brunette coiffure was gone and, in its place, a sassy, spiked-blonde style. The brown tinted contacts were gone as were the frumpy clothes. In their place were the newest clothing styles fresh from Milan. Prada heels replaced the cheap Russian-made slip-ons. Instead of the tattered woolen coat was a leather and minka jacket. A Gucci purse, a diamond-studded Cartier watch and over-sized Armani sunglasses completed her image makeover. She looked more like a jet-setting pop star than the wife of a proletariat bureaucrat. Everyone would surely notice her as she entered the terminal, but only Günter would recognize and know this was the real Polya Primakov, the dedicated and, up until two days ago, deeply embedded mercenary and former agent posing as the wife of Boris Ivanov. She had spent the last twelve months carefully manipulating Boris with her sexual charms to mesmerize and control his every move until he would do exactly as instructed. Twelve very long months as far as Günter was concerned, for they were lovers. Both, however, knew the rewards justified the sacrifices that had to be made to achieve their and Aioka's goals.

Günter was confident neither agent would recognize Polya, but still wanted to leave nothing to chance. He followed one of the FSB agents into the restroom just a few minutes before the passengers were cleared to leave the ship. He noiselessly pulled his silenced Walther PPK from its holster as he walked up behind the agent as they entered the bathroom. He lifted the pistol till it was almost touching the head of the agent and fired one shot then slipping the pistol back into the holster. The bullet pierced the skull as it entered behind the left ear then ricocheted around the brain shredding it, killing the agent instantly. Günter caught the agent before he could fall.

"My friend drank a little too much," he said in his thick German-accented English.

The man washing his hands at the sink nodded his head in acknowledgement. Günter kicked open the door to one of the stalls. "Sit here and relax a while, Hans, while I get you a bottle of water," Günter said for the benefit of the other man in the washroom. Günter sat the agent backwards on the toilet with the front of his head leaning against the back wall. He ripped the toilet paper roll from the dispenser and stuck it as carefully as he could in the hole made by the bullet, so it could absorb any blood that flowed from the wound before gravity pulled it all out of the head and into the lower extremities. He pulled off the agent's coat and threw it over the top of the door to keep it closed. He washed his hands making sure no one was in the other stalls and nonchalantly left the restroom and reentered the terminal. Within a minute Polya walked out of the exit with all the flair of a movie star and greeted Günter with a big kiss, drawing the attention of several men who wished to be in Günter's shoes at that moment.

"I've missed you so very much," Polya said, as they walked hand-in-hand from the terminal.

"I too have missed you more than you will ever know," Günter replied, "but we must not linger here long." Günter glanced at the other FSB agent who was noticeably agitated by the absence of his partner.

Günter and Polya entered the waiting limousine and were soon on their way to a long awaited, and desired, reunion.

"This is Hilton security," a voice answered.

"I seem to have lost my friend," the marine started to explain. "I'm assigned to security for the Congressmen who are here on the island attending William Casey's party. I just heard about the bombings at Honolulu and we have been ordered to return to the plane immediately for security purposes. The problem is I've looked everywhere for Romeo Gonzalez, my partner, and he's just not around and he's not answering his cell phone."

The security officer pulled up Romeo's room information on his computer.

"He's not on the grounds," security replied. "According to his room information he rented a car shortly after check-in and left immediately."

"Did he say where he was going?"

"I'm afraid the computer doesn't have that information. I suggest you check with the parking valet. They would have brought the rental car to the door for him. Maybe he said something to one of them."

"Thanks for your help," the marine replied. "I guess I'm on my own. Could you please arrange for me to return to the airport?"

"Let me connect you with the concierge. I'm sure they can help you with that," the security agent responded politely.

"Romeo, Romeo, where the hell are you, Romeo? You be in deep shit boy," the other military escort sang to himself.

Aioka was sullen as he stared at the waves breaking offshore at Honoli'i Cove. He sat on the veranda looking down the river at the surfers testing their skills on the crashing waves.

"Why have you failed me?" he asked Satochi. "Why have so many failed me?"

Satochi knew that he was not expected to reply.

"You made a grave error killing the CIA agent's brother. Now he will be cautious and vigilant. He will know it was you."

"I was fooled by the resemblance, but I know that is no excuse for my failure," Satochi replied. Aioka did not respond, but it was as if Satochi could read Aioka's mind and could hear the word *rokudenashi* repeated over and over. He glared at Aioka who failed to see the menacing expression.

"We must put our failures behind us and move quickly to take the FBI's focus from here and place it on the mainland," Aioka resumed. "I had Günter contact two of those men we had freed from prison. The two who failed to eliminate Jim Rikey. They will meet you in Denver, Colorado. You will give them the suitcase and reaffirm the instructions on where and when it is to be delivered."

"Will they know the contents of the suitcase?"

"No, Günter told them it was a highly contagious virus and they would die if they opened it. All they will know is that a man will meet them outside the gate by the shipping warehouse. They were told that they are to give him the suitcase. You will be back here in Hilo with me before that meeting."

"How can we be sure they will follow your orders if I'm not there to see to it?" Satochi asked.

"These men have failed me once, they will not dare to fail me again, and to be sure I will have them under surveillance from the time they receive the suitcase until they reach Wichita to make the delivery."

Satochi nodded his head and started down the veranda steps towards his waiting car. As he neared the driveway, he was sure he heard Aioka call him *rokudenashi* under his breath. A seed that had been planted in his brain was beginning to bloom into severe paranoia. He did not wish to be the next of Aioka's assassins to pay the ultimate price for failure. "No, it shall not be me!" Satochi said, as he climbed in the back seat.

CHAPTER ELEVEN

"Have you seen anyone around my jet in the past couple of hours?" Jeff asked one of the two security guards at the Kailua-Kona general aviation gate. "Like possibly my partner in charge of plane security."

"As a matter-of-fact, I did," one of the men replied. "I think it was a little more than two hours ago. That other marine, you know, the one with that gnarly scar, he came by to pick up a suitcase he said he had left. One of the senator's assistants was still here unloading luggage to take up to the Four Seasons."

"Did you see him leave?" Jeff asked.

"No, I didn't. I figure he probably left in the van and headed back to the Four Seasons. He never walked out."

"Was there anyone else around?" the marine asked.

"Just the catering truck and the maintenance crew, but they were gone before the van left," the guard replied.

It was then the marine noticed the radiation detector in the hands of one of the guards and that they both were carrying M-16s. "What's up with that?" he said pointing to the detection unit. "You guys look ready for serious confrontation."

"We got a call from naval operations at Pearl. One of their spy satellites reported radiation somewhere here at the airport, but we sure as hell can't find any. Only the normal x-ray machine low-level signal."

"Another waste of taxpayer's money as far as I'm concerned, but with what went down at Honolulu we're taking no chances," the other guard replied.

"If a satellite picked up a signal, it was a hell of a lot stronger than any x-ray machine can produce. Those satellites are designed to pick up dirty bombs and nukes," Jeff told them. Both the security guards turned white and were visibly shaken by the marine's comment.

Suddenly, Romeo's comments on the way to the hotel came rushing into Jeff's mind. "Oh, shit! Romeo figured it out."

"Figured what out, sir?" one of the security guards asked.

"Listen to me carefully." Jeff instructed. "I need an immediate roadblock set up at the main highway. Nobody is to leave until their car or truck is thoroughly searched. Get on your radio and get as many police personnel here as you possibly can to assist."

"Just what is it we are looking for?" the guard asked.

"We're looking for the same thing the Russians were looking for when they wouldn't let us leave Perm. We're looking for a nuclear bomb."

"That's strange," one of the National Guard men said to his partner as he picked up, labeled, and bagged what he knew was a gas tank cover from a 747.

"What's strange?" his buddy replied.

"This is the second one of these I've found."

"What's so strange about that? Three planes just blew apart, there is debris everywhere."

"Yeah, but look at that cap. Just like the other one I found, it is in one piece and there's not a burn mark on it. Don't you think that's a little strange? It had to have fallen out before the explosion. Why would two gas caps fall off their respective planes on the same day?" the guardsman asked.

109

"They wouldn't unless for some reason they couldn't be screwed all the way on," his buddy replied. "I think you better report this to the captain."

"Don't shoot the messenger, don't shoot the messenger," Viktor's assistant repeated to himself as he went to update Viktor on the latest news from Helsinki.

"The report from our agent in Finland is not good."

"I'll be the judge of that," Viktor replied. "You just relay to me the facts."

"Our agent reports that his partner was killed by an unknown assailant and there was no one who even closely resembled Polya Ivanov."

"The fool," Viktor shouted. "She got off the ferry. Why else would his partner have been killed?"

"Should I make arrangements for us to go there?" his assistant asked.

"No, we will deal with Polya Ivanov at a later date. The missing devices are not in Finland. I am sure they are in America by now. Where is the Congressman's plane? Has it arrived in Washington yet?"

"No, it is in Hawaii. At the Kailua-Kona airport on the Big Island. Our sources tell us the Congressmen stopped for some big party on the island."

Viktor felt the air rush from his lungs. Why had he not realized it before this? "Tell me again about those bombings in Hawaii."

"Three 747's blown apart at the Honolulu airport. CNN is now reporting of an anthrax attack on a cruise ship off the coast of the Big Island."

A smile crossed Viktor's face. "That *sukin sin* is back in Hawaii."

"What son-of-a-bitch would you be referring to, sir?" his assistant asked.

"Aioka, Aioka Matsuura, the same *sukin sin* who kidnapped our top genetic scientist last year. The same *sukin sin* who I would bet a year's salary is behind the theft of our four suitcase nukes."

"That is the name of the leader of the terrorist organization that is now claiming responsibility for the attacks in Hawaii. CNN says he is the leader of the terrorist group the Red Summit out of Japan."

"Out of Hawaii I would say is more accurate. This will not be a popular decision, but the Kremlin needs to contact the President of the United States and tell them about the four stolen bombs," Viktor explained.

"Yes, but who is going to contact the Kremlin and explain to them why we believe four Russian suitcase nukes are now in the hands of terrorists on American soil?" the assistant asked. "It doesn't seem possible this man could steal our bombs."

"I believe nothing is impossible for Aioka Matsuura, nothing at all," Viktor said as he pulled out his cell phone. "Sometimes he even surprises me," Viktor thought as a smile crossed his face.

CHAPTER TWELVE

The final notes of 'Amazing Grace' lingered heavily in the morning mist as the last breath of air escaped from the bagpipes. Haruko clung to Jim's arm with a death grip unaware of the bruises and abrasions that lay under the sleeve of his suit coat. As they walked towards the waiting limousine, few words were exchanged.

"He was going to call you the day he was murdered," Haruko explained as the car slowed to allow one of the numerous tour busses to unload several dozen tourists by the Tomb of the Unknown Soldier. "He wanted you to be the first to know that we had planned to marry and he wanted you to be the best man."

"I'm so sorry Haruko. I guarantee we will find the men who did this."

"The man who did this was Aioka. Those two men who pulled the trigger were only doing as they are told. They will pay for their actions."

"You know they have put me in charge of the team. We will be meeting tonight when Eddie arrives in town. I would like you to be there," Jim said.

"You forget that I have been removed from the team. I will be in Haskell, Texas, investigating one of the six Ebola outbreaks."

"You said that the Ebola deaths are related to Aioka's terror plans. As far as I'm concerned, that still makes you active in the terror investigation. Just make sure you report your findings to me before any of those other greenhorns get hold of what you find out."

"You can count on that, but in return I expect you to keep me informed about the team's progress."

"Haruko, you are part of the team regardless of what these clueless bureaucratic horse's asses say, and don't you ever forget it."

Haruko tried to smile through her tears and reply, but the words wouldn't come. She squeezed Jim's hand and turned so he wouldn't see her crying.

At that moment Jim wanted nothing more than to go with Haruko. He just wasn't sure if it was because he still loved her or that he was homesick for Haskell.

By Monday morning there were over two hundred military personnel combing through every inch of the Kailua-Kona airport. Not only was there grave concern over the nuclear signature reported, but the President had been informed about the stolen suitcase nukes suspected to have been smuggled out on the Congressional plane. Forensic experts were also called in when quite a bit of blood was found near where the baggage would have been unloaded. Much too much blood to be from a cut or abrasion. It had been confirmed that the blood had come from two people and one was the same type as Romeo's blood. Positive identification as to if it was Romeo's was pending confirmation by the DNA tests. Jeff had no doubts.

When Eddie arrived in Washington, he was not the bubbling extrovert they all were used to. Then again, when your little brother is mistaken for you and murdered, it would tend to make anyone a little surly.

"It's good to see you Eddie. I'm sorry about your brother, but I swear we will catch the asshole that did it," Jim said.

"I am sure the asshole is Satochi. Who else would do such a thing?"

Jim and Haruko both had to agree.

"I'm very sorry I missed Jotty's funeral and I'm even more sorry for your loss," Eddie said turning to Haruko.

"Thank you, Eddie, and I too am sorry for your loss as well." Haruko turned to face Jim. "I must go. I have to catch a plane this evening to Dallas."

"What the hell are you talking about?" Eddie exclaimed. "You're the expert on Aioka."

"It's a long story that I will tell you about later," Jim interrupted, not wanting Haruko to have to suffer through her grief and anger by once again retelling the story of her dismissal.

Both Jim and Eddie kissed Haruko on the cheek as she left the McClean headquarters and headed to catch her flight.

"Obviously, there is a lot more going on than I know about," Eddie said. "Tell me what you meant when you said it looked like all hell was about to break loose. It seems to me it already has."

"You don't know the half of it," Jim said, and began a synopsis of what the NCTC now knew.

"Four nuclear bombs." Eddie almost yelled. "You've got to be shitting me."

"We aren't convinced that Aioka is behind that theft. He has claimed responsibility for the anthrax attack on the *Grand Maui* and the airport bombings in Honolulu. Haruko is convinced he's also behind the Ebola attacks. I have to agree with her, because someone used the Ebola scare to break those four white supremacists out of prison in Haskell. They were the ones who killed Jotty and tried to kill me."

114

"Maybe Aioka just saw an opportunity with all the chaos that was happening with the Ebola outbreaks," Eddie suggested.

"That seems to be the thinking of the bosses here in Virginia, but I tend to agree with Haruko, that somehow Aioka is involved in this."

"What about the nuclear bombs?" Eddie asked, "you said you aren't convinced Aioka is responsible."

"Several major international corporations have received extortion notes threatening their factories or offices will be the target of one of these missing nukes if they don't pay twenty million dollars to some bank account in Bahrain."

"Hell, that seems like a simple matter. Just make a fake wire transaction and follow the trail."

"It is not that easy," Jim said. "Besides, when the money doesn't show up, what's from keeping this guy or group from setting off the nukes when he realizes he's been fooled?"

"Good point," Eddie said. "Is Al Qaeda behind it?"

"We don't know yet. However, you haven't heard the worst of it. Remember our friend Colonel Viktor Cheznov of the FSB?"

"Yeah, he's the one who took out the coffee plantation and kidnapped the Russian scientist back to Russia. What's he got to do with this?" Eddie asked.

"It seems the colonel was also responsible for overseeing the facility where these four suitcase nukes were stolen. Russia claims they were taken out of Russia on a Congressional jet."

"Not the one that was held at gunpoint on the tarmac in Perm last week?" Eddie said. "That's absolutely preposterous."

"I thought so too, until I heard one of Lord Farrelton's hydrogen planes picked up a nuclear signature coming from the Kailua-Kona airport. The same airport where that Congressional jet is parked."

"Holy shit, did they find anything?" Eddie asked.

"No bombs, but they're still looking. They did find a pool of blood by the plane. Most of it belonged to one of the marine escorts assigned to the Congressmen. The rest they think belongs to the senator's assistant who is also missing. They believe the assistant is the one who stole the nukes."

"That doesn't sound good," Eddie replied. "Do you think somebody killed the assistant to cover their tracks?"

"That would be my guess. Aioka doesn't like to leave any loose ends," Jim replied. "What's even worse is that our friend Colonel Cheznov will be assisting in our investigation. We are to give him full access to all we know about the bombs as well as the Red Summit."

"What ignorant jackass decided that?" Eddie asked.

"That jackass would be our President. He accepted the offer from the Russian President. Viktor seems to believe that Aioka and the Red Summit are behind the theft of the bombs. We are to meet him in Kona tomorrow. All I can say is you better damn well have watered my garden while I was gone."

Eddie grimaced.

"You were wonderful, Marlin. This has been just a marvelous two weeks that I shall never forget," Barbra said, as she finished packing the small suitcase of clothing she had brought with her off the *Grand Maui* when she came to William Casey's party.

"Must you leave so soon, my love?" Marlin purred.

"As much as I've enjoyed your wonderful company, I'm afraid that I must return to the mainland. My family is concerned for my well being and I haven't a thing left to wear. All my clothes are back on the *Grand Maui* and I was told it may be weeks before they can be sent to me. Besides, with the delays in commercial flights leaving the islands, I couldn't pass up Bill's offer of the use of one of his private jets to return home."

Marlin marveled at the shallowness of Barbra's existence. Thousands were dead in the Honolulu airport bombings and the anthrax attack on the *Grand Maui*, and by all rights she should be dead as well, but yet she acted as if those things didn't happen to people of her stature and social class. It really pissed Marlin off. "Well, I hope you will return soon so we can spend more time together."

"I'm sure I will," Barbra said, kissing him gently on the cheek knowing full well the chances of that were remote at best. "I'm sorry to leave you here on the Big Island. I know you want to get back to Oahu as soon as you can, but that may take a few days until all this nonsense is settled at the airport. I've left you a little something to tide you over until they open up the airport." Barbra placed an envelope on the dresser near the door. "This room is also paid for until next weekend. By then I am sure you will be able to return home."

"You are so beautiful and kind," Marlin said in his most charming and sincere voice.

Barbra set down her suitcase and sat on the edge of the bed next to Marlin's nude body. "You could brighten anyone's day," Barbra said, as she kissed him deeply on the lips while her other hand caressed Marlin's finest asset. "You were wonderful," she said as she rose and left the room.

Marlin wasn't sure if Barbra's last comment was directed to him or to what she was caressing. Either way, she was now gone and he could concentrate on what to do about

the anthrax attack. He knew the FBI would come calling. He
needed to be prepared when they did.

Polya was a trained professional. She had been
recruited by the FSB right out of college and adored the
lifestyle and privileges her covert duties required of her. She
was what the American intelligence agencies sometimes
referred to as a swallow. But she was much more than that.
Her early assignments did involve obtaining information from
unsuspecting businessmen and foreign government officials
in that special way that gave agents such as Polya their nom
de guerre. Soon she proved to be far more efficient at her job
than most others in the service of the FSB. She was selected
for advanced training which was how she ended up at one of
the most secretive terrorist training camps in Chechnya. It
was there she made some very powerful and intimate
friends, one of whom was Günter. Günter Marx was born in
East Germany to a family of privilege, several years before
the wall came tumbling down. Soon after the collapse, he
moved with his family to South Africa. It was the streets of
Johannesburg where he learned his hatred for blacks, Jews,
and anyone else who wasn't white and Anglo-Saxon. He even
hated them if they were too goddamned liberal or stuck their
nose where it didn't belong. Americans seemed to be the
worst at meddling in another country's business and he had
grown sick of it. That is what drove him into his anarchist
ideals and that is what led him to seek terrorist training. It
was at the camp in Chechnya where he met Polya and they
had soon become lovers. It was also Günter who convinced
Polya that opportunities existed beyond the FSB that could
offer her a lifestyle far beyond any she had ever dreamed of.
Plans were made and schemes were hatched that would

make them both wealthier than they could have ever imagined. Aioka would play a major role in those plans.

"Who called it in? the police sergeant asked.

"Anonymous tip, but I heard the tape and it sounded like some stoned local looking for his weed patch."

"Anonymous tip would have sufficed," the sergeant said, staring at the patrolman.

"Any identification on the bodies?"

"No, not unless you want to call those petroglyphs carved on their chests identification. We think they're tourists. This is a rental car. We have somebody checking with the rental company as we speak. We should have a name shortly."

"Somebody is sending us a message," the sergeant replied, looking in at the two posed dead men. "Damn, what an awful smell. Have the coroner get the bodies out of the car as soon as possible. The sun is baking those poor souls."

"Did I hear you say there are petroglyphs carved on their chests?" one of the ambulance drivers who first responded said.

"Yeah, they're carved in the chest of both men. Probably some type of warning. Why do you ask?" the sergeant said.

"Cause my brah up in Waimea told me about some FBI agent near Hawi who was murdered a couple of days ago. He had a petroglyph carved in his chest too."

"Shit, the FBI," the sergeant said. "That means a whole lotta shit is going to hit the fan down here too. You better give them a call and tell them what we got," he said to one of his patrolmen. "Seems like all hell has broken loose on the islands the past few days, but I can't say I'm surprised.

The Menehunes will only put up with so much. Paradise may be hard to find for a few days."

CHAPTER THIRTEEN

"Just how long had you been having an affair with Mr. Cheney?" Haruko asked the secretary.

"Excuse me?" the secretary replied, sounding shocked. "Who said I was having an affair? Mr. Cheney was a married man."

"I don't have the time to waste while you play your little charade," Haruko said angrily. "Everyone knows about the affair, including his wife. You were probably closer to him than anybody, so that's why I am talking to you."

The secretary looked nervously at the FBI agent standing by the door.

"Would you feel more comfortable if he left the room?" Haruko said, sensing the secretary's discomfort.

"Please," she responded softly, and waited for him to go. "Ver Dell and I have been sleeping together at least three times a week for the past ten months. Bill was a very virile man for his age," the secretary said.

"I would guess so. His wife told me that this past year he seemed to come to life. She says they were having sex at least three times a week as well," Haruko replied. Ver Dell's secretary seemed shocked. "He told you he and his wife hadn't had sex in months, I bet." The secretary just nodded her head.

"Was Ver Dell a fitness nut? Did he keep in good shape? Did he take Viagra regularly, or any other stimulants?" Haruko asked.

"No Viagra that I know of and I would have known. He didn't do anything extreme as far as working out, but he was in fairly decent shape," she replied. "You know, I do remember some herbal supplements he received in the mail every couple of months, but I have no idea what they were for."

Haruko had a pretty good idea what was probably in those supplements. Jotty also had received his package in the mail every couple of months as well. "Are there any of those supplements still around here?"

"Let me check," the secretary said, picking through one of the boxes of Ver Dell's belongings she had packed to send to his wife. "Here it is," she said, holding up a box.

Haruko smiled, it was the same brand found at the homes of two of the other victims, the same brand that she insisted Jotty take.

"Oh my God," Haruko said out loud. "It was meant for Jotty!"

"Agent Rikey, I trust you have recovered from that traumatic incident in Kauai," Colonel Cheznov said as he greeted Jim and Eddie upon their arrival at the airport.

"You're kind of like a bad penny to me, Colonel. You keep turning up when you're not really wanted," Jim replied, as Eddie stood back sensing the tension.

"Please call me Viktor, but you are wrong, I am wanted here, Jim. Wanted and needed, at least according to your president."

"Bullshit!" Eddie coughed into his hand at Viktor's reply, causing the two men to turn towards him.

"Allow me to introduce my opinionated colleague, Eddie Popp."

"Nice to finally meet you, Eddie. I understand I just missed you at the coffee plantation last year on Maui. It will be a pleasure working with you," Viktor said.

"I hope I will soon be able to say the same," Eddie responded.

"I want to say how sorry I am to hear about the death of your good friend, Jotty Joplin," Viktor said turning back to Jim. "It came as quite a shock to me. I was looking forward to working with him. I was also very relieved to hear you survived the assassination attempt on your life."

"You are surprisingly well-informed, Viktor. I assume you also know Eddie's brother was killed up in my house in Hawi. The body was placed in the exact position that your dead agent's body was found," Jim said.

"I am truly sorry for your loss, Eddie, but Jim I don't know what agent you are talking about."

"Horse piss," Jim replied. "If you're going to be working with us, I expect you to be honest."

"Forgive me, Jim, you are right. That was one of my agents killed at your house. I only hope we can avenge both his and Eddie's brother's death by putting an end to the Red Summit."

"Thank you," Jim said.

"Where is the lovely Haruko? I expected that she would be here to meet me as well," Viktor said.

"Haruko is following up on some leads back on the mainland," Jim replied, not wanting to elaborate.

"Having to do with the Red Summit, I would hope," Viktor replied.

"No," Jim hesitated, "she is following up on some random Ebola cases back in my hometown in Texas."

"That's ridiculous," Viktor said.

"I couldn't agree more, but it's not my choice, so let's just leave it at that," Jim replied.

Viktor continued, "Haskell, Texas, I believe that is where the file said you lived before you moved to Hawaii."

"You are well informed Colonel, but it's still where I live. I'm just visiting here in Hawaii for a spell," Jim replied.

"Well, I certainly hope Haruko will be joining us later. She is the expert on Aioka Matsuura," Viktor said. "So, tell me what have you found out about the missing bombs?"

"Very little beyond what we learned from your report. The Congressional plane was thoroughly searched and allowed to leave yesterday. We do believe one of the marine escorts was killed by someone here when he came back to check on the plane. We also know that a radioactive source was identified for less than a minute about the same time the guard was presumed killed," Jim explained.

"That means somebody had to open one of the suitcases. Those nukes are shielded so as not to produce any radiation signature. Tell me, was the marine who was killed, the one with the large scar circling his head?"

"Yes, Romeo was his name," replied Jim.

"Poor soul. I warned him in Perm to be careful whom he shared his concerns with. He should have listened."

"You should have stopped the bombs from ever leaving Russia," Eddie requested.

"I did try and it almost caused an international incident. You need to stop and realize that it was a member of your Congress or his assistant who stole them in the first place," Viktor replied tersely.

"Not without the help of someone in your own security agency I'm sure," Eddie replied sharply.

"I reckon that's just about enough bickering for now, boys," Jim said in his elongated Texas drawl. "Whether we all like it or not, we are in this together so we need to start acting like it. Now what is it you can tell us about these nukes and don't give me any of that 'it's classified' horse manure," Jim said.

"If it's okay with you, Jim, I would rather be out in the field chasing down leads from the airport bombings or the anthrax attack on the ship," Eddie said.

"And I would hope track down your brother's murderer," Viktor remarked.

It wasn't so much what Viktor said, but the tone in which he said it that set Eddie off. In a flash, the two adversaries were throwing punches.

"You boys let me know when you're finished so we can get to work," Jim said walking away from the two men. Immediately they stepped away from each other. Neither was much interested in fighting and both were hoping Jim would break it up. When he didn't, they were smart enough to stop themselves.

"Sorry, Colonel." Eddie said. "I'm just a little on edge about losing my brother."

"I understand completely and apologize as well," Viktor replied. It was a shaky truce at best.

"I don't like taking Instructions from some slant-eyed sum' bitch," one of the white supremacists sent to meet Satochi said to his partner.

"Relax, he's just a gopher for Günter. He takes orders just like us."

"Meb'be so, but we're the ones drivin' an old Buick and he arrived in a jet plane," the man said disgruntled.

"You jus' worry bout what we gots to do. We's already screwed up once and I ain't plannin' on screw'n up again. You got it?"

"I got it," he replied. "But I still dun' know how that sum' bitch lived. We both shot him and he fell off the damn cliff. One lucky sum' bitch is all I gots to say."

The two men had driven all night, snorting meth to stay awake. They were given explicit instructions on where and when they were to deliver the suitcase Satochi had placed in the trunk. They had arrived in Wichita three hours before their scheduled rendezvous. The meth had taken their hunger for food, but not for the Lone Star beer that filled the ice chest in the back seat of the Buick.

"Ain't you the least bit curious to open that suitcase?"

"Hell no," his partner replied. "I gots no wish to be kilt by some germ. Let's just do like we was told and get the hell back to Texas. I ain't never cared much for Kansas. Pass me another beer." As his partner turned to grab a beer from the cooler, he and everything within one hundred yards were vaporized.

It was sudden, unexpected, and devastating but, unlike 9/11, the horror of the attack did not unfold for all to see on their 46-inch plasma screen televisions. At first there were a few breaking news bulletins on radio and television stations around the country. Then a few television stations started running nonstop broadcasts with their news anchors speculating as the newsroom writers scurried to obtain eyewitness reports and video footage of the nuclear blast carnage, neither of which materialized. All land and cell phone service in and out of the Midwest had been blocked. Air traffic was halted except for specific emergency personnel with special authorization. All public satellite transmissions were blocked. When a news copter from station KOCO in Oklahoma City defied the air traffic ban and sent a news crew to video the scene, National Guard jets ordered it to land and, when it did not comply, it was shot down killing the station's prominent anchorman. The government was not going to lose control of the situation! Even prior to 9/11, specific protocols had been put into place to deal with this exact scenario and unlike the Katrina debacle where the FEMA emergency plans completely collapsed into chaos, CBIRF, the marine expeditiary force designed to deal with this exact situation, was prepared, very prepared. Within six hours of the blast, CBIRF was on the ground, had established a secure perimeter, and had begun rescue and recovery operations. Immediately upon detonation of a nuclear device on American soil, Martial Law goes into effect. The chemical biological incident response force is a group of 2800 Marines stationed in Indian Head, Maryland. They are the first responders to any weapon of mass destruction attack on American soil. They know exactly what agencies and resources to call upon and do so with utmost haste. There was of course a major uproar by the media giants about access to the site and the violation of their rights. The Supreme Court was quick to point out that those rights became moot once Martial Law was declared. It would be several days before CBIRF lifted the media and communication blackout and allowed the press access to what was now a sanitized and viewer-friendly ground zero.

Jim wanted to punch Viktor when news of the nuclear blast first reached them. "Why in tarnation did the KGB even need suitcase nukes?" Jim asked.

"Don't be so naive, Jim," Viktor replied. "Your nation has had such devices since the mid-sixties, just as we have. That was the nature of the Cold War. We all knew it was only a matter of time till something like this happened. Just thank God we know who is responsible and are not about to destroy each other's country."

"I'm not totally convinced that Aioka is the one responsible," Jim replied. "Several international corporations received extortion threats, allegedly from Aioka, advising them that, if twenty million dollars was not wired to a certain bank account, there would be dire consequences. I would consider blowing up Wichita, Kansas, fairly dire"

"That makes no sense," Viktor replied, "Aioka is a terrorist, not an extortionist. He is driven by a cause, not by financial gain."

"That's exactly what Haruko said," Jim responded.

"Then again, terrorism is expensive, and Aioka has lost many of his assets," Viktor said. "Did any of them pay the money?"

"Three that we know of and who knows how many will now that someone has followed through on their threat," Jim replied.

"Are you saying that there was a specific target in Wichita?" Viktor asked.

"Seymour Pharmaceuticals, more precisely their nutraceutical division. The largest manufacturer and shipper of herbal remedies in the western hemisphere," Jim replied.

"They received the extortion letter and they decided not to pay. From what we know, a couple of dozen other companies around the world, including two other pharmaceutical companies in Germany and one nutraceutical company in Finland, also received the threat. The Finnish company paid the money as did a couple of oil companies."

"If they knew there were still three more bombs the rest would surely pay," Viktor responded. "Does your President plan on telling them?"

"What the President does is up to the President, but I would bet those companies contacted already know there are three more nukes missing," Jim replied.

When the bomb detonated, Aioka was delivering the second suitcase nuke to Günter in Helsinki to fulfill his part of the original agreement. Günter had supplied the Ebola strain in exchange for a suitcase nuke. Aioka was not pleased that the scientists at Zetanutra were not further along on the preparation of the tainted supplements.

"We had difficulty acquiring the Level 4 bio-safety equipment," Günter explained. "Such equipment is not readily available. We had to pay a premium to a Chinese university whose order was about to be delivered. It only arrived last week. We paid them three times the cost as well as paid for their new order."

"What about the smallpox virus? Were you able to obtain it?" Aioka asked.

"No, but we were able to obtain a voracious flu strain that is extremely contagious. It will work just as well."

"I hope so," Aioka replied sounding somewhat skeptical. "I grow weary of your failures and all this bad news."

"You have a lot of audacity to come here and speak to me in such a way. I am here as a favor to you. I do not work for you nor do I believe in your cause. Our relationship was mutually beneficial and nothing more. I have only stayed to assist your men until you fulfilled your side of the bargain. Now that you have done so, our business is concluded," Günter replied.

"Forgive me if I misspoke," Aioka replied bowing. "I am deeply indebted to you for the assistance you have so kindly provided. You are the expert in dealing with such contagions and I thank you for your help."

"Your apology is accepted," Günter replied, "and I too thank you for making my extortion plot feasible. Had you not blown up the bomb in Kansas, no company would have been inclined to pay."

"You see we are both dependent on one another," Aioka said. "I would be most grateful if you would stay here until the chimera was complete. My staff needs someone like you to oversee and motivate their work, if you know what I mean."

"I do," Günter replied, "and I will, if you in turn will help me by reissuing the extortion threat. It is so much more affective coming from a known terror group such as the Red Summit."

"Consider it done," Aioka replied, "but don't forget one-third of the money you collect belongs to me."

"Sixty million has already been deposited in your account and I expect that amount to triple within the week."

"I'm sure it will! I will contact you soon," Aioka replied.

Neither man trusted the other, but both depended on the actions of the other, and depending on another was something neither Günter nor Aioka were willing to do for long. Günter was tempted to tell Aioka about Haruko being in Texas, but thought it better to wait. He knew Aioka despised her and wanted her dead, but did not want Aioka to know Haruko was assigned to follow up on the Ebola case and suspected Aioka was behind it. He would have his men handle the Haruko problem. The less Aioka knew, the better, or so he thought.

CHAPTER FOURTEEN

"We should have kilt' 'er when we kilt' 'er boyfriend," the man said to his partner. "I don't like cum'n back here and I don't like that she got that FBI agent with 'er."

"I don't like it anymore 'n you, so shuddup and keep watch'n for 'er car," his partner replied. "Sooner we kill 'um both, sooner we gits out of dis shit-hole."

"Did you recognize the man in the video that came to visit those inmates before they escaped?" the FBI agent asked Haruko.

"No," Haruko replied quickly, hoping the agent assigned to accompany her would get the hint and keep his mouth shut.

"Well, he looked foreign to me," the agent continued, missing Haruko's hint. "For sure the man ain't from around here. No Texan in his right mind would dress like that unless he was look'n to get beat-up and tied to the bumper of a truck."

"I hope you didn't mean what I think you mean," Haruko replied, extremely agitated.

"No ma'm, whatever it is you thought I meant, I sure as hell didn't mean it," the agent replied contritely.

His reply seemed to calm Haruko's anger. "Are you from around here?" Haruko asked.

"No ma'm, I'm from Dallas."

"Do you know an agent named Jim Rikey that is from this area?" Haruko asked.

"Yes ma'm, I do know a Jim Rikey, but he's no FBI agent. He is a Farm Service Agent and a real pain-in-the-ass. Pardon my French."

"Why do you say that?" Haruko said.

"He's an anachronism ma'm. Him and those 10-inch barreled, pearl-handled Colt 45 six-shooters he carries. He's a gun-slinging cowboy who belongs back in the 1890's. He's a loose cannon who always seems to be stick'n his nose where it doesn't belong."

"Really," Haruko replied. "He's one of my best friends."

The agent seemed to shrink into the car seat. "And they are bison grips, not pearl-handled," Haruko added.

"Ma'm, I'm truly sorry if I offended you or your friend, Mr. Rikey. Truth is, he's one hell of a man who has solved more big cases than just about any agent at the Dallas office. It's just that we all feel a little jealous of Jim Rikey. The man's got a PhD, was special ops in the military, and a football star in high school. Why in tarnation he chooses to work as a Farm Service Agent is beyond me."

"Does everybody in Texas use the phrase tarnation?" Haruko asked. "Just what is a tarnation?

"Sorry, ma'm, but I don't rightfully know," the agent replied.

Haruko made a mental note to ask Jim next time she saw him. She was actually missing Jim and it bothered her greatly. She had loved Jotty and it had been less than a week since his murder, yet it was Jim she couldn't stop thinking about. She was beginning to question her own morality.

"There's a truck coming up behind us mighty fast," the agent said staring into his rearview mirror.

As Haruko turned to look, the truck slammed into the rear of their car, causing it to fishtail wildly. "It's the two men who killed Jotty, call for backup now." The back window shattered into a thousand shards of glass.

"Ma'm, I think I had better get us the hell out of here before I make a phone call. Do you have a gun?"

"No," Haruko replied.

"Then take mine, and tighten your seatbelt," the agent ordered. He turned his car and headed down a dirt road.

"I don't know if this is such a good idea," Haruko said.

"It's the only one I had," the agent replied.

"Hit that sum' bitch again, then pull next to him so I can get a clear shot," said the man who had blown away half of Jotty's head.

"There's a big tractor coming at us," the agent said. "I don't know if we can get through."

"Well, we sure as hell can't stop and wait for it to clear the road," Haruko replied. "Floor it and pray that he gets out of our way." A pickup truck hooked to a trailer was parked on the right side of the road ahead. The tractor pulled as far to the left as possible to get out of the way of the speeding car and truck fast approaching.

"The tractor pulled over, but we're not going to make it. He will be right next to that truck when we get there," the FBI agent said.

"We have no choice!" Haruko replied.

The Ford Crown Victoria reached the tractor just as it pulled opposite the parked truck and trailer. The front bumper hit the large tire on the tractor while the right side of the car scraped the pick-up truck. The car exploded from in-between the tractor and the pickup and trailer like a splinter festering out from a wound, but not before the rear wheel well caught the edge of the trailer flipping the trailer Into the air and sending the Crown Vic spinning violently into a ditch.

A stunned farmer watched from atop his tractor as the collision transpired.

"Hit the brakes, hit the brakes," the passenger yelled to the driver. The truck that had been chasing Haruko slid to a stop just inches from the overturned trailer that was partially blocking the road. The tractor turned into the tall corn stalks that seemed to embrace the road.

"We have to get out of here," Haruko screamed to the FBI agent, but there was no answer. His face was covered in blood and he lay motionless against the broken steering wheel. She reached over and felt for a pulse. She thought she may have felt a weak one, but did not have time to find out for sure. Haruko unfastened her seat belt, but her door could not be opened. It was pressed against the bottom of the ditch. She looked around for the gun, but it had disappeared during the violent accident. She scrambled quickly over the seat and out the rear window that had been shot out. She ran to the driver's door to try to pull the agent free, but quickly changed her mind when a bullet slammed into the body of the car. Haruko dove towards the front of the Crown Vic then rolled to the bottom of the ditch. She could hear the two men running towards her car. She crawled up the other side of the ditch, then ran as fast as she could into the corn field.

"Shoot 'er, don't let 'er gets away," a voice yelled out.

Bullets ripped through the corn stalks on both sides of her, but Haruko kept running. Soon she heard the sound of the stalks snapping as the two men chased after her into the field. Haruko's head began to throb. When she reached up to rub the pain, her hand became sticky. Her head had smashed into the side window when the car spun out, opening up quite a gash on the right side of her scalp. Not only was she leaving a trail of broken stalks for her pursuers to follow, but a trail of blood as well.

"You can't get away bitch. We gonna kill you just like we kill't yer boyfriend," one of the men yelled.

Again, bullets started ripping through the corn stalks all around her. Haruko dove to the ground, her head was beginning to spin and she felt faint.

"No way," Haruko said to herself. "There is no way those two are going to get me." She struggled to her feet and began circling back towards the wrecked car. At least she hoped she was circling back. The height of the corn made it impossible to see where she was headed. Every few moments she would stop and listen for the men that were following her, then angle away from them.

"The bitch is headed back for the car," one of the men said.

"We know what you're try'n to do, and it ain't gonna work," one of the men yelled at Haruko.

"Joe, you head back to the truck and I'll keep a following her. We'll run 'er down, then shoot 'er in the head," the other man said.

Haruko turned and headed deeper into the field away from where she thought the road was. Her movement began to slow and she grew dizzy from her loss of blood. Then she heard the sound of the truck coming towards her as it tore across the corn field flattening everything in its path. She stumbled and fell hard on the ground, too weak to get up.

"Well looky here," the man said holding his gun on Haruko. "Guess you're not as tough as you thought ch' were, huh bitch?"

Haruko stared, feeling seething hatred for the man who had murdered Jotty.

"I am going to…" Haruko stopped talking and stared towards the cornfield behind the man.

What they had thought was the approaching truck was a giant combine bearing down on the two of them.

Jotty's murderer turned and fired his pistol towards the cab of the combine, but was blinded by the glint of sunlight reflecting off the massive machine. The combine raised its cutters like a giant claw preparing to grasp the frightened man. Haruko used what strength she had remaining and flung her body away from the monster. The murderer saw her move and turned to complete the task he was assigned to do. Before he could fire, a loud blast from a shotgun exploded, lifting the murderer into the air knocking him backwards, his arms flailing and the gun soaring into the corn. The engine of the massive machine shut down and the farmer, who had been on the tractor when the Crown Vic went out of control, slowly climbed down from the cab, making sure to keep his shotgun pointed at the now maimed and crying murderer.

"We need to get you to the hospital, ma'm," the farmer said in a slow Texas drawl. "An ambulance will be here shortly as will the state troopers."

"What about his partner?" Haruko asked.

"You needn't worry yourself bout him, ma'm. I got him hog-tied in the back of my old pickup truck."

"What about the FBI agent, is he alright?" Haruko asked.

"Well, he ain't dead, and I 'spect he ain't gonna die either, but he is in need of some doctoring."

Haruko heard the sirens approaching and slowly closed her eyes.

"I understand you have something you would like me to see," Eddie said to the agent in charge at the Honolulu Airport.

"A couple of our technicians found these on the tarmac," the supervisor said.

"They look like gas caps," Eddie said, examining one carefully.

"Correct, 747 gas caps to be precise," the agent replied.

"What makes these so important?" Eddie asked.

"No burn marks, no heat distortions, and nowhere near the explosions," the agent replied. "We believe these fell off the three planes before they were bombed. It is rare for one of these to fall out on the taxiway, let alone three in one day."

"You think whoever is responsible for gassing the planes may be responsible for planting the bombs," Eddie replied.

"Well, if he was, we may never know. He was killed when the third plane blew apart at the gate."

"That doesn't mean he didn't do it. Just makes it harder to find the man that paid him to do it," Eddie replied. "What was his name?"

"Toyoyuki Nagatoshi, but everyone called him Yoyo although, from what I hear, he didn't care much for the nickname."

"Did he have a wife and family?" Eddie asked.

"No, at least not here in Oahu. His file says he comes from Honuapo on the Big Island. His 'notify in case of emergency' information lists his parents in Na'alehu."

"Na'alehu I've heard of," Eddie replied. "Isn't that down on the southern most tip of the island?"

"Yeah, down where haoles are not welcome and where even most of the native Hawaiians avoid after sunset," the agent explained. "Be careful when you go there and take one of the agents who grew up on the Big Island. You might

137

also want to get in touch with the local police. They can probably help you get some answers or at least they can tell you where to look."

"And where not to look," Eddie replied.

"Shima, I'm afraid I bring bad news," Satochi said to one of the workers deep inside a lava tube of the Great Crack. "Your brother, Toyo, was killed performing his assignment at the Honolulu Airport.

"Eh brah, you said goin be klea da ehyapoaht befoa da ting explode," Shima said.

"And he should have been," Satochi quickly replied. "Something must have delayed his escape."

"Wen Toya had money he took kea o' my mada and fada. Whateva he neva bow on drugs or eteh girls," Shima said, changing the subject.

"Don't worry about your parents. My boss is a very generous man and will make sure your parents will continue to be taken care of," Satochi replied. He pulled an envelope thick with hundred-dollar bills from his pocket. "Take this to your parents. They will need you with them as they grieve."

"Yea boss," Shima replied his eyes brightening at the sight of so much cash.

"Have you broken through to a lower lava tube?" Satochi asked.

"Two times, as all. Da tube got hot. Pele not happy!" Shima replied.

"Pele will be very happy when we send the haoles running back to the mainland," Satochi replied. "We must be close to an active lava flow. We will meet back here in two days. I will bring more supplies and dynamite. I want you to head down the tube a couple of hundred yards and try blasting a few test holes."

"Yea boss," Shima replied.

"Soon we will take our islands back from the imperialists who stole them from our Queen," Satochi said.

Shima believed in, and would fight for, a sovereign Hawaii but, at the moment, he could only think about the drugs he would buy with the money and surfing at Honoli'i Cove.

CHAPTER FIFTEEN

"This isn't exactly what I expected when I finally returned to Haskell," Jim said. "I just thank God you're safe and alive."

"You can thank your friend Gordon for that. If he hadn't driven his combine into the cornfield, there would have been quite a different outcome," Haruko replied.

"That's what I hear," Jim said. "I also hear he used his Winchester Model 97 shotgun on one of the men. I've been trying to buy that gun off of him for ten years. Boy howdy, am I glad he never sold it to me."

"I'm so glad you're here, Jim, I've been so very sad, but seeing you helps more than you can imagine."

"Take that towel off your head and let me have a look at your scalp."

"Only if you promise not to laugh. They cut off almost half of my hair and had to shave my head," Haruko replied, as she removed the towel.

"Whooeee," Jim hollered.

Haruko pulled her long hair over the side that had been shaved. "You promised not to laugh."

"I didn't laugh," Jim said smiling, "but I reckon even Donald Trump couldn't come close to the comb over you can do with your hair."

Haruko smiled.

"What's a comb over?" Viktor asked, strolling into the hospital room.

"What's he doing here?" Haruko asked Jim.

"I'm sure you remember Colonel Viktor Cheznov of the Russian FSB," Jim started to explain.

"She remembers me. I saved her life," Viktor said. "It is a pleasure to see you again, Haruko, I'm just so sorry it is under these circumstances. Your superiors are fools for not keeping you on the team hunting down Aioka."

Jim could see that Haruko was surprised by Viktor's knowledge of the situation. "Viktor has been assigned to work with the NCTC task force by the President of the United States. I have been instructed to include him in on all aspects of the investigation. We believe Aioka is behind the tragedy in Wichita. You did hear about that, I assume."

"I haven't heard much. The news blackout has kept very little information, other than that propaganda the government has been spewing, from getting out," Haruko replied. "I was hoping you could fill me in on what really happened and what we plan to do about it."

"We're not doing anything about it, at least not until the doctor says you're good to go," Jim replied.

"Does that mean I'm back on the team?" Haruko asked.

"You were never off of it as far as I was concerned," Jim replied. "And before you ask, yes, the director back at NCTC has given the okay for you to return to Hawaii with us. He will send someone else here to work on the Ebola investigation."

"No, this is part of the Aioka investigation. I'm sure he's behind the Ebola outbreak," Haruko insisted. "I've been researching it for the past two days while stuck here, and I believe I know how it was done. What I cannot figure out is how those two murderers knew I was here in Texas."

"They probably followed you from Washington," Jim suggested. "Or tapped into your computer and discovered your travel plans."

"That's not possible. All the arrangements were made by the office, nothing would have been on my computer about the trip even if they were smart enough to hack into it, which they are obviously not."

"Then they've had you under surveillance and followed you here," Viktor said.

"No, that's not likely, either. According to receipts found in the car, they started driving here the day before I even arrived in Dallas," Haruko replied.

"Then somebody had to tip them off about your plans. Somebody back in Virginia that knew you were coming. That's not a very pleasant thought," Jim replied. "There's somebody 'dirty' at the NCTC."

"Either that, or it was just a random coincidence that we both showed up in Haskell at the same time," Haruko suggested.

"That seems highly unlikely," Viktor replied.

"I have to agree with Viktor. This was not some random encounter. They were here for a purpose and I believe eliminating you was their purpose," Jim said.

A chill ran down Haruko's spine. "And they almost succeeded," she said softly.

Jim caressed her gently. "We need to find the leak back in Virginia and plug it permanently."

"You said this Ebola case is somehow related to Aioka and the Red Summit. How did you arrive at that conclusion?" Viktor asked.

Haruko looked at Jim to see if she should answer. He nodded once. "Aioka has to be behind the Ebola deaths. That's why I came to Haskell. I believe the death of the warden at the prison and the scare that followed was planned as a means for breaking those men out of jail. And we know that they were working for Aioka, or why would they have tried to kill Jim and Jotty?"

"I thought it was Jim and Jotty who originally arrested the four men. Perhaps they were just seeking retribution against the men who put them in prison," Viktor suggested.

"Perhaps," Jim replied, "but it's much more likely they were freed by Aioka as a means for seeking his own revenge for the grief we've caused him. Remember, it was his assassin Satochi who killed Eddie's brother in an attempt to kill Eddie. He wanted the entire team dead."

"Except for Haruko," Viktor replied. "Why did he decide to spare her life?"

"You sound like those bastards at the NCTC who questioned me. They asked the same question," Haruko replied.

"And what was your answer," Viktor asked.

"Her answer is what got her kicked off the team to start with, so I don't feel we need to rehash that," Jim said.

"No, I want to answer," Haruko interrupted. "I originally thought Aioka had something much more devious in mind for me, though, after this attempt by these two, I am starting to wonder myself."

"Tis' a might peculiar," Jim replied,

"Why don't we ask them?" Viktor replied. "Maybe they'll tell us why Aioka ordered the murders and went to all of this trouble with the Ebola infections, if indeed it is Aioka who is behind all of this."

"What about the man who came to visit the four prisoners a while back. Have you found out anything from it?" JIm asked.

"He of course used a false identification when he signed in. The photo on the license is too blurry to be of any help. The name and address were of course made up," Haruko replied.

"What about video surveillance, don't they have him on tape?" Jim asked.

"This guy was a pro, he knew not to look up or look at any cameras. There was only one clear shot of his face. Preliminary analysis back at NCTC thinks he is Northern European. They said they would run his face through the data base, but so far I haven't heard back," Haruko replied. "I'm sure the bombing in Wichita has tied up the computers and the techs back at the NCTC."

"I'll put in a call and see if I can move the process along. As far as I'm concerned, this is probably one of the best leads we have in finding Aioka."

"Are you sure we should trust them back in Virginia?" Haruko asked.

"I don't think we have much choice," Jim replied.

"If you say so," Haruko said.

"When we get back to McClean we'll try to find the leak."

"What about the two prisoners?" Viktor asked.

"I plan on having a few words with those two good ole' boys tonight. Maybe I can find out a little something from them."

"I guarantee I would if you allowed me to interrogate them," Viktor added. "The FSB is very good at making people talk."

"And very good at making people disappear," Jim replied sarcastically as his phone began to ring.

"Hello!"

"Man, this is good bread. I could eat this all day," Eddie said.

"You do, brah, and you'll start to look like me," the portly FBI agent assigned to assist Eddie replied.

"No brah, I could never eat that much Hawaiian bread," Eddie replied.

"Actually brah, it's called Portuguese sweet bread, brought by one of the many immigrant cultures to the islands. We kind of made it our own."

"Good thinking!" Eddie replied as he munched another big roll.

"When did the local police say they'd meet us?" the agent asked.

"He said to be at the Punalu'u Bakeshop at 10 o'clock. I figured that's when he'd be here," Eddie replied.

"You still got a lot to learn about Hawaiians, brah. Ten o'clock means between eleven and noon to the locals," the agent laughed.

The two men sat down beneath a Monkey pod tree on the lush bakery grounds. They were parked in the gravel parking area near Highway 11 and away from the tourist lot at the back of the property. Several of the bakers were near them at the picnic tables enjoying their lunch break. Eddie watched as another tour bus disgorged its load of tourists racing to see who could be first in line at the bathroom.

"Didn't I read somewhere that Mark Twain planted a monkey pod tree around here somewhere?" Eddie said.

"Just up the road a'ways, but it blew down sometime in the fifties," the agent replied.

"You must be Eddie," the local police sergeant said as he approached the two men sitting on the lava stone wall relaxing in the shade.

"That's right, I'm Eddie, Eddie Popp like in soda pop."

145

The sergeant looked over the tanned beach boy standing before him. "You sure don't look FBI, brah."

"Well, actually, I'm CIA on loan to the FBI, but now that I told you, I got to kill you," Eddie replied. "Just kidding, brah."

"I'm Sergeant Hale, Kamejiro Hale. You can call me Jiro," the sergeant replied laughing. "Get it? Ka-me-jiro, call me hero."

"Very funny," Eddie moaned.

"I'm agent Smith," the FBI man said, standing and extending his hand.

"You're kidding, right? Agent Smith?" Jiro replied.

"That's really my name, but you can call me Dano like in Hawaii Five-O."

"You're the one who called in those two tourists with their chests carved up, right?" Dano asked.

"What did you just say?" Eddie said, visibly upset.

"Two bodies found in a car down hidden in the grass at Punalu'u Beach. They had what looked like petroglyphs carved on their chests. I called it in to the FBI when one of the ambulance drivers told me that someone up near Hawi was carved up the same way," Jiro replied.

"That somebody was my little brother," Eddie replied. "Did you know about this?"

"I thought everybody knew about it," Dano replied.

"I'm sorry for your loss," Jiro replied. "I'll help you in any way I can."

"I appreciate that, and will take you up on it, but first I need to know about Toyoyuki Nagatoshi."

"Bad news. Toyoyuki is a troublemaker," Jiro began.

"Was a troublemaker, he was killed in the Honolulu airport bombings," Eddie interrupted.

"Well, I can't say I'm sorry. Toyo and his brother Shima caused me more than enough grief over the past few years. Always getting into fights, smoking and selling weed, racing around in that old beatup station wagon, and fighting their roosters. I bet I've arrested the two of them half a dozen times," Jiro explained.

"What do you mean fighting their roosters? asked Eddie.

"You are a haole, brah," Dano replied. "Rooster fighting is their entertainment."

"Especially down on this side of the island. It's about all there is to do for fun, but it's illegal."

"Why aren't they in jail?" Eddie asked.

"Brah, this is Hawaii. We tend to cut our people slack. Even if we did press charges, no jury would even consider finding Toyo and Shima guilty. At least nobody who valued their own life," Jiro explained.

"Where's this Shima now? Does he still live around here?" Dano asked.

"I haven't seen Shima around for a couple of months. Spends a lot of time surf'n over near Hilo, especially this time of the year when the waves are bigger. He and Toyo both spent a lot of time surf'n, when they weren't getting into trouble around here."

"I was told their parents live in Na'alehu," Eddie said.

"Just across the street and behind those houses. You can see their house from here," Jiro said, pointing down Kaalaiki Road. "It's that rundown looking one with all the junk in the yard."

"Which of the junky rundown ones are you pointing at?" Dano asked.

"The one with the station wagon parked out front. Between the Hana Hou Restaurant and the high school. Looks like Shima is visiting his parents," Jiro said.

"I think this would be a good time to visit the Nagatoshi family," Eddie said.

"I think it would be a good time to visit the Hana Hou, I'm kind'a hungry," Dano said.

"Have another piece of taro bread," Eddie said, tossing him a roll.

"Just let me do the talking to start with," Jiro said. "Like most folk around here, they don't look too kindly upon haoles."

As the three men walked across the road towards the house, they could see the parents sitting outside on the steps and a large man, Shima, leaning against a tree with a beer in one hand and a joint in the other.

"Eh brah, what you smok'n?" Jiro asked in a hybrid pidgin.

"Not smokin nahtin, brah," Shima answered as he threw the joint on the ground.

"Good morning, folks," Jiro said to Shima's parents. "I want to tell you how sorry I am to hear about Toyoyuki."

Both parents nodded. "He was good boy," the mom said. "He take good care of parents," she said, both looking at Shima in disgust.

Shima paid no attention and reached into a cooler for another beer.

"Haven't seen you around lately, Shima, whacha been up to?" Jiro asked.

"Dakine who like know?" Shima replied looking at the two FBI men.

"I'm Eddie, Eddie Popp, you know like in soda pop and this is Dano."

148

"Cops?" Shima replied. "I not say nahtin to you guys."

"If you don't talk to us here, I'll have to take you to the station. One way or the other, you're going to have to answer a few questions," Jiro said.

"Ah brah wat! Wat you like know?" Shima replied.

"Do you know who your brother worked for?" Eddie asked.

"No brah, he wen pump gas in da airplane."

"How long had he been working at the airport?" Dano asked.

"Oh, like six months ago."

"When was the last time you talked to your brother?" Dano asked.

"Oh, like six months ago."

"Did your brother say..." Dano began to ask.

"Where have you been the past two months?" Eddie interrupted.

"Stay workin and surfin," Shima replied.

"Where you been surf'n, brah? No good waves around here. At least none I can find," Eddie said.

"Dakine, these wave not fo haole pretty boys," Shima replied.

"There ain't no waves on the Big Island, and from what I've seen it doesn't matter because there don't seem to be any real surfers here either," Eddie said, challenging Shima.

"Brah you like go? Bring your haole ass down Honoli'i and we goin see who can surf," Shima challenged.

"Thanks for the offer, but I have a couple of murders I have to solve first. You wouldn't know anything about a couple of dead haoles found at Punalu'u with their chests carves up?" Eddie asked.

"Somebody carved a petroglyph on them," Dano added.

"Don't know nahtin bout no ded bodies," Shima replied.

"Where you been working?" Jiro asked.

"Around," Shima replied.

"We can do this at the station if you like," Jiro said.

"Been doing construction for dis guy I met surfin. I stay workin in Puna."

"This guy got a name?" Jiro asked.

"Bobura, dat all I know."

"Is he from Japan?" Jiro asked.

"Nah brah, kama 'āina."

"Where can we find this Bobura, or old Japanese man?" Dano asked.

"Dunno, he pick me up, he take me home, he pay cash, as all I know. Brah I no like ask."

"Where does he pick you up?" Eddie asked.

Shima didn't immediately answer. "Honoli'i Cove," he said. "When I stay surfin."

Shima's parents sat quietly during the questioning, seemingly oblivious to what was happening around them. "Shima not a bad boy, just not take care of parents like Toyo," his dad said.

"Quite old man!" Shima said. "I not sayin nahtin else to you befoa I talk to my cuzzin, he one lawyer."

"No, I think you answered my questions for now," Eddie replied.

"I don't want you driv'n until you sober up a bit, you understand," Jiro said.

"Yea boss," Shima replied.

"One last question," Eddie said, "just what does Shima mean anyways?" Shima turned and walked into the house without responding.

"Island dweller," his dad said.

"Thanks for your help," Eddie replied. He knew he would be seeing Shima again real soon.

CHAPTER SIXTEEN

"Polya, my love, I'm happy to see you, but I told you it was not safe to come here," Günter looked around to make sure none of the workers had heard him.

"I'm afraid I bring bad news. The two men you sent to kill the Japanese woman failed. She suffered no more than a concussion and minor head wound. Both of the men were captured. One of them may not live. Let's hope he dies before he can tell them anything."

"What is there to tell? They know nothing but my name," Günter replied.

"They may know nothing, but that Japanese woman, Haruko, she has figured out much," Polya replied. "She suspects Zetanutra may be the source of the Ebola outbreaks in America."

"Suspects or knows?" Günter asked.

"I'm told she only suspects it for now, but she has returned to Washington to further her investigation. There she has the tools and personnel she needs to thoroughly research her suspicions. They say she is extremely bright; it will not take her long to figure it out," Polya replied.

"She has the video with your image on it and they know you are northern European. They will be comparing it to all European photo data bases. Eventually, they will find a match. All airports now scan faces of all passengers for terrorists entering the terminal. The ferry terminal will also have your picture. They undoubtedly will scan the faces since the FSB agent was murdered."

"Did our contact have any advice on how we should proceed?"

"He suggested we take the package and a sample of the chimera and leave Helsinki as soon as possible," Polya replied. "He believes we still have three or four days before the NCTC can take any action."

"It will be impossible to manufacture the required number of chimera-tainted capsules by then. My scientists have only today begun manufacturing the freeze-dried duplexed virus. They begin loading the capsules into the bottles tomorrow."

"Can the operation be moved to another location?" Polya asked.

"That would not be feasible. We are dealing with a Level-4 biological agent. Even a minor spill or leak could cause mass deaths. Helsinki would be virtually wiped out," Günter replied.

"Will you contact Aioka?" Polya asked.

"And tell him what? That his entire bio-terror scheme is about to implode. I think not," Günter replied.

"Maybe some of the Ebola-tainted capsules can be sent before they confirm Zetanutra as the source. If it is as contagious as you claim, maybe his plot won't fail." Polya suggested.

"That might be the only way to keep him from trying to kill us," Günter said. "Aioka is not one to tolerate failure."

"What will happen when he finds out you tried to kill Haruko without his permission?" Polya asked.

"Let's hope he doesn't find out until we can make our escape."

"You know he'll eventually find us, and kill us if he thinks we betrayed him," Polya said.

"We still have much to offer him. Remember we do have one of the suitcase nukes you helped steal. We also control his share of the extortion money and we can package a quantity of the chimera-tainted capsules and move them away from the facility to someplace safe in the next two days. That will be our insurance policy," Günter explained. "Then you and I can live worry-free in a place where no one can find us,"

"We will never be free as long as Aioka is alive," Polya replied.

"Heh, Jim, are you still dating that fine-looking British aristocrat?" It was Eddie's voice. Jim turned to see if Haruko had overheard.

"What is it you need, Eddie?"

"Can you get your friend Lord Farrelton to give you a little viewing time with one of those hydrogen spy planes flying around the islands? I need to track a car for a couple of days."

"We already have two hydrogen planes dedicated to our investigation over the islands looking for more nukes. Just call the base in Oahu and tell the tech what you need, should be no problem."

"Thanks Jim. How's Haruko doing?" Eddie asked.

"Just fine, would you like to talk to her?"

"Maybe later, I'm a little lost right now. I'm in Pahoa searching for an address."

"What in tarnation are you doing there? That place is still stuck in the sixties."

"You need to get out a little more, my friend. This place has more million-dollar homes than the Kohala Coast," Eddie said.

"I seriously doubt that," Jim replied.

"Maybe so, but it has to be close. I'm trying to find an art studio of this guy who makes some of the best authentic weapons and tools on the Big Island. I spoke with this professor who wrote the book *Hawaiian Petroglyphs*. Not only did he explain the meaning of the symbol carved on Michael, but he's trying to decipher the petroglyphs carved on the two tourists. He told me about this guy Rick who makes the kind of ancient Hawaiian weapon he believes was used. That's who I'm now looking for."

"What two tourists?" Jim asked.

"It's a long story that I'll tell you about when you get back here."

"That may be a while. We're staying here tonight and leaving for Washington in the morning," Jim replied

"Damn!"

"Now what?"

"I found this Rick guy's studio, but there's a sign saying he's down at Kahena Beach for the day." Jim tried to muffle a laugh. "Did you say something?" Eddie asked.

"No, but I have heard of it. Down off of Highway 137." Jim replied.

"Dano says he knows how to find it. Dano's the FBI agent sent to babysit me, if you were wondering," Eddie said.

"Just be careful and keep me informed," Jim instructed.

"No problem, brah," Eddie said, as he closed his cell phone.

"I haven't been around here for at least fifteen years," Dano said. "Things sure have changed. They used to call the Puna District the 'Wild West'."

"Why did they call it that?" Eddie asked.

"No outsiders were welcome. All the braddahs grew their weed around here. If an outsider came to one of the local beaches, he would either get beat up or his car would be torched, maybe both."

155

"You sure you know where this beach is? I don't want to wander into some brah's weed patch," Eddie said.

"We're almost there. See all the cars parked on the side of the road. Just park behind that truck and we can walk down. If I recall, it's kind of steep, so be careful."

As Eddie and Dano climbed down the hill through the trees, they heard what sounded like several drummers rhythmically pounding away and they caught glimpses of several people through the trees. "Looks like it may be crowded. We will have to ask somebody to point out this Rick guy to us," Eddie said.

"Let's just hope they will. We don't particularly look like we belong here," Dano replied.

"Well I do," Eddie said. "I told you to lose that FBI look. Take off your shirt, maybe that will help."

"Why don't you take off all your clothes? That's how nature meant us to be," said a beautiful and naked redhead, as the two men emerged from the trees.

Dano and Eddie stopped dead in their tracks. "Welcome to Kahena Beach, would you like a hit of some outrageous homegrown," she said, offering a joint to Eddie.

"Thank you for the offer, but not at the moment," Eddie replied.

"Are you two a couple?" the redhead asked, as another strikingly beautiful and naked brunette exited the water and joined her friend.

"What do you mean, are we a couple?" Dano asked, unable to take his eyes off the two women.

"I mean are you guys a couple, you know, gay lovers? Because if you aren't, or even if you are, I would sure like to get to know your friend here better," she said, reaching out and holding Eddie's hand.

"I'm Cheshire and this is my friend Summer."

156

"It's a pleasure to meet the both of you," Eddie replied with a dazzling smile, turning up his beach boy charm. Cheshire became weak in the knees. "I'm Eddie, Eddie Popp, you know like in soda pop. And this is my friend Dano."

Both of the girls were mesmerized by Eddie's charm, barely acknowledging Dano.

"Eddie, take a look around," Dano said, breaking the spell Eddie had cast.

Eddie looked around. There were at least seventy people, all naked, on the beach and in the water. Several were playing drums, and a few towards the far end of the beach seemed engaged in some very amorous pleasures.

"Are those two guys doing what I think they are doing?" Dano asked.

"I believe they are, Dano, I believe they are," Eddie replied. Eddie continued to scan the beach and noticed that there were several male couples who were more than just friends. He also noticed that not everybody was naked, but pretty close to it.

"So, are you going to take your clothes off and join us?" Cheshire asked. "If you are wondering, we're not lesbians, although many of the girls here are. This is just a safe place we can come and be natural like God meant us to be."

"I can think of nothing more beautiful than harmonizing with you in such a natural state," Eddie replied, caressing her hand, "but I'm afraid I'm unable to devote the time necessary to share such a wonderful experience this day."

Cheshire almost cried. "Maybe tomorrow?" she said hopefully.

"I cannot promise you tomorrow, but I will promise to meet you here again very soon," Eddie replied. "Today, I am here to find an artist. They call him Rick. Do you know him?"

"I do. Everyone knows Rick. He's the tall black-haired man playing the bongos," she said, pointing down the beach. "Promise me you'll call," Cheshire said, handing Eddie her number.

"On my honor," Eddie replied, pulling her to him and kissing her gently on the lips. When he released her to walk away, she remained standing with her eyes closed as if in a trance.

"Eh brah," Dano said as they were walking away, "you got a real talent for that. You good with words! But let's go over and do some natural harmonizing with that braddah, and get out of here. These mahu creep'n me out."

"Hi Rick, I'm Eddie, Eddie Popp. Somebody told me you make the best authentic weapons on the islands."

Rick stopped beating the drum and set it down on the ground, revealing the fact that he too was naked. "I'm not gay if you're trying to hit on me," Rick said.

"I'm not either, I actually work for the CIA and need to get your help on an extremely important case." Eddie said.

"Let's go over here and talk," Rick said.

"You know, I feel a little weird talking to a naked guy in the middle of a crowded beach," Eddie said.

"Especially with that stuff going on," Dano said, nodding towards two men in a rather provocative position.

"Is he CIA too?" Rick asked.

"No, he's my driver, Dano," Eddie replied.

"Why don't we meet back at my studio in an hour, I'm just about through here," Rick said. "You can wait for me up at the Aloha Outpost. It's near my studio and they make a great cup of coffee."

"We'll do that, see you in an hour," Eddie replied.

As Eddie and Dano walked back towards the trees, several men stared at Eddie.

"Looks like you could make a lot of friends here," Dano laughed.

"I think I made the friends I wanted today," Eddie replied, as he smiled and waved at Cheshire and Summer.

"What did Eddie want?" Viktor asked.

"He wants to direct one of our surveillance planes to follow a car around the island for a couple of days. It must have something to do with that worker from the Honolulu Airport. They think he may have been the one to plant the bombs in the planes that exploded," Jim replied.

"Is he in custody?" Viktor asked.

"No, he's dead. Eddie went to check on his family on the Big Island. Something there must have made him suspicious."

"Did you say that two of the planes have been monitoring the island since before the attack on WIchita?" Haruko asked.

"Yes, actually, they've been monitoring the islands since the airport bombings," Jim replied.

"If I remember right, didn't you say they have several cameras that are always recording and they keep a digital file of all of it," Haruko said.

"That's how we found Aioka's hideout in Hawi and how we followed the dive boat that discovered the anthrax in the lava tube," Jim explained.

"You must be talking about that new experimental hydrogen plane we've heard so much about at the FSB. I understand it can stay in the air for weeks at a time," Viktor said.

"I'm afraid I don't know what you're talking about," Jim said, "and, if I did, even the President doesn't have the authority to direct me to tell you about it."

"I understand completely," Viktor said with a smile.

"Didn't they halt all commercial air traffic for a couple of days after the airport bombing?" Haruko asked.

"Yes, but private jets were allowed to depart from the other islands the next day. Commercial flights didn't start up for two days after that," Jim said.

"There couldn't have been many private jets leaving the Kona Airport between the time the plane picked up the radiation signature and the day of the explosion in Wichita," Haruko said. "Wouldn't they show up on the recordings made of the planes leaving?"

"They would. There also will be flight plans that had to be filed," Jim replied.

"Yes, but who is to say if the planes followed the flight plan?" Viktor said.

"Our surveillance capabilities should be able to give us some information about that," Jim said.

"And what yours doesn't show, I am sure the Russian satellites will," Viktor boasted.

"That's something we need the techs at McClean working on immediately," Haruko said.

"I'll make the call to my supervisor in Moscow. I'm sure he can convince our President to supply your agency with the needed information," Viktor said.

"Well, if he can't, I'm sure our President will," Jim replied.

CHAPTER SEVENTEEN

"Eh, dis haole guy, Eddie Popp, brah he come go Na'alehu, ask pleny questions," Shima said.

"What answers did you give him?" Satochi asked.

"I neva tell him nahtin, boss," Shima replied.

"Who was with him?"

"Kamejiro and dis one braddah name Dano. Dey come askin all kine questions about Toyo. Dey was drillin' me about what I do, where I been. Brah, I had tell em I was work fo da one guy I meet surfin."

"Did you tell them my name?"

"I tell em, I don't know nahtin. I jus sed I call you Bobura," Shima replied. "I tell em dakine, you pick me up at park and take me to job in Puna."

"Did they say anything else I should know about?"

"Yea boss, dey wen ask about da dead haoles with chests carved up in Punalu'u. Da Eddie haole bad news, brah."

"I need you to go back to the camp and blast those test holes I told you about. Take plenty of supplies. I will try to come by in two days but, if I don't show, I want you to stay there until you hear from me. Take the phone, but don't turn it on except at night when I will call to check in. Do you understand?"

"Yea boss," Shima replied.

"Have one of the men drop you off and return your car here. I don't want it parked anywhere near the camp or near Punalu'u."

"Yea boss."

"Did you give the money to your parents like I told you to do?"

Shima hesitated, "Plenty, brah."

"Next time make sure they get it all."

"Yea boss."

"Get out of here," Satochi said.

Satochi continued to sit at the table watching the surfers. After a few minutes, he started slowly up the stone steps that led back to the road, made difficult by the throbbing pain from the wound to his leg. The wound Eddie inflicted with Satochi's own 'lei o mano'. It would have been much quicker to just cut across the beach and through the trees to get to Aioka's house, but no one, not even Satochi, was to be seen entering the house from the beach. "You will pay for this Eddie Popp, yes, you will all pay."

"It's only for a few days," Jim tried to explain.

"That's horse crap and you know it, Jim. They plan to never let me rejoin the team in the field," Haruko complained.

"That's not true. The doctor just wants to keep an eye on you for three more days. If your MRI shows you're fine, then you can fly to Hawaii and join us. Besides, you said you needed a few days with the big computers and the research techs to try to figure out which planes flew in and out of Kona and to where," Jim reminded her.

"My President, in his desire for cooperation between our countries, has generously offered the information you requested from our satellites about flights in and out of Kona as well," Viktor replied.

"As well he should have," Jim said. "We really need you to do this, Haruko."

"I know, but it's so busy around here I can barely get any search time on the big computer. I need to search the email accounts of all the Ebola victims. I got a hunch that I'll find what I'm looking for, but they won't give me any time on the computer. The nukes are priority," Haruko complained.

"Just write down what you need, I have a friend down at Texas A & M that works in the Internet Research Lab. They got this big room full of machines they call the 'Monster Computer' and I know from experience that it can find just about anything you're looking for on the internet. It shouldn't take much time at all to find what you need," Jim explained.

"That would be a big help," Haruko replied, "but I still wish I was going with you." Haruko held Jim's hand tightly. "I just hate being left alone."

"Maybe I should stay and give you a hand," Viktor offered. "I'm pretty good with a computer."

"I think I would rather have you stick with me," Jim replied.

"Like the old saying," Viktor responded, "keep your friends close and your enemys closer."

"Something like that," Jim replied.

"I'll have my friend at the IRL call you the moment they find anything," Jim assured her.

"Viktor and I have several debriefings we must attend before we return to Hawaii tonight. CBIRF and a few other agencies need to find out all they can from Viktor about the remaining nukes."

"May I suggest you also try to find out which companies have been threatened and which companies have paid the ransom to keep their factories from being destroyed," Viktor said. "There must be a reason the pharmaceutical company in Wichita was targeted first."

"Thanks, but I have already thought of that and I'm working on it," Haruko replied.

"A little homophobic are we, Mr. Dano," Rick said as the two men entered his studio.

"Not really, I would have been just as uneasy had it been a guy and a girl doing that on the beach," Dano replied.

"Well, you needn't worry about me, I'm not gay. It took me a while to get used to the changes around here, too, but I eventually did. Pahoa has always been a very accepting community."

"I see Cheshire seemed to take a liking to you, Eddie," Rick said. "I've been asking her out for years and have gotten nowhere. You must have the gift."

"That's what people say," Eddie replied. "Thanks for meeting with us."

"You said you were CIA. That didn't leave me much choice if I want to continue to live a normal life."

"I think you have read too many thrillers. We're really not like that, well, maybe just a little." Rick laughed at Eddie's joke.

"These are beautiful," Dano said, looking at several koa wood weapons and tools displayed on the studio wall.

"Go ahead, you can hold them," Rick said. "Just be careful, those tiger shark teeth can give you a nasty cut."

"I understand it's a lot harder to get both koa and tiger shark teeth these days," Eddie said.

"Extremely difficult. You just need to know where to look. You can find anything for the right price," Rick replied.

"I have a few pictures I want you to see, it may be a little gory, but I need to know what made the mark," Eddie explained.

"Oh man, Those poor guys." Rick sighed as he took the photos.

"What can you tell me about them?" Eddie asked.

"Somebody has a real anger issue," Rick said. "They also don't know their petroglyphs. This one is called Rainbow Man; he is the protector of the island. These others I've never seen before and actually don't even look like petroglyphs to me," Rick replied.

"That's the same thing the professor who gave me your name said," Eddie replied. "What do you think was used to make them?"

"If it was a knife, it was really dull and nicked up. I would say they were made by a tiger shark tooth. A really big tiger shark tooth," Rick said.

"Who were these guys, and who did they piss off so bad?" Rick asked.

"These two were tourists found down at Punalu'u, but this one was my brother. It was meant for me," Eddie replied.

"Oh man, I'm really sorry, did they catch the guy who did this?" Rick asked.

"No, but I will," Eddie replied. "Do you think the same man did both of these?"

"From the photos, I would say yes," Rick replied.

"I believe the man who did this is named Satochi, Satochi Yomane. I also think you might have made the weapon that did this," Eddie said.

"Whoa, back up there partner. A lot of people make these replica weapons and tools. A few of us make authentic and custom ones for the big dollars, but they are mass produced in several places in the South Pacific. There is no way you can tell just by looking at those pictures," Rick replied.

"I'm not accusing you of anything, I am just asking for your help," Eddie said. "In the past six months, have you made any custom weapons that could do this, because the man I am looking for would only buy the best, and from what I've been told you're the best at making these on this island," Eddie explained.

"The best on any of the islands, but who's bragging," Rick said.

"The man who bought this would not have told you his name. He looks Japanese and has a fairly severe limp."

"Bingo," Rick replied. "I made a cane sword for this guy. A cane sword with a giant tiger shark tooth hidden beneath the handle. He needed it right away and said money was no object. Words that are music to my ears. It usually would take me at least six months to make something like that but, for him, and his money, I was able to knock it out in a couple of weeks. Man, I'm really sorry. Most people who buy my stuff just display it. I never thought this guy would use it."

"Any chance he left you his name, address, and phone number," Dano asked.

"Yeah, right," Rick replied. The guy paid half the price up front in cash and said he would be back in two weeks and double the price if it was ready and if my work was as good as people said it was. There is no question about the quality of my work. I was only worried about getting it done in time."

"I guess you finished it in time?"

"For twice my normal price, you damn right I did," Rick replied.

"Did the guy give you any name at all?" Eddie asked.

Rick thought for a moment. "You know he did. He said to call him Bobura, you know, a Japanese guy," Rick replied.

Eddie's muscles tightened when he heard the name.

"Looks like you've heard that name before," Rick said. "I hope you catch the babooze before he does something else crazy."

"Thanks for all your help. Here's my number, call me if you see this Bobura again," Eddie said.

"No problem, brah. Can I see those photos of the two tourists again?" Rick said.

"Sure," Eddie replied.

Rick looked at them for a minute. "These aren't supposed to be petroglyphs. He wrote a word. Look, if you turn them sideways and put this guy first, next to the other guy, it makes a word."

Eddie looked at the pictures. "You're right, it does kind of look like a word: KAPU."

"It means 'keep out' or 'forbidden'," Rick said. "I guess these guys were someplace they shouldn't have been."

"Now I just need to find that place," Eddie replied. "That's where I'll find Satochi, at this kapu 'āina!"

CHAPTER EIGHTEEN

"More bad news, can't I trust anyone anymore?" Aioka yelled.

Satochi knew not to answer.

"My own men turning against me," Aioka continued.

"I have not turned from you or from your cause," Satochi replied. "You alone are capable of stopping the American imperialism before it destroys Hawaii and the rest of the world."

"Then why do my men forsake me?" Aioka asked.

"Tell me who has turned against you and I will destroy him," Satochi pledged.

"Günter ordered the murder of Haruko without asking permission. His men failed and now the crux of my entire plan is about to collapse. My informant tells me Haruko has suspicions about the cause of the Ebola outbreaks. They say within two days she will know it was Zetanutra that produced the tainted capsules of 'tongkat ali' sent to the six victims. He has jeopardized all we have worked for. He must pay for his disloyalty."

"He controls one of the bombs and the money paid as ransom," Satochi said.

"That is why you must go there immediately and convince him to return the bomb," Aioka said.

"What about the money?" Satochi asked.

"He has already transferred our share of what has already been paid. With the bomb, we do not need any more of the money. Soon they'll connect the money transfers to him and to the company as well. You must retrieve the bomb at all costs. Günter has become a hindrance to our plans."

"What about the tainted capsules, are they ready for distribution?" Satochi asked.

"Günter says no, but that's what you must also find out. Even if it's ready, the NCTC will stop the shipment at the ports. It will never enter America as planned. You must acquire samples of the virus while you are there. The time will come when we can again use the chimera. This is just one battle in the long war we are destined to fight. The day will come when American imperialism is stopped forever. It is warriors like us who will bring about that day."

"I will leave at once for Helsinki," Satochi said.

"Yes, but you must not fly there directly. I have been informed that Haruko has several people analyzing satellite photos and the filed flight plans of all jets leaving the Kona airport since the Honolulu bombings."

"Then we have nothing to fear. We flew from the Hilo airport when we delivered the bombs," Satochi said.

"Don't be foolish, they'll eventually search all the airports for the information. I have already moved our jets to safer locations. Take a helicopter to the Honolulu Airport. I have booked you a first-class ticket to Los Angeles. One of our men will meet you there and take you to the Ontario Airport where one of the Zetanutra jets will take you on to Helsinki. I will make arrangements with the pilots for your return trip. The plane has been fitted with the necessary safeguards to protect and store the chimera virus. I will prepare an appropriate facility in Oahu to keep the virus safe. Do you have any questions?" Aioka asked.

"I understand what I'm to do," Satochi replied, but instead of leaving as he knew he was expected to do, he hesitated.

"You have something you wish to ask me?" Aioka said.

"No, I have information that I believe you need to know," Satochi replied.

"Quickly then, you must not be late for your flight," Aioka replied.

"This Eddie Popp is becoming a serious problem," Satochi said.

"As I said he would be when you failed to kill him in Hawi. You have awoken a giant and now you must fight and destroy him, Bobura," Aioka replied.

Satochi was shocked by the name Aioka had called him. "You have heard," Satochi asked.

"My network of informants is vast," Aioka began. "I know he visited the family of Toyoyuki in Na'alehu and spoke with your man, Shima. He is loyal but not very smart. He gave away much information to this Eddie Popp."

Satochi was surprised by Aioka's knowledge, for he himself had only heard of this a moment ago outside on the beach. "That was what I was about to tell you," he said. "He may know a name, but nothing more," Satochi replied. "It's a name with no significance. That will lead him nowhere."

"Do not underestimate you adversary. I should never have assigned you the task of killing Eddie Popp. It was too personal, but I thought it only right that you kill the man who made you a *bikko*," Aioka said.

Satochi's anger began to swell. "I may be a cripple, but I am not 'rokudenashi'" Satochi snapped back.

"Nor did I say you were not worthy or capable," replied Aioka. "You are still my most trusted assassin."

"At least you haven't said it to my face," Satochi replied still angry.

"All stories told are not necessarily true. You must listen carefully to discern why you are being told this information in the first place and what the teller has to gain by spreading such falsehoods," Aioka explained. "For if I deemed you not worthy or capable you would no longer be in my service. You would be dead."

Satochi knew this to be true. Aioka was not a man to tolerate disobedience or failure. Satochi himself had killed many a cell member who did not perform as Aioka instructed. "Forgive my ignorance. I was blinded by my own paranoia. It shall not happen again."

"I'm sure it won't. Now you must go if you are to catch your flight," Aioka said.

Satochi bowed and left the house. Aioka sat watching the surfers challenge the waves of Honoli'i Beach. "Should I have told Satochi that Eddie Popp already knows that he is the Bobura?" Aioka said to himself. "This is a place of so much beauty, I'm sorry that I must leave soon, but I must prepare. I always must prepare." Aioka said softly to no one.

There were almost two dozen messages on the machine when Eddie returned to Jim's house in Hawl. He had not been back to the house since his brother's murder. The cleanup crew hired by the FBI did an excellent job removing the bloodstains from the desk and the floor beneath. Eddie started to sit down at the desk and listen to his messages, but remembered that was where both his brother and the Russian FSB agent's bodies were placed. Instead he decided to open a beer and listen to the messages from the couch.

The first five messages were from NCTC headquarters back in McClean. They had been trying to reach him to tell him about Jotty's murder and to warn him that he may be at risk as well. The next nine messages were condolences from friends about the loss of his brother. Two messages followed

171

from women friends that seemed to be in dire need of his companionship. The sixteenth message piqued his interest.

"Hi, this is Marlin. We met at Bill Casey's party the night of those god-awful terrorist attacks on Honolulu and the *Grand Maui*. You were with Seneca Willows and I'd just come from the ship with Barbra Chenoweth. Thank God we left the ship when we did. That was quite a spectacular exit you and the Captain made from the 18th green. I understand they're still trying to fix the ridges the helicopter put on the green. Have you had any luck finding out who is responsible for the attacks? Barbra told us that you're some sort of secret agent or something. The news said it was some terrorist group called the Red Summit. I hope they've left the island. Oh, the reason I called is that I have a lady friend you may be interested in coming to town and I'm already booked up. Give me a call, I'm still at the Four Seasons. Aloha!"

"I wish I had the time, my friend, I really wish I had the time," Eddie said.

There were two more messages of condolences, then another from Marlin.

"Aloha Eddie, I was just wondering if you received my previous message. I could sure use some help with a scheduling snafu. Believe me, you won't be disappointed."

"I'm sure I wouldn't be," Eddie said to himself. It suddenly struck him how convenient it was that Marlin, Barbra Chenoweth, and the Captain all left the *Grand Maui* just prior to the anthrax attack. Why hadn't anyone thought to question them?

"Aloha Eddie, it's Marlin again. Sorry, but I made other arrangements for my lady friend from the mainland. Maybe next time. If you're not busy, stop by the Four Seasons. I'm still staying here and there is plenty of action to keep a man interested and occupied. Give me a call. Aloha."

"I think maybe I'll come by for a little chat. I have a few questions that need to be answered and they are not about your personal life," Eddie said to the empty room.

There were still two more messages on the machine.

"Aloha, it's me again, Marlin. Please call me, I think we really need to talk. I'll be gone a couple of days with a lady friend, but I really need you to call me in two days."

The call had been made that morning. "Your sounding a little desperate there, my friend." Eddie knew Marlin needed to tell him something important and he was sure it had nothing to do with womanizing. Marlin was scared and Eddie could think of only one reason that Marlin would be scared. He must know something about the anthrax attack. The trouble was, Eddie would have to wait for two more days to find out. He just hoped Marlin wouldn't say something stupid to the wrong person and get himself killed.

There was one final message on the machine.

"Hello Eddie Popp. Do you recognize my voice?" Eddie leaped from the couch; it was the voice of Satochi. "You have caused me much grief, Eddie Popp. You should be dead. Very soon, you will be. Goodbye Mr. Eddie Popp."

Eddie dove to the floor expecting a bullet to tear through the window and rip into his body, but none came. Satochi had called hoping to instill fear into Eddie and had succeeded for the moment, but just for the moment. Eddie went back to the couch to finish his beer.

"Now you've really pissed me off," Eddie said to the answering machine. "Things are about to get ugly."

Six hours after giving the information to the technician at the IRL in College Station, Texas, Haruko received her data.

"Five of the six names you gave me all received the Malaysian herbal Viagra supplement, tongkat ali, from a

173

nutraceutical company in Helsinki, Finland, called Zetanutra," the technician said

"Let me guess, the one name you couldn't connect with was the one from Washington, D.C.?" Haruko asked.

"Exactly," the technician responded. "I also did that search for Bio-level 4 safety equipment you requested."

"And?"

"And Zetanutra has not purchased any Level-4 bio-gear from the manufacturer."

"Well, thanks for all your help," Haruko said.

"Not so fast," the technician replied. "A university in China did place an order for that type of safety equipment and it had been sent to an export house for shipment. Then they placed a second order for the exact same equipment. It seems that before the exporter could ship it, the university called and asked that it be sent to Zetanutra instead."

"That's fantastic news, thank you so much," Haruko replied.

"No problem, anything for a friend of Jimbo," the tech replied.

Tears welled in Haruko's eyes. Jotty was the only person she ever knew that referred to Jim as Jimbo. Haruko quickly dialed Jim's cell number.

"Hi Haruko, before you say anything, I want to remind you are on speakerphone so our Russian friend can hear everything. Tell me, did you get the information you needed?" Jim asked.

"More than I expected," she replied. "I think you two had better cancel your flight to Hawaii and start making plans to visit a somewhat cooler climate. Five of the initial six victims all received the same herbal supplements from a company called Zetanutra in Helsinki."

"What about the sixth victim?" Jim asked.

"That would be the NCTC agent. Apparently, he never ordered anything from Zetanutra," Haruko replied.

"Then how was he infected?

"The same as the others, by the herbal supplement," Haruko replied.

"I thought you said he had never ordered anything from Zetanutra," Jim said. "How did he get a tainted capsule?"

"I gave it to him," Haruko replied. "Actually, I gave it to his wife. She had confided in me that he was having some difficulties in the bedroom, so I suggested he try one of Jotty's supplements. The tainted capsule was meant for Jotty."

"Aioka has to be behind this," Jim said.

"Wasn't Zetanutra one of the first companies to pay the ransom to the extortionists?" Viktor asked.

"You're right," Jim responded.

"And what better way to build a market to distribute your tainted supplements than to vaporize your main competitor and steal their market share," Viktor said.

"Have you had a chance to sort through the satellite imagery of the flights out of Kona?" Jim asked Haruko.

"Not yet," Haruko said sarcastically. "It seems the cooperation we were promised by the Russians is not as forthright as we expected."

"Give it a little time," Viktor replied. "Some of our generals do not understand our President's new policy of cooperation and the free exchange of ideas and technology. Let me make a call to the Kremlin and see what I can do to speed up the process."

"Jim, I don't think we should wait. I took the liberty of directing a satellite camera on the Zetanutra manufacturing and shipping plant in Helsinki. There seems to be much more security around this middle warehouse than around any of the others. In the past six hours only one truck has entered the middle warehouse. We've got people on the ground watching in case the satellite goes out of position. I think we need to move on this warehouse as soon as possible."

"I'll have our State Department contact the Finnish government. These things take time to set up," Jim explained.

"We need to head there now, so when the Finnish government gives the green light, we can be ready to move," Haruko said.

"I've had much experience in dealing with the Finnish authorities and, believe me, they won't allow any of us close to the plant when they raid it," Viktor said.

"Our President may convince them otherwise," Jim replied. "Haruko is right, we need to head there while the State Department sorts out the details."

"Does that mean I'm clear to go back into the field?" Haruko asked.

"They have no choice but to let you go, you know the situation better than any of us. But don't even think about participating in the raid on the plant. You're there in an advisement capacity only. Is that clear?"

"Let's just hope we aren't too late," Haruko replied, avoiding the question.

"I'll make the arrangements. We'll pick you up in an hour and head to the airport. Get packed and make sure we have somebody monitoring that satellite to let us know if things change," Jim said.

"Thanks for getting me back on the team, Jimbo," Haruko said softly ending the call before Jim could respond.

"Don't call me Jimbo," Jim started to reply. "The last person who did got...."

CHAPTER NINETEEN

"Not there," Günter ordered, "It's too close to the Level-4 containment lab. Aioka may be willing to wipe out half a country's population with the duplexed virus, but I'm not. If that lab was breached, Helsinki would be a ghost town in a matter of days. Place the Claymores just inside the outer walls of the warehouse and connect the trip wire to the door. Those walls will barely slow down the steel bearings when the mines are triggered."

"According to our contact, the NCTC team will be in Helsinki in approximately fourteen hours," Polya advised. "He says there are several field agents watching our facility. But most troublesome are the satellites. They have us under constant surveillance and, according to our comrade's sources, they have the computer capability to follow all vehicles that enter and leave the facility."

"How long have they been watching us with the satellite?" Günter asked.

"Not long, six hours at the most. They suspect it is Warehouse 2 where we are manufacturing the Ebola capsules, but they have no idea it is now a chimera."

"So, if we attempt to relocate the cases of tainted capsules, they'll be able to follow the truck with the satellite. What a complete waste," Günter said.

"They'll also be able to follow us as we leave," Polya reminded him.

"Don't worry about that, there's a way to leave here safely along with samples of the chimera," Günter replied. "I'm more concerned about Satochi than I am the NCTC."

"Yes, but the Finnish authorities may take matters into their own hands at any time now," Polya said.

"I have several very loyal men, who are paid exceedingly well, who will put up quite a battle when the time arrives. I'm sure they won't attack until the NCTC agents arrive. They aren't willing to anger the Americans by moving too quickly. Remember, one nuclear bomb has already been detonated on American soil. They won't tolerate any country getting in the way of bringing those responsible to justice regardless of whose country it is," Günter said. "It is Aioka's assassin that we need to fear,"

"Why is he coming here?" Polya asked.

"Supposedly to check on the progress of the chimera-tainted supplements, but that is not true," Günter said.

"How do you know that?"

"Because I know Aioka, and I know how Aioka thinks. He wouldn't send Satochi to inquire on our progress. Satochi is too valuable for such a task. No, there is much more to Satochi's visit. I'm afraid Aioka discovered my attempt to kill Haruko without his permission. Had my men succeeded, I'm sure I'd have been able to reason with Aioka and convince him it was necessary to protect his plan. But, by failing to accomplish Haruko's death, I'm afraid we are now condemned and Satochi is our executioner."

"What about our comrade, can he not intervene in our favor?" Polya asked.

"That is a possibility I've considered, but I'm afraid it's too late for that. We'll be blamed for the failure of the bio-terror plot Aioka so carefully constructed. I'm sure he'll try to retrieve the suitcase nuke that was part of the deal as well."

"What about the money, what will happen to our share of the money?" Polya asked.

"It's safe and waiting for us. I've already transferred Aioka's share to his secure accounts. Our half of the money will be divided three ways just as our comrade planned."

"And the money that is yet to be paid in our extortion plot?" Polya asked.

"I doubt we'll be sharing any of that with Aioka, especially since he wants us dead," Günter laughed.

"Set some of those mines in the access tunnel where I showed you," Günter instructed, "but by no means arm them, I'll do that."

"What have you done with the suitcase nuke? I hope it's safely away from here." Polya said.

"Of course. It's gone from here and hidden in a secure spot. It's our future. As long as we have it, we have our own money-making machine," Günter replied.

"Do you plan to kill Satochi?" Polya asked.

"I don't plan to kill him personally, but I do intend for him to die," Günter replied. He should be arriving two hours before the NCTC team gets here. If all goes as planned, Satochi will be waiting here in the warehouse when it's attacked, and you can be assured, Satochi will never surrender."

"So, you finally got your top-secret clearance," the Hydrogen Solutions technician said.

"I had no choice." Eddie replied. "Jotty Joplin arranged it for me, so I could come keep you company in this cracker box."

"Hey, it may not be big and pretty, but I call it home," the tech replied. "I heard about Jotty and your brother and I'm really sorry. If there is anything I can do, let me know."

"Thanks, but you're already doing it. That old station wagon I asked you to track may show me where my brother's murderer is hiding. The guy who owns it works for Satochi, Aioka Matsuura's number one assassin," Eddie replied.

"Isn't Satochi the guy whose leg you almost took off when you stopped that anthrax attack in California?" the tech asked. "I remember Lord Farrelton telling the base commander that you used some ancient Hawaiian weapon to do it."

"It's called a 'lei o mano' and I was really lucky that it was his leg and not my neck. I was very fortunate indeed, my arm was only broken in three places," Eddie said.

"Damn, I sure envy you guys in the field," the tech replied.

"What do you have for me?" Eddie asked.

"Well I picked up the wagon in Na'alehu, where you said it would be. It made a few stops. They are all marked on this map. Two of them are liquor stores. Then it headed to Hilo. It stopped at a bar on Kinoole Street for a while, then two people, one of them female came out, got in the car, and stopped at this sleazy motel in town. About an hour later, one person exited the hotel, got in the car and drove to Honoli'i Cove. He parked along Kohoa Street. I lost him when he went down to the beach. There must be at least a hundred surfers there today."

"Shima told me he spent a lot of time there. It's where all the local braddahs go to surf," Eddie replied.

"Until someone gets into that car, I'm afraid there isn't much more I can do for you," the tech said.

"Well, I hope you don't mind company for a while, 'cause right now that's my only lead," Eddie said.

"No problem, make yourself at home, mi casa es su casa. I even have some beers in the fridge if you promise not to tell anyone."

"Boy Howdy, what in tarnation did you just do, Haruko?" Jim asked

"I just couldn't get that comment about Donald Trump and our comb overs out of my head, so I decided to shave my head."

"Just now in the washroom you decided to do that?" Viktor asked.

'No, I decided to do it before we left for Helsinki, but didn't have time. I brought everything I needed with me so I could do it during our flight. Including this," Haruko replied, pulling a wig from out of her carryon. What do you think?" she asked.

"I think it looks beautiful on you," Viktor replied. "Very natural!"

"And you, Jim," Haruko said turning and posing for Jim.

"I kinda think I'd like to see you as a blonde," Jim said smiling.

Before Haruko could reply, her computer buzzed telling her that she had a message from her office.

"My assistant at McClean just received information from Interpol that you may find interesting," Haruko said, "especially you Viktor."

"Oh," Viktor replied cautiously.

"It seems Günter, our mystery man in the video visiting the four prisoners in Haskell has been matched to a man wanted in Helsinki, who is thought to be responsible for a murder at the ferry terminal. They have identified him as Günter Marx, a former KGB agent known to work in Germany, these days thought to be a freelance agent available to anyone willing to pay the price. They also say this murdered man was a current Russian FSB agent."

"The FSB is a very large organization. I know very few outside of my superiors and my own office staff," Viktor replied.

"Tell us Viktor, who in the FSB helped steal those four nukes?" Haruko asked.

"Don't be absurd," Viktor replied, "you know it was the senator's assistant."

"Don't play dumb, Viktor," Jim said. "Your security is poor, but not that poor. There had to be someone on the inside, probably even a high-ranking FSB agent, to pull something like that off. Just what all haven't you told us?"

"I thought it was an internal matter and of no concern to your investigation," Viktor replied. "Now I see I was wrong. His name is Boris Ivanov, the FSB agent in charge of the weapon storage facility. He accompanied the congressmen on their tour. He also is the one who relayed the Kremlin's order to allow the plane to depart, an order that never was issued by the Kremlin. By the time we discovered this, Boris was gone, as was his wife Polya, another former KGB agent."

"And no one has found them?" Haruko asked.

"Oh no," Viktor replied. "We found them both. Boris was found floating in the Kama River. Polya was seen boarding a train to St. Petersburg."

"That's a thirty-hour trip," Jim replied. "Were you able to catch her?"

"She was an excellent KGB agent when she worked for us. The sleeping woman we believed to be her, turned out to be a murdered look-alike. Polya had taken a plane to St. Petersburg and then the ferry to Helsinki. It was one of my men who was murdered in the Helsinki ferry terminal. My second agent never recognized her when she exited the ferry."

"And you didn't think it important to tell us this?" Haruko asked.

"I had no idea that the murderer was this Günter Marx you refer to. And it was obvious that Polya did not have the weapons with her. I decided that I would deal with her at a later date."

"Didn't you think that by questioning her you could discover who stole the weapons?" Haruko asked.

"I knew who stole the weapons. It was someone on the Congressmen's plane. I thought it more important for me to follow the weapons rather than spend my time searching Helsinki for Polya," Viktor explained. "Of course, I do have agents that are looking for her in Helsinki."

"Do you think Polya and Günter are behind the distribution of the tainted supplements?" Jim asked Viktor.

"According to Haruko, those supplements were shipped several weeks ago. Polya was still working in Perm at that time, so I doubt she's directly responsible. I believe it's safe to say that this Günter is involved since he seems to have helped plan the prisoner escape in Texas," Viktor explained.

"Yes, but Günter did kill one of your agents sent to stop Polya." Haruko replied.

"That's true. They very well may know each other since they both seem to be working for the same boss, Aioka. However, I believe they're both nothing more than mercenaries hired to perform a specific task. Polya doesn't strike me as a believer in any ideological cause other than her own financial well-being." Viktor replied.

"Is it possible Günter and Polya knew each other when they both worked for the Russian government?" Jim asked.

"Not just possible, but likely," Viktor replied.

"Our observers did report that a man matching Günter's description and a woman were seen entering the

Zetanutra facility and have not yet reported seeing them leave," Haruko replied.

Jim's Blackberry chimed, signaling an incoming scrambled text message.

"When did you start carrying one of those?" Haruko asked.

"Since I became team leader and they said I had to carry one," Jim replied, patiently waiting while the built-in decoding system unscrambled the message.

"We've finally heard back from the Minister of the Interior's Supreme Police Command. They're mobilizing their counter-terror strike team and will be in place by the time we arrive. The Helsinki Police Department has been notified and are securing and evacuating the area surrounding Zetanutra. The Commander of the National Bureau of Investigation is heading up the operation and has assured our President no action will take place until we arrive. That's as long as we arrive by 9:30, which is when they plan on going in. However, we're there as observers only," Jim read to Haruko and Viktor.

"What about the Ebola, who'll secure the laboratory and ensure the safety of the strike team?" Viktor asked.

"The Finnish military has a biological and chemical containment unit," Haruko replied. "I'm sure they'll be deployed."

"Boy howdy, I hope so," Jim replied, "for everyone's sake."

Satochi was awoken by the chiming of his cell phone. He looked at his watch. It was still several hours till he was due to arrive. The perpetual dusk glowed through the jet's window. He opened the phone but did not speak.

"Hello, my trusted friend," Aioka said softly. Satochi knew there was trouble if Aioka called during an assignment.

"Aloha, braddah," Satochi replied as planned if all was well and it was safe to talk.

"I have word that Günter has turned against us. He has removed the suitcase from the facility and some of the chimera virus. He knows the facility will soon be raided by the Finnish Police and NCTC agents and has arranged your meeting to correspond with that raid. He intends to kill you," Aioka informed him.

"Just as you said it may be," Satochi replied. "You were wise to place the tracking device in the handle of the suitcase."

"Günter must pay for his disloyalty," Aioka stressed.

"What about the woman who assisted in stealing the bombs, should I kill her as well?" Satochi asked.

"She is loyal and an asset that continues to prove its value. Do not harm her if possible," Aioka replied, "but if she interferes, kill her."

"What about the chimera?" Satochi asked.

"It's easlly replaced," Aioka replied. "The NCTC has identified Günter and believes he is behind the Ebola outbreak. They also know that he's tied to the nuclear bombs. It's possible he'll have already made his escape. If that is the case, make sure he can never stop running."

"I understand completely," Satochi replied. "I will not fail you."

CHAPTER TWENTY

"I'm very glad you were all able to join me today," William Casey said to the select crowd of Hawaii's rich and famous. "It's terrible, simply terrible, what these terrorists are trying to do to our world today. I want to say how sorry I am and express my deepest condolences to those honored citizens who lost their lives in the tragic airport bombings in Honolulu, the anthrax attack on the *Grand Maui*, this great ship berthed behind me, and the thousands in Wichita, Kansas, who died in that cowardly attack."

"Somebody should have told him two of the planes blown up at the airport were headed for Asia," the technician said to Eddie, as they watched the news broadcast of the event. "I heard this was a black tie invite only."

"Yeah, I don't see a lot of local braddahs joining in the festivities. Just what's going on?" Eddie asked.

"Casey is about to send the freshly sterilized *Grand Maui* back to sea," the tech replied.

"I hate to admit it, but I do recognize quite a few of those people," Eddie said.

"I heard you've been working the circuit," the tech replied.

"Whoa, I didn't know people kept track of that sort of thing," Eddie replied.

"Please join me in a moment of silence to honor our friends and neighbors who died at the hands of these terrorists," Casey continued.

"Nobody really keeps track, it's just that you've been seen in the company of some of the richest and finest looking divorcees to visit the island," the tech replied, realizing he had said too much.

"And just where and who saw me?" Eddie asked, but he could tell the tech didn't want to answer. "It's okay I do have top secret clearance."

"Promise me you'll tell this to no one, not even Jim Rikey," the tech replied.

"Scout's honor," Eddie said holding up two fingers.

"An agency of the government, which will remain unnamed, encourages us to keep an eye on certain gatherings of notable people around the islands. Your face has appeared at several such gatherings. And I must say with some extraordinary beautiful and wealthy women."

"Now ladies and gentlemen, to show that we Americans will not kowtow to any cowardly terrorists, and that we refuse to let terrorists scare us away from the life we love, let the festivities begin," Bill Casey shouted.

"So, you guys use those hydrogen planes to spy on our own citizens?" Eddie said.

"According to the Attorney General, the Patriot Act gives the government the right to do that," the tech replied.

"And you believe that right-wing crap?" Eddie snapped back.

"Hell no, I think they have gutted the Constitution, but I do have a job to do," the tech replied, sounding somewhat ashamed by his lame response. "In fact, we have cameras on William Casey's party as we speak. Let me show you."

The tech punched several buttons, and three separate views of the Aloha Tower Marketplace and *Grand Maui* came on the screens in front of them.

"Looks like security is pretty tight, no tourists are being allowed anywhere near the party," the tech replied, pointing to several manned barricades around the pier area.

"Are they holding machine guns?" Eddie asked, pointing at a screen.

"Yep," the tech replied. "Looks like William Casey just may be a little worried about terrorists crashing his party."

"Give me a close-up on the crowd so I can see if I recognize anyone," Eddie asked.

"No problem," the tech replied, pushing a slider switch that operated a very powerful zoom lens on one of the hydrogen plane's cameras.

"Holy cow," Eddie said. "That's unbelievable."

"Watch this," the tech said, pushing a button that lit up another screen and a second button that activated a small square frame hooked up to a mouse on the desk next to him. He moved the mouse to the face of a lady in the crowd and right-clicked. Within seconds her name, address, and several options to display personal information appeared on the screen.

Eddie couldn't believe what he was seeing. "How in the world do you do that?"

"A very advanced facial recognition software connected to a data base that you just wouldn't believe, and some of the fastest computers in existence," the tech replied.

"Click on that guy, I know him," Eddie said, seeing Marlin's face in the crowd. "It figures he would be at a classy party like this."

Within seconds Marlin's whole life was laid bare on the screen in front of them.

"He sure doesn't report an income to support that life style," the tech commented. "He's got a flag on his file."

"What does that mean?" Eddie asked.

"It means he is on a watch list."

"Whose watch list?" Eddie asked.

"Let's have a look," the tech replied. "I don't know for sure who flagged him, but they did it because he has been seen associating with members of Hawaii-Nation."

"Who's that?" Eddie asked.

"It's the group that wants independence and sovereignty for the Hawaiian Islands. They think the United States stole the islands from the native Hawaiians and they want them back. They are progressively getting more active and more violent."

"And Marlin is part of this?"

"No, not according to the file, but he is on the watch list," the tech replied.

"Look," the tech said excitedly, "looks like somebody's taking the station wagon for a spin in Hilo."

Immediately all thoughts of Marlin were gone as all the screens switched to the station wagon.

"Let the show begin," Eddie said. Suddenly, his phone began to ring

"Yes," Satochi replied, "I'll meet you just as we planned in the warehouse at 9:00 o'clock."

"It will be good to see you, my friend. I can show you the cases of chimera-tainted supplements ready to ship as well as the timeline for the remainder of the production. Based on how many orders we have for the herbal Viagra, I'm amazed that American men are capable of reproduction," Günter said laughing. "See you soon."

Satochi activated the tracking screen on his laptop. Just as he had thought, the bomb was nowhere near the Zetanutra facility. He doubted that Günter was at the facility either, but there was the possibility since he wanted Satochi there early. That half an hour would allow Günter time to kill Satochi and still make his escape before all hell broke loose. If that was the plan, Satochi would be ready, for he knew of the access tunnel that led to the waterfront. Aioka was the one who initially had it built. He would wait there, far enough away from the facility to be safe, yet close enough to hear the attack and to kill Günter.

"I don't wish to wait here any longer," Polya said. "I'll wait for you at the safe house."

"Satochi will be here shortly and there's nothing to fear from the Finnish police. My gunmen and my preparations will allow us ample time to make our escape," Günter said.

"I don't wish to be here when you kill Satochi. I haven't jeopardized my relationship with Aioka and don't wish to be in a position where he's forced to kill me. I am your lover, not your accomplice," Polya explained.

"Our comrade wouldn't be pleased if he heard you speaking like this," Günter said

"Our comrade is a businessman, a very practical businessman. I'm not so sure he would approve of your plans," Polya replied.

"You forget, Satochi is on his way to kill me. It is kill or be killed. How practical is that?" Günter replied.

"Why not just leave while we have the chance. Contact Aioka and bargain with him. Tell him you will return the nuclear weapon if he guarantees no contract will be put on your life. Tell him you'll steal more of the Ebola virus to use in the future. We each have over thirty million dollars that is more than enough to live anywhere and anyway we choose. Let's just leave together," Polya begged.

"You don't understand what kind of a man Aioka is. I acted on my own, defying Aioka's wishes. To him, I was disloyal, and all disloyalty deserves death. Satochi has been assigned to kill me and he'll stop at nothing till he has completed the assigned task. I must stay and kill him," Günter explained. "I have no other choice."

"I will wait for you at the apartment," Polya said, and hurried down the access tunnel towards a car she and Günter had parked there two days earlier. "I'll leave you the boat. I love you."

Günter just nodded his head.

"Two hundred meters and no closer," the commander of the Finnish assault team said to Jim, Viktor, and Haruko. "One of you may join me in the command truck to watch the video feeds from each squad leader."

"That would be me," Jim said.

"I'll give you two radios so you can follow the assault. Don't even think about moving up until I personally tell you it's safe. I have several sharpshooters in the area and I don't want to have to explain why two Americans were shot. Understood?" the commander asked.

Both Haruko and Viktor nodded their heads. "One American, one Russian," Viktor replied.

The commander smiled and handed them the radios. Neither Haruko nor Viktor realized that they would understand absolutely nothing that was said unless they spoke Finnish, which the commander seriously doubted.

As Jim stepped up into the mobile command center, he was greeted by a uniformed woman in her late twenties. The uniform failed to disguise her exquisite physique and beautiful looks.

"You must be Mr. Rikey from the NCTC. My name is Taru and I'll be your translator."

"What a beautiful name," Jim replied. "Does it have a meaning?"

"It means legend or myth," Taru replied with a sly smile.

Taru put her hand to her ear as a message came across the radio.

"A limousine just cleared the outer gates and is headed for the middle warehouse. It's impossible to see who is inside," she translated.

Jim looked at his watch. It was still a half-hour until the teams would be ready to storm the building.

"We've been had," Haruko said to Viktor. "That's why the commander was smiling when he handed us these radios. He knew we wouldn't understand a damn thing."

"Speak for yourself," Viktor replied. "I do know a little about the Finnish language."

"So, what then was that last transmission?" Haruko asked.

"Something about a car and the middle warehouse," Viktor replied.

"Big help you are," Haruko replied.

Haruko and Viktor both resigned themselves to being left out of the operation until it was complete. "Maybe we can find a building near here where we can get a better view," Haruko said.

Viktor was busy sending a text message and wasn't paying any attention. "Viktor," Haruko shouted, finally getting his attention. "Let's go find someplace where we have a better view."

"Looks like a couple of taller buildings that way," he replied. "Let's head there."

The limousine pulled up to the middle warehouse and honked twice. A large roll-up door began to rise and an unarmed guard strolled out to talk to the driver. "Can any of the observers see inside?" the commander asked.

"Negative," replied several voices. "It does appear the guard is unarmed," one observer added.

The guard stepped back as the limousine pulled into the warehouse. He looked around for a moment at the surrounding buildings before reentering the warehouse and lowering the door.

"Do you think he saw something?" the commander asked.

"If he did, his body language would have told us," one of the observers replied.

Taru furiously translated the conversations for Jim.

The limousine pulled up next to the interior structure that housed the lab. Several dozen cases of the Ebola-tainted supplements were stacked high just in front of the limousine. Surrounded by the cases was the door that led down to the access tunnel. The tunnel carried the power and water lines for the entire Zetanutra facility. It also led down to the waterfront where, hidden in a small storage shed, was the tunnel's exit. Aioka had arranged for the construction when he first bought the Zetanutra facility several years before.

The driver turned off the engine and exited the car.

"Is Günter here?" the driver asked several men stacking more cases of the supplements.

"I think he's inside the lab. He should be out in a moment," one of the men replied.

Satochi's driver became wary when he noticed the bulge of a pistol beneath several of the workmen's jackets. He wasn't Satochi's normal driver, but had been hired that morning through a temporary labor bureau. "Mr. Yomane advised me to inform you that he'll remain in the car until Günter arrives." Sensing he was in a dangerous situation, the driver started slowly moving towards the door where the original guard let the limo into the warehouse.

"I think you should wait by the car until Günter arrives," the guard told the driver.

"I was just going outside for a smoke. The sign says I can't smoke in here," the guard replied, continuing towards the door. Out of the corner of his eye, he noticed several other guards who were all carrying machine guns. Without hesitation, he broke into a run for the door. Two marksmen who were hidden in the rafters both shot. The bullets ripped into the side of his skull blowing away most of the driver's head before the body crumpled to the floor.

Two other guards took cover behind the cases next to the limousine, covering both sides of the car should Satochi try to exit.

Günter stepped out from behind the cases of supplements in front of the car.

"Satochi, come out of the car before it's too late. Any minute now an elite squad of Finnish National Police counter-terrorist officers is going to attack the warehouse. I have a way out. We both want to live, let's make a deal," Günter called out.

He waited for an answer.

"Those were gunshots," the commander said. "Let's move in now!"

Over sixty police officers trained in counter-terrorist operations surrounded the warehouse. Each man carried an assault rifle and wore full body armor. There were four doors into the warehouse. Within seconds each of the doors and two areas designated as entrance points in the walls were set with charges of explosive cutting tape.

"In place and ready to cut and burn," came the call from all six team leaders.

"This is it," Taru said to Jim. "All charges are set and they're awaiting the commander's signal."

Several more gunshots were heard inside the warehouse. Jim looked over at the commander sitting in front of the wall of video screens.

"What are you waiting for," Jim said to himself.

"Go, go, go," the commander shouted into his radio.

The six ECT charges exploded almost simultaneously. Several smoke and flash grenades were thrown into the newly created holes. Jim watched the screens as the men started into the breached walls even before the smoke had cleared. Suddenly several explosions rocked the mobile command center and the screams of the men filled the air.

"Shoot out the window and see if he's in there," Günter ordered one of his men.

A short burst from his automatic rifle blew both side windows out of the limousine.

"It's a setup, the car is full of explosives," the guard shouted.

At that very moment, the explosive tape ripped off the warehouse doors and cut two large holes in the side walls. Flash grenades came sailing into the room, exploding and momentarily blinding several of the guards. Police started to rush into the warehouse, but the claymore anti-personnel mines that had been placed just inside the walls of the entire warehouse started exploding. The body armor of the strike teams was no match for the ballbearings streaking out from the claymores, ripping through the walls and the bodies of everyone within twenty yards of the building. Not one policeman escaped unscathed. Over half of the officers died instantly, their bodies shredded by the steel balls. Several more would die before they could make it to safety away from the warehouse. Some of the survivors lost one or more limbs. The guards inside the warehouse started firing randomly through the open walls.

Günter paid no attention to the attack. He knew Satochi had bested him. He dove down into the access tunnel breaking several ribs when he landed. He leaped to his feet and began running as fast as he could, ignoring the excruciating pain from his shattered ribs.

"Not this time, Satochi," Günter yelled as he ran.

"Did you hear that? It sounded like gunshots," Haruko said to Viktor.

Viktor looked at his watch. "It's too early. They're not going in for another fifteen minutes," he replied. "We'll hear several explosions when they attack the warehouse. First they'll blow off the doors and then they'll throw flash grenades before they enter."

Seconds later the explosions Viktor spoke of occurred.

"I guess you're right, they've started the attack," Viktor said.

"What are they saying on the radio?" Haruko asked. The claymores started exploding and Viktor quickly turned to look. As far back as they were, they could hear the screams of the injured policemen.

"They knew we were coming," Viktor said. "Those last explosions were claymore mines. It was a trap."

"We had better get back there to see if we can help," Haruko said.

"Who's that man over there? He looks familiar," Viktor said.

"It's Satochi, Aioka's assassin," Haruko gasped. "We have to...Ouch, what are you...", but Haruko was unconscious before she could finish her sentence.

Viktor removed the needle from Haruko's arm. "That'll knock her out for at least five hours," Viktor said.

"Put her in the trunk," Satochi ordered his driver. "If I were you, I'd get as far away from here as possible. It's about to get really messy. I wouldn't recommend breathing the air around here."

Just as Satochi gave his warning, the ground shook as a massive explosion erupted from the limousine turning both the inner Bio-level 4 laboratory and the outer warehouse into rubble.

Jim jumped from his chair and ran outside with Taru close behind.

"I want all secondary teams to move up, we need to pull those men out of there," the commander yelled into his radio. Only two of the cameras were still carrying a signal and both of those belonged to men who were down on the ground. One was stationary, indicating the team member wearing it was not moving. The second screen was erratic, moving too quickly to fully focus, indicating the man wearing it was writhing in pain. With most of the strike teams now dead, policemen in support roles rushed forward to help their comrades, as did Jim and Taru. They had barely exited the command center when the massive blast of explosives erupted, knocking them off their feet, obliterating the warehouse and raining debris down upon their heads.

"We've got to fall back," Jim shouted at Taru.

"We must help the injured," Taru insisted.

Thousands of supplement capsules littered the ground along with pieces of building materials from the warehouse. A dust cloud hung over the area in the moist Helsinki air.

"Get on the radio and tell everybody to pull back," Jim ordered Taru. "Anyone who goes near the blast site risks death from Ebola. That's what's in these capsules," Jim said, pointing to the ground. "Anyone coming near here needs bio-hazard protective gear."

Taru understood and started translating Jim's instructions into her radio. Immediately the policemen started pulling back.

"One of our military bio-chemical teams is suited up and moving in to begin recovery," Taru translated. "There are showers and a clean room set up about three blocks north of here in a parking structure. All personnel in the debris zone have been ordered to head there."

"You'll get no argument from me," Jim replied. Then he remembered Haruko and Viktor.

Günter was about halfway down the access tunnel when the massive blast knocked him to the ground. Debris-filled air rushed by him as he held his breath. He ran past the claymores he had his men place in the tunnel, but now there was no reason to arm them. He knew the explosives in the limo more than likely sealed the tunnel. There would be no one following him. Smoke hung thick in the air making it almost impossible to see.

"Mein Gott," Günter said, as he cleared the debris from his body and opened his eyes. Mixed in the debris were hundreds of the tainted supplement capsules both whole and in pieces. Much of the air was filled with the powdered herbs, which included the chimera virus. Covering his nose and mouth, Günter struggled to his feet and staggered towards the hidden exit at the end of the tunnel.

The door covering the access tunnel exit blew open from the blast and debris and smoke poured from the tunnel.

"Don't go near the smoke," Satochi warned. "It may have the Ebola virus mixed with it."

"I must get back before I'm missed," Viktor replied. "I'll be in touch." Viktor started running back towards the perimeter making sure to stay away from the plume of smoke that continued to grow.

Satochi and his driver moved further from the tunnel exit, away from the potentially deadly smoke and fumes, waiting in case Günter miraculously escaped the massive blast.

The police abandoned the mobile command unit and moved towards the triage and decontamination areas. It was essential to remove their contaminated clothing and shower as quickly as possible.

"Has anyone seen my two partners?" Jim asked several people who had joined him and Taru as they headed for the showers.

No one answered or even understood what Jim was saying. They all were frightened for their lives and ran on towards the designated decontamination area.

"They don't understand you," Taru said trying to catch her breath.

"I've got to find Haruko and Viktor," Jim said to Taru.

"They were behind the barricades. They should be safe," Taru replied trying to assure Jim.

When they arrived at the triage area, all modesty was out the door, as workers in bio-hazard suits ordered everyone to strip and throw their clothes into large plastic barrels. Taru swiftly removed her clothing revealing a stunning body, but Jim was a bit more hesitant.

Taru smiled, "I assure you I won't look, Mr. Rikey. Although I find the modesty of you Americans a rather curious trait."

One line formed as people patiently waited for their turn in the portable showers.

"Jim. Jim," Viktor called from behind a barricade. "I can't find Haruko."

Günter knew that his chances of contracting the Ebola virus were great. He had many cuts and abrasions caused by his leap into the tunnel and the subsequent explosion. All of them easy access for the chimera virus to take hold. The tunnel was dark with smoke and Ebola-laden dust from the explosion debris, but Günter could make out a lighter patch in the smoke and knew he was near the exit. He rushed through the door coughing and wheezing.

"I've been expecting you," he heard Satochi say.

Günter knew Satochi wouldn't have a gun, preferring to kill his victim's up close and personal. Günter was in no condition to fight. Without hesitation, he sprinted the twenty yards to the edge of the wharf and leaped into the frigid water. By the time Satochi made it to the spot where Günter had jumped, there was no sign of him.

"Climb down the ladder and see if you can locate him," Satochi ordered his driver. "He must be hiding under the wharf."

Before the driver even made it to the ladder, the rumble of a powerful Merc 357 engine echoed loudly as it roared to life. The 18-foot fiberglass boat shot out from beneath the wharf as if fired from a cannon and was out of rifle range in seconds.

"What now, boss?" the driver asked.

"We go collect the suitcase nuke," Satochi responded. "And if we're lucky, we'll find Günter there."

A cold rain began to fall and, as the drops fell to the ground, they brought with them the chimera virus that hung in the debris cloud above the blast sight.

"The rain will make the cleanup easier," Taru said to Jim.

Jim, however, was focused on what Viktor had yelled. He was hoping he had heard wrong. He waved at Viktor, cupping his hand to his ear, the international sign for 'what did you say?'.

"I can't find Haruko anywhere," Viktor yelled again.

Jim started towards where Viktor was standing, but one of the men in the bio-hazard suits started yelling at him.

"He says, you must not get out of line, if you want to live," Taru translated.

"I don't think it's quite that serious," Jim responded, but did as he was told.

Viktor tried to get closer to the triage area, but was forcibly stopped by armed military personnel.

"One of my team members is missing," Jim said to Taru. "I know that it may seem minor compared to the horror we've just witnessed, but is there anyone you can get to help search for her?"

Taru knew there was more to Jim's concern than just finding a missing team member.

Viktor yelled for Jim to get a radio so they could talk, for he still had the one the commander had given him.

Taru heard Viktor and asked one of the haz-mat team members to give her one from the pile of possibly contaminated equipment. After a rather heated debate, the man gave in, handing her the radio, but not until it had been heavily sprayed with a green liquid.

"I hope that thing still works after all that," Jim said, as Taru passed him the still dripping radio.

Viktor held up four fingers, telling Jim to set his radio on channel four.

"Can you hear me, Jim?" Viktor asked.

"How in tarnation did you lose Haruko?" Jim asked.

"We were both looking for a better vantage point to watch the raid," Viktor said. "I went in a warehouse down by the wharf to see if we could get on the roof. I was halfway up the steps when I heard her scream Satochi's name. By the time I ran back to the wharf, all I saw was the back of a car turning the corner and this was laying on the ground." Viktor held up Haruko's radio.

"Jim, I spoke with the commander. He can't spare anyone at the moment to help find your friend," Taru said.

"Viktor, I need your help. Neither the Finnish National Police nor the Helsinki Police can spare anyone to help find her. You said you had several FSB agents in Helsinki. Is it possible they can help you search for her?" Jim asked.

"I'll see what I can arrange," Viktor replied.

"You'll be on your own. I have to stay in quarantine for at least two days," Jim said. "I'm count'n on you, buddy."

"Should I call Eddie and request he and some more agents be sent to help?" Viktor asked.

"I'll call Eddie, but I need him in Hawaii. I find it hard to believe Satochi is here and not there, but I wouldn't put anything past Aioka," Jim replied. "Eddie knows Hawaii and may be able to find out something on that end."

"What happened during the raid?" Viktor asked.

"The warehouse was booby-trapped with claymores. The claymores took out most of the police. A gun battle was beginning when suddenly it was like a bomb was dropped on the place."

"Was that part of a planned trap?" Viktor asked

"I can't imagine. All the men inside were killed. It doesn't make any sense," Jim said.

"None of it makes any sense," replied Viktor.

CHAPTER TWENTY-ONE

"Aloha," Eddie answered.

"Eddie, are you still at the Hydrogen Solutions?" Jim asked.

"I sure am, and things are finally getting interesting, the ..."

"Eddie, you need to be quiet and listen very carefully," Jim said interrupting. "Haruko's been kidnapped. We think by Satochi."

"How is that possible?" Eddie asked.

"Listen Eddie, I don't have time to explain everything now. I may have been exposed to the Ebola virus, me and several thousand Finns. I'm standing here in the cold, butt-naked, waiting for decontamination. Viktor is using his people on this end to see what he can do to find her. The raid turned into a catastrophe here. From what I've been told, I'll be in isolation for at least two days to see if I was infected."

"What do you need me to do?" Eddie replied.

"I need you to convince the HS tech to pull up all satellite or hydrogen plane footage of Helsinki for the past two hours. I also need a plane monitoring everything going on here. It may help in finding Haruko," Jim explained.

"Are you sure it was Satochi that kidnapped her?" Eddie asked.

"From what we've been able to learn here, Satochi was here to meet this Günter Marx who runs Zetanutra. We aren't sure if the meeting ever took place, or if either of them is even alive. Viktor swears he heard Haruko yell out the name Satochi just before someone pulled her into a car and took off."

"I'll get right on it. Is Washington sending some agents to help?" Eddie asked.

"The Finns won't allow it. They aren't even accepting offers to help with containing the virus and de-con," Jim replied. "And from what I've been told, as soon as I clear isolation, they'll want Viktor and me out of the country. They say they'll work with our embassy personnel in trying to locate Haruko."

"That's a bunch of crap," Eddie replied.

"This is an open line, so I have to be careful with what I say but, believe me, we'll find Haruko."

When Polya heard the roar of the speedboat's engine as Günter pulled into the boathouse next to the warehouse loft, the tension in her shoulders finally eased for the first time in days. She watched him exit the boat on one of the security monitors that kept watch over the entire warehouse complex. She could tell immediately that something had gone wrong.

"At least he's alive," she said to herself. She guessed that Satochi must have also survived their encounter. She watched as Günter stripped off all his clothes, then turned and looked directly into the camera and picked up the intercom phone.

"I was so worried," Polya said, as she answered.

"Be quiet and listen to me," Günter demanded. "Satochi is still alive and I've been exposed to the chimera virus. I have no doubt that Satochi will find us here soon, so you must take the nuke and leave here quickly."

"What will you do?" Polya asked. "I'll wait till you're gone then try to decontaminate myself. Then I'll move to the safe house for a few days to see if I was infected. If not, I'll join you as we planned. If I was..."

"You'll be fine," Polya interrupted. "We'll meet just as you planned."

"Let us pray that will be so," Günter replied.

As they talked, a perimeter alarm signaled that a car had turned on the restricted road that led to the warehouse. A camera automatically zoomed in on the intruders.

"It's Satochi, he must have followed you here," Polya said.

"That's not possible," Günter replied. "There must be a tracking device on the bomb. Find it."

Polya ran to the suitcase that housed the nuclear weapon. There was no apparent device on the suitcase, so she opened it and carefully began looking for the tracking device.

"Polya, Polya!"

She could here Günter yelling over the phone line and picked it up.

"Yes, I'm here," she replied.

"Don't waste your time searching the inside of the suitcase. It's shielded and no tracking device could work from inside. It must be on the outside."

"The only thing on the outside is the handle and the two wheels," she said.

"Tear the handle off, that must be it," Günter ordered. He could here Polya struggling as she followed his instructions.

"That's it, the device is here," she said, picking up the phone.

"Throw it to me from the window. Also throw me some warm clothes. I'll head out in the boat and he'll follow me believing I have the bomb. Use the dolly and load the suitcase into the car. Leave by the south road. I'll head north over the water."

Polya was too much of a professional to question or waste valuable time. She grabbed some clothes and placed the handle in a zippered pocket of the windbreaker, then tossed them to Günter who was waiting by the boathouse.

"Be careful," Polya yelled. Günter only waved. She pushed the suitcase onto a hand truck and took the lift down to the car which was packed and ready to go. She struggled with the suitcase nuke but managed to get it into the trunk of the car without wasting too much time. As she entered the car, she again heard the roar of the speedboat's engine as it left the boathouse. When she pulled the car from the garage, she thought she heard gunshots on the other side of the complex.

"I'll see you soon, my love," she said to herself, although she knew there was little chance of that.

Satochi watched the speedboat disappear across the water. He knew the shots would attract unwanted attention. It was time to leave Helsinki. Aioka would not be pleased that Günter escaped with the nuke, but Satochi did capture Haruko and this he knew would please his boss. As he prepared to leave, his phone began to ring.

"Yes," Satochi answered.

"Tell Aioka that I have the nuke," Polya said.

"He'll be pleased to know that," Satochi replied.

"I'll contact him once I've safely left Finland," Polya replied. "I'm sure we can come to a mutually beneficial business arrangement. Oh, and tell him Günter believes he was exposed to the chimera virus."

Satochi smiled. Aioka was indeed a wise man. He knew all along Polya was not committed to any cause but her own financial gain. It was time to return to Paradise.

"Colonel Cheznov, I hope all is going well with the Americans," Viktor's assistant in Perm said.

"As well as can be expected under the circumstances," he replied.

"We've been monitoring the raid like you requested. Do you think there's much danger from the virus because of the explosion?"

"I think the rain will keep it from spreading. Did you pull up the satellite images I requested?"

"We did, and discovered something you may find interesting," the assistant replied.

"Explain," Viktor demanded.

"We were able to isolate an image of two men and the woman struggling on the wharf, but there is very little clarity. Identification is impossible."

"Were you able to follow the car?" Viktor asked.

"For a short distance, then we lost it in traffic. However, about three miles north of the wharf, we had a reading of a nuclear signature that we believe is one of our suitcase nukes."

"Are you still receiving the reading?" Viktor asked.

"No, it lasted only for a moment, then disappeared, but if we were able to pick it up, you can be sure the Americans did as well. Should we send our agents to the location?"

Viktor hesitated before responding. "No, I believe you're correct in saying we weren't the only ones that picked up the radiation signature. I'll inform the Americans, but keep me updated. Is there any chance the suitcase has been moved?"

"The area seems to be a secure complex of some sort. One car did approach, quite possibly the one from the wharf we were following, and a second car did leave an adjacent warehouse a few blocks away. However, we did see a speedboat leave the area heading north, right after we detected the radiation. It seemed to draw the attention of the vehicle, for it turned to try to follow on land."

"Are you still tracking the car and boat?" Viktor asked.

"Unfortunately, we have lost them both. The assets we have in the area are not as sophisticated as we would like. You must remember, Finland is not a high priority," the assistant said.

"Well, I think it is now." Viktor replied.

CHAPTER TWENTY-TWO

"Eh brah, I tink you bettah take yo mada guys and go outta Na'alehu," Shima's partner said as they walked towards their camp inside a crevasse at the Great Crack.

"How come ladat?" Shima asked.

"Bobura sed dat when bomb explodes, gonna make big wave dat to hit islands. Mebbe land break apart," the man said. "Mebbe goin move them mauka to Waimea or Hawi."

"Bobura nevva tell me dat," Shima replied.

"Mebbe he goin' tell you when he get back," Shima's partner replied.

"When he goin' come back?" Shima asked.

"I dunno, mebbe two, tree day or sumptin. He tell me keep blasting holes till he come back."

"Mebbe tomorrow I go Na'alehu goin' move dem," Shima replied.

"Shoots," his friend replied. "Mebbe I go wit you den." Suddenly the earth began to shake.

"Brah, Pele no like us makin dakine holes in island," Shima said.

"You feel dat? Dat shake shake is da lava stay flowin ova hea," his partner replied. "Mo betta we be careful where we blast."

"Yeah brah, I stay feel warm down here," Shima replied. "Maybe we go Na'alehu today, brah. Just work when Bobura come back."

Shima's partner hid the supplies behind a pile of rocks in the crevasse. "Holes can wait, brah. We go Na'alehu," he said as he lit a joint, inhaling deeply, and then passing it to Shima.

"Bobura not goin' be happy," Shima replied.

"We jus go only one day. When we come back, goin' blast mo'big holes, Bobura dunno."

"Yeah brah, but Pele gonna know." Shima replied.

"Sorry Jim, but Hydrogen Solutions have no surveillance planes anywhere near Helsinki," Eddie explained over the phone.

"What about satellites?"

"We have a couple for weather. Britain has one near there, but it lacks the technology to be of any real help. The Russians have a couple in the area, but we don't know their capabilities, only that they aren't anywhere near as sophisticated as our newer ones. That's a question Viktor needs to answer," Eddie replied.

"He already did. He said that the high zoom lens is down on the one satellite that would have been able to help, but they're working on it," Jim said.

"Sounds a little fishy to me," Eddie responded.

"I sorta got that feel'n too," Jim replied. "The boys back in McClean have any ideas?"

"I was getting to that," Eddie replied. "That tech we have working on flight plans of planes leaving Hawaii did a check on private jets coming and going between Helsinki and the USA. A Zetanutra Citation X jet landed there from Ontario, CA, about four hours before the raid."

"Do we have a manifest of the passengers?" Jim asked.

"Yeah, right," Eddie replied. "But we got something even better. The same plane left there less than two hours after the raid went down. It stopped to refuel in Montreal, and is scheduled to arrive in Ontario in exactly one hour.”

“Boy howdy, that’s the first good news I’ve heard all day,” Jim replied.

“The local FBI office, along with Homeland Security, will be there with a couple of dozen agents to meet them,” Eddie said.

“Better have a SWAT team available,” Jim suggested.

“Already been arranged, buddy,” Eddie replied. “If I had more time I’d head there too. McClean also told me they’re just about finished with crosschecking flight plans and actual destinations with all private jets that left the Big Island between the arrival of the Congressmen’s plane in Kona and the bombing in Wichita. No flights flew to Wichita, although one went to Kansas City, a couple to Colorado, and a half-dozen to Texas. Most flew from the Big Island to California. It’ll take a few hundred more man-hours to follow up on possible secondary general aviation flights to the Midwest from those original destinations. They promised me the info for flights from the other islands in that time frame by this evening. Something is bound to come out of it. Now tell me how are you doing?”

“De-con went well, although I nearly froze my ass off waiting in line,” Jim said.

“Yeah, nothing more fun than standing around naked with a bunch of Finnish police,” Eddie said.

“You might be surprised,” Jim replied.

“Whoa there buddy. You’re beginning to creep me out,” Eddie replied.

“Not all Finnish police are men. I’ll tell you about it later,” Jim said. “I’m supposed to remain in isolation for another thirty-six hours, and I don’t see any way around it. My guess is that Satochi and Haruko are on that flight, so I see no need in trying to stick around any longer than necessary.”

“What about Viktor? Where is he?” Eddie asked.

“Actually, he’s looking at me through the window as we speak. I’ll fill him in on the news about the jet and try to find out why the Russians don’t seem to want to share their satellite information. I need you to arrange a live feed, so I’ll know what’s happening in California when that Zetanutra jet lands.”

“You and me both. I’ll take care of it. Just make sure you have your laptop with you,” Eddie replied.

“Keep in touch,” Jim said, and pushed “end” on his Blackberry. He turned and saw that Viktor was holding the intercom phone.

“Any news from your end?” Jim asked.

“As a matter of fact, yes, and it’s not so good,” Viktor replied.

“We did have a satellite in the area, but its camera wasn’t working properly.”

“I’ve heard,” Jim replied.

“You’re well informed,” Viktor replied, “but what you haven’t heard, because I ordered it not released to your government, is that our satellite did pick up a radiation signature characteristic of our suitcase nukes.”

“Are you saying one of the stolen nukes is here in Helsinki?” Jim asked.

“Precisely,” Viktor replied. “It was in a warehouse complex a few miles north of here. I have agents watching the complex.”

“Have you informed the Finnish government?” Jim asked.

"No, I thought it better that such bad news come from your President, since your country is running this investigation."

Jim wanted to respond, but thought it best to hold his tongue. He didn't care much for Viktor and didn't really care what Viktor thought of him, but if the President wanted them to work together, Jim would do his best to do what the President asked.

"What have you heard from Eddie?" Viktor asked.

"Eddie thinks he's found Satochi and Haruko," Jim explained. "The NCTC is following a Zetanutra jet headed for Ontario, California. It had arrived a few hours before the raid and left two hours afterwards."

"What makes Eddie think Satochi is on that jet?" Viktor asked.

"Just seems logical. If it was Satochi who kidnapped Haruko, he'd want to get out of Helsinki and back to Hawaii as quickly as possible."

"Do you think he has the suitcase nuke with him?" Viktor asked.

Jim hadn't thought about that. "When exactly did your satellite pick up the radiation signature?" Jim asked.

"I don't know, I'll have to contact Moscow to find that out," Viktor replied.

Before Viktor had finished his reply, Jim was already calling Eddie back. "Eddie, it's Jim."

"I was just about to call you back. We were just informed that the British picked up a radiation signature in Helsinki identical to the one we picked up in Hilo. Looks like Satochi took one of the nukes to Finland," Eddie said.

"Maybe he went to pick one up," Jim suggested. "What time did they record the radiation?"

"Less than an hour after the attack on Zetanutra,"
Eddie replied, "Why?"

"The Russians also picked up the radiation signature.
Viktor thinks the nuke could be on the plane with Satochi,"
Jim said.

"That would be bad," Eddie said. "I think we better
rethink our tactics for meeting that jet in Ontario. If Satochi is
on that plane and has that nuke, he wouldn't hesitate
detonating it if cornered."

"I have to agree," Jim said. "I'll contact Washington.
They may want the military involved, but I need you to get in
touch with whomever is in charge in California and warn
them. They may want to shoot it down."

"There's not enough time for the military to mobilize
and I don't think shooting down the plane based on our
opinions is a good option, even though I'm guessing that's
what the President will order. Anyways, I don't think
interceptor jets could be scrambled in time," Eddie replied.
"The team already assembled in Ontario will have to adjust
their tactics. I'll call you back as soon as I know something."

"Good luck," Jim replied, "God knows we're going to
need it."

"There are just way too many unknowns," Viktor said.
"I think trying to stop Satochi in Ontario is too risky. We
should wait till they leave California and are over the Pacific,
then force them down to a remote airstrip or shoot them
down."

"We don't know for sure they'll continue on to
Hawaii," Jim replied. "According to the flight plan, Ontario is
the final destination."

"It's your government that has to live with the
consequences," Viktor replied brashly.

If he wasn't behind a thick pane of glass, Jim would have punched him despite the President's order to cooperate. Jim just wanted Viktor to get out of his face. Exactly the reaction Viktor expected. "I think you should go see if the nuke might still be in that warehouse complex," Jim suggested.

"I'm sure by now the Finns have been notified and sent in their military," Viktor replied. "But there is little I can do here. I'll contact you if I find out anything."

Jim watched as Viktor headed down the hallway and into the elevator.

"I don't trust that Russian son-of-a-bitch," Jim said to himself, but whatever it was Viktor was keeping secret would have to wait. Jim had more important matters to deal with. Mainly, trying to save the life of the woman he loved.

Satochi was awoken by the pilot. Aioka needed to speak with him immediately.

"How soon till you land in California?" Aioka asked. Satochi, in turn, asked the pilot.

"In less than a half an hour," Satochi replied, sensing trouble. He had spoken with Aioka when the plane departed Helsinki several hours ago. Aioka was pleased that Haruko had been captured and seemed to have expected that Polya would end up taking the nuke. He was not happy that Günter had escaped. He would have rather had Satochi kill Günter than count on the chimera to do the job, but even that was not totally unexpected.

"The FBI knows you're on the plane and they believe Haruko is with you. They also think you have the suitcase nuke on board. There is a SWAT team awaiting your arrival."

Satochi knew not to question the validity of Aioka's information. "What do you suggest?"

"This is their plane right here," the Ontario controller said to the FBI agent as he pointed to the radar screen. "They're in the pattern and should be on the ground in about five minutes."

"Did everybody copy that?" the agent in charge said over his radio.

"Roger that," six different team leaders called in. Jim was listening on his laptop in Helsinki, as was Eddie in Oahu.

"Cessna Citation 240J, you are north of the pattern, please acknowledge," the controller said.

"What's happening?" the agent in charge asked.

"The Citation is not responding and has left the pattern," the controller explained.

"Try them again," the agent ordered.

"Cessna Citation 240J, please acknowledge," the controller repeated the call several times, still with no response. "He must have changed frequencies."

"Cessna 240J is coming down," one of the other controllers said. "Looks like northwest of here. He's landing at Cable."

"Oh shit," the agent replied.

The Cessna Citation pilot turned his radio to frequency 123.00. "Advising all Cable traffic, this is Citation 240J entering the pattern five miles northeast of runway 246."

"What is this airport?" Satochi asked the pilot. It's called Cable Airport. It's a small private airport a few miles away from Ontario. They have no tower. They use a UNICOM system. You just announce to all other traffic that you are in the pattern and landing. If anyone else wants to use the airport, they'll let you know."

"Citation 240J, this is Maniac Mike. I run the restaurant here. Make sure you put down right on the numbers."

"Roger that, Maniac Mike," the pilot replied.

"What did he mean?" Satochi asked.

"It means that the runway is not that long, so I have to set down immediately in order to stop before the runway ends. But don't worry, we've got reverse thrusters on this model, so we'll stop before we're halfway down the runway."

"I don't need it in twenty minutes, I need a helicopter right now!" the FBI agent in charge yelled into his radio. "How long will it take us to drive to this other airport?"

"About fifteen minutes, ten minutes if we go Code Three," one of the airport police officers replied.

"You drive," the FBI agent said. "I want everyone following us now."

He turned to one of the other agents. "Call the local police and have them keep that plane from taking off, but do not, I repeat, do not approach the plane till we arrive."

The FBI arrived at the airport eight minutes later. Several local police cars were on the runway and the Citation was sitting near the restaurant with its door open.

"Everyone's gone," a local police officer said to the lead FBI agent. "When we arrived, this is how we found it."

"Anybody see who got off?" the agent asked.

"I saw them," a man with a big moustache said. "Five people got off, four men and a woman. The woman looked sick."

"Why do you say that," the lead agent asked.

"Two of the men, the Asian ones, were supporting her or holding her up. It was like she was having trouble walking."

"What did the woman look like?"

"She was small and Asian as well. The other two guys were the pilots. At least they had on pilot uniforms. Both white guys," the mustached man volunteered.

"What about the two Asian men, anything you remember about them?"

"Sure, one was huge, but he seemed to be taking orders from the smaller man, the one with the cane."

"Did you see where they went?"

"They headed around front. I thought they were helping the woman to the restroom. It's out front. I was busy in the restaurant. I didn't notice they were gone until all the police cars started rushing in."

"This is very important. Did you see them carrying any large suitcases?" the agent asked.

"Not at all, the pilots each pulled two small suitcases on rollers, and the two Asians weren't carrying anything, except the woman."

"Why would somebody walk away from a new Citation X? It must have cost close to 4 million dollars," said one of the airport policemen.

"The plane's clean," one of the agents radioed to his boss. "No suitcase nukes in here."

"Did he say what I thought he just said?" the mustached man asked.

"You didn't hear him say anything," the lead agent said in a threatening tone.

"I think you're right, I need to get back to work," the man replied.

"Work will have to wait. You'll need to tell one of my men exactly what was said and what you saw." An agent led the mustached man into another room.

"Somebody tipped them off," the lead agent told his team members over the radio. "The NCTC is not going to like this one bit."

"No, we're not," Jim said listening to the fiasco unfold, but at least he was now certain Satochi had captured Haruko. Even more important she was still alive. Jim was raring at the bit to get out of isolation and out of Helsinki. He needed to get back to Hawaii and find Haruko. He knew that was where Satochi would take her. He would have every commercial and private plane arriving in the islands searched. Now more than ever Jim was convinced Aioka had someone on the inside feeding him information, and as soon as he found Haruko, he would find that informant. His phone began to ring.

"This is Jim."

"Finnish military just searched the warehouse complex. The suitcase nuke is gone, if in fact it was ever here. They did find clothes belonging to a man and a woman. More troubling is they found some men's clothes in a boathouse that were covered with the same residue from the Zetanutra blast. They are testing them for contamination now. How did the raid on the plane go?" Viktor asked.

"Not well, I'll tell you about it when you return," Jim said, closing his phone. Jim looked out the window at the Helsinki skyline. He thought about the suitcase nuke and about Wichita. Then he thought about Haruko and Jotty. A cold rain continued to fall.

CHAPTER TWENTY-THREE

Four FBI agents were assigned to every major airport on the islands, except for Honolulu, which had reopened, where eight agents were assigned. Every private jet arriving at the airports was searched by these agents and customs officials. At the Honolulu Airport, five of the agents watched monitors displaying the faces of all arriving passengers, while the other three searched the incoming jets. Jim, as head of the NCTC team, had ordered the searches, but not without stirring up controversy in Washington. Several of the senior NCTC agents felt such a heavy deployment of manpower could best be used elsewhere. They agreed catching Satochi and rescuing Haruko was very important, but not nearly as important as finding the remaining suitcase nukes.

The agents in Honolulu were kept very busy by all the incoming commercial flights. In Lihue, Kona, and Hilo the pace was far from hectic, with few direct flights arriving from the mainland and even fewer incoming private jets, although, at least two an hour seemed to arrive in Kona. Maui was an entirely different situation. A constant stream of commercial passengers arriving on direct flights from the mainland were more than the FBI agents assigned to the airport could handle. The closed-circuit video monitoring system did not cover all arriving gates, causing two of the agents to stand at the doors watching as the passengers disembarked. Another sat in the security room watching those gates that were covered by cameras. The fourth agent was constantly on the run between helping his partners in the commercial terminal and rushing to meet all arriving private jets when the controller notified him of an approaching aircraft. Such was the case with a particular jet arriving from the Burbank Airport in California.

"Excuse me," the agent yelled to a couple about to enter a chauffeured Lincoln waiting next to a Learjet 45.

"What can I do for you," a very tanned and sporty looking man in his late fifties replied.

"I'm with the FBI, can you please tell me where you arrived from?"

"Burbank, I'm Sullivan Taylor, President of Taylor Productions."

"Does this jet belong to you or is it a charter?" the agent asked.

"Technically, it belongs to my production company, but I'm the only one who uses it. Is there a problem?"

"No sir, we're just looking for somebody whom we believe will arrive on a private jet from California," the agent replied. "How many people were on your jet?"

Sullivan Taylor did not like to be questioned about anything and was growing tired of the agent's questions. I and my lady friend here," he replied, gesturing to the girl standing slightly behind him. "My assistant, Mr. Tang, and my two pilots."

"Where is your assistant, this Mr. Tang?" the agent asked.

"Collecting the baggage, I believe. Mr. Tang, could you come here please?" Sullivan called out.

The agent turned to see a giant of a man struggling to fit through the Learjet hatch.

"This is my assistant and bodyguard, Mr. Tang." Sullivan replied. "Anymore requests?"

"No, but if you don't mind, I need to look inside your jet. With your permission, of course."

"By all means, be my guest," Sullivan replied, as Mr. Tang finished loading the trunk.

The agent entered the plane, looked in the bathroom on board and then poked his head in the cockpit.

"Can I help you?" one of the pilots asked.

"Sorry to bother you, I'm with the FBI. Are you Mr. Taylor's regular pilots?"

"That we are," one of the pilots replied.

"You fly Mr. Taylor to the islands often?" the agent asked.

"Just about every weekend. Sullivan has an estate up by Kapalua," the pilot said.

"He likes to bring his young starlets here to audition, if you get my drift," the other pilot replied.

"I noticed," the agent replied, "The one outside barely looks eighteen."

"No comment," the first pilot replied, "but I bet he got real nervous when you said you were with the FBI."

All three men laughed. "Thanks for your cooperation," the agent said.

"Well, did you find anything?" Sullivan asked with an attitude.

"Thank you for your cooperation," the agent said. "Have a nice stay in Maui."

Sullivan didn't reply, he just entered the car and it sped away.

The agent turned as a large 747 touched down on the runway. He needed to get back inside and help look at passengers.

"You look like a busy man," the second pilot said as he carefully stepped from the Learjet using his cane to keep his balance.

"Too busy," the FBI agent replied as he hurried away.

Another Lincoln pulled up next to the Learjet. "As soon as he's out of sight put her in the car." Satochi said. "We have a boat to catch in Maalaea."

"Somebody tipped them off," Eddie said to Jim. "Why else would they switch airports like that?"

"The switch could have been planned all along," Jim replied. "But leaving a new Citation X behind like that, they had to know we were closing in quick."

"We could use a few more agents helping out at the Honolulu and Maui Airports," Eddie said. "The agents there are overwhelmed, especially in Maui."

"There's no way," Jim said. "McClean is already questioning my ability to lead the team. They already think I'm wasting too many man hours covering the airports. I'm just giving it one more day, then I have to scale it back to just Kona and Hilo. I should be out of isolation in just a few hours, and then Viktor and I will head back to Hawaii."

"I did just receive the list of private jets that may have transported the nuke to the mainland," Eddie said.

"Any good possibilities?" Jim asked.

"As a matter of fact, there were three that look like possibilities," Eddie replied.

"Two belong to William Casey. He flew several of his guests, including seven passengers that were on the Congressional jet back to the mainland. One flew directly to Dallas, then returned to Kona. A second jet flew to Los Angeles, then to Washington, but stopped in Kansas City."

"Both sound like good possibilities," Jim said. "Are you following up on the passenger list?"

"As much as we can with the man power we have but, like I said, our guys are pushing it right now."

"What about the third plane?" Jim asked.

"I saved the best for last," Eddie said. "The third plane flew out of Hilo, stopped in Burbank, and then flew to Denver. It was there for less than an hour and headed back to Hilo, stopping again in Burbank."

"What makes this plane so special?"

"Other than the registered owner, Taylor Productions, doesn't seem to exist anywhere but on paper," Eddie explained. "And it arrived in Maui from Burbank, about seven hours after the Citation X was abandoned in Upland."

"How far is Burbank from Upland?" Jim asked.

"About an hour or less."

"What did the agent find when it landed?" Jim asked.

"Nothing, or I probably would have heard about it," Eddie replied. "But like I said, Maui is where we are short-handed. If there wasn't a Japanese woman screaming for help, I doubt the passengers or crew were even questioned." Jim didn't immediately reply. Eddie knew he shouldn't have made the comment about Haruko. He knew Jim still loved her.

"Get a hold of the agent who searched the plane, see what he has to say," Jim ordered.

"I've already made the call, I'm waiting to hear back," Eddie explained.

"Keep me informed, I should be there within twenty-four hours," Jim said.

"We'll get her back. I just know we will," Eddie replied.

Jim didn't respond.

"Eddie, it's Marlin calling again. I hate talking to these damn machines, but you're never home. I hope you got my earlier messages. I really need to meet with you. I have some information that may help you find the person responsible for

225

the anthrax attack on the *Grand Maui*, but I think I'm being followed. I was at the re-christening party for the *Grand Maui* and these two men tried to grab me, but a security guard showed up and they took off. I'm scared, Eddie. Real scared. I'm afraid to return to my house in Oahu and afraid to stay at the Four Seasons any longer. I'm staying at a friend's house down near Na'alehu for a couple of days while he's out of town, but I don't even feel safe here. My cell number is 332-0809. Call me and we can meet at the cliffs at Ka Lae. Nobody can sneak up on us there. Pease call, I beg you."

"Why Southpoint?" Eddie said to himself. He wasn't sure what to make of Marlin's request. Marlin seemed like a nice enough guy, but he was a prime suspect in the anthrax attack on the *Grand Maui*.

"What did you say?" the Hydrogen Solutions technician asked.

"I said Southpoint. A suspect in that anthrax attack wants to meet me at Southpoint on the Big Island," Eddie replied.

"Doesn't sound like a smart thing to do. That place is pretty isolated," the tech said.

"I know, but that's why he wants to meet me there. He says he has some important information about the attack. He thinks they're trying to kill him or something."

"Who's they?" the tech asked.

"I guess I'm going to have to meet him to find that out," Eddie said.

Eddie dialed Marlin's cell. "Aloha, this is Marlin, sorry I'm unable to come to the phone right now, but your call means a lot to me. I really would enjoy talking with you. Please leave a message and I'll call you right back. Mahalo."

"Aloha, Marlin, I have received your messages, but I've been really busy. I would like to hear what information you have about the anthrax attacks, but do you really think it's necessary to meet at Southpoint? I'd rather meet someplace more convenient, but if I don't hear back from you tonight, I'll be at the cliffs at 9:30 in the morning. Mahalo."

"Do you think it's safe to meet him there?" the tech asked.

"Probably not," Eddie replied. "But I'll take another agent with me and, like Marlin said, you can see if anybody's coming for several miles, so it should be safe. Marlin is a pretty harmless guy. It's taking the time to do it that I am worried about."

"Agent Rikey won't be back till later tomorrow evening so you can head out now and stop by the Maui Airport to interview the agent about that Taylor Productions jet. I'm sure the base can arrange a helicopter to at least get you to Maui," the tech explained.

"Good idea, that way I can see this jet for myself. I'll give Dano a call and have him meet me in Kona."

The tech started singing the Hawaii-Five-O theme song. "Very funny," Eddie chortled.

"Don't be too concerned about your meeting in Southpoint," the tech advised, "I'll keep an eye on things from above and send in the cavalry if necessary."

"Thanks," Eddie replied.

"Oh, just one more thing before you go," the tech said. "Just for me, let me hear you say 'book'm Dano'."

Eddie smiled and waved one finger in the air as he left to catch his helicopter.

"Oh, mein Gott! Scheiße!" Günter said, falling into his thick German accent. He had not wanted to admit he had contracted the virus, when his joints began to ache the night before. The dull red that had replaced the white of his eyes, staring at him from the mirror, left little doubt he was a doomed man. He dialed Polya's cell, but there was no answer and no voice mail. She was smart, she knew where to hide herself and the bomb, and how to transfer the extorted money that would undoubtedly continue to pour in.

The safe-house was a small cottage located in the forest not far from Helsinki. A man and his wife, both former Russian FSB agents, managed the large lodge and the hundred plus acres surrounding it. The property was sometimes used for hunting but, more often than not, it was used as a retreat or hideout for a team of former and current Russian agents. These agents used their training to freelance their unique talents to those countries and individuals able to afford the steep cost of their services. There were several cottages, or kesämökki, as the locals called them, that were actually well equipped and secure living quarters that could accommodate extended stays if necessary. A quiet place for Günter to die or fight like hell to live. And if his body did manage to survive the Ebola virus, it would be so decimated, Günter might wish he had died.

CHAPTER TWENTY-FOUR

"Yes sir, I've already canceled the surveillance at both the Honolulu and Lihue airports," Jim explained to the director. "I'm still keeping the teams in place at Kona, Hilo, and Maui for another twelve hours. We have reason to believe Satochi may have arrived at the Kahului Airport in Maui late yesterday and will attempt to fly from there to the Big Island. One of our agents checked a private jet arriving from Burbank. It belongs to Taylor Productions, out of Hollywood, but that turns out to be a shell corporation. The agent also reported one of the pilots matched Satochi's description."

"Then why the hell didn't he stop him?" the director asked.

"At the time, the agent had not reviewed the file on the suspects," Jim replied.

"Dammit Rikey, we can't afford sloppy mistakes like this."

Jim knew the director wasn't happy with his performance. "We're taking care of the problem, sir," Jim replied. He was beginning to hate this job.

"Have your agents searched the jet for any corroborating evidence that Satochi was on the plane?" the director asked.

"No sir, the jet was gone before we figured it out," Jim replied.

"Well, search it when it arrives back in California," the director said.

Jim, of course, had already planned to do this, but he let the director talk.

"And have our L.A. people find out who is behind this Taylor Productions."

This too was already happening, but Jim wasn't going to tell the director, especially since the jet did not arrive as scheduled in Burbank and no one had any idea what happened to it. This too the techs back in McClean were working on.

"Is that Russian where he can hear our conversation?" the director asked.

"No sir, not at the moment," Jim replied.

"Good, I don't know what the President was thinking when he told us to keep that Russian S.O.B. in the loop. We have received a report from our friends at the CIA that the Russian satellites picked up some interesting video of what happened in Helsinki."

"I was told their satellites didn't have the capabilities to really be of much help," Jim replied.

"Don't believe everything you hear," the director replied. "The informant wasn't specific about what the video shows, but the CIA will have a copy of it within the next forty-eight hours and will send one to us. My guess is they already have it and will release it to us once they are through with it. I want these guys caught. I expect some results, Rikey," the director said.

"You will have them, sir, I guarantee it," Jim replied, as the phone disconnected before he even finished speaking.

"What a horse's ass," Jim said out loud. "He never once mentioned Haruko."

"Hello my friend," the voice said over the phone.

"Greetings also to you my friend," Viktor replied, according to a pre-arranged code.

"I have news that may interest you, Viktor," the caller said.

"Don't use my name over the phone, this conversation is not scrambled," Viktor instructed.

"Sorry, comrade," the caller said.

Viktor decided not to scold the caller again for his lack of discretion. The man had spent his life as a diehard KGB bureaucrat for Mother Russia, not a covert agent, so his old habits were hard to break.

"What news do you have, and don't use names," Viktor said.

"The friend you mentioned has stopped by for a visit, but he is not well. Not well at all," the caller said.

"Is his wife with him?" Viktor asked.

"No, only the gentleman, but I'm afraid he won't be staying long."

Viktor knew Günter was close to death. He must have contracted the Ebola virus during the raid on the warehouse.

"Did he bring his luggage?" Viktor asked.

"No, only a knapsack," the caller replied.

That meant Polya had the suitcase nuke, but where had she gone? She was supposed to be at the hunting lodge with Günter.

"Let me know when his wife arrives or when he leaves," Viktor ordered.

"Of course," the caller replied. "I'm sure I'll speak with you again very soon."

Viktor was too angry to reply. He now had to make a call he dreaded making more than when he called the Russian President to tell him the nukes were missing.

Haruko glared at Aioka from the doorway. Satochi had just removed her blindfold and the affects of the drugs used to render her unconscious still clouded her eyes. Satochi knew better than to release the plastic ties that still bound her wrists or the leather straps on her ankles limiting her steps to a mere shuffle.

"Inside, woman," Satochi ordered, shoving Haruko.

"Allow me to remove the tape from your mouth," Aioka said, approaching her.

Haruko tried to back away, but Satochi grabbed her roughly, holding her in place.

Aioka carefully removed the surgical tape from her mouth, trying not to cause Haruko pain. "There, isn't that better?" Aioka asked.

Haruko remained silent.

"Please, have a seat," Aioka said pointing to a chair. Haruko remained stiff, refusing to move. Again, Satochi had to shove her towards the seat and push her to sit down.

"My darling Haruko," Aioka began, "I just don't know what to do with you. You have caused me more grief than you can imagine. By all rights I should just kill you."

Haruko still did not respond or react.

"But perhaps you can somehow assist me in my goal to punish America for ruining the world with its imperialistic ideas."

"Please, no more of your terrorist manifest philosophy," Haruko finally spoke. "I have read it and find it at best absurd."

Aioka smiled, "So you can talk."

"Satochi, tell them to bring us some tea" Aioka said. "And perhaps some rice. I'm sure Haruko is hungry after her journey."

Haruko was in fact famished. It had been over two days since she had eaten, although she did not realize it since she had been unconscious for most of that time. She knew she was no longer in Finland. Hawaii was the obvious choice based on the heat and humidity and the fact that was where Satochi was believed to be. Her clothes were also damp and spotted indicating that she had been momentarily in the rain. The sun did not shine brightly through the curtained windows indicating a likely cloud cover. Her mind started working furiously as she continued trying to decipher her probable location and what Aioka intended to do with her. A large Asian man brought in the tea and rice.

"Please eat and drink some tea," Aioka said.

Haruko hesitated, more out of an ingrained cultural politeness than of fear of poisoning, until she saw Aioka begin to eat and drink. As hungry as she was, she remained calm and slowly ate her rice.

"I'm sure by now you've figured out you're in Hawaii," Aioka said, as if having read Haruko's thoughts. "You'll have to die. I can't allow you to continue to harass me forever."

"Not forever," Haruko replied, "just until I kill you."

Aioka laughed. "Very brave words, but a ridiculous thought. You are in no position to kill anyone, and now you are beginning to try my patience." Aioka nodded to the Asian man who brought in the tea. He grabbed Haruko around the neck with one hand and lifted her into the air.

"Perhaps we will have a chance to talk again later," Aioka said, gesturing to the man to remove her.

Haruko tried to reply, but the man squeezed her throat tighter allowing no words to escape as she was carried from the room.

"You should kill her now," Satochi said to Aioka when the door closed behind the guard carrying Haruko.

"Oh, I will kill her. You can be assured of that," Aioka replied. "I just want her death to serve a purpose and send a message. I must decide how best to use her death to my advantage."

Satochi nodded his understanding. "I feel I failed you in Finland," Satochi finally said.

"You failed to bring me back the bomb, if that is what you mean," Aioka said. "However, you did bring me Haruko."

"Yes, but I failed to kill Günter as well," Satochi said.

"No, you did kill Günter, but just not as you had planned. I have been told he is near death with the Ebola virus."

Satochi smiled. "What about the bomb?"

"I'll have that back when I need it. Polya took it and has already offered it back in exchange for her life and of course her and Günter's share of the extortion money that she already has."

"You were wise to let her live," Satochi replied.

"Polya is a mercenary. A very wise mercenary. Terrorism is her business, not her ideology. I expected her to take the bomb. She knew Günter had to die when he acted on his own."

"You must allow me to deal with this haole CIA agent who has been asking too many questions," Satochi said. "I believe he poses a great danger to your plans."

"I have already taken care of that," Aioka replied. "He should be dead within the hour."

"I only wish it was me killing him," Satochi replied.

"Eh brah, are you sure we need to go all the way to Southpoint to meet this guy?" Dano asked Eddie.

"Relax and enjoy the scenery," Eddie replied. "I don't know if Marlin has any information we can use, but he is a prime suspect in the anthrax attack, so I need to hear what he has to say. Besides, I want to check out these cliffs I've heard so much about."

"I came here once when I was a kid," Dano said. "Those brahs crazy who jump off them cliffs."

Eddie smiled and continued to check out the scenery and look for any possible traps he and Dano might be driving into. When their car reached a series of old broken-down giant windmills, the road turned to one lane.

"That's kinda spooky looking," Dano said looking at the windmills. "You'd think with all the wind out here these things would be working."

"Looks like those over there nearer the water are working," Eddie said, pointing to a series of fourteen windmills turning quickly in the wind.

"Those are huge," Dano said. "I'd say they're at least two hundred feet high and those blades must be fifty feet long."

"At least fifty feet," Eddie replied, turning to check out a car full of tourists pulled to the side to allow them to pass. "A little early in the morning for tourists, don't you think?"

"No brah, you forget all those mainlanders are at least three hours ahead in time. To them it is already late morning."

"I guess you're right," Eddie replied.

They rode in silence until they reached a fork in the single lane road.

"I think the cliffs are to the right," Dano said. "The other road leads you to the green sand beach."

Eddie turned to look behind them. He could still see the car of tourists about three miles away heading up the single-lane road. "Marlin was right. Nobody is going to sneak up on you here."

They turned to the right and drove about three hundred yards when they came upon a parking area. There were three other cars already there and several people were standing near the edge of the cliffs.

"Which one is Marlin?" Dano asked.

"I don't see him," Eddie replied. "Let's go have a look."

Eddie and Dano both exited the car, but Dano stayed next to it while Eddie walked towards the cliff. "Are you coming?"

"No brah, I feel a little safer staying away from those cliffs."

"Scared of heights?"

"No, scared of cliffs. That is a pretty strong wind blowing."

"Well, I don't think you need to worry about getting blown off,' Eddie laughed. "I'll go see what I can find out."

Dano watched as a helicopter flew near the old derelict windmill farm they had just passed. Eddie walked towards one of the wooden platforms that protruded from the cliff over the ocean.

"If you're gonna jump, you better take off your shoes," a young boy said to Eddie as he ran by and threw himself from the cliff.

"Where'd he come from," Eddie said out loud. He had passed no one as he walked up to the cliff. He looked back at Dano who was still turned, looking up the road at the helicopter flying around the windmills.

Eddie looked over the edge and saw the boy just surfacing from the clear blue water. Several other people were in the water. He followed the line of swimmers and saw most were climbing back up the cliff to the south of him. That's when he saw Marlin slowly climbing an old metal ladder hanging down the side of the cliff next to one of the platforms. He was about to call Marlin's name, but thought better of it when he saw Marlin slip and almost fall from the slick, spray-covered rungs. As he waited, another man had climbed up the rocks and walked behind him. Eddie turned to keep an eye on this man when he suddenly jumped in the air and seemed to disappear before Eddie's eyes. Eddie ran over to where the man had been standing and saw a huge crevasse with ocean water splashing within it, but no sign of the man.

"Aloha, Eddie," Marlin called. "Planning on jumping?"

"I don't think so, today," Eddie replied. "So, what has you so scared we had to meet down here?"

"Who's that?" Marlin asked, pointing to Dano.

"He's my partner. My liaison with the locals," Eddie said.

The helicopter had flown from the windmills to the ocean and was now headed towards the cliffs causing Dano, Eddie, and Marlin all to turn to look at it. Several of the cliff jumpers also started waving, thinking it was taking video of their jumps.

Two gunshots exploded from behind Marlin and Eddie. They both turned, just as Dano was falling to the ground. A man had climbed out of one of the many crevasses in the cliff and had shot Dano twice in the back. As he was going down, Dano managed to pull his Glock 9 from its holster and return fire hitting the man squarely in the face with three shots.

"Dano," Eddie yelled and started running toward him. Instantly chips of lava started flying in the air as the sound of an automatic rifle exploded from the helicopter. Bullets ripped into the body of one of the young boys standing on the wooden platform. His body crumpled and he fell sideways off the platform, bouncing against the cliff as his body tumbled into the water. Three other cliff jumpers nearby leaped without hesitation, hoping to avoid the bullets. Marlin ran for the cliff and the safety of the water below, but bullets ripped through his body before he could reach the cliff. The distraction of Marlin heading for the cliff gave Eddie just enough time to scramble to the crevasse where he had watched the man leap into less than a minute earlier. Eddie took a leap of faith praying the water was deep enough to break his fall. The shooter from the helicopter had already turned and Eddie could hear the bullets ricocheting off the lava at the top of the crevasse. Eddie hit the water and winced in pain. He thought he had hit his leg on a sharp outcropping of lava. He disappeared under the water. He came up gasping for air, but the helicopter was now directly over the crevasse and the shooter continued to spray the pool with bullets. Eddie was fortunate that, when he came up, he was at the edge of the crevasse inside a lava tube that connected to the ocean and to another crevasse further inland.

"Eh brah, try come in hea," a voice yelled. The man he had seen leap into the crevasse a moment before was waving him further inside. "It safe in hea."

Eddie couldn't argue with that, but something told him to be careful. The shooting stopped from the helicopter, but Eddie could hear that it continued to hover just overhead. As he started to swim towards the man, he noticed the trail of blood in the water coming from his leg. The other man noticed it too.

"Brah da sharks goin come in hea," the man said.

Eddie could see that the idea of sharks troubled the man more than the bullets from the helicopter. Not a good sign.

"I'm a little weak," Eddie said, "give me your hand." Eddie wanted to make sure the man had nothing in his hand as Eddie approached. He also wanted the man to think he was in worse shape than he actually was. The man lifted his left hand out of the water to grab Eddie, but left his right hand under the water. Eddie also reached out with his left hand, grabbing the man's wrist. When the man raised his right hand and it held a large diver's knife, Eddie was ready, but his attacker wasn't. Eddie yanked the man towards him with his left arm smashing his head into the man's face. Blood poured from the man's nose, turning the churning water even pinker than it already was. Eddie grabbed the wrist holding the knife and the struggle began. The knife was dropped and lost almost immediately. For what seemed like hours to Eddie, the two men wrestled in the water. Eddie began to feel his body weaken from the loss of blood from his injured leg. His attacker got behind Eddie and had his arm around Eddie's neck choking him. The attacker had braced himself against the smooth worn lava that lined the side of the tube, making it impossible for Eddie to escape the hold. It was nature that intervened as a dorsal fin of a small tiger shark approached the two men through the tube opening. Eddie had been correct in sensing the man's fear of sharks. Instantly the grip loosened and the man struggled to climb out of the water and up the crevasse. Eddie was too exhausted to move and hoped the shark would not attack. As the man quickly climbed, a loud shot rang out startling the man, causing him to fall backwards, smashing his head on the rocks knocking him unconscious as he slipped past Eddie into the water.

"Adios, brah," Eddie said to the man's floating body as he now started to climb out of the crevasse. The sound coming from the helicopter was not as it had been. It was as if someone was constantly revving the engine. As he reached the top and peered out of the crevasse, he saw that the helicopter was struggling to hover. Fluid was pouring from the engine. He looked towards the car and saw Dano leaning against it holding a hi-powered rifle. A second shot rang out from Dano's rifle and the man holding the machinegun toppled out of the helicopter. Dano turned to where he had seen Eddie climbing from the crevasses and winked.

"They just can't keep a good brah down, man," he called to Eddie.

The helicopter pilot managed to turn the helicopter away from the cliffs and headed north towards the giant windmills. He struggled to keep the helicopter from crashing and it appeared he would succeed.

Slowly Dano lifted the rifle and took careful aim. The shot rang out and hit its mark. The copter suddenly turned to the right towards the windmills. The bullet had hit the rear stabilizing propeller. An expression of sheer terror was on the pilot's face as the copter turned into the blades of one of the giant windmills. The helicopter blade slashed into the steel superstructure supporting the windmill just as its giant blade caught the helicopter underneath the passenger compartment tossing it like a toy towards the next windmill in line. This time the blade slashed down across the helicopter cleaving it in two, both halves bursting into flames and falling to the ground.

"You better call for some help, brah," Eddie said. "It looks like you started a fire."

"No brah, I put out a fire," Dano replied.

"That you did, braddah, that you did." Eddie replied.

Less than a minute later, two police cars were racing down the Southpoint Road, a Coast Guard helicopter was hovering near the crash scene, and two Navy fighter jets were circling overhead.

"I told you I would send in the cavalry," the tech back in Oahu said the moment Eddie answered his phone. "You boys put on quite a show. Everyone and their braddah was watching the show."

"Thanks for the help," Eddie replied.

"An air ambulance is on its way. I saw Dano take the two shots to the back and it looks like there were other casualties," the tech replied.

Eddie had forgotten about Marlin and turned around when he heard some of the cliff jumpers making their way back up now that the shooting was over. He saw Marlin's body crumpled on the edge of the cliff.

"Do you think he was part of the setup?" Dano asked, "or was this to take him out?"

"Probably both," Eddie said. "Aioka doesn't like to leave any loose ends."

Dano turned over the body of the first attacker he had shot. "Do you recognize him?"

"No, nor did I recognize anyone in the helicopter," Eddie replied.

"Eddie" the voice over the phone said several times, trying to get Eddie's attention once again.

"Sorry, I forgot you were there," Eddie told the tech.

"Just thought you might want to know the helicopter came from the Hilo Airport, but it made a stop on the way there."

"Made a stop where?" Eddie asked.

"In the middle of nowhere, but that nowhere is real close to the spot on the road where that old station wagon pulled over and let those guys out."

"What about the station wagon, has it made any more trips?" Eddie asked.

"It's still sitting at Honoli'i," the tech answered.

"I told Jim all about it and he ordered a couple of agents there to check the area out," the tech said.

"I hope they are braddahs. Tell them to be careful, the local surfers don't care much for outsiders coming to their beach."

"Sorry, but the only two available were haoles. Jim told them to look like tourists." the tech explained.

"That shouldn't be too hard. Those FBI guys look out of place wherever they go. Is Jim back in Hawaii?"

"He should be landing here in Oahu shortly," the tech replied. "He wants to review some video we've been taking of the islands."

"Did he say anything about Haruko?"

"Just that they're still looking for her Jim is convinced it was her and Satochi on the Taylor Production's jet," the tech replied.

"Any word on the jet?" Eddie asked.

"No, it seems to have disappeared. It never arrived as scheduled in Burbank. That's one of the things Jim will be checking out when he gets here. Cell phone reception is a little sketchy out here, so tell Jim I'll head for Hilo."

"Shouldn't you and Dano see a doctor first?" the tech asked.

"I'm not bad, just a cut on the leg from a ricochet in the crevasse. They're planning on flying Dano out. He took two shots into his vest. He may have a broken rib or two," Eddie replied.

"Eddie," Dano called, as they were putting him in the helicopter. "You may need these." Dano tossed Eddie the car keys. "I put the rifle back in the trunk. If you need anything, I've got an arsenal in there. Just take care of my ride, brah."

"I'll see you in Hilo," Eddie replied.

"Heh, Eddie, you're not going to believe this, but the station wagon is on the move again," the tech said.

"Where's it heading?" Eddie asked.

"Looks like it may be heading back towards Volcano City again," the tech replied.

"Same place as before, you think," Eddie asked.

"Maybe," the tech replied. "I didn't even notice this before, but where the helicopter landed and the station wagon pulled to, is a fairly well-known landmark."

"What is it?" Eddie asked.

"They call it the Great Crack," the tech replied. "They say if it ever broke off, the resulting tsunami racing across the ocean would be over a half-mile high."

"Where did you hear that?" Eddie asked. "I saw a special on the Discovery Channel. They said if it happened it could kill millions of people living along the West Coast of North, Central, and South America."

"Oh shit," Eddie said. "Tell me that mile marker again."

"Between marker 46 and 47 on the mauka side. Looks like a paved pullout near an overgrown dirt road."

"Thanks," Eddie replied. "I'll be in touch."

"One more thing," the tech said, "one of the men getting into the station wagon had a pronounced limp. Just thought you'd like to know."

"Thanks, brah," Eddie replied. "I think it's time for a little revenge."

"Be careful," the tech said.

"Just send me some backup," Eddie requested.

CHAPTER TWENTY-FIVE

"Welcome back to Oahu, Jim," the tech said, meeting Jim at the gate separating the Hydrogen Solution's facility from the rest of the Navy base. "I think you'll like what I found for you."

"I hope so," Jim replied. "You guys are the miracle workers."

Viktor stood behind Jim.

"This is Colonel Viktor Cheznov of the Russian FSB. The President has instructed me to keep Viktor informed on all aspects of the investigation for finding the suitcase nukes," Jim explained.

"It's a pleasure to meet you, Colonel but, unfortunately, I cannot allow you into this facility," the tech said.

"Your President has authorized me to receive full access to all phases of this investigation," Viktor began to explain.

"That may be true, but the President has no authority to grant access to British facilities or soil. This cordoned off section of the base has been given diplomatic status and is under the authority of the Queen, not the President."

Viktor turned to Jim in hopes he would intervene. "Sorry, Viktor, I guess you'll have to wait for me out here."

"I'll arrange for you to stay at one of the base VIP guest houses," the tech said.

"I won't be long," Jim said. "It'll give you a chance to freshen up a bit before we head to Hilo. I believe we're going to have some business there. At least I hope so."

"My President will not stand for this," Viktor shouted.

"I'm sorry, Colonel, but I have my orders. I suggest you have your President contact our Prime Minister," the tech replied.

"I'm sure he will," Viktor said, pulling out his cell phone and walking back to the car.

Jim was having a difficult time not smiling as the two men argued. As soon as he and the tech were inside the door, he smiled. "Yippee-ki-o-ki-ay," Jim whooped, "You wouldn't believe how happy I am to get rid of that Russian jackass for a while. I didn't know this place was a sovereign British facility."

"It's not," the tech replied. "But there's no bloody way Lord Farrelton would allow a Russian FSB agent anywhere near any of this, regardless of what your President says."

"What do you have that's so important?" Jim asked.

"This," the tech replied, pushing a switch.

"Is this in Hilo?" Jim asked.

"Yes, it's a park just north of Hilo. It's called Honoli'i Cove. It's the main surfing area on the East side of the Big Island."

"Eddie said something about that place. We have two agents watching it," Jim said.

"That would be these two men right here. They stick out like a sore thumb. If you look closely here, you can see part of a house along the Honoli'i Stream that feeds into the ocean."

"Looks like a pretty big house from what I can see," Jim replied.

"It is," the tech said. "It was considered one of the finer houses along that area until they built the highway bridge right above it. There is a long private drive leading to it from the main road behind it. It also has a clear access to the ocean by boat."

"That bridge and the jungle hide it pretty well," Jim said.

"Not from our eye-in-the-sky. Watch! See this car coming down the road?" the tech said, pointing to the screen with a laser pointer.

Jim watched as a large SUV pulled off Highway 11 and down Kahoa Street Road. A gate was opened and the car turned down an overgrown driveway toward the house.

"We lose sight of the car along the driveway and it parks under some trees, but keep watching right here."

Jim continued to watch. Suddenly, a man using a cane walked from beneath a tree, turned, and watched as a second much larger man came into view holding a woman who shuffled across the short distance to the door of the house.

"That was Haruko," Jim said. "And the man with the cane has to be Satochi."

"It appears that the girl was handcuffed and her feet were shackled," the tech said.

"Can you get me a close-up of their faces?" Jim asked.

"Sorry pal, but that's as good as it gets. The hi-powered cameras were focused elsewhere when this went down."

"Well, it's clear enough for me. We're going into that house," Jim said emphatically. "That is, if they're all still in there. How old is this tape?"

"It was recorded about three hours ago. We believe the girl...."

"Haruko," Jim interrupted.

"We believe Haruko is still inside along with the larger man who held her when they entered. The man with the cane left there about an hour ago. He and two of the surfers from the beach got into this station wagon and headed towards

Volcano National Park. We think they're headed here to a place near the Great Crack."

"The what?" Jim asked.

"The Great Crack. It's this big fissure that bisects the southern end of the Big Island. Eddie is on his way there right now."

"I can pull them and Eddie up on the screen if you'd like," the tech said.

"No, show me what's going on at the house in Honoli'i," Jim said. "I'm getting Haruko back."

Aioka knew it was time to leave the Honoli'i House. Like always, he knew this time would eventually come and he had prepared for it. His men had reported that two FBI agents were now watching the beach and the house. Viktor had contacted him to warn him that they knew Satochi and Haruko had returned to Maui and were believed to have continued on to the Big Island. He also warned him of Jim's visit to the Hydrogen Solutions facility in Oahu. Aioka was well aware of the surveillance capabilities of Hydrogen Solution's unmanned high-altitude planes and was taking new precautions because of them. Viktor's biggest concern was that Haruko knew he had been involved in her kidnapping.

"She must die," Viktor insisted to Aioka.

"She will die when she has served her purpose," Aioka assured him. "She will give us the time we need to put the next phase of our plan into action."

"I don't like it," Viktor insisted, "she must die before they discover she's there."

"You should have taken better precautions in masking your involvement if you're so concerned," Aioka replied. "I assure you that my man, Shima, will kill her before your involvement can be revealed. You are too valuable of an asset to lose."

Aioka's response seemed to calm Viktor's concerns. "I'll be in touch," Viktor said and ended the call.

Aioka did not like someone questioning his decisions. Viktor was becoming a liability. A liability that knew too much about Aioka's plans.

"Prepare the suitcase for my departure," Aioka said to Shima. "Have it taken to the van at the Makakai house."

"Yea boss."

The Makakai house was on the hill above Aioka's river house at the end of Makakai Place. Aioka had leased this house for this very purpose. If the river house was being watched from the beach or from the air, it was possible to sneak across Kahoa Street below the Mamalahoa Highway Bridge crossing Honoli'i Stream without being seen from above or from the beach or ocean.

"Have my bags taken there as well. I must prepare for out next attack on the imperialists," Aioka said.

After the suitcase nuke and his other bags had been transferred to the van, Aioka explained the next task to Shima.

"Soon government agents will come to this house. You must follow my instructions carefully if you wish to survive and if you truly want the sovereignty you so desire for your Hawaiian Nation. Satochi and I are about to begin the final phase of our operation that will drive these imperialistic Americans from this sacred forbidden land and stop their world domination. When the attack comes, you must call me so I can activate the countermeasures that I've put in place. That is extremely important. It'll buy you the time you need to move to the upper house. Let the attackers see that the woman is still alive, especially the tall one that will lead the attack. Place her by the window where they can see her. You also will be able to see her from the Makakai House. There you will find a rifle already in position that you will use to kill her, but not until the tall leader is about to release her. Do you understand?" Aioka asked.

"Yea boss," Shima replied.

"It is imperative that you do not kill her until the tall man is present. Once she is dead, use the motorcycle to escape. A helicopter will be waiting for you at the Hilo airport. Do not fail me."

"Yea boss," Shima replied, although he was unsure what some of Aioka's words meant.

Aioka knew he was taking a risk relying on Shima to kill Haruko. He did not doubt Shima's loyalty, but he questioned his ability under pressure. He wished he had some of the ninjas he had personally trained, but most were killed when his yacht, the *Kona Snow*, was destroyed along with the anthrax in Catalina Harbor several months back. He didn't yet have the opportunity or the time to recruit and train others in the art of terrorism to take their place. Like Shima, these Hawaiian terrorist recruits were faithful, but lacked the skills necessary to be ruthless assassins. He knew, however, even if Shima failed, his plans would not be affected. In fact, if Haruko lived it meant the end of Viktor and that wasn't necessarily a bad thing. Viktor was turning into more of a liability than an asset. Besides, Viktor no longer controlled the final suitcase nuke. With Günter either dead or near death, it was Polya that controlled the fate of the fourth suitcase nuke. Aioka knew that, above all, Polya was a mercenary and a business woman. Her loyalty to Viktor could easily be bought, as could the suitcase nuke he believed was now in her possession.

When Aioka reached the Makakai house, he took one final look at his Honoli'i Stream house before climbing into the van. He could see Shima already moving Haruko into position by the window. It would not be long until the FBI agents on the beach relayed the sighting to the control center where Jim Rikey and Viktor waited and watched. Nor would it be long until that entire area was washed away. That is, if what Satochi and the Discovery Channel had said proved to be true.

It was Shima's station wagon. There was no doubt about that and it was parked exactly where the tech told him it would be. Eddie at first drove past to see if there was anyone around. When he saw no one he, called the tech to see if he had a view of the area.

"Sorry buddy," the tech said, "but your boss has pulled seniority on you."

"Jim's there?" Eddie asked.

"He arrived about twenty minutes ago. I believe we've found Haruko."

"Where?" Eddie asked.

"At the house on the Honoli'i Stream by the park," the tech replied.

"The same park that the station wagon is always visiting?" Eddie asked.

"That's the one," the tech replied. "We also got a report from one of the agents on the beach that a woman fitting Haruko's description can be seen sitting inside. Jim's on his way there now with a team."

"Sounds like a setup," Eddie replied.

"Jim thinks so too, but says they have to move in. He's taking a SWAT team and Navy SEALS as backup if needed," the tech replied.

"Do I still have backup on the way?" Eddie asked.

"Dano was cleared by the hospital and he and some policeman named Kamejiro Hale. I'm guessing they're about an hour or so behind you. Dano said to tell you to take the AK-47 and extra clips if you go in before they arrive."

"Tell him thanks, and I will."

"He also said there is a box of grenades if you need them in with the spare tire. Who is this guy, Rambo?" the tech asked.

"Just be glad he's on our side," Eddie replied. "If you talk to Jim, tell him Eddie said 'Good luck, cowboy'."

"That's funny, that's the same thing he told me to tell you."

CHAPTER TWENTY-SIX

"I stay skehd man, is kinda hot. I tink Pele stay mad."

"Just keep placing that dynamite where I showed you," Satochi yelled to the man in the crevasse. A second man was pouring another bucket of cement over the rocks that had been piled around the suitcase nuke.

"Long time already?" the brah asked.

"We still have two hours until it goes off. More than enough time to finish our work and get to a safe distance," Satochi assured them.

"I dunno, boss, Pele stay mad cause we stay doin."

"Pele wants our sacred land back as much as we do. She is here to help us; this is her kapu 'āina." Satochi said to ease the man's concern.

The man mixing and pouring the cement climbed up the ladder in order to lower more water down into the crevasse to mix with the cement. He picked up the binoculars to scan the horizon as Satochi had trained him to constantly do.

"Ho boss," the brah said, "who dat pullin in by da station wagon? Brah he comin' by us, eh he got one gun."

"You know what to do," Satochi said, moving behind an old lava formation on the far side of the crevasse.

"Grab the other end of the ice chest," the young man told his partner as they exited the pickup truck. The man reached into another smaller chest and pulled out a beer.

"What the hell is in here?" he asked his partner.

"Two radios, four armored vests, four auto-assault pistols, and several spare clips," his partner replied.

"What, no ham sandwiches?"

"Smartass! Let's just get this down to the beach."

Both the men were members of the SWAT unit Jim had requested to assist the raid on Aioka's house. They looked no different than the other local surfers on the beach, but immediately raised the suspicion of all the other surfers. Honoli'i Cove was the finest surfing area on the east side of the Big Island and everyone there knew who the local surfers were. Outsiders were not welcome. Especially outsiders trying to pass themselves off as surfers. The two men carried the ice chest to a spot near several large rocks that could serve as cover. They sat down on the chest and pretended to watch the surfers.

"What da hell dat?" said one of the brahs sitting under the lanai of Aioka's house.

One of the local tour helicopters had suddenly appeared from around the point and was slowly cruising down the coast towards downtown Hilo.

"Look like some haoles on tour of da coastline," Shima replied.

The brah lifted his middle finger and waved it at the helicopter.

"Aloooohaaaa, you haole assholes. Go back to Cali."

"Where's your aloha spirit?" Shima said.

"Wat, I sed aloha," he responded, as both men laughed.

"That is Haruko sitting by the window. Looks like she's tied up," Jim said as the helicopter continued slowly by the cove.

"Why isn't she hidden?" Viktor asked.

"They know we're coming. It's a setup," Jim replied. "I think they intend to kill her when we attack."

Viktor felt a sense of relief hearing Jim's opinion, but of course did not show it. "How do you intend to save her?" Viktor asked.

"We need to get our men in as close as possible then go in fast," Jim said.

He turned to the pilot, "I need to speak to our men on the fishing boat." Seconds later he was connected.

"I need two sharpshooters in position to take out any bad guys in that room where Haruko is sitting."

"That may be difficult. There is no way we can position the boat to see the entire room," the captain replied. "And these waves have us bobbing like a cork."

"I need no excuses," Jim replied. "It may be the only way to save Haruko's life."

"We'll do what we can," the captain assured him.

Jim called the tech back in Oahu. "What's the status on the Navy cruiser?"

"It is about thirty minutes to the North, heading your way, but sticking close to the coastline. The team leader has informed us he will drop four men in the water who will approach from below near the stream outlet and have three additional men on wave-runners hidden behind the boat if necessary."

"Just tell him to be careful, they're expecting us," Jim said.

"Will do," replied the tech.

"Circle around and put this thing down," Jim ordered the pilot. "It's time to saddle up."

Eddie had a bad feeling he was walking into a trap. He tried to call the tech back in Oahu to get an overhead view of the situation, but the phone continued to be busy. Eddie had no idea where he was headed, only a general direction the tech had given him. He stuck mostly to the old road, which at times was nothing more than a tall patch of grass with impressions where someone had recently walked. Eddie had been walking about a mile continuing on the road as it turned several times. The road turned towards the ocean and began to parallel a large, not so ancient flow, of black lava. Eddie saw several cairns built out across the expanse of lava. Eddie left the road and began following the stacked lava rock trail markers. Only a couple of hundred yards onto the barren lava, Eddie began to make out what appeared to be a fence.

"Damn, I wish he'd get off the phone," Eddie said to himself as he tried once again to call the tech.

As he continued towards the fence, he suddenly came upon the Great Crack. He was not prepared for the massive crevasse that now lay before him.

"It's huge," Eddie said to himself, as he carefully approached the crevasse. He stopped several feet from the edge when his footsteps took on a hollow sound.

"That's not good," he said to himself, backing away from the sheer cliffs of the crevasse. That's when he noticed the boxes of dynamite stacked near a pile of rocks.

"Drop the rifle or die now, Eddie Popp," a voice called out from behind him.

Eddie recognized Satochi's voice and knew he was in trouble.

Aioka boarded the *Grand Maui* as it prepared to leave the Hilo harbor. He had booked passage for the entire re-christening voyage that left three days ago from Honolulu.

Hawaiian Cruise Lines had heavily promoted the cruise in hopes that the exceedingly rich and famous would return after the horrific anthrax attack that killed so many of the passengers. Bill Casey and several dozen of his influential friends, many of them shareholders in the cruise line, all had joined the weeklong party when it started with the live telecast from the Aloha Tower. The cruise was scheduled to end in two more days back in Honolulu with a larger party than the sendoff party. Aioka had one of his men carry his two suitcases to his stateroom. One was the suitcase nuke that Aioka would use to end America's imperialism.

"I want men all along Kahoa Street," Jim said to the SWAT team leader.

"We have six men in place along the beach, the two agents that have kept the place under surveillance and four who are undercover," he replied over the radio.

One of the SWAT team called in from the beach, "Looks like several of the locals have been slowly making their way to the house. I think they know we're here."

"They've known that for quite a while," Jim replied. "We won't be sneaking in from the front. What's it look like from the road?"

"There are only two men behind the house near the garage. Neither appear to be armed. My men can easily take these two out without making a sound, if you're sure these guys are hostiles," the head of the SWAT unit said.

"Anybody associated with that house is to be considered a terrorist," Jim replied. "Everybody listen up. We have seen at least four men inside, two behind the house, and at least six on the lanai or in the front yard. That number could grow. We know Satochi has left the house, but he is not the number one man. Aioka Matsuura is in charge of the Red

Summit. Satochi answers to him, as do all these other men. Don't underestimate him. He's always thinking three steps ahead and seems to have a contingency plan to deal with any situation. I have personally seen him use explosives on several occasions and he wouldn't hesitate to kill his own men if it was to his benefit. Our main objective is to rescue Haruko, but be careful, there is a reason he has her sitting in the window like that. There's a good chance either she or the room is wired to a bomb."

"What about a sharpshooter? Could this Aioka have one assigned to take out Haruko if we attack?" one of the team members asked.

"That's a possibility, but the only boat in range is ours. It might be smart to check out the jungle up to the road just in case," Jim replied.

"I'll handle that," one of the SWAT team sharpshooters said. "I need to find a good spot to set up anyway."

"Good," Jim said. "If Aioka is inside, he'll have several escape routes planned, so be on your toes. He probably even has a tunnel leading out of there, so I want all the local police manning the perimeter to pay close attention. Search all vehicles trying to leave the area. We'll also need to check out and evacuate all nearby houses. The men in the boat need to keep an eye on any other boats trying to enter the area. That's how he got away once before. Are there any questions from the team leaders?"

"What if the house is booby trapped?"

"We have two FBI bomb experts en route. They'll be here before we make our move. I saved our biggest concern for last. Some of you are already aware of this, but those of you who are not, you need to know that there may be one or more nuclear weapons inside the house."

A deafening silence greeted Jim's remark.

"We believe Aioka is responsible for the nuclear blast in Wichita. We also believe Satochi either delivered, or went to retrieve another of the stolen Russian nukes in Helsinki. Either way, we know one of the nukes is still in Finland. That means there are two left unaccounted for. Chances are they're still here on the Big Island. Team leaders have been given pictures of the suitcases housing the nukes. If you see one, don't move it. Don't even touch it. However, it becomes your main objective to guard it until my FBI experts can check it out, even if you have to sacrifice the life of the hostage to do so."

Saying the last sentence was very difficult for Jim. He loved Haruko dearly, but knew the safety of the thousands who would die if one of the nukes was detonated far outweighed his selfish love.

"If there are no more questions, everybody move into position. We'll start our approach in twenty minutes. Don't make a move until you hear from me," Jim ordered.

"How's it look from above?" Jim asked the tech back in Oahu on the secure phone line that remained open.

"Besides the barriers set up by the local police, everything looks normal. No boats coming in, no helicopters in the area, and no radiation signatures. I wish I could tell you how many men are inside the house, but that metal roof screws up my heat sensing equipment. That's something Hydrogen Solutions needs to take care of," the tech said.

"Any word from Eddie?" Jim asked.

"There is no way he can reach me if you want this line to remain open," the tech explained. "I did take a look from the wide-angle camera and it appears his car is now parked next to the station wagon along Highway 11, but with that camera I can't really see people. I can put it on your computer screen if you like?"

"No, I have enough to look at with the overhead shot you're already sending and the views from the camera on the boat and the camera our man has on the beach. Is back-up on the way for Eddie?" Jim asked.

"Yes, but still at least an hour away," the tech said.

"See if you can find a helicopter to pick up Dano and the cop," Jim said. "I don't like Eddie facing Satochi alone."

"I'll see what I can do," the tech replied.

Jim closed his eyes and sighed.

"Ding, ding, ding…" a soft bell began to chime in Aioka's Honoli'i house.

"Dat bad," Shima said, "somebody break into da Makakai house."

"Brah, you bettah call da boss, I know like" one of the brahs left to guard the house said.

Shima dialed the phone. "I tink deh find da rifle in Makakai house," Shima said when Aioka answered.

Aioka could hear the alarm in the background. "You know what to tell the brahs," Aioka said. "Have the men lead them away from the house. Use the wave-runners, I'll launch the sub. That should distract them enough for you to get to the motorcycle. I'll have the helicopter waiting for you as we arranged. Use the woman as your shield if necessary. They won't shoot as long as you have her."

"Yea boss," Shima answered. He didn't like the way things were going, but what Aioka said made sense. He would have one of the men place the suitcase on the lanai, then have everyone head for the beach creating chaos. He would have the two guards behind the house escort him up the hill. He knew they were both armed and trained for combat. As were the three brahs who would be on the wave-runners. They were to exit the mouth of the river, take a sharp right and follow the coast towards Hilo, after taking out the fishing boat which Shima knew was part of the FBI team watching the house. Although he couldn't see it, some of the surfers from the beach had told him about the Navy cruiser just around the point. Aioka predicted this. That was what the sub was for.

Aioka removed a second cell phone and binoculars from a small waist pack. The phone was programmed to call and activate the submarine. He leisurely walked to the rail on the starboard side of the *Grand Maui*. The guests joining the cruise and Bill Casey's party in Hilo had all done so and the passengers who opted to visit the shops in Hilo had all returned. The ship slowly began to pull away from the pier.

"It's show time," Aioka said, showing just a hint of a smile.

Eddie allowed the rifle to gently slide from his hands to the ground.

"Now step away from it," Satochi ordered.

Eddie had never known Satochi to carry a gun. He still had not seen Satochi and for a moment contemplated diving to the ground for the rifle and spinning away firing. That idea quickly vanished when he saw another man, who was holding a gun, exit the crevasse from a ladder about ten feet to his left.

Eddie turned around to face the murderer of his brother. It was fortunate that he had not gone for the rifle. Satochi held a 9-mm Glock in his right hand and held a cane in his left.

"So nice of you to come to me," Satochi said. "It saves me the trouble of hunting you down."

"Whatever I can do to help out," Eddie replied staring at the head of the cane with the large Tiger-shark tooth embedded in the koa wood.

"A beautiful piece, don't you agree," Satochi replied, "and very deadly."

"Is that what you used to kill my brother?"

"Killing your brother was a mistake. Not a regrettable one, for you see, it has brought you to me."

"Is that what you used to carve up those tourists found down at Punalu'u?" Eddie asked struggling to remain calm.

"They, like you, stumbled upon this very site. We couldn't allow them to tell anyone what they found."

"What did they find?" Eddie said. "Three men playing with dynamite in the middle of a lava field? How serious is that?"

"I guess you don't watch much educational television," Satochi said. "This is called the Great Crack."

"So I've been told," Eddie replied.

"Oh, so you are an educated man," Satochi sneered. "This crack is over eight miles long and in some places, like right in front of you, over eighty feet deep. It bisects the Ka'u District. According to research, if this crack ruptured and the southern flank collapsed into the ocean, they estimate that a tsunami almost a mile high would slam into the coasts of the Americas, killing millions."

"Impossible," Eddie replied.

"Don't be a fool, Eddie Popp. How do you think all of these cliffs got here in the first place? They all are a result of a catastrophic flank collapse," Satochi replied.

"Even so, do you really think a few dozen cases of dynamite will make that happen? If you do, you are crazier than I thought," Eddie laughed.

"Eh boss," the man down in the Great Crack called out. "Get plenty steam coming up. Not safe, eh."

"I'm sending down Mr. Popp. I would like to get his opinion about the situation," Satochi said. "Down the ladder Mr. Popp."

Eddie had no choice but to do as Satochi ordered. The further down the ladder he climbed, the hotter and fouler the air became.

"Me tink it not safe too, boss," Eddie yelled at Satochi, mimicking the man still at the bottom of the crack.

"Now move over to that pile of rocks and have a seat," Satochi ordered when Eddie had reached the bottom.

The other man quickly ran to the ladder and climbed out, pulling the ladder up and out of the Great Crack as soon as he reached the top.

"It looks even deeper from down there, don't you think?" Satochi said, looking down at Eddie.

Eddie looked around at the walls. It would not be impossible to climb out, but very difficult and time-consuming he decided.

"You plan on just leaving me down here so I can get a steam-bath?" Eddie asked.

Satochi smiled at Eddie's humor. "Look where you are sitting," Satochi said. "Look what's under that pile of rock."

Eddie tried to pull off the top layer of rocks. He could see that cement had been poured over them but he wasn't sure why. He kicked at one of the rocks, knocking it loose from the fresh cement.

"Looks like a cheap suitcase," Eddie yelled up to Satochi.

"You were correct in saying that a few cases of dynamite would have no affect on the crack," Satochi said. "However, the nuclear device in that 'cheap suitcase' is equivalent to 1000 tons of high explosives. I think that's more than enough to rupture this Great Crack."

Eddie wiped the sweat from his face and coughed. The temperature was rising noticeably in the crack and the volcanic gasses hung heavily in the air. Eddie thought he could see a dim red glow up one of the lava tubes.

"Don't inhale too much of that vog," Satochi said. "I want you awake when the nuke detonates. Unfortunately, I'm afraid you'll miss the tsunami."

Eddie knew he had at least twenty minutes until the bomb exploded. At least that is how long he figured it would take for Satochi to reach a safe distance from ground zero.

"Hell, I'm ground zero," Eddie said to himself as he tried to remember what he had been taught in that nuclear terrorism class the CIA made him take.

"Ten minutes," Jim said into the radio.

"Those two men behind the house just disappeared," one of the SWAT team members said over the radio.

"Disappeared where?" Jim asked.

"I think they went back inside," the man replied sheepishly, knowing he should have been more alert.

"Jim, they're closing the drapes, I can no longer see Haruko," the agent in the boat said.

A loud roar erupted from upstream as the engines on two wave-runners and a small speedboat came to life. "What in tarnation is that?" Jim asked but, before anyone answered, the three boats exploded from an overhang of vines hiding a boathouse next to the main house.

"Jim, one of the men from inside just sat a large suitcase on the lanai, opened it up for a second, and then took off running. It's like a jail break, there are people running in all directions," the observer from the boat reported.

The tech back in Oahu was monitoring all the transmissions. "Jim, it's not a nuke. If that suitcase is a nuke, my plane would have registered the radiation signature when it was opened. There was none, I repeat there was none."

One of the terrorists on the wave-runner opened fire on the fishing boat. As the sound of the machine gun burst echoed across the water, everyone on the beach dove to the sand and those still surfing sought shelter below the water.

The four undercover SWAT team members, as well as the two FBI agents in position on the beach, had all drawn their weapons, but were not sure whom or where to shoot. The beach was complete chaos. Just as Aioka had envisioned.

A loud blast came from the horn of the Navy cruiser as it raced around the point north of Honoli'i Cove. Three Navy SEALS on wave-runners rushed past the cruiser in pursuit of the two who had fired on the fishing boat and of the speedboat racing down the coast.

"I count two people and a driver on the speedboat," the observer from the fishing boat reported. The wave-runners raced in and out of the crashing waves, cutting sharp turns sending up a blinding spray, all the while firing their machine guns. Stray bullets were heading in all directions, hitting several in the panicked crowd trying to flee the beach.

"Was it Aioka and Haruko?" Jim asked.

"Impossible to tell," the observer replied.

"I'll take care of the speedboat," the pilot of the helicopter said. I've got a sharpshooter on board with me."

"Just make sure you hit no hostages," Jim ordered.

Things seemed to be quickly spiraling out of control, but Jim knew that was how Aioka wanted it to appear. Jim knew things were not always what they seemed to be.

"I need a team in that house now," Jim exclaimed. "We need to find Aioka and free Haruko. I'm sure they haven't left the house. Don't touch the suitcase on the lanai. It's not a nuke, but it still could be a bomb.

Shots rang out near the house. "Jim, we got shots fired from the side of the house," one of the agents on the beach reported.

"Watch your back, guys. Any of those people on the beach may be a hostile," Jim warned.

"Roger that," the agent replied.

"Jim, I've got a clear shot at a man shooting out of an upstairs window," the sharpshooter on the hill above the house called in.

"Take the shot." Before Jim could finish his sentence, the crack of a hi-powered rifle echoed off the cliffs.

"Positive impact, man is down," the sharpshooter said.

Shima entered the office next to the living room. There was a large screen that showed several views of the beach and hill area behind the main house. On the desk was a panel with more than a dozen toggle switches. Each switch controlled a cache of C-4 hidden beneath the sand and ground.

"Time to ma-ke die dead," Shima said and flicked the first switch.

Aioka watched as the wave-runners tore from their hiding place and raced towards the fishing boat. The speedboat seemed to be getting away until a helicopter swooped in behind it. The sound of gunfire was louder than he expected and several passengers moved to the rail to see what was happening.

"Are those gun shots?" one of the passengers asked.

"I believe they're fireworks," Aioka replied. "It looks like a wedding celebration."

"How wonderful," one of the ladies replied and the entire group headed back towards the bar. The band started to play and the gunshots were soon forgotten.

The Navy cruiser had rounded the point and he saw the two Navy wave-runners pull forward and begin firing on his men.

"Now it's time to suffer some real consequences," Aioka said, and pushed a button on the phone. Silently a small submarine left the boathouse. Aioka only wished he would be around to see what would happen next, but the *Grand Maui* had left the harbor area and was quickly heading toward the next stop on Bill Casey's traveling party.

Eddie knew he couldn't stop the nuke from exploding. His only chance was to get out of the Great Crack and then run like hell. He headed straight to a pile of supplies Satochi's men had left at the bottom of the crack. There was some dried fish and fruit, a little water, two flashlights, and three cases of dynamite.

"I think this will do," Eddie said.

He grabbed several sticks of the dynamite and tied them together. He stuck a fuse into the centerpiece. He looked around the crack trying to decide the best placement. His plan was to try to blast the sheer wall of the crack and create a rubble pile he could use to climb out. It was a great plan until he realized he had nothing to light the fuse.

The ground began to tremble as a small earthquake rocked the area. Eddie knew it was caused by the magma moving beneath the ground. He looked to where he thought he had seen a slight red glow earlier. Even through the thickening vog, Eddie could see that lava was slowly moving down a tube towards the crevasse that entrapped him.

Eddie made two more bundles of dynamite. He knew the ancient lava above the new flow would be weakened by the severe heat. He tossed the first bundle of dynamite into the tube that contained the pool of lava. Immediately the dynamite exploded, showering the crevasse with shards of broken lava and a few fresh gobs of molten lava. Part of the tube containing the fresh lava collapsed, but was of no help to Eddie. In fact, the explosion had caused the lava to begin pouring from an open fissure at the bottom of the tube.

"That's not good," Eddie said, trying to plan his next move. He took the second bundle of dynamite and used one of the glowing gobs of lava to light the fuse. He considered placing it in the pile of rocks that covered the suitcase nuke, but had second thoughts.

"No use ending this any sooner than I have to," Eddie said.

This time he placed the dynamite in a small tube on the side of the crack near where the ladder had been. He ran to the far end of the crevasse and lay on the ground behind a large lava boulder. He had made the fuse extra-long to give him a chance to better protect him from this explosion. Once he had placed the charge, he realized too late that it was in the direct path of the flowing lava.

Satochi had heard the first explosion and decided he had better investigate. He sent one of his men ahead to get the car and come down the road as close as possible to pick them up. He and the other man headed back to the Great Crack. They arrived just as Eddie dove behind the boulder. They thought Eddie was hiding to keep from being shot.

"Why would I want to shoot you, when I can watch you burn up in the lava," Satochi yelled down to Eddie. The lava was moving along the edge nearest Satochi, towards Eddie, and away from the suitcase nuke.

"See boss, I tole you Pele stay mad," the man said.

"Don't get too close to the edge," Satochi warned.

Satochi realized too late that he was not the reason Eddie stayed hidden behind the boulder. The ground in front of him flew into the air as the dynamite Eddie had placed directly below them exploded. The man standing in front of Satochi now lay battered and bruised by the chunks of flying rock.

"Brah, try help me," the man called out to Satochi.

Inside the Great Crack much rubble had fallen from the walls, but not in a position to help Eddie escape. It had created a damn blocking the ever-increasing flow and the lava began to pool around and below the suitcase nuke. In the crevasse wall where Eddie had placed the charge, the blast had collapsed the wall of another tube parallel to the crevasse undermining the ground above. Lava rushed in to fill this new void.

"Boss help me, I tink my foot stay broken," the man called to Satochi.

Satochi took a step towards the man, but quickly stopped when he heard the hollow echo of the ground beneath him.

"Looks like you will be joining me for the fireworks," Eddie said, pointing to the lava that was coming closer to the nuke. "I don't think you'll be able to limp away in time."

In his anger, Satochi pulled his gun and fired several shots at Eddie, who easily ducked behind the boulder.

"If I were you, I'd be thinking about getting away, not getting revenge," Eddie called out from behind the rock.

Another small earthquake shook the Great Crack, causing rocks to tumble from the walls and opening a large lava tube at the end of the crevasse away from the flowing lava. The tube was nearly seven feet tall at the entrance.

The man with Satochi started dragging his body across the lava, away from the cliff, towards Satochi. Satochi could hear the lava cracking as the man pulled himself across the smooth lava.

"Stop," Satochi yelled. "The lava cannot support both our weights."

"Help m-me," the man pleaded and continued to pull his body away from the cliff.

"Don't move," Satochi yelled, but the man didn't listen. Satochi turned his pistol toward the man and continued to fire until the clip was emptied.

Satochi slowly took a step backwards trying to move safely away from the edge, but the lava below combined with the explosion had weakened the top of the lava tube where Satochi stood. Eddie heard a sharp crack as the roof of the tube collapsed sending the dead man skidding into the molten lava below. Satochi had used his cane as a mountain climbers pick, lashing out away from the crack, catching the tiger-shark tooth in a small indentation and now hung precariously on the tilted lava shelf.

The quake opened up other fissures in the crevasse and lava began to pour into the crack, moving closer to Eddie.

"Wish I could stick around for your big ending," Eddie said, "but Pele has shown me favor." Eddie picked up one of the flashlights left by Satochi's men. "Your brah was right. I tink you made Pele angry." As Eddie turned to run down the lava tube, the tiger-shark tooth on Satochi's cane snapped from the strain, sending Satochi down the smooth lava shelf as if he were on a children's slide. He screamed as his body hit the molten lava, but only for a second, before his body burst into flames.

"Hope you saw that little brother," Eddie said and sprinted down the open lava tube.

"Jim, I've got a visual of what may be a submarine leaving the mouth of the stream and heading into the ocean," the tech back in Oahu said, watching the events unfold from the cameras on the hydrogen plane high above the island.

"Captain, did you hear that?" Jim asked.

"Affirmative, we have it on sonar and will intercept," the captain of the Navy cruiser replied.

"Just be careful, it could be another of Aioka's tricks," Jim warned.

"The speedboat looks to be headed for the Wailuku River Bridge in downtown Hilo," the helicopter pilot said. "I won't have a good view once it goes under the bridge and up the river. Better get some backup in here."

Jim started to call for the local police to head to the area, when the pilot interrupted.

"Jim, the driver of the speedboat just bailed out into the bay. The boat is heading straight into the bridge at full speed."

A huge explosion ripped the metal grated bridge apart as the speedboat plowed into one of the bridge supports.

"It was a bomb," the pilot said.

Before Jim could respond, the picnic shelter in Honoli'i Park exploded in a giant fireball killing and wounding several of the beachgoers who had ran there for protection from the bullets. Screams now drowned out the random gunfire still happening on the ocean.

Shima smiled as he watched the chaos on the beach. He scanned the several screens on the office wall to decide which switch to hit.

"I tink dis one," he said flicking the toggle next to the number five on the board. Immediately, another explosion ripped apart a Volkswagen van parked on Kahoa Street next to the staircase leading away from the park.

"Jim, the entire area must be booby-trapped, we got to get those people out of there now," the observer said.

Out in the ocean the three Navy SEALS had finally killed the two terrorists on the wave-runners.

"This is priority, I want all team members on the beach to move civilians into the water immediately," Jim ordered. The park is wired with explosives."

No sooner had Jim made the order than another bomb exploded near the SWAT team members with the ice chest, injuring two of them, but not seriously. Following that, another truck on Kahoa Street blew apart, sending shrapnel in all directions.

"Stay time to go," Shima said moving another of the toggle switches. This time the Makakai house exploded killing the SWAT sharpshooter and sending burning debris into the jungle-covered hillside.

Haruko sat dazed, still tied to the chair in the living room. She had been kept drugged from the day Satochi kidnapped her in Helsinki, her brain in a constant haze.

"Let's go, we outta hea kotonk," Shima said, cutting the ropes holding Haruko to the chair. Haruko still had her ankles bound to keep her from moving quickly. However, she had been sitting for so long, she was barely able to stand, let alone walk. Shima had to carry her to the back door. He leaned her against the wall while he looked to make sure the way was safe. Haruko slid down the wall.

"Eh wake up I sed," Shima said, slapping her hard. "Time to go."

The flashlight did little to light the lava tube, but it was enough for Eddie to see the floor in front of him. The bottom and sides of the tube were smooth, although the floor was covered with a few smaller rocks that had fallen from the ceiling. Eddie had gone only about one hundred feet when a large explosion shook the tube, bringing down some larger rocks from the ceiling.

"That couldn't have been the nuke," Eddie said. Then he remembered the cache of dynamite. The lava had reached the crates of dynamite, blowing a huge hole in the bottom of the crevasse causing more lava to come pouring out of new fissures and into the tube Eddie had entered. Eddie could see the glow of the rapidly moving lava coming nearer. It was moving almost as fast as he was down the tube.

"This is not good," Eddie said, "not good at all," and he picked up his pace.

The small submarine headed straight out of the Honoli'i Stream and into the ocean. It remained around ten feet below the water and could easily be seen by the cameras on the hydrogen plane.

"We've got the sub on sonar," the captain of the Navy cruiser reported to Jim. "We'll intercept it."

"Jim, tell the captain that the sub is not trying to get away, but is heading directly for his ship," the tech in Oahu reported.

"It's another bomb," Jim said. "Captain, destroy the sub before it hits your ship."

"Are you sure? Your hostage may be aboard." the captain replied.

Jim paused for a second. "Blow it up, Captain, you cannot risk your ship."

"That might be easier said than done," the captain replied. "I don't think our deck guns will be effective and I cannot risk launching a torpedo or depth charge this close to shore."

"Jim," the tech said, "He better do something quick."

On deck, the twenty-millimeter computer operated Mk 15 Phalanx locked on to the approaching sub. A loud buzz emanated from the gun signifying that it was spitting out almost three thousand rounds a minute. Whether it would be successful the Captain didn't know.

"Brace for impact," the Captain announced to the crew. The buzz lasted less than four seconds before a huge explosion rocked the cruiser. The bow of the ship lifted out of the water and came crashing down, knocking several men to the deck and tossing two overboard.

"Damage report," the Captain ordered.

"Sir, the gun worked. The sub blew up twenty feet from the ship," the computer operator reported.

"We have several men bruised up and a couple of broken bones," the lieutenant reported.

"Some damage to our rudder," the engineer reported. "She'll be difficult to maneuver.

"Sorry, Jim, but we're going to have to pull back to a safer location. I won't be much help if I can't steer this thing," the Captain explained.

"I understand, take care of your men," Jim replied.

No explosions had occurred on the beach or in the vicinity for almost a minute, but it was still chaos on the beach as the SWAT team tried to get everyone into the water and off the beach.

"There are too many people here, we're going to need some help," one of the FBI men on the beach called in.

"What's happening at the house, anybody have a clear view?" Jim asked.

"As soon as these shock waves settle down, I should have a clear view," the observer on the fishing boat called in.

"SWAT six, can you see the back of the house?" Jim asked. "SWAT six do you read me?" Still no answer came.

"If he was in that house on the hill behind the target," the tech said, "SWAT six won't be answering anytime soon. One of the explosions took it out."

"Jim," the observer from the boat called, "I see no activity in or in front of the house."

"Roger that," Jim replied.

"Wait a minute," the observer said, "I see two people crossing the street behind the house and heading into the jungle."

"Are they civilians or bad guys?" Jim asked.

"One of them is your hostage. It's Haruko," he said excitedly. "The man seems to be dragging her along."

"Who do we have in the area?" Jim asked.

"Nobody," the SWAT leader replied. "All my men are on the beach side except for six whom we assume are down."

"What about local police?" Jim said.

"Most have headed to the bridge explosion in town," the leader replied.

"Then I guess it's you and me," Jim said, turning towards Viktor. "It's up to us to save Haruko."

The heat was oppressive as was the foul air in the lava tube. Each time Eddie turned to look behind him, the red glow of the advancing lava was brighter. The tube began to shake as another earthquake brought on by the moving magma shook violently. Eddie had to cover his head to protect himself from the rocks falling from the ceiling of the tube.

As soon as the shaking stopped, Eddie continued running. He had no other choice. His biggest fear was that the lava tube would suddenly end. As he ran, he continued to mull over in his mind what affect the lava would have on the nuke. He knew Hawaiian lava tended to be on the hot side, between 1100 to 1200 C. He also knew this was above the melting point of uranium and of plutonium.

"So, if the nuke was submerged in the lava long enough it would just melt," Eddie decided. "But according to Satochi, it was set to go off in about twenty minutes, and that was almost ten, no fifteen, minutes ago," Eddie continued to talk to himself. "The lava may not even have reached the nuke by then."

Another earthquake shook the tube, but no rocks fell from the ceiling. Eddie turned and could now see the lava and not just the glow from it. He was quickly running out of time.

"Whoa," Eddie said. "The uranium might not melt too quickly, but the control circuitry is plastic, copper, and solder. That would melt in no time!"

Another earthquake, this time much stronger, knocked Eddie off his feet. Rocks from the lava tube's ceiling rained down upon his head and then night turned to day. A skylight had formed when the top of the tube collapsed into the tunnel. Eddie leaped to his feet and scrambled up the debris left by the collapsing ceiling. It was just high enough for him to grab the ledge and try to pull himself out of the tube. His first two tries were unsuccessful, as the lava shelf broke off from his weight. With the molten lava just yards away, he was at last able to pull himself from the tube and roll away from the skylight. When he thought he was far enough away, he stood up and began running toward the ocean, angling away from the tube. His footsteps echoed from the hollowed tubes just below the surface. Tubes that may also be flowing with the fresh lava.

He had run for about five minutes without stopping and was nearing the ocean when he heard the sound of an approaching helicopter.

"Eddie, Eddie," it was Dano calling him. The helicopter landed near him. "Damn, I'm glad you are safe, you had us real worried."

"We've got no time to talk, there's a nuke up there set to explode any second," Eddie yelled over the sound of the whirling blades. He jumped into the copter and the pilot began to lift off before the door was even closed.

"Head low and towards the ocean," Eddie ordered, but at that very second a huge explosion blew the helicopter towards the ocean.

Jim's six-shooters were strapped to his sides even though he had not fired them since accidentally killing the tourist in Kauai several months before.

"You had better give me a gun," Viktor said, as they exited the mobile command center and headed down Highway 19 towards the jungle where the observer had seen Haruko.

"Ain't gonna happen, partner," Jim replied. "My orders were to keep you informed as to what was happening. Giving you a gun is not part of my orders."

Viktor wanted to argue, but knew Jim would not change his mind. His hope was that Shima would kill Haruko before she could tie him to her kidnapping.

Shima struggled as he tried to move through the jungle while carrying Haruko. "You gotta walk," Shima said to his prisoner as he pulled out a large knife and cut the bindings securing Haruko's feet. She was still groggy from the drugs and stumbled to the ground. "If you no get up, I ganna shoot you right hea," Shima told her. He yanked her to her feet and started to pull her behind him. Twice more she stumbled before gaining her balance.

"Anybody got a visual on Haruko?" Jim said into the radio.

"I see movement near the top of the hill by the bridge, but I can't say for certain it's Haruko," the observer from the boat replied.

"I can," the tech said. "Haruko and a large man are about to exit the jungle not more than fifty feet in front of you. Be careful, he has a gun in his hand."

"Thanks," was all Jim replied.

At that instant Shima stumbled from the jungle pulling Haruko behind him.

"Drop the gun," Jim yelled, pulling his six-shooter from its holster for the first time in months.

Shima pulled Haruko in front of him and placed his gun under her chin. "I swea I goin blow her head off."

Viktor knew Jim was an expert shot and could have easily shot Shima before he could pull the trigger, but Jim froze. Just like he had at the coffee plantation back on Kauai.

Shima started backing onto the bridge crossing over the Honoli'i Stream over two hundred feet below.

"Shoot him, Jim" Viktor said, trying to force Jim into a bad shot.

"Shut up, Viktor," Jim replied.

"Yea, yea, yea, shut up Viktor," Shima laughed, for he too could tell Jim was afraid to shoot.

Slowly Shima backed across the bridge keeping Haruko between him and Jim and staying close to the edge.

"You can't let him get away, Jim," Viktor said continuing to badger Jim.

"I said shut up, Viktor."

"If you shoot me, she comin over da rail wit me," Shima threatened.

Without warning the bridge began to sway and a rumble rose from the ground.

"It's an earthquake," Viktor yelled, sprinting off the bridge fearing it would collapse.

Shima too began to panic, losing his grip on Haruko's neck, but still standing behind her with the gun. Haruko's hands were tied behind her, but her feet had been freed and her drug-clouded mind was beginning to clear.

"Sayonara, asshole," Haruko said to a stunned Shima, as she leaped into the air and kicked him squarely in the throat, collapsing his larynx.

Shima grabbed for something to hold to keep from falling over the railing. He grabbed Haruko's hair, knowing it wouldn't stop his fall, but at least he would take her with him. To his surprise, Haruko's wig was all he grabbed and he tumbled over the railing and onto the lanai of the Honoli'i house below. His impact was just enough to move the mercury switch on the fake suitcase nuke causing a large quantity of C-4 to explode, destroying most of the house. Again, the bridge shook violently, but continued to stand.

Jim ran to where Haruko had collapsed on the bridge. He picked her up and carried her back to the mobile command center where ambulances had begun to arrive.

Haruko looked at Jim and smiled. "Is it over?" she asked. "Did we finally get Aioka?"

"It's over for now," Jim replied. Haruko knew then that Aioka had gotten away again."

"Jim, Jim," the tech was calling. "My sensors report that a nuclear incident just occurred on the South side of the island."

"What do you mean nuclear incident?" Jim asked, knowing what the answer had to be.

"Somebody just exploded a bomb," the tech replied.

Eddie had forgotten to figure in a key component when he ran the various bomb scenarios through his head. The lava had reached the nuke and began to surround the rocks and cement protecting the suitcase. Eddie had forgotten about the several pounds of high explosives that encased the plutonium core of this nuke. The heat and pressure of the lava detonated those explosives but, asymmetrically, gave a low yield explosion of the plutonium.

"Hold on," the pilot yelled, "we may get wet."

The shockwave of the blast had disrupted the air around the helicopter, forcing it down, but only momentarily. Once the disruptive air passed by, the helicopter shot up like a rocket.

"I guess I overcompensated," the pilot said.

"Just stay away from windmills," Dano replied.

"It was a fizzle," Eddie said.

"A what?" Dano asked.

"A fizzle. The outer explosives failed to fully detonate the inner plutonium and the nuke basically fizzled out."

"It sure caused one hell of an eruption," the pilot said, pointing to several large fountains of lava shooting over a hundred feet in the air.

"Look at that car and house shake. It must have caused one big earthquake too," Dano said.

279

"Yeah, but it didn't do what Satochi wanted it to do. The nuke failed to collapse the southern flank of the island into the ocean."

"Where to?" the pilot asked.

"Take us to Hilo. That's where Jim and the rest of the team should be. Call Volcano Park and tell them to close Highway 11 south. Dano, I need you to call that sergeant we met in Na'alehu. What was his name?"

"Hale, Kamejiro Hale," Dano replied. "I was supposed to meet up with him in Na'alehu on my way here, but the helicopter changed my plans."

"That's right, call Kamejiro and tell him to evacuate everyone from Na'alehu to the park. It may have been a fizzle, but there will still be radiation spread all over the place."

"Not to mention lava flowing everywhere," the pilot added.

"I've got to call Washington," Eddie said. "They might be a bit curious about what happened here." Eddie opened his cell phone, but before he could push a button he blacked out.

CHAPTER TWENTY-SEVEN

"Welcome back," Jim said to Eddie. "You had us pretty worried."

"What happened?" Eddie asked.

"The doctor said a combination of exhaustion and exposure to some pretty nasty gasses," Jim replied. "After what I heard happened at Southpoint, I can't even imagine how you made it out of that lava tube."

"Did you find Haruko?" Eddie asked.

"Yes, she's safe and in the room next door."

"Where are we?" Eddie asked.

"Hilo Medical Center. I told Dano to fly you straight here when he called."

"So, you know Satochi is dead?" Eddie said.

"No, we thought that was probably the case but, you forget, you passed out before you could tell anybody what happened," Jim explained.

"He fell in the lava and burst into flames. Him and one of his men whom he had shot trying to save himself," Eddie said. "There was a third man, but I don't know where he went."

"He's here at the hospital. He was the only person who took a big dose of the radioactive plutonium when the bomb went off. The doc says his chances are good, but he'll know for sure if the man survives the next twenty-four hours."

"What about Aioka? Were you able to capture him?" Eddie asked.

"No, he wasn't in the house or, if he was, he managed to get away somehow. And there was no sign of the other suitcase nuke. He either took it with him or it was already someplace else," Jim replied.

"Then I guess we still have some work to do," Eddie said, starting to climb out of bed.

"Not so fast. The doctor has to clear you first. He's checking on Haruko as we speak."

"As we speak about what?" Haruko said, entering the room with the doctor.

"She's in better shape than me," the doctor said, sensing Jim's concern. "She has no physical injuries. The drugs have been flushed from her system, but her recent memory is still a little foggy. She's free to go."

"What about me?" Eddie said.

"You probably will have a cough for a few days and possibly a headache, but I can see no reason to keep you here either," the doctor said. "Just take two aspirin and call me in the morning if it gets worse."

Haruko, Jim and Eddie all smiled.

"Now for the bad news," Jim said. "Washington has ordered my NCTC team to stand down until they sort through what happened at Honoli'i Cove."

"What do they mean, stand down?" Haruko asked.

"It means we're on vacation until they decide what to do with us," Eddie said.

"That's ridiculous," Haruko shouted.

"No, that's American politics," Jim said.

"Where's Viktor? Eddie asked. "Was he ordered to stand down as well?"

"Viktor headed back to Oahu all bent out of shape because I wouldn't give him a gun when we rescued Haruko. I'm sure he called his President to complain about how we weren't allowing him to fully participate in the recovery of the suitcase nukes. That's probably half the reason we've been told to stand down."

"Well, we might as well enjoy Hilo while we can," Eddie said. "I heard they have a great farmer's market and I could sure go for some papaya. I forgot to ask, did the earthquake from the bomb blast cause a tsunami?"

"The tsunami warnings did sound, but nothing really hit any of the islands. They did report a three-foot tidal surge along southern Mexico and parts of Central America, but no serious damage or deaths have been reported," Jim said.

"Let's go have some fruit," Haruko said, and the three of them headed for downtown Hilo.

"That fool failed to kill her," Viktor said to Aioka. "Soon she will remember that it was me who helped kidnap her. What am I supposed to do?"

"I would return to Russia if I were you," Aioka suggested. "Either that or kill her yourself."

"I can't return to Russia. They'll soon figure out I was the one behind the theft of the nuclear bombs."

"Then I guess you didn't plan things as well as you thought," Aioka remarked. "I guess you'll have to kill her then."

Viktor ignored Aioka's last remark.

"With Günter dead and Polya missing, I have no way of even getting my share of the extortion money."

Aioka knew Viktor was leading to his next request.

"I know Günter sent you your share, perhaps you could give me three or four million until I can contact Polya."

"I'm afraid I, like you, are not in a position to access that money at the present time," Aioka replied.

"Where are you? Maybe I can help you get away," Viktor offered.

"I have already gotten away," Aioka replied. "I would suggest you do the same. Goodbye Viktor, I'll be in touch."

Viktor slammed the phone down on the desk of his hotel room.

"That *sukin sin,*" Viktor said, lapsing into Russian. "He used me like he used everyone else and I fell for it." There was a knock at the door.

"Who is it?"

"I have what you asked for, comrade Colonel," a voice with a heavy Russian accent replied.

"Quiet, you fool," Viktor said, opening the door. "No one must know you're here."

"Forgive me," the man replied, handing Viktor a designer bag. Inside the bag was a Yarygin 'Skyph mini', the same type of handgun Viktor carried when he was in the Motherland.

"Thank you, my friend," Viktor said when he saw the pistol. "You must go before someone finds you here. All of Russia is grateful for what you have done."

"That may be true, but I still do not understand what is happening," the man replied.

"Just remember the words of the famous Russian poet, Fyodor Tyutchev: 'You can't understand Russia with your brain.' Just go, knowing you have done a heroic deed."

"What is that?" Jim said, looking at the huge fruit covered in spiky thorns that Haruko was holding in her hand.

"It's a durian, it tastes fabulous," Haruko replied, smiling. "It's only nine dollars."

"Nine dollars for that? It'd better taste fabulous at that price," Jim replied.

"Don't worry, I'll pay for it," Haruko said. "You just need to try it."

The old Filipino man behind the table wrapped several layers of newspaper around the durian before carefully placing it in a plastic bag and handing it to Jim.

"Guys, you have to try this coffee, it's terrific," Eddie called to Jim and Haruko.

They both went over to sample the coffee.

"It's good," Jim said, looking around on the ground. "Do you smell anything?"

"Probably some rotting fruit in one of the booths," Haruko replied.

"No, it smells worse than that, like a backed-up sewer," Jim said, but Haruko and Eddie had moved on to another vendor and didn't hear him.

Jim could tell he wasn't the only person to notice the smell. He could see several other tourists were looking around with a distressed look on their faces.

The three friends left the produce section of the market and crossed Mamo Street to the clothes and souvenir stalls. Many of these had taken on a semi-permanent look and could almost be considered stores. Jim followed Haruko into one that specialized in women's dresses.

"See, that smell is even in here," Jim said turning to Eddie. "It smells like a sewer."

"Excuse me sir," the clerk said to Jim. "Do you have a durian in your bag?"

"Why yes, I do," Jim replied, surprised. "I'm afraid I'll have to ask you to leave it outside. It stinks up the store way too much."

Haruko and Eddie were both laughing at the joke they had played on Jim.

"Why didn't you tell me it was me stinking up the place?" Jim asked.

"What, and ruin all our fun?" Haruko replied.

"Well, I'm throwing this thing away, it must be rotten," Jim said.

"I don't think so," Haruko replied. "I paid nine dollars for that durian and you promised me you would try it. Trust me it's delicious."

Jim had his doubts. "Okay, but I'm not carrying it around anymore, so if I have to try it, let's do it now."

They took the durian back across to the vendor where they had purchased it and asked the clerk if he would cut it open for them. He pulled out a large knife and in just a few seconds had removed and discarded most all of the durian except for several firm, cream-colored, peanut-shaped pulpy chunks and passed them to Haruko.

"That's it?" Jim asked. "That's the part you eat?"

"It's delicious, try some," she replied. Haruko took a plastic spoon and scooped a spoonful out for Jim.

It had the consistency and taste of a highly-flavored almond custard, but sprinkled with a variety of delicious, complex, and incongruous subtle flavors, that all worked together to create an unsurpassed taste experience.

"This is incredible," Jim said. "Who would have thought something that smells so bad could taste so good."

"In most of Asia it is illegal to take these on public transportation and even into many buildings," Haruko said.

"Understandably so," Jim agreed.

Their fun was interrupted by a phone call from Washington.

"Jim, this is Director Conyers." Jim knew he was in trouble, for up until a couple of days ago he had never even spoken to the director of the NCTC. Now for the second time in three days he had called Jim directly and Jim had a feeling it was not a social call.

"Yes sir, how can I help you?"

"I just got off the phone with the President and, needless to say, he's not very happy about the progress you've made in recovering the warheads. The Russian President called him to complain that you aren't allowing Colonel Cheznov to fully participate in the investigation."

"If that includes giving the Colonel a weapon, then the President is correct," Jim replied. "The Colonel has been privy to every bit of information as soon as I became aware of it. As for my team's performance in finding the suitcase nukes, I would suggest you take the time to read the report that was submitted by all parties involved." Jim was losing his patience with Conyers and didn't really care if he was fired. "And thank you for asking, Haruko is now safe."

"I will be arriving in Oahu at 4:00 p.m. Hawaii time. I expect you to meet me at the Hydrogen Solutions facility at Pearl at 6:00. We will be discussing the future of your investigation."

"Yes sir," Jim replied. "Should I inform the Colonel of this meeting?"

"That won't be necessary, but I would like Haruko and Mr. Popp to be available if I wish to speak with them."

"We'll all be there," Jim responded.

"Do you know the present location of Colonel Cheznov?" Conyers asked.

"I believe he's staying at the rooms the agency has provided for us at the Ohana Islander Waikiki," Jim replied.

"Good," Conyers said, and disconnected the call.

"What was that about?" Eddie asked. "Mr. Conyers requests my presence in Honolulu later today. I think the

287

President is sending him to Hawaii to personally tell me I'm fired."

"Well, at least he isn't sending Donald Trump," Haruko said, trying to ease the tension.

"He also would like the two of you there in case he has any questions," Jim added.

"Well, I have a few questions for him, too," Haruko said. "Like when is he going to pull his head out of..."

"Haruko," Jim interrupted sounding very serious. "That will be my job to ask him that."

CHAPTER TWENTY-EIGHT

"Two cars were waiting for Jim, Eddie, and Haruko, when the Navy helicopter sent to pick them up in Hilo touched down at Pearl.

"Mr. Rikey," one of the drivers said, "I have been asked to bring you directly to the Hydrogen Solutions facility. Mr. Popp and Ms. Ozawa are to be taken to the hotel in Waikiki. I was also told to remind both of you that you are still under orders to stand down. Mr. Conyers requests that you stay at the hotel in case he needs to speak to either of you. If you do go to dinner or need to leave the hotel for any reason, please notify the desk clerk as to where you'll be."

"Sounds like we're under house arrest," Eddie said.

"No sir, not as far as I know," the second driver replied. "However, I've been ordered to stay with you at the hotel."

"And for what reason?" Haruko asked.

"To protect you," the driver replied.

"Protect us from what?" Eddie asked.

"I don't know, sir. I was only told to protect you."

"Somebody is not telling us the whole story," Jim replied. "I'll see what I can find out and give you a call. Until then, the two of you should enjoy the Waikiki Beach Walk. It's right next to the where our rooms are at the Ohana."

"Here, take my Blackberry," Jim said. "I know you both lost your phones, and I may need to get a hold of you." He handed it to Haruko.

"Any dinner recommendations?" Eddie asked.

"The agency is still paying, so I'd say Roy's is your best bet, but you better call for reservations."

"I'll just show them my badge," Eddie joked.

"Give Mr. Conyers my regards," Haruko said, as she climbed into the car.

When Haruko and Eddie arrived at the Ohana, there was already another armed shore patrol officer at the hotel.

"I thought you said we're not under house arrest?" Eddie said.

"You're not," the driver replied. "We're here to protect you."

"Then should I make dinner reservations for four?" Haruko asked.

"No ma'm, we won't be joining you for dinner. But please let the desk clerk know where you're going," replied the driver.

"That makes no sense," Eddie said. "You say you're here to protect us, but yet you'll let us go to dinner by ourselves?

"Ma'm, can I take that bag for you," the driver asked Haruko, ignoring Eddie.

"Maybe Viktor knows what this is about," Eddie said That got the driver's attention.

"I think it'd be best if you didn't speak to Colonel Cheznov just yet," he said to Eddie.

Haruko and Eddie looked at each other. "I better give Jim a call," Haruko said.

"I'm afraid that won't be possible," the driver said.

"Eddie, you were in the CIA, what is all this crap?"

"If I knew, and told you, we'd probably have to kill each other," Eddie joked.

"Well, that makes about as much sense as everything else at the moment," Haruko replied. "Let's go have dinner."

"Have a seat, Jim," Conyers said when Jim entered the room.

Jim thought about cracking a joke, but changed his mind when he saw a picture of Viktor lying on the table.

"I read the report and I must say, given the extent of the explosives in and around the Honoli'i house, I commend you for only losing one man."

"Yes, but three civilians were killed and fourteen injured, including four of my men," Jim added.

"True, but you did free Haruko, and several of Aioka's terrorists were killed. It's unfortunate that Aioka got away with the suitcase nuke, but I agree with your assessment that someone within the agency was feeding him information."

"What are you getting to," Jim asked. "Do you know who leaked the information?"

"We believe we do. We think it was the same man who helped in the kidnapping of Haruko. Look at these photos."

Conyers passed Jim several photos taken from a satellite over Helsinki at the time of the kidnapping and attack on Zetanutra.

"I was told we had no satellites in position at the time."

"We didn't," Conyers replied, "but the Russians did."

"That's not what Viktor told me," Jim said.

"And for good reason. Have a look at these enhanced photos."

Jim grabbed the stack of photos from Conyer's hand. "That son-of-a-bitch. He helped Satochi kidnap Haruko."

"That's not all," Conyer's said. "The FSB believes Viktor was behind the original theft of the nukes. He and a few former KGB agents that are now freelancing to the highest bidder."

"And Aioka was the highest bidder," Jim said

"So it seems," Conyers paused while Jim sorted through the photos. "The President has asked me to personally convey his apology for forcing you to include Viktor in the investigation, as has the Russian President."

"I guess I take back all those things I called him," Jim said, smiling.

"I want to apologize as well. I should have listened to you and I should have never taken Haruko off the team. If it wasn't for her, who knows how many would have died from the chimera."

"What do you mean, chimera?" Jim asked.

"It was not the plain Ebola virus that Aioka first tested in those Zetanutra capsules. This one was duplexed with a very contagious strain of flu virus. Had the capsules been distributed, our experts estimate up to one hundred and fifty million Americans would have died and over twice that number throughout the world."

"Whoa," Jim said. "When did you find out Viktor was dirty?"

"The Russian President contacted us as I was on my way here to chew you out."

"That's good to know, I was expecting to be fired," Jim said.

"We usually don't fire our heroes," Conyers replied. "Even if they do screw up."

"Why haven't you arrested Viktor?"

"We were hoping he'd lead us to Aioka or to the last nuke."

"You mean the last on American soil?" Jim corrected.

"True," Conyers replied. "We know the fourth one is somewhere in Finland. According to the Russians, it's in the hands of one of those former KGB agents. Chances are, they'll be able to purchase it back in the near future."

"Does Viktor know we're on to him?"

"Not yet, at least as far as we know."

"Where is he now?"

"Still in his hotel room I'd guess. I have two military police watching the hotel and the hotel has allowed us to tap into their closed-circuit video of the sixth floor."

"The hotel allowed that?" Jim asked.

"What they don't know won't hurt them," Conyers said, smiling. "God bless the Patriot Act. We also have Agent Smith, the one they call Dano, covering the room with a hi-powered rifle, just in case."

"What's the plan?" Jim asked.

"We believe he's about to run. That's why we have men covering the hotel. We thought you should be the one to take him down."

"Then let's saddle up and do it," Jim replied.

"I hate it when the sun goes down," the Hydrogen Solutions tech said to his assistant.

"Why is that?'

"No more sunbathers to zoom in on," he said, laughing.

"What you need is another FBI raid to keep you occupied," the assistant said.

"That would be nice, but I'm just now starting to recover from the last three I monitored," the tech replied. "Let's see, what's on the schedule for tonight?"

"You'll like this," the assistant said, "the *Grand Maui* returns this evening to Honolulu with the final party extravaganza scheduled at the Aloha Tower."

"Good idea, let's check out the facial ID software. Maybe we can get the numbers of some of those high-end call girls Casey supplies for his guests," the tech replied.

"Even if we did, you couldn't afford to have coffee with one," his assistant replied.

"You got that right."

He moved a few switches and used a toggle like you would find on a video game to move the hi-power zoom camera to the *Grand Maui* which was just clearing Diamond Head on its way to Pier Four at the Aloha Tower.

"That ship is lit up like a Vegas casino. There are more lights on it than on Molokai," the tech said.

"There are more lights in this room than on Molokai," the assistant joked.

"Let's see if we can recognize anyone," the tech said.

"Turn the recorder back on, I turned it off when you were scoping out the topless beach," the assistant replied. "That way, we'll have proof if Lord Farrelton wants to know if we're working."

"Good thinking," the tech replied.

They locked on to several faces identifying several politicians, the governor of Hawaii, a couple of beach boys, and three beauties that the tech swore had to be hookers.

"Try that guy," the assistant said. The tech pushed a button and snapped a picture of the man's face. Instantly, the computer software started processing the image. Ten seconds later the screen began to flash red.

"Holy shit," the assistant said.

"I've got to contact Jim Rikey immediately," the tech said, dialing Jim's Blackberry.

"I'm eating light tonight, I think I'll have the crab wrap," Haruko told the waiter.

"Yeah, me too," Eddie said to Haruko. "I'd like the steak and lobster," he said to the waitress.

"Whaaa-t?" Eddie said, as Haruko stared at him. "Jim said the agency is paying."

Jim's Blackberry began to ring.

"Hello."

"Who's this?" the tech asked.

"Who's this?" Haruko answered back.

"I'm trying to reach Jim Rikey," the tech said. "I'm the tech at Hydrogen Solutions."

"Jim isn't here, this is Haruko."

"I guess I can tell you, but you need to give Jim the message immediately."

"I promise I will," Haruko replied.

"Tell him I've found Aioka."

Haruko almost dropped the phone. "Where is he?"

"He is on the *Grand Maui*. It's about twenty minutes from docking at the Aloha Tower pier. He's in the crowd of party revelers celebrating with Bill Casey."

"Who else is on that ship?" Haruko asked.

"At least ten senators, two governors, and probably the CEOs of more than half the Fortune 500 top fifty US corporations."

"Thanks," Haruko said. "We're on our way there now."

"I'll keep an eye on you from above," the tech said.

"On our way where?" Eddie asked.

"To stop Aioka from destroying Honolulu."

"Where is the other policeman?" Jim asked, as the car dropped him at the Ohana.

"He's on the sixth floor by the elevators," the shore patrol policeman replied.

"Do you know what rooms Eddie and Haruko are in?"

"No, but I do know where they went to dinner. They left word that they could be reached at Roy's. It's just down at the end of the Beachwalk."

"Viktor still in his room?"

"Haven't seen him since we arrived, but your man Dano said that he's been taking a nap."

Jim knew Haruko would want to be there once she knew that it was Viktor who had helped Satochi kidnap her. He was about to send the policeman to get Eddie and Haruko so they could participate in arresting Viktor when Dano called in to say that Viktor was up and it looked like he was planning on going out.

"I reckon it's time we pay Viktor a visit," Jim said. "Tell your partner I'm on my way up." Jim decided he would call Haruko as soon as Viktor was restrained. She deserved the chance to face him before he got caught in a diplomatic tug-of-war.

Jim's Blackberry began to ring as Haruko and Eddie were headed by cab to the Aloha Tower. Haruko saw that it was the Hydrogen Solutions tech calling back.

"This is Haruko."

"The *Grand Maui* has anchored off the beach at Waikiki. I just heard they have some big fireworks show planned to coincide with the Hilton Hawaiian Village display. The ship will not pull into port for at least two more hours."

"Was this planned or is it something new?" Haruko asked.

"Apparently, they had it planned all along, but it was meant to be a surprise for all the party goers," the tech replied. "They say it'll be the biggest fireworks display the islands have ever seen."

"Turn left here," Haruko yelled at the cab driver.

"This ain't the Aloha Tower," the driver said.

"I know, but now I need to rent a boat."

The cab turned sharply from Ala Moana Boulevard onto Holomoana Street and into the Ala Wai Boat Harbor.

"This place looks familiar," Haruko said.

"Don't tell me they showed Gilligan Island reruns in Japan when you were growing up," Eddie said. "This is where the Minnow set sail from."

"I knew it looked familiar," Haruko replied.

The two jumped out of the cab and Eddie hurried to commandeer a speedboat while Haruko paid the driver.

There were two men just docking one of their company boats used for para-sailing along Waikiki Beach.

"Is this boat pretty fast?" Eddie asked.

"Fast enough for what we use it for," the man replied. "You can sign up in the office if you would like to go up first thing in the morning."

"I'm afraid you boys are going to have to help me out tonight," Eddie said, pulling his FBI credentials. "We need to be taken out to the *Grand Maui* immediately. I know it sounds like a cliché, but it's a matter of life or death."

"You are going to have to check with our...," one of the men started to say.

"We don't have time to check with anyone, either you can radio them on our way out, or you can walk over and tell them after we take your boat," Haruko interrupted pulling out her credentials.

Both men looked at each other. "What the hell," one of them said, "the FBI is going to pay for the gas, right?"

"You can count on it," Eddie replied. "Let's go."

CHAPTER TWENTY-NINE

"Dano, do you still see him?" Jim called over the radio.

Jim heard nothing but static.

The elevator chimed, signaling he had reached the sixth floor.

"The radio can't reach Dano from the elevator, but I heard you. I relayed your message. Dano says Viktor is still getting dressed. He also said he thought he saw a gun," the officer assigned to the sixth floor said.

"A gun? Dano, did you see a gun?" Jim called.

"I'm really not sure, I don't have that great of an angle to see the entire room. He had his back turned towards me when he pulled something out of a paper bag. Then he untucked his shirt and I saw him messing with the back of his waistband like he was putting a gun there. Maybe I'm just being paranoid," Dano said.

"No, we don't need any surprises like that," Jim said. "We're going in so let us know if things change."

"You got it," Dano replied.

Jim and the officer walked down to the end of the hallway and knocked on the last door on the left. The room faced Lewers Street and provided as good visibility as possible for Dano who was across and down the street on the seventh floor of the Wyndham Vacation Condominiums. The officer stood behind Jim and had pulled his service revolver. Viktor opened the door slightly and saw that it was Jim.

"Hello Jim, how's Haruko?" Viktor said.

"Can we come in?" Jim asked.

"Do I have a choice," Viktor replied, seeing the gun in the officer's hand.

"No, not really," Jim replied.

"I see you still have your six-shooters on," Viktor said. "Too bad you're still too scared to use them."

Jim didn't reply.

"How'd you find out?" Viktor asked. "Did you monitor my calls?"

"Your own country sold you out," Jim answered. "They sent us the satellite video of Helsinki. It shows you helping Satochi kidnap Haruko."

"Believe it or not, I'm glad she's safe. I like Haruko," Viktor said.

"Where's Aioka and the other two suitcase nukes?" Jim asked.

"If I knew that, I'd be using it to bargain with," Viktor said.

"We know one of the nukes is still in Finland. Does your friend Günter have it?" Jim asked.

"Günter is probably dead by now. He contracted the Ebola virus."

"Then who has the nuke, Polya?"

"You are well-informed," Viktor said. "I haven't seen or heard from Polya. She has disappeared with my and I imagine Günter's share of the extortion money."

"So, this was all about money?" Jim asked.

"For me and my people, yes. For Aioka it was all about the cause. We were just able to mutually assist each other in moving towards our goals," Viktor explained. "Having Aioka make the extortion threats gave it much more credibility. Plus, the fact that it was his own company that was first to meet the extortionist demands. Many others followed."

"Does Aioka have the fourth nuke? Jim asked

"I'm sure of it," Viktor replied. "He has something big planned for it. What, I'm not sure. I do know he plans to use it very soon."

"Why did Aioka give one of the nukes to Satochi to use? Is Aioka part of the sovereignty movement?" Jim asked.

"Aioka believes America will try to take over Japan in the same way they stole the Hawaiian Islands. He views the sovereignty movement as the same fight against imperialism that he has fought for Japan. He believed it would ultimately benefit his own cause," Viktor said.

Jim turned to the officer, "better check for a gun before you cuff him."

"Put your hands, on top of your head," the officer said, as he stepped towards Viktor.

Suddenly, the officer spun around and fell to the ground as the sound of breaking glass was heard. Blood began to pour from his shattered shoulder. Viktor dove to the ground as four more bullets ripped into the wall directly behind where he had been standing.

Jim also dove to the ground. "Dano, what in tarnation are you shooting at?"

"That's not me," Dano replied. "I'm not sure which direction they're coming from."

When Jim looked up, Viktor was gone. "Viktor is on the run," Jim said to the officer waiting downstairs. He took the back stairs. I'll follow him, but be careful, he's probably armed. Tell the desk clerk to call for backup and for paramedics, your partner's been shot."

"How bad is he," the officer asked.

"He took a slug in the shoulder. Should be fine, once they stop the bleeding. And call my cell phone and tell Haruko and Eddie what's going on. We could use their help."

Viktor was down the back stairs in no time. The stairwell exit emptied right onto the lower walkway of the new Waikiki Beachwalk. It was packed with hundreds of tourists checking out the shops or heading to one of the restaurants. Viktor was skilled at blending into a crowd and disappearing. He moved quickly and crossed Lewers with a group of several drunken college students, weaving through the oncoming traffic. He walked past the Fendi Purse Store and turned right on Kalakaua Avenue

"Jim. I saw him exit the hotel and cross Lewers going mauka, then I lost him."

"What in tarnation is mauka?"

"Towards the mountains, sorry," Dano replied.

Jim just caught a glimpse of Viktor as he rounded the corner. The plate glass window of Fendi's shattered as the sniper took another shot at Viktor, missing by inches. Viktor sprinted to the escalator shoving people out of the way and ran up the steps to the second floor of the Royal Hawaiian shopping center.

"Someone's trying to take out Viktor. The shot came from one of the high-rises on the north side of Kalakaua," Jim said into his radio. "Let the local police know."

"Roger that," the shore patrol officer responded.

Jim hoped it was only Viktor that the sniper was shooting at when he too passed by the shot-out window of Fendi's. He knew he was just seconds behind Viktor, but those seconds would be more than enough time for a professional like Viktor to disappear in one of the myriad of shops in and around Waikiki. When Jim reached the second floor of the shopping center, he was pleased to see that very few shops had opened in the new center. The stairs leading to and from the second floor were not yet completed. It was easy to see that Viktor had not entered any of the first three stores that Jim ran past. In the middle of the floor was another set of escalators still under construction and wrapped in plastic. Jim caught a glimpse of Viktor as he ran past a group of about thirty tourists taking a beginning ukulele lesson.

When Viktor reached the end of the mall, the escalators located there were also wrapped in plastic and nonfunctional. There was an elevator, but the panel showed it was on the first level and Viktor could not afford to wait for it. He climbed the rail and leaped to a palm tree next to the railing and shimmied quickly down it.

"Give it up, Viktor," Jim yelled from above.

Viktor turned to run, confident Jim was still too traumatized to shoot him. He was right.

Jim was about to follow Viktor's lead and jump to the tree when the elevator door opened. He entered, and quickly closed the doors. When the doors opened on the first level, Jim didn't see Viktor, but heard the screeching of car brakes and crunching metal up ahead. Jim ran past the Royal Hawaiian and towards the entrance of the Sheraton Waikiki.

Viktor had contemplated hi-jacking one of the cars that had collided to avoid running into him or one of the others pulling up to the Sheraton for valet parking, but there was too much traffic to allow him to safely escape. He turned and saw Jim just coming out from the garden area between the Royal Hawaiian Hotel and the new shopping complex. He knew Jim had also seen him. Viktor rushed into the lobby looking for some way to slow Jim down. He pulled his Yarygin 'Skyph mini' from a holster on his back and fired one shot into the ornately painted light fixture on the ceiling, causing it to shatter throwing glass everywhere, but more importantly causing mass panic in the lobby area. Viktor barely slowed down as he continued down the hallway past several stores.

"What the hell was that?" one of the salesmen at the Starwood Vacation Gallery said when he heard the first shot and the screams. He ran out into the hallway and saw Viktor running towards him. He didn't see the gun in Viktor's hand and tried to block Viktor's path. Viktor was moving fast, but saw the collision coming. He lowered his head and bowled into the salesman, knocking him through the front plate glass window of the bikini store, creating even more panic in the hotel.

The broken light fixture did slow Jim down, but only slightly. He heard the crash of the salesman flying into the plate glass window and saw Viktor running outside past the Hula show taking place by the pool at the Sand Bar. Viktor had turned to the left leading toward the Royal Hawaiian Hotel just next door. The pathway was narrow and crowded as tourists watched and played in the waves breaking over the railing. Jim had lost sight of Viktor, but could hear the complaints of the crowd as Viktor ran by shoving people out of the way, even knocking some over the rail and into the water.

Viktor did not cut down to the sandy beach when he came to the steps leading down to the beach. He continued on the cement path. He was able to move quicker because no people were now in front of him. He soon discovered why.

"Chort poberi," Viktor exclaimed in anger. He had come to a locked gate and cursed his misfortune in his native Russian. He quickly jumped over the railing on his right and onto the sandy beach. He stayed away from the water and near the retaining wall that ran all along the grass area by the Royal Hawaiian Hotel. The going was slow, but he knew Jim would have been slowed by the deep sand as well.

"Give it up, Viktor, you can't get away," Jim yelled when he reached the steps down to the beach and saw Viktor fifty yards ahead of him.

Hearing Jim's voice gave Viktor a burst of adrenaline and he leaped onto a stack of chaise lounges the attendants had stacked near the wall for the night. He used them as a springboard to leap over the wall, landing in the middle of the band performing at the Royal Hawaiian Martini Bar. He knocked the guitar player forward into several tables of tourists enjoying their cocktails. He barely broke stride as he ran across the patio knocking people to and fro. He ran past the dinner buffet and jumped over a railing and right onto a couple laying in lounges inside a private cabana by the pool. The woman took the brunt of the hit as Viktor tumbled over her onto the pool deck. Her husband reacted quickly, grabbing Viktor and a struggle ensued. They wrestled towards the pool. Viktor could not afford the delay and pulled his pistol, shooting the man squarely in the chest, blowing him into the pool. The underwater lights highlighted the red cloud of blood as it began to spread through the water. Several parents leaped into the pool to pull their screaming children away from the floating body and the scarlet water.

The struggle had cost Viktor much time. Jim was now right behind him. Jim watched as Viktor took the first set of steps leading from the pool area in one leap, but needed two strides for the second set. Jim, being so much taller, needed only one stride for each set of steps, cutting the distance between him and Viktor.

"Where's my back-up?" Jim said into his radio.

"The police are en route, what's your location?" Dano asked.

"I'm leaving the pool area of the Royal Hawaiian and headed I believe for the lobby," Jim said. "We also need paramedics in the lobby of the Sheraton and the pool area here."

"Already on the way to the Sheraton, I'll call in the Royal Hawaiian," Dano replied. "I still have no location for the other sharpshooter."

"Just let everyone know about him, but I think his target is Viktor," Jim said, starting to breathe heavily.

"Did anyone reach Eddie and Haruko?" Jim asked. No one responded immediately.

"Not yet," Dano replied, purposely lying in order not to distract Jim from the task at hand. For, at that very moment, Eddie and Haruko were somewhere on the *Grand Maui*, trying to stop a second nuclear holocaust and catch the man responsible for the first.

CHAPTER THIRTY

The speedboat pulled up next to the *Grand Maui* despite warnings from a crew member standing on the gangway.

"All boats are supposed to be out of this area," the ship's mate yelled at the driver of the speedboat. "The fireworks display is about to start."

"FBI," Eddie yelled. "How long till the fireworks start?"

"Ten minutes," the ship's mate said, looking at his watch. "What's the trouble?"

Neither Eddie nor Haruko responded. "Aioka may not have known about the fireworks display. That means he may have already activated the timer on the nuke. If that's the case, he'll either be trying to get off this ship quickly or he'll try to re-set the nuke's time clock," Haruko said to Eddie.

"A guy was just down here asking about going to shore," the ship's mate said, overhearing their conversation.

"What did he look like?" Haruko asked.

"Asian, possibly Japanese. I told him because of the fireworks no boats were coming in or going out right now. He didn't seem too happy about it."

"Did he say anything else?" Eddie asked.

"Yeah, he asked where his luggage had been taken," the man said. "I told him the valets had already locked it away in the lower hold for unloading when we docked."

Eddie and Haruko looked at each other knowingly. "Can you take me there?" Eddie said.

"Sure, but I can't let you in. I don't have a key. The cruise line is very strict about who can handle the guest's luggage. I guess they had a theft problem at one time."

"Call someone who does have a key and have them meet us there," Eddie told the ship's mate. "I also need to speak to the Captain."

"He's at the party and doesn't have a radio."

"I'll find him," Haruko said.

"Give me the key to the boat," Eddie said, turning to the two men who had brought them on the speedboat.

Both men hesitated.

"Look," Eddie said, "that wasn't a multiple-choice question. The FBI is commandeering your boat. Go up and enjoy the party."

"Good luck," Haruko said to Eddie.

"You be careful," Eddie replied. "Aioka could be desperate."

Aioka, in fact, was anything but desperate. He had returned to the party and was sipping a glass of very expensive champagne while he listened to a senator tout the President's newest foreign aide package to help rebuild Africa and oust Islamic terrorists.

"What about other terrorists?" Aioka piped in. "My company just paid a fortune to some Japanese terrorist organization who threatened to nuke my entire manufacturing operation."

"Probably the same bastards who set off that nuclear device in Wichita," the senator replied. "I'm Senator Fitch, from Idaho."

"Shōwa Tennō." Aioka replied, holding out his hand to shake the senator's. "I'm CEO of Zetanutra."

"A pleasure to meet you, Mr. Tennō," the senator said, vigorously shaking Aioka's hand.

Aioka smiled at what a fool the senator was. He had used the name Emperor Hirohito was given upon his death. It

307

was a name known to every man, woman, and school-aged child in Japan, but obviously unknown to the senator.

"I understand it was the same terror group responsible for the anthrax attack on this ship," Aioka said.

"I hadn't heard that, Mr. Tennō," the senator replied. "Where did you hear that?"

"I think I read it in a Japanese newspaper. If you'll excuse me, I see a friend I must say hello to," Aioka said, tiring of his little game with the senator.

Aioka checked his watch. The fireworks were scheduled to begin at any moment and the helicopter he had called was due in fifteen minutes. More importantly was how much time was remaining on the suitcase nuke's timer. Aioka did not know about the planned fireworks extravaganza and had set the timer on the nuke believing the *Grand Maui* would be reaching port in another fifteen minutes. That would have left him a little less than a half-an-hour to get a safe distance from ground zero. He had already arranged for the helicopter to pick him up at the Aloha Tower, so it wasn't a problem arranging for it to fly to the *Grand Maui* instead. He would be safely on the ground in Kauai before the explosion. Or so Aioka thought.

Aioka had really wanted the nuke to explode when the ship reached the pier at the Aloha Tower. Several thousand people were expected to be there to join in the finale of Bill Casey's party. In fact, more than ten thousand people had already jammed the area listening to the free concert Casey had arranged. Carlos Santana and the re-united Eagles were featured artists at the concert, along with several of Hawaii's own top bands.

Still, it would be a spectacular and just as effective explosion. In fact, now there was a possibility for even more deaths and damage. The nuke would no doubt level several of Hawaii's famed beachfront hotels which were sure to be packed with tourists.

Aioka was confident all would work out just fine.

"Where's the crewman with the keys?" Eddie said impatiently.

"I just spoke with him on the radio, he needs the first mate's okay before he can just unlock the hold," the man told Eddie.

Eddie looked around for something heavy. The ship was a vision of organization, there was nothing lying about. He punched the glass door that held a large fire extinguisher.

"This will do," Eddie said, and smashed the extinguisher into the lock area of the door until it broke free and the door swung open.

"Now show me where the light switch is," Eddie ordered.

The mate walked into the hold, revealing a room packed with hundreds of suitcases and turned on a computer attached to the bulkhead.

"Tell me the person's name and I can pinpoint his or her luggage in this maze," the mate said.

"I don't think you'll find anything listed under Aioka Matsuura on that list, but you might as well give it a try," Eddie replied.

"I've heard that name before," the mate said. "Funny, I don't see it here."

"Aioka's the one responsible for the anthrax attack on this ship," Eddie said. "That's why you've heard the name."

The man turned white. "Is he going to release anthrax again? Is that what this is about?"

"No, this time he plans on blowing up this ship and all of Honolulu with the suitcase nuclear bomb that is somewhere in this room. And it's up to you and me to stop that from happening," Eddie explained.

The man visibly shook and almost wet himself in fear.

"We're looking for a larger suitcase, probably not very stylish, and very heavy, around eighty to one hundred pounds, but don't try to pick it up. Don't even touch it if you find it. Should be fairly easy to spot among all this designer stuff," Eddie said, gesturing with his hand."

"What do I do if I find it?" the mate asked.

"Just call me. I'll start over here on the right, you take the left," Eddie said.

Eddie moved quickly, picking his way through the large areas of luggage. Near the front was the luggage from all the first-class suites and cabins. Eddie figured that was probably where he would find the suitcase. He was right, it was in the first-class area, but it wasn't he who found it.

"I think this might be it," the mate yelled. "It's big, old, and cheap looking, and doesn't look like it belongs in first-class," the mate yelled.

Eddie quickly made his way to where the mate stood.

"I think you may be right," Eddie said.

"What the hell is going on in here?" the crewman with the key had finally arrived.

"Quiet please," Eddie said.

"I asked you a question," the man said, rushing towards Eddie. "You have no business being in here. I don't care if you are FBI."

The shipmate who had helped Eddie find the suitcase stepped in front of the crewman to explain, but was shoved out of the way. Eddie was busy concentrating on the suitcase locks and didn't even notice the man approaching until he grabbed Eddie's shoulder.

Instinctively, Eddie whirled, breaking the man's grip, then planting a closed fist squarely in the man's chest knocking him backwards. "I would appreciate a little cooperation here," Eddie said. "This is a nuclear bomb that could explode at any minute, and I really need to concentrate. Is that too much to ask? Now I need both of you to stand away until I need your help. We're going to try to get this nuke to the speedboat waiting at the gangway. Any questions?"

The man slowly stood up and backed away to the door where his shipmate was standing.

Eddie carefully felt and looked at every inch of the suitcase that was visible and accessible. He slowly tried the latch on the left side of the case, but it was locked. He them tried the right latch, but it too was locked.

"Anybody got a pocket knife?" Eddie called out, without turning.

"Yeah, I do," said the crewman who had brought the key to unlock the hatch.

"Bring it over, I'm going to need your help," Eddie replied.

The man moved next to Eddie and handed him the knife.

"I'm going to use the knife to break off the piece of metal that holds the latch locked. When I do, that latch will spring open. You, my friend, will make sure that doesn't happen. When the lock breaks, you need to hold that latch down until I take over. Do you understand?"

The man nodded his head, his mouth was too dry to answer.

It only took a couple of seconds for Eddie to pick the lock and release the latch. Although it was very cool in the hold, the crewman was pouring sweat and the latch was slippery. When Eddie went to place his finger where the crewman's had been, his finger slipped and the latch sprung open with a loud snap. The crewman passed out with fear.

"Damn good thing that wasn't booby-trapped," Eddie said. "Come help your friend. I think he needs some water, but don't leave. I'm going to need you both in a minute."

This time Eddie was able to break the lock and hold the other latch by himself. He was able to determine that it, too, was not booby-trapped. The suitcase was now unlocked, but still closed. Eddie took the blade of the knife and ran it around the edges of the suitcase several times. Each time he opened the case ever-so-slightly until he could get down and look into it to make sure the lid wasn't wired to set off an explosion.

"Do you have a flashlight? It's hard to see inside." Eddie asked.

"I can go get one," the mate said, still tending to his shipmate.

"We can't afford to wait," Eddie said. "Let's just pray for the best."

Eddie took a deep breath and lifted the lid.

Haruko knew Aioka had plastic surgery since the last time she had seen him, but she had no doubt that she would recognize him. As she entered the Grand Ballroom amidship, the party was in full swing. Most women were in expensive evening gowns that cost more money than Haruko earned from two-month's salary. She was sure she looked extremely out of place but, in fact, her simple Japanese dress had a sense of elegance that allowed her to move about relatively unnoticed in the room. Unnoticed to everyone but ship security and Aioka Matsuura.

The room was filled with people. Many more than the fire marshal would have approved. Haruko moved to the Grand Staircase so she could better view the room. Trying to find Aioka in this mass of people would be extremely difficult. She tried to do grid scans, but the dynamics of the crowd was in constant flux, with people dancing and moving about the room. Haruko wasn't even sure Aioka was on the ship, let alone in the room. That's when she remembered the tech back in Pearl who originally identified Aioka. She quickly pushed redial on Jim's Blackberry.

"I need your help," Haruko said. "Is the party still being televised?"

"Yes, but Casey just announced the fireworks were about ready to begin, so the broadcast is about to shift to watching the display."

"I need you to help me locate him in this room," Haruko said.

"No problem," the tech replied. "Once I have his image, which I have, I can let the computer do the searching. Give me a minute. Where are you located?"

"I'm about half-way up the staircase," Haruko replied.

"I see you. Wave to the camera," the tech said.

"Do you see Aioka yet?" Haruko asked.

"Not yet, but it looks like ship security has figured out you don't belong there. Two are moving towards you, one from above and one from below."

"Good, I need to let them know what's going on and get some backup here," Haruko said.

"I got him," the tech yelled. "He's moving away from you towards the door on your right. No, no! I mean on your left. Sorry, I got turned around. He's about one hundred feet ahead of you. You better move fast."

"I see him." Without hesitation, Haruko started running down the stairs, forgetting about the two security guards moving towards her. When she reached the bottom of the steps, the guard stepped in front of her.

"Excuse me, ma'm, but I don't believe we've seen you on the ship earlier. What…"

"You have to get out of my way or he'll get away," Haruko interrupted, stepping around the guard. The other guard had caught up to her and now he stepped into her path.

"Ma'm, what's your name and what cabin are you in?" the second guard asked.

Haruko leaned to the side to try to see around the guard. "I'm with the NCTC. You need to move, before I lose him."

"Lose who, ma'm?" the guard said, trying to be patient.

"Aioka, Aioka Matsuura. The one responsible for the anthrax attack, now move," Haruko yelled.

The mention of the anthrax attack tensed both guards and their pleasant demeanor suddenly disappeared and one of them grabbed Haruko's wrist. She still held Jim's Blackberry in her hand.

"You need to come with us so we can figure this all out," the guard said.

"You don't understand," Haruko said, but knew any more conversation would waste precious seconds. Seconds that would allow Aioka to once again disappear.

"Sorry," Haruko said. She allowed the phone to drop as she reversed her wrist, slipping the guards grasp and striking him in the neck causing his entire body to go momentarily numb. The second guard was reaching for a baton when Haruko kicked him squarely in the groin, dropping him to his knees. "I'm really sorry," Haruko said, running off in the direction where she had last seen Aioka.

Most of the partygoers paid little attention to the confrontation, since it happened so fast and the room was so crowded. Those that did assumed the gentlemen became fresh with the lady and she put a stop to it. Ship security, however, was very aware of what was going on, at least as far as knowing an unidentified guest just took down two of its guards. As of yet, they were still completely in the dark about the terrorist threat Aioka and the suitcase nuke posed to the *Grand Maui*.

Aioka didn't see the two security guards attempt to question Haruko. Had he seen the confrontation, he would no doubt have been able to exacerbate her predicament. According to his watch, the helicopter was due in less than ten minutes. It was time for him to make his way towards the helipad. As he neared the door the first fireworks, coming from the Hilton Hawaiian Village, lit up the sky. The crowd rushed to exit the Grand Ballroom for a better view as the ship dimmed its lights to provide its guests a most spectacular show. Aioka was stopped in the flood of people. He cursed himself for not having brought a bodyguard with him, but he needed to leave him back at the Honoli'i house to insure all went according to plan. Somehow, Haruko had discovered his presence on the *Grand Maui*, but from what he had seen, she must be acting alone. Even the ship's security was unaware of her being aboard.

"That woman back there tried to kill me," Aioka said frantically to one of the security men moving against the flow of guests and towards Haruko.

"She has a gun," he added.

The security guard's demeanor instantly changed and he relayed Aioka's message to all the other security men.

315

"Just keep moving with the crowd, sir. We'll handle the situation," the guard replied.

"Thank you, thank you for saving my life," Aioka said, then turned and smiled as he rejoined the crowd

CHAPTER THIRTY-ONE

A large red nuclear symbol began to flash on the screen of the control room, as a warning buzzer began to sound.

"We have a confirmed radiation signature consistent with a nuclear device," one of the other technicians in the Hydrogen Solutions facility said.

"Is it where I think it is?" the tech asked.

"If you think it's located just off the coast of Waikiki, then it is," the second tech responded.

"That would put it on the *Grand Maui* and somebody just opened the suitcase," the tech said.

The tech picked up a phone and relayed the information to the base commander, who had already been informed of the situation on the *Grand Maui*. A SEAL unit was already standing by with a helicopter if a device was discovered and a second unit had already left by boat to backup Haruko and Eddie on the *Grand Maui*.

"We have a hot one, get the chopper in the air," the commander said to the SEAL leader.

"This doesn't look good," the tech said as he watched the screen on which the security guards were approaching Haruko. Suddenly, the image shifted to a camera located at the Hilton Hawaiian Village showing the fireworks display.

"Haruko, Haruko!" he yelled into the phone, but heard only the noise of the crowd and the fireworks exploding off the starboard side of the ship.

"Haruko, put the phone to your ear!" he continued to yell.

"Who is this?" a man's voice asked into Jim's Blackberry.

"This is the goddamned FBI and you guys are keeping our agent from stopping your ship from being nuked," the tech said. "You should be helping Haruko, not trying to stop her."

"Sir, I'm afraid I have no way of knowing if you're telling the truth."

At that moment, the guard Aioka had spoken to came face to face with Haruko, and drew his weapon.

"Put your hands where I can see them and get down on the floor," the guard said.

"You're letting him get away!" Haruko screamed.

"I'm not going to ask you again, get down on the floor," the guard repeated.

Just at that instant, a partygoer who had a little too much to drink bumped into the back of the guard, distracting him for just a second. It was more than enough time for Haruko to act. In a flash, she spun and landed a full roundhouse kick to the guard's head, knocking his radio earpiece across the room and his gun to the floor where it was kicked under a couch by another guest rushing by to watch the fireworks. The man was down, but not out. It gave Haruko the head start she needed to try to catch up to Aioka. She saw him as he squeezed through the door with dozens of other guests but, unlike most, he turned away from the starboard side, heading towards the steps leading up to the Sky deck and helipad.

"Sir, your lady friend is in serious trouble," the security guard said to the tech over the phone.

"She's an FBI agent that is trying to stop a tragedy from occurring, you moron," the tech yelled.

"Sir, you too are in serious trouble by…" the guard stopped in mid-sentence as he listened to the radio call from the crewman for the Captain.

"Tell the Captain that the FBI agent has found a nuclear bomb on board and is attempting to disarm it," the crewman who had brought down the key said over the radio. "Also tell him that a second FBI agent, a woman, is on the ship after the terrorist who brought the bomb on board

Every security guard suddenly froze.

"There's a nuclear bomb on board. Another of your FBI agents is trying to disarm it," the security guard said excitedly into the phone. "What should we do?"

"Tell your Captain that a team of Navy SEALS is on the way to your ship, both by boat and by helicopter. Don't tell anyone in order to avoid a panic. Do you understand?" the tech asked.

"Yes sir."

"I no longer have a visual of the ship, so please find our agent and help her," the tech said. "And get this phone to the agent with the bomb, ASAP!"

"Yes sir," the guard said, and went running to find Eddie.

Eddie winced as he opened the suitcase. He prayed it was not booby-trapped and set to explode when opened. It wasn't. The suitcase itself was very thick and made of some sort of metal that helped to shield the device. Inside was an inner case made of six-inch thick Plexiglas. Beneath the top layer of Plexiglas were a timer and the circuitry for the bomb. Somewhere below the timer was the plutonium wrapped in a sphere of high explosives. The upper Plexiglas panel was held in place by four keyed locks, one of which had wires running to the circuitry.

"I don't think I'll be breaking into this," Eddie said to himself.

"The timer was not very sophisticated, but did count down the seconds. Eddie still had seventeen minutes and thirty-three seconds before the nuke was set to detonate.

"Come help me carry this," Eddie said to the two crewmen standing by the door.

They started into the room when a huge explosion shook the ship causing both of them to dive to the floor. The fireworks show had begun. Both men were visibly shaken.

"If you guys don't get over here now, there'll be one hell of an explosion, but nobody within three miles will know because they'll all be dead," Eddie said.

Eddie closed the suitcase and fastened the latches.

"Let's get this down to the speedboat, but be careful, dropping it could set it off," Eddie reminded them.

Both crew men were shaking as they helped Eddie carry the suitcase and one cried.

"I'll get in. Pass that side to me. You jump in and take the other handle," Eddie explained as they carefully placed the suitcase nuke in the speedboat.

"Are you Eddie?" the security guard with Jim's Blackberry asked. "Is that the nuke?"

"I don't have time for twenty questions," Eddie said preparing to start the boat.

"I was told to give you this phone," the guard said, tossing Jim's Blackberry to Eddie.

"Where's Haruko? She should have the phone," Eddie said.

"She lost it fighting with me," the guard said.

"What?" Eddie said, stopping what he was doing.

"That was before we found out she was FBI, now she's after that terrorist. Our men know to help her. The man on the phone told me to give it to you."

Right," Eddie said, as the boat's engine roared to life. "Don't let that son-of-a-bitch get away."

Eddie pushed the throttle all the way forward and the speedboat shot away from the *Grand Maui*.

Jim carefully rounded the corner, wary of Viktor lying in wait. He saw Viktor up ahead with his back to Jim. Viktor held his pistol in his hand and turned just as Jim saw him. He contemplated taking aim, but knew it would take too long for he had already heard the sound of approaching sirens. Jim ducked behind one of the columns that formed the portico. The covered hallway was over forty yards long and had at least twenty columns supporting it on both sides. To the right were several shops. To the left was a lavishly landscaped garden of the Royal Hawaiian Hotel. The portico was designed to protect guests from the occasional rain storm when they traveled from the lobby to the restaurant and pool area.

Viktor had reached the lobby of the hotel. To the left, the lobby opened up to the large grassy area that Viktor had run past moments before. It was flooded with scared guests fleeing the bar, restaurant, and pool area where a madman with a gun had just run through. None realized Viktor was that madman and he quickly blended into the on-rushing crowd. As he reached the front entrance of the hotel, Jim was turning the corner into the lobby, not fifteen yards behind. However, the crowd brought his progress to a near stop.

"FBI, everyone down," Jim yelled, but nobody ducked or got out of his way.

Jim pulled one of his six-shooters and for the first time in months contemplated firing it into one of the ceiling's wooden beams, hoping to get the crowd out of his way, but he couldn't do it. When the crowd saw the gun in his hand, several screamed, causing a panic. People were now running and screaming in every direction, making Jim's progress even more difficult.

Viktor leaped down both sets of steps leading from the driveway to the hotel entrance. Police cars were pulling into the street leading from the Sheraton to the circle drive in front of the Royal Hawaiian, blocking Viktor's escape route. His only escape would be through the lobby he had just exited. It was time to end his flight and begin to fight.

As Viktor reached the bottom of the steps, an exquisitely dressed Asian couple was exiting a Hummer limousine. The woman was about the same height and had the same build as Haruko. Viktor grabbed her around the neck, sticking the barrel of his Yarghin under her chin, and pulled her down the pathway and under the large Banyan tree in the middle of the garden area directly in front of the Royal Hawaiian.

"Just let me walk away or she is dead," Viktor said to Jim, as Jim reached the landing between the two sets of steps.

"Give it up Viktor, even your own people are trying to kill you."

"You know I won't do that, Jim. There are plenty of other countries where a man can get lost," Viktor said. "You know I could have killed Haruko if I had wanted to."

"You're damn lucky you didn't, or you'd be dead already," Jim replied.

"Who would kill me? You, a gun-shy mental case afraid to even pull your gun from its holster, let alone shoot and risk killing another innocent bystander. Do you still hear the cries of his wife and children when you try to sleep at night? Do you still see their faces when you look at yourself in the mirror? No, you won't shoot, you don't have the balls to shoot"

"Drop the gun," a policeman said who had slowly worked his way behind Viktor.

A huge explosion thundered, as the first fireworks from the Hilton burst into the air. It was just enough of a distraction.

Like a flash Viktor pulled the gun from the woman's throat and put two shots into the policeman's face and had the gun back to her throat.

"See Jim, you're afraid to shoot. How many more do I have to kill before you let me walk away?" Viktor asked.

"None, partner" Jim replied, pulling both six-shooter like a gunslinger.

Viktor's eyes got wide, but before he could react to pull the trigger, the first two bullets entered his forehead less than an inch apart. As he stumbled backwards three more bullets from each of the pistols ripped into his body, but he was already dead.

"Are you alright, ma'm." Jim said to the woman.

She, nor her male companion, understood, for neither spoke English.

"Clint Eastwood, Clint Eastwood," the Asian man said as he pulled out a camera handing it to one of the valets. He and his wife ran to either side of Jim and posed for a picture. Jim didn't feel much like smiling.

CHAPTER THIRTY-TWO

As the guard lay on the floor, he saw his gun kicked under one of the couches and was able to retrieve it. His radio, however, flew across the floor and under the feet of the guests stampeding toward the deck to watch the fireworks display. It was completely smashed.

"I don't need no damn radio as long as I got my gun," the guard said, picking himself off the floor. "That terrorist bitch is going to pay for that kick."

Haruko had pushed her way through the door and turned in pursuit of Aioka. The usually well-lit passageway was dark and full of shadows.

"Looking for me," Aioka said, coming out from behind a wall and smashing his fist into Haruko's face knocking her to the deck.

"I've grown weary of you constantly interrupting my plans," Aioka said, as he kicked Haruko in the side. Haruko curled tightly into a fetal position trying to protect her face and head.

"This time I'm afraid you're too late to stop the inevitable," Aioka said, as he circled, continuing to kick at Haruko.

"We know about the bomb," Haruko shrieked.

"So what. There's no way you can stop it. If you try, it's booby-trapped and will explode."

Haruko thought of Eddie.

"I'm willing to be a martyr if that is necessary," Aioka responded, as if reading Haruko's mind. "There are many with the passion to continue the struggle against American imperialism. All of them willing to take my place. Many have been prepared for the battles ahead." Aioka kicked Haruko again.

"Of course, this is not my ideal, as to where the battle must be fought," Aioka continued. "But where else is America's raping of an indigenous people more blatant than here in Hawaii. Their land was stolen from them, their Queen deposed, their population deliberately poisoned by drugs to make them subservient, the people relegated to the poorest living conditions imaginable, an entire people whose existence is to serve as slaves to the desires of the rich American bourgeoisie."

"You forget that the Japanese are just as guilty as the Americans," Haruko said through her pain. "We may not have originally stolen the land, but over the past thirty years it is our culture which has stolen Hawaii from the Americans. We're just as responsible for your so-called enslavement of the Hawaiian people."

"You know nothing," Aioka yelled, kicking Haruko savagely in the head area.

"You are worse than the Americans you hate," Haruko continued. "You don't care about the Hawaiian people, all you care about is money. You use your twisted ideology to justify your greed."

"Bitch!" Aioka spat, turning when he heard the sound of an approaching helicopter. He started to kick her again when an explosion, much louder than the others, shook the boat. The *Grand Maui* was now beginning to shoot off some of its fireworks display. Aioka flinched at the sudden explosion, missing the hard kick he had aimed at Haruko's head. It was the opening she was waiting for. Like a cat, Haruko's arm shot forward, grabbing Aioka's ankle as his kick

325

missed its mark, pushing his leg sideways, using the momentum of the kick to cause his balance to waver. As he tried to steady himself, Haruko rolled into the back of his leg, bringing Aioka down on top of her. Haruko knew Aioka was much stronger than she was and her grappling skills were not nearly as good as her fighting skills. She rolled out from under him and quickly got to her feet. The kicks had taken their toll on her body and she struggled to maintain balance in her fighting stance.

Another thunderous explosion lit up the sky and the *Grand Maui*. Aioka saw a security guard approaching with his gun drawn.

"Help me. She's trying to kill me. She has a gun!" Aioka cried out to the security guard. Haruko turned to look and Aioka bolted for the steps leading to the helipad.

"Not this time," Haruko said and ran after him.

"Stop," the guard yelled as he chased Haruko. "Stop or I'll shoot."

Haruko did not stop and caught Aioka as he was running up the steps. She was about to grab him when the wood right above her head splintered and the sound of the shot brought both her and Aioka to an abrupt stop.

"I said stop. Put your hands in the air and step away from the gentleman," the guard said, aiming his gun at Haruko.

"Thank God you saved me, officer, she's trying to kill me," Aioka said.

"Don't listen to him," Aioka said. "That man is Aioka Matsuura, the leader of the Red Summit terrorist organization."

"She's delusional," Aioka said. "She's been stalking me for months. She even killed my late wife."

"He's lying to you," Haruko told the guard. "He's the one responsible for the anthrax attack on your ship. He's trying to escape on that helicopter you hear."

The guard could hear a helicopter.

"I'm trying to get on that helicopter, but to escape from this crazed killer," said Aioka as he started to walk up the stairs.

"You must stop him," Haruko said. "Call the Captain he'll tell you." Haruko was hoping the Captain had by now received the message about Aioka being on board. "He has planted a nuclear bomb on your ship."

The guard now didn't know who to believe. "Sir, I need you to stop and come back down here until I can find out who's telling the truth."

Aioka continued slowly up the steps.

"Please sir, I need you to stop," the guard said again.

"If I come down she'll kill me," Aioka said.

"I won't allow that to happen," the guard said, but Aioka kept walking.

"Stop him," Haruko yelled. The helicopter was close to the helipad, but hadn't landed yet.

"You must stop now," the guard said to Aioka.

"You won't shoot me, I've done nothing wrong. It's the woman who is the killer." When the guard's eyes looked back at Haruko, Aioka sprinted around the landing on the staircase and up the remaining steps.

"He's getting away," Haruko screamed and ran after Aioka.

The guard couldn't shoot, he wasn't sure who to believe. He ran after Haruko.

"Unidentified aircraft, you're in extreme danger. You've entered a restricted area," the radioman from the

Grand Maui repeated to the helicopter trying to approach and land on the ship.

No reply came.

"Unidentified aircraft, what the hell are you thinking? There are fireworks exploding all around you. You will be blown out of the sky."

Inside the helicopter, Aioka's pilot was dripping sweat, cringing with every explosion and praying he would not take a direct hit.

"Unidentified aircraft, please…"

"Shut up!" the pilot yelled, ripping the radio headset from his head. "Of course, I see the freak'n fireworks."

The fireworks were now coming not only from the Hilton Hawaiian Village, but from a barge lying between the *Grand Maui* and the beach, as well as from the *Grand Maui* itself. It was the fireworks coming from the ship that troubled the pilot the most. They seemed to be coming from several locations on the ship, but by far the largest of the fireworks seemed to be coming from the helipad itself.

"Should we stop the display," one of the crewmen asked the first mate in charge, while the Captain attended the party.

"Is it possible just to stop the fireworks coming from our ship?" he in turn asked the computer operator.

"If I interrupt the program, the entire show will shut down, the hotel, the barge, and the ship. It would be impossible to restart the program without starting the show over from the very beginning," he replied. "Are you sure you want to do that?"

"No, but I don't want to blow a helicopter out of the sky, either. Keep trying the radio. The Captain will be here in a minute." A second military helicopter had approached, but was staying a safe distance from the ship.

"This is Nav-air 23, holding one half mile from your location. We need to land on your ship immediately."

"Nav-air 23, this is the *Grand Maui*. Our helipad is covered with high explosives fireworks and is unavailable at the moment."

"Then stop the show. We have a report of a nuclear weapon aboard your ship and need to deploy our team now."

"Nav-air 23, the weapon was removed by an FBI agent who took the suitcase on a speedboat and headed out to sea five minutes ago."

"Does he have a radio with him?"

"No, but I understand he has a cell phone with him."

"Do you have the number?"

"No," the radioman replied. The crew on the bridge watched as the Navy copter turned and headed out to sea.

Aioka reached the top of the steps and started waving his arms at the pilot.

"Land, dammit," Aioka yelled, continuing to look up at the copter.

The pilot switched on his spotlight to illuminate the helipad and try to find a safe place to set the copter down. The glare of the light blinded Aioka and he tried to cover his eyes while still waving to the pilot.

"Whoosh, whoosh!" Two large canisters gave off a muffled roar as they rocketed their giant explosive payloads one hundred yards into the sky above. The pilot saw the flash and rocked the copter quickly to the left.

"What are you doing?" Aioka yelled. "Come back."

Haruko had reached the top of the stairs leading to the helipad. She started to run towards Aioka, but the guard had caught up to her and yanked her back.

Aioka saw his two pursuers out of the corner of his eye and began to run towards the helicopter, unaware of the high-explosive fireworks surrounding him.

"Whoosh," another canister roared to life shooting its payload skyward just three feet from Aioka. Startled he turned to the right tripping over a canister and falling atop two others.

"Croosh, whump." Two more canisters ignited. The first was the canister directly under Aioka's face. The payload projectile crushed into his skull pushing his face four inches into his brain cavity lifting him into the air. The second canister fired less than a second later burying its payload into Aioka's chest cavity. The thrust of the two explosions lifted Aioka's body into the air, propelling him backwards twenty yards over the side of the ship.

Haruko and the guard stared in awe as Aioka's body flew above them. Arms and legs were flailing, but Aioka had died instantly at the first canister's payload impact. Twenty feet above the water the firework payloads both exploded, disintegrating Aioka's head and torso in a brilliant display of pyrotechnical splendor. The crowd of partygoers cheered loudly at the closeness of the spectacle, unaware they had just cheered the disintegration of Aioka's body.

The helicopter pilot knew landing would be impossible and continued his banking left turn down close to the water and headed back towards the airport.

"No amount of money is worth this," he said to himself, still cringing with each explosion.

Haruko stood dumbfounded by what she had just witnessed. Aioka was dead, yet Haruko felt cheated somehow.

"I should have been the one to kill him," she said.

The security guard looked at her, then turned and vomited on the staircase.

"Whoosh." Another of the canisters hurtled its payload skyward. Two seconds later the payload exploded and a 'happy face' lit up the sky.

CHAPTER THIRTY-THREE

"Holy shit! Did you see that?" the tech said. Several of Hydrogen Solution's technicians had gathered to watch the events unfold on the *Grand Maui*. They watched as Haruko and Aioka fought and they watched as Aioka's body was blown into a million little pieces when the fireworks embedded in his body exploded. Now the attention shifted to the two helicopters. One was dancing in and around the exploding fireworks display, while the other, the one belonging to the Navy SEALS, hovered at a safe distance.

"What are they waiting for? That nuke could go off at any second," one of the techs said.

"Relax," another replied. "If it does, we won't be around to complain about it."

Suddenly, the Nav-23 copter banked right and headed out to sea.

"Where the hell are they headed?" someone said.

The head tech panned back with the hi-zoom camera they had been using to follow the events. They found the Navy copter and then found the small speedboat that had left the *Grand Maui* moments before heading away from Oahu. On board, they could see Eddie, and behind him, the suitcase nuke that was set to explode in less than five minutes. However, they were unaware of just how little time they had left since no one had yet heard from Eddie.

For the past three minutes, since Eddie had left the *Grand Maui*, his only thought was to get the nuke as far away from Honolulu as possible. The waves were rough the further he went from shore and the speedboat was starting to crash hard into them, slowing down his progress. Eddie reached back and undid both the latches on the suitcase nuke.

"Boy howdy," Eddie explained. There were only four minutes and twenty seconds left on the timer, which continued its relentless countdown. "I'm starting to talk like Jimbo," Eddie said to himself. It was then he saw Jim's Blackberry flashing on the deck next to the nuke. He had forgotten about the phone and the engine noise had drowned out the ringer.

"I hope you got a good plan for stopping this thing," Eddie said to whoever was calling.

"How much time is left?" the tech asked

"Four minutes and seven seconds," Eddie replied. Just then the boat hit a large wave yanking the wheel from Eddie's hand causing the speedboat to turn sharply to the left almost swamping the boat. Eddie dropped the phone, grabbed the wheel and turned the boat back out to sea and away from land.

"Where's that phone?" Eddie said, looking around. He didn't see it and couldn't waste any more time searching for it.

He pulled off his belt and tied the steering wheel securely to the rail running along the side of the boat. He stood up and looked back towards Waikiki.

"Damn," he said. "not far enough." Eddie could still see the lights of the hotels on the beach and the fireworks exploding above them. He knew that a six-foot-tall man could see almost four miles to the horizon when standing at sea level. That meant he was still too close to Oahu. This size of the suitcase nuke, if what Viktor had said was true, could do serious damage up to four miles away. He wasn't that far yet. The speedometer showed the boat's speed to vacillate between twenty-five knots when it crashed through a wave to thirty knots on smoother water. At that speed, the speedboat could be another mile-and-a-half to two miles farther out before the nuke detonated.

"That will do," Eddie reassured himself. He checked to make sure the steering wheel was secure, then climbed over the seat to the platform where the parasailors stood awaiting to fly into the air. He strapped on one of the parachutes, making sure it was securely attached to the rope wrapped around the winch. Normally the rope would be slowly unwound, allowing the parasailor to gently float into the sky above. Eddie didn't have the luxury of time. He would have to release the winch and hope that the chute wouldn't rip apart when it jerked him off the deck.

"No, don't do it!" the tech yelled, as he watched the action on the screen in front of him. "Wait for the SEALS. You won't be able to float far enough away from the blast." He knew it was useless to yell, but he didn't know what else to do. Eddie was his friend, and he was about to watch his friend commit suicide.

"The Navy copter is less than two minutes away," one of the other techs said out loud. "That's not enough time to rescue Eddie and get a safe distance away before the blast."

Another of the techs spoke up, "The boat should be almost five miles from shore when the nuke detonates. If the size of the warhead is consistent with the one that exploded in Wichita, most of Oahu should be spared."

"Which way are the Trade Winds blowing?" someone asked.

"Due East at 16 knots."

"Should we contact the authorities on Molokai and Lanai?"

"It's not big enough to generate a plume that can reach that far. At most the radiation plume will only be a mile wide and dump most of the radioactivity within ten miles. It's Eddie we need to worry about," the tech said.

"Haruko, I sure as hell hope you made that son-of-a-bitch pay for what he's done and what he's about to make me do," Eddie said, out loud. "Here goes nothing."
Eddie released the winch so it would free-wheel out the rope holding the parachute. Eddie had been holding the parachute in a tight ball in front of him. He double checked his harness and glanced once more at the timer on the nuke. It was down to three minutes. Eddie turned and tossed the parachute behind him. It immediately caught in the wind and Eddie was yanked off the speedboat like he was shot from a canon. He quickly rose to about three hundred feet, but was still drifting further behind the speed boat.
"Yeah baby," Eddie screamed. "What a rush." He pulled out the knife that the crew man had given him and started to cut the rope. What he didn't expect was the jarring shock when all six hundred feet of the rope finally reached its end and snapped taut. The knife flew out of his hand and his harness cut into his back.
"That's going to leave a bruise," Eddie said, trying to decide what to do next. His inner clock told him that he had less than two minutes till detonation. He knew if he undid the harness and dropped into the ocean, chances were he wouldn't survive the fall. If he did, he most certainly wouldn't survive the blast. If he did nothing, he would have an incredible view of a nuclear explosion for about a millisecond before he turned to dust. Neither choice was very appealing.
"What the hell?" Eddie said, as a Navy attack helicopter swooped in below him. One of the men was trying

to signal Eddie, but Eddie had no idea what he was trying to tell him.

"Get out of here, before it's too late!" Eddie screamed, throwing his thumb into the air to signal them to leave. The man who had signaled him flashed a thumbs-up sign as the copter moved forward. The rotor cut through the rope tying Eddie to the boat like it wasn't there. Eddie began to drift backwards and down.

"Thank God for the Navy!" Eddie yelled, thinking that he may have a chance after all.

As the helicopter circled up behind him, he tried to turn and watch them leave, but his parachute collapsed and he started to fall towards the ocean.

"Now what?" Eddie screamed. He heard the helicopter and realized it was the wind from the rotor that collapsed his chute. Eddie felt a strong jerk and he started hurtling through the sky at what seemed like a hundred miles an hour. The pilot had purposely collapsed Eddie's chute and hooked it on the skid of the copter. What Eddie thought was a hundred miles an hour was closer to one hundred and fifty miles an hour. Eddie's face burned from the rushing air. His body banged constantly against the skid.

"Ten seconds," the tech calmly said over the radio to the pilot. "Better sit her down."

Back in Waikiki the fireworks show had started the climactic finale. Dozens of giant explosive packs, shot high into the sky from the Hilton, the barge, and the *Grand Maui*, were all exploding at once in a cavalcade of colors. Thousands of people had gathered along the Waikiki beach front to watch, the guests on the *Grand Maui* had all crowded to the starboard side and two hundred thousand others were all watching their television screens, but the crew of the *Grand*

Maui along with Haruko all had moved to the port side of the ship and gazed out to sea.

Dano had finally told Jim about Haruko, Eddie, and the nuke. He and Dano moved to the lawn outside the Royal Hawaiian to watch and wait.

"I've got the speedboat at 4.8 miles off shore," one of the techs said. "That should be a fairly safe distance."

"How deep is the water there?" the tech asked

"About 1800 -1900 feet that far out. The explosion will not impact the ocean floor," someone answered.

"What's the chance this thing will cause a tsunami?"

No one had given any thought to that possibility. "Even if there is no tsunami, there will be one hell of a swell caused by the shock wave," someone else said.

"How big?" the head tech yelled. "I need to know how big?"

"Give me a minute to run the figures," someone replied.

"We don't have a minute, we have ten seconds," the tech said. He pushed a button to activate the tsunami warning system. It had been installed at the facility when Hydrogen Solutions had been doing their sea temperature experiments the previous year.

The helicopter dove down towards the water. The pilot dipped it sharply throwing Eddie free of the skid. He dropped about twenty feet into the water. One of the Navy SEALS jumped in right behind him with a rope and harness to secure him. The helicopter had stopped its engines and came down hard on the water, about fifty feet in front of the three men.

337

"Put this on and hold on, this may hurt a little," the SEAL said to Eddie, handing him a helmet. Eddie barely had time to slip the helmet over his head, when the blinding white flash came.

In Waikiki, the fireworks show had reached its zenith, or so everyone thought. As the last glow of the grand finale faded into the darkness, and as the crowd thundered their approval with applause, the sky was lit up by the detonation of the suitcase nuke. It turned the night into day revealing the mushroom cloud as it continued to billow upward. The applause was replaced by the roar of the explosion cascading across the water and then by the wailing of the tsunami warning sirens. The beachfront hotels shook and several of the upper floor windows facing the ocean shattered. The awe of the crowds lining the beach quickly shifted to fear as the realization of what had occurred began to register in their minds. Thousands began running for the safety of the hotels, trampling one another as they fought to reach higher ground. Dano and Jim were among those who ran but, because of the shootings that had occurred moments before, the crowds had been kept away from the Royal Hawaiian, allowing Jim, Dano, and the rest of the authorities at the scene to easily scamper to safety.

"Look, isn't that a helicopter out there?" Haruko shouted, pointing to the Nav-23 as it settled into the water.

"Everyone cover your eyes, five seconds till detonation!" yelled one of the crewmen who had helped Eddie load the nuke onto the speedboat.

Most of the partygoers were still on the starboard side of the *Grand Maui*. The bright flash was at their backs, but they heard the massive explosion and felt the shockwave as it hit the upper decks of the ship, causing it to list sharply towards the island. Several people tumbled over the railing and into the water.

Haruko and a few of the crew members who heard the warning dropped to the deck, looked away, and clung to the rail. Many of the others tumbled backwards, suffering a variety of injuries.

The Captain had returned to the bridge and immediately sounded the alarm, notifying the crew that there was a man overboard. In this case, it was more like two or three dozen men and women overboard.

The Captain could hear the tsunami sirens on shore and knew he should turn his ship into the approaching waves. To do so would require him to start the engines and, with so many people in the water, that would be impossible. Even if he loosened the anchor chains in order to ride out the waves, he risked crushing those who had gone overboard. The *Grand Maui* would be their only protection from those incoming waves. He knew his ship was about to take a thumping.

The helicopter had just made it far enough from the blast for the initial shock wave to blow over them. The pilot had already restarted the engine and was lifting out of the water, knowing that a big wave was surely on its way. He knew if he wasn't in the air, before it reached them, the helicopter would be lost. The SEAL had Eddie in the harness and connected to him. He signaled for them to be pulled in. The copter began to rise as a large swell over thirty feet high bore down on them. When the swell struck, the helicopter was just inches above the top of the swell. As the crew looked out the door, Eddie and the SEAL rode the crest of the wave and looked straight in at the other crew members. As the swell passed, the two men were now dangling beneath the helicopter.

"Man, would I have liked to surf that wave," Eddie said.

"Next time, surfer boy. I think you've gone on enough thrill rides for the day," the SEAL replied. "Let's head home."

"Take me to the ship," Eddie insisted. "My partner is on that ship."

The two men looked towards the *Grand Maui* just as the wave smashed into it.

"Sorry, sir, but we have orders to take you immediately back to Pearl for de-con and medical evaluation. I was told to inform you that your friend Haruko is safe on the *Grand Maui* and will see you back at Pearl."

"My partner Haruko," Eddie corrected. "What about Jim? Jim Rikey. He's our team leader. Is he safe?" Eddie asked.

"Sorry, but I wasn't given any further information," the SEAL replied.

"The helicopter is back in the air," one of the crewmen shouted. "At least I think it is."

Haruko lifted herself from the deck and looked towards the blast. In the moonlight, she could see the perfectly formed mushroom cloud. It was just how her grandmother had described the Hiroshima blast to her when she was a little girl.

"I thought I would never see this," Haruko said to no one in particular. She resolved to work to never allow a terrorist group to do this again. She knew that would be a difficult vow to keep, but one she was determined to follow through.

"Everyone inside and hold on," someone yelled, "there's a huge wave coming."

Haruko could see what looked like a giant black strip stretching from beyond Diamondhead to her left, and disappearing into the darkness to her right, growing larger and larger as it approached. A crew member handed her a life jacket and dragged her through a door as she pulled it over her head.

"This is the Captain, everyone hold-on tight, we are about to be rocked by a large wave," the ship's public address system blared. "Secure the life boats, but get those life jackets and preservers into the water."

The wave hit with such a fury that the *Grand Maui* was pushed almost fifty yards closer to the shore. The anchors were dragged behind the ship and ripped large tears in the hull, but held the ship firm. Unlike the pressure wave that hit the top of the ship and caused it to list, the wave hit and lifted the ship solidly but evenly, pushing it towards the beach. The ship also cushioned the impact of the wave on the rescue boats that had just entered the water, as well as the passengers who had been thrown overboard.

The guests aboard the ship were scared, but didn't panic. Since the anthrax attack, the crew had been trained on how to handle such an emergency. Those with specific rescue tasks performed them flawlessly, and those designated to calm and control the passengers did so with equal skill, exactly what one would expect from one of the most elite cruise ships in existence.

It was fortunate that the blast created the large wave instead of a massive tidal surge. The wave hit the beach with a fury crushing boats and buildings within thirty feet of the normal high tide line. Water rushed into many of the hotel restaurants and bars along the beach front, breaking windows and destroying furniture, but doing little structural damage. Most people had retreated to a safe distance, but those few caught by the giant swell were pulled out to sea. Luckily, the *Grand Maui* had lowered several of its life boats to rescue the passengers knocked overboard and they were able to rescue many of those swept out by the undertow. Within an hour, the *Grand Maui* had rescued all the people who were nearby in the water and was ordered by the Coast Guard, who had several ships now in the area, to return to its pier at the Aloha Tower.

Marshall Law had been declared on Oahu and all non-emergency traffic was ordered off the streets. Military units from Pearl and Hickam were put in place to enforce a curfew along with Hawaii National Guard units. The local news and media kept the public informed and assured them that authorities were confident life would return to normal by the following afternoon. For many people, life would never be normal again.

CHAPTER THIRTY-FOUR

Jim and Dano were waiting for Haruko when the *Grand Maui* reached its berth at Pier Four next to the Aloha Tower.

"Has anyone heard from Eddie?" Haruko asked the minute she got off the ship.

Jim was disappointed that she asked about Eddie before asking about him. But then again, Eddie had just taken on a nuclear weapon and Jim had only fought Viktor.

"He's back at Pearl being checked out," Jim replied.

"Was he hurt?" Haruko asked.

"No, just a few cuts and scrapes. They just wanted to make sure he didn't get a dose of radioactivity. He should be fine. What about you? I heard you took quite a beating."

"No worse than the one my sensei gives me during my training sessions," Haruko replied.

"I don't think your sensei leaves foot print bruises all over your arms and back like this," Jim replied holding Haruko's arm up and spinning her around.

Jim continued to hold her hand and Haruko didn't mind.

"He's finally dead," Haruko said softly. "Aioka is finally dead."

Jim put his other arm around Haruko and pulled her close. She began to cry.

"It must have been awful," Jim said trying to imagine what an exploding head must have looked like.

"What is awful is that I didn't get the chance to kill him," Haruko replied. "I wanted him to pay for killing Jotty."

She could feel Jim's body tighten when she mentioned Jotty's name. "But I still have you," Haruko added, pulling Jim closer.

"We better get going," Dano said. "I don't think some of the other passengers on the ship appreciate the fact they are restricted on board and Haruko gets to leave."

Jim and Haruko looked up at several scowling faces.

"I think you're right," Jim replied. "Anyway, Eddie is probably pretty anxious to see us by now."

"At least pretty anxious to get out of the hospital," Haruko added.

Haruko and Jim rode silently in the back seat of Dano's car. A trip that normally would take at least twenty minutes only took ten due to the curfew in affect. Dano had called ahead and Eddie was waiting when they reached the base medical center.

"Boy howdy it's good to see all of you guys," Eddie said. "Damn, I really am starting to sound like Jimbo."

Haruko turned quickly to look at Jim's reaction and Eddie braced himself and closed his eyes anticipating the punch that he knew was coming. Nobody got away with calling Jim Jimbo.

"It's great to see you, too, Eddie," Jim replied, hugging him.

Haruko stared for a moment, surprised at Jim's reaction, and then she too gave Eddie a hug.

"You would think you guys are Hawaiian with all the hugging going on," Dano said, as he then gave Eddie a hug.

"Where's Viktor?" Eddie asked.

Dano looked to Jim. "Viktor was a traitor, both to us and to his own country. He was the one who originally arranged for the nukes to be stolen. He was telling Aioka our every move. When they called me to the Hydrogen Solutions facility to meet Conyers, I thought it was to fire me. Instead, they showed me a Russian satellite surveillance video of Helsinki. It showed Viktor helping Satochi kidnap you," Jim said, looking at Haruko.

"That son-of-a-bitch!" Haruko said.

"My words exactly," Jim replied. "The Russians by that time had figured out Viktor was behind the theft of the nukes, along with two other former KGB agents."

"How did Viktor hook up with Aioka?" Dano asked.

"Aioka became aware of Viktor last year when Viktor raided Aioka's coffee plantation to take back that research scientist Aioka had kidnapped," Jim explained. "Aioka most likely contacted Viktor when he discovered Viktor was in charge of the security at the nuclear storage facility. At the risk of sounding too cliché, I'm sure he made Viktor an offer he couldn't refuse."

"Did you arrest Viktor?" Haruko asked.

"Viktor ran, and Jim had to shoot him," Dano said.

Haruko looked at Jim, knowing the emotional breakdown Jim had suffered when he accidentally shot the tourist in Kauai. The fear and sadness that had shown in his eyes since that shooting were gone. She knew then that Jim was back to his former self.

"He killed a couple of tourists and left me no choice," Jim said. "If I hadn't done it, the Russians would have. I didn't want to give them that pleasure."

"Yeah," Dano said, "a Russian sharpshooter was trying to take out Viktor, too. I guess he had a few secrets they didn't want him to tell in case he wanted to cut a deal."

"What about the fourth suitcase nuke?" Eddie asked. "Where is it?"

"Not in the USA," Jim replied. "At least as far we know. Several intelligence agencies picked up the radiation signature of the nuke in Helsinki when we went to take out Zetanutra. From what we've learned, Günter Marx, the man in charge at Zetanutra, had a partner, a female partner. They were working with Viktor and Aioka in the nuclear extortion plot. Aioka must have given them one of the nukes."

"Any idea where we can find them?' Haruko asked

"No, but we're working on it," Jim replied.

"I'll leave the three of you to sort things out," Dano said. "I'm still on the FBI payroll and my boss wants me back on the Big Island to help sort through the mess at the house in Honoli'i Cove."

"What mess?" Jim asked.

"I guess Aioka left several bombs buried under the sand and hidden around the house. We have closed the area, but the surfers still manage to sneak in there to catch the waves. My boss wants me to try to find out which of those surfers may have helped Aioka and which ones may still be involved with the sovereignty movement. I need to head to the North Shore and practice my surfing. I got a feeling I'll be working under cover for a while."

"Be careful," Eddie warned, "those are big waves up there and the locals don't take kindly to strangers."

"What else did Conyers have to say?" Haruko asked.

"He asked me if I wanted to take over as the head of the Southeast Asia terrorist task force. I told him no.

"Why did you do that?" Haruko asked.

"I told him I was no longer interested in working for the NCTC. I'm moving back to the Big Island, at least for a while, and working for the Farm Service Agency. Someone needs to stop all this GMO crap before it ruins the Big Island."

Haruko started to tear up.

"I also told him you were by far more qualified than anyone else to lead the team," Jim added.

"Thank you, but it'll never happen," Haruko replied.

"Why's that?" Eddie asked.

"First off, if you hadn't noticed, I'm a female. Secondly, even though I'm now an American citizen, the NCTC is a 'good ole boy' system made up of 'good ole boys' Need I say more?"

"Then I guess you aren't interested in this letter offering you the position. Conyers told me to give it to you. I was just waiting for the right moment," Jim said.

"Congratulations, Haruko, it will be an honor working for you," Eddie said, giving her a hug. "Can I take a two-month vacation?"

"If I recall, you've been on vacation for the past six months," Haruko said.

"You already sound like a boss," Eddie replied.

"I am the boss, but I'll see what I can do," Haruko replied laughing.

"What about you, Jim? I was hoping you'd be coming back to McClean with me," Haruko said. "I don't know if I want the job if you're not there."

"Who says you'll be working in McClean?" Jim said.

"What do you mean?" Haruko asked.

"Conyers told me the President decided it made more sense to move some of the NCTC offices away from McClean and make them not so highly visible and subject to so much Congressional scrutiny. A little more covert with a free reign to conduct investigations as you see fit."

"I like the sound of that," Eddie piped in. "Just like it was back in the CIA."

"More or less," Jim replied.

"I'm not so sure," Haruko said. "Just where do they plan on setting up this covert facility?"

"It's already up and running," Jim replied. "It's right next to the south end of the runway at the Kailua-Kona Airport."

"Are you talking about the Natural Energy Laboratory at Keahole Point?" Eddie asked.

"Well, that's the name of the umbrella facility. There are several individual corporations that are commercial tenants at the facility."

"The lobster farm? The lobster farm is a front for the NCTC?" Eddie asked.

"There are a few more businesses there besides the lobster farm. Our front organization supplies specific deep-water enzymes for use in nutraceuticals in Japan. The NSA was using it, but they've moved elsewhere," Jim said.

Haruko's eyes lit up when she realized that she and Jim could be together.

"All right!" Eddie said, excitedly. "But if you're moving back, that means I have to find someplace else to live."

"Looks that way," Jim smiled.

"I guess I need to start looking for a place too," Haruko said.

"Oh, I think I can help you with that," Jim said, and pulled Haruko close.

"I think it's time for me to curl up in a bed and sleep for the next twenty-four hours," Eddie said. "It's been a long week." Eddie remembered his encounter on Kahena Beach. "Better yet, maybe I just need a little Summer and a smile. A Cheshire smile."

"I'm not exactly sure what you're talking about, but I'm sure that'll be fine," Haruko said, already sounding like the boss. "Just make sure you're around for debriefing on Monday morning. We have another nuke we need to find."

"See you, Jimbo," Eddie said, smiling, remembering the first time he said that to Jim and got punched in the mouth.

Jim and Haruko both smiled, "Don't call me Jimbo," Jim replied.

For the first time in ten years Haruko felt at peace. Aioka had consumed her thoughts above all else. Now that he was dead, Haruko felt like she could finally move on. "I know Jotty would be happy knowing we're together," Haruko said.

"I know you loved him," Jim said.

"I did, but I always loved you too." Haruko said.

 "But you lived with Jotty. I thought you two were going to marry?" Jim said.

"When Aioka was alive, I could never have truly loved either of you. It's true, Jotty and I were lovers, but had you lived in McClean and Jotty somewhere else, you and I would have been together. Only now that Aioka is dead can I give my heart to someone."

Jim held her close. He knew Haruko loved him, but wondered if it would last. Even though Aioka was dead, another terrorist would soon take his place. Was Haruko's love for Jim stronger than her ideology for a world free of terror, hate and fear?

"Let's go home," Haruko said.

CHAPTER THIRTY-FIVE

An old man wearing a heavy coat made from the hide of a reindeer, and his wife who was wrapped in a heavy fur shawl, trudged through a fresh blanket of snow in the thick birch forest. The going was slow, due more to their age than to the weather. Their breath froze when it hit the crisp night air. They stopped twenty yards from a small kesämökki and stood silently catching their breath from the tiring journey. It had taken over twenty minutes to travel from their own cottage to this one hidden deep in the forest in the middle of their property.

"Should we burn it down?" the old Russian man asked his wife. "He hasn't picked up the food in two days and the dacha remains dark. No smoke comes from the fireplace."

"Patience, my love, you must have patience. Günter has paid us very well and has always been good to us," his wife replied. "It's too soon for such harsh action."

"I'm frightened," the man replied. "Didn't you see those pictures of the poor souls in Helsinki who contracted the virus? I'm sure the virus has taken our friend Günter. Though I'm old, I don't wish to die such a horrible death."

"Nor I, my love, but give it more time. We owe it to our friend. Do you not still hear the radio inside?"

"I have heard the radio since the day our friend arrived. It means nothing."

"Patience, we must be patient."

The couple turned and started the long hike back. Snow gently began to fall.

Günter lay motionless on the hard-wooden slats of the bed. He had burned the blood-soaked mattress days earlier. His right eye was closed and his left eye stared blankly towards the ceiling, although it was more a gelatinous orb filled with blood than it was an eye. His body was not much more than a skeleton as he lay there laboring to maintain his shallow breaths. Günter was still alive, but just barely. He had defied the odds and managed to survive for two weeks with the deadly virus. Most men would have succumbed to death long before this, if not from the virus itself, then from the loss of will to live. He had not thrown up any blood for the past four days. The rash that had covered Günter's body had started as small raised papule lumps that turned to blood-oozing lesions, but now had begun to dry and scar over.

The radio had been his constant companion, but he hadn't listened to music. He heard the news reports of Satochi's death at the volcano and of Aioka's death aboard the *Grand Maui*. He listened to reports of the nuclear explosion off of Oahu and of the dozens of deaths it had caused, but not the millions Aioka had desired. He thought he had heard a report about a Russian FSB agent turned traitor who was killed, but he couldn't be sure if it was real or had been a hallucination during one of his delirious states.

The worst had now passed and Günter knew he would live. He also knew it would be several weeks before he recovered enough strength to leave the dacha. Several weeks he would spend thinking about Viktor, Polya, and the money he believed they had stolen from him. Several weeks planning how to retrieve and use the last suitcase nuke. Several weeks until a new reign of terror would begin.

ACKNOWLEDGEMENTS

So many people to thank:
Berch Papikyan for help with Russian questions.
Kouichi Ikeda for help with Japanese questions.
Bob McGavren, United Airlines pilot, for help with pilot info and cockpit dialogue.
Francis Sansone at SOEST University of Hawaii.
Roger at Claremont Travel.
Jeff Wyckoff for the rose information.
Charles Kumlander and his friend, Helelä Matti from the University in Helsinki, for the Finland information.
Mike at Cable Airport.
Officer Cabot for arranging the Kauai pidgin translations.
Natalie Kaululaau for the Kauai pidgin translation.
Fred Ilyan for showing me the Russia tourists never get to see and for the wonderful mission work he does there.
Andrew Karam PhD, my guru for nuclear, biological and radiological terrorism. I met Andy at a book signing for *Taka*, at the Hilton Waikoloa. He then invited me to one of his trainings and has always answered my technical questions, or knew someone

who could. I guess he wanted to make sure I got it right for the next books.

Mike Corwin, who continues to inspire me and research those peculiar questions I seem to always come up with.

Jennifer Boen, my main editor.

Gary Corwin, the man I call the finisher, who does a terrific job making sure I am grammatically and mechanically sound.

Booklines-Islander Group and all their sales reps, for their support and for keeping my books in the stores.

G. Brad Lewis for the incredible photos he has allowed me to use on all of my covers.

David Cook, at InstantHawaii.com, for his help getting the Big Island pidgin translations. It was David who suggested I write about the east side of the Big Island. It was also his description of the Great Crack hike that helped inspire this book.

Brandon Beirne for his help with my Navy questions.

Katy, Scott, and Lance for their continued support.

All the resorts where I stayed while writing or that I have used as settings in *Kapu 'āina.* Specifically:

Hilton Waikoloa Village	Hilton Hawaiian Village
Kona Coast Resort	Honoli'i House
Four Seasons	Royal Hawaiian
Ohana Islander Waikiki	Kona Village Resort
Waikoloa Sheraton	

Most of all I need to thank my wife for putting up with my hours spent at the computer. I couldn't have done this without her support.

Addendum: I thought KAPU 'ĀINA was the conclusion to my Bio-terror series but now that Thrillogy Press is releasing new edited versions I've decided to write a fourth book in the series. Look for it in 2021.